INVERTEBRATA
ENIGMATICA

STRAND MAGAZINE (1893)

INVERTEBRATA ENIGMATICA

Giant Spiders, Dangerous Insects,
and Other Strange Invertebrates
in Classic Science Fiction and Fantasy

CHAD ARMENT, EDITOR

COACHWHIP PUBLICATIONS
Landisville, Pennsylvania

Invertebrata Enigmatica
Published 2008 Coachwhip Publications
Coachwhipbooks.com

ISBN 1-930585-65-9
ISBN-13 978-1-930585-65-2

Front cover image: © Laurie Knight

Contents

The Sphinx
Edgar Allan Poe

During the dread reign of the Cholera in New York, I had accepted the invitation of a relative to spend a fortnight with him in the
retirement of his *cottage ornée* on the banks of the Hudson. We
had here around us all the ordinary means of summer amusement;
and what with rambling in the woods, sketching, boating, fishing,
bathing, music, and books, we should have passed the time pleasantly enough, but for the fearful intelligence which reached us every
morning from the populous city. Not a day elapsed which did not
bring us news of the decease of some acquaintance. Then as the
fatality increased, we learned to expect daily the loss of some
friend. At length we trembled at the approach of every messenger.
The very air from the South seemed to us redolent with death. That
palsying thought, indeed, took entire possession of my soul. I could
neither speak, think, nor dream of any thing else. My host was of a
less excitable temperament, and, although greatly depressed in
spirits, exerted himself to sustain my own. His richly philosophical intellect was not at any time affected by unrealities. To the sub-
stances of terror he was sufficiently alive, but of its shadows he
had no apprehension.

His endeavors to arouse me from the condition of abnormal
gloom into which I had fallen, were frustrated, in great measure,
by certain volumes which I had found in his library. These were of
a character to force into germination whatever seeds of hereditary
superstition lay latent in my bosom. I had been reading these books
without his knowledge, and thus he was often at a loss to account
for the forcible impressions which had been made upon my fancy.

A favorite topic with me was the popular belief in omens—a
belief which, at this one epoch of my life, I was almost seriously

disposed to defend. On this subject we had long and animated dis-
cussions—he maintaining the utter groundlessness of faith in such
matters,—I contending that a popular sentiment arising with absolute spontaneity—that is to say, without apparent traces of suggestion—had in itself the unmistakable elements of truth, and was
entitled to as much respect as that intuition which is the idiosyn-
crasy of the individual man of genius.

The fact is, that soon after my arrival at the cottage there had
occurred to myself an incident so entirely inexplicable, and which
had in it so much of the portentous character, that I might well
have been excused for regarding it as an omen. It appalled, and at
the same time so confounded and bewildered me, that many days
elapsed before I could make up my mind to communicate the circumstances to my friend.

Near the close of exceedingly warm day, I was sitting, book in
hand, at an open window, commanding, through a long vista of
the river banks, a view of a distant hill, the face of which nearest
my position had been denuded by what is termed a land-slide, of
the principal portion of its trees. My thoughts had been long wandering from the volume before me to the gloom and desolation of
the neighboring city. Uplifting my eyes from the page, they fell
upon the naked face of the bill, and upon an object—upon some
living monster of hideous conformation, which very rapidly made
its way from the summit to the bottom, disappearing finally in the
dense forest below. As this creature first came in sight, I doubted
my own sanity—or at least the evidence of my own eyes; and many
minutes passed before I succeeded in convincing myself that I was
neither mad nor in a dream. Yet when I described the monster
(which I distinctly saw, and calmly surveyed through the whole
period of its progress), my readers, I fear, will feel more difficulty
in being convinced of these points than even I did myself.

Estimating the size of the creature by comparison with the diameter of the large trees near which it passed—the few giants of the
forest which had escaped the fury of the land-slide—I concluded it
to be far larger than any ship of the line in existence. I say ship of
the line, because the shape of the monster suggested the idea—the
hull of one of our seventy-four might convey a very tolerable conception of the general outline. The mouth of the animal was situated at the extremity of a proboscis some sixty or seventy feet in
length, and about as thick as the body of an ordinary elephant.

Near the root of this trunk was an immense quantity of black shaggy hair—more than could have been supplied by the coats of a score of buffaloes; and projecting from this hair downwardly and laterally, sprang two gleaming tusks not unlike those of the wild boar, but of infinitely greater dimensions. Extending forward, parallel with the proboscis, and on each side of it, was a gigantic staff, thirty or forty feet in length, formed seemingly of pure crystal and in shape a perfect prism,—it reflected in the most gorgeous manner the rays of the declining sun. The trunk was fashioned like a wedge with the apex to the earth. From it there were outspread two pairs of wings—each wing nearly one hundred yards in length—one pair being placed above the other, and all thickly covered with metal scales; each scale apparently some ten or twelve feet in diameter. I observed that the upper and lower tiers of wings were connected by a strong chain. But the chief peculiarity of this horrible thing was the representation of a Death's Head, which covered nearly the whole surface of its breast, and which was as accurately traced in glaring white, upon the dark ground of the body, as if it had been there carefully designed by an artist. While I regarded the terrific animal, and more especially the appearance on its breast, with a feeling or horror and awe—with a sentiment of forthcoming evil, which I found it impossible to quell by any effort of the reason, I perceived the huge jaws at the extremity of the proboscis suddenly expand themselves, and from them there proceeded a sound so loud and so expressive of woe, that it struck upon my nerves like a knell and as the monster disappeared at the foot of the hill, I fell at once, fainting, to the floor.

Upon recovering, my first impulse, of course, was to inform my friend of what I had seen and heard—and I can scarcely explain what feeling of repugnance it was which, in the end, operated to prevent me.

At length, one evening, some three or four days after the occurrence, we were sitting together in the room in which I had seen the apparition—I occupying the same seat at the same window, and he lounging on a sofa near at hand. The association of the place and time impelled me to give him an account of the phenomenon. He heard me to the end—at first laughed heartily—and then lapsed into an excessively grave demeanor, as if my insanity was a thing beyond suspicion. At this instant I again had a distinct view of the monster- to which, with a shout of absolute terror, I now directed

his attention. He looked eagerly—but maintained that he saw noth-
ing- although I designated minutely the course of the creature, as
it made its way down the naked face of the hill.

I was now immeasurably alarmed, for I considered the vision
either as an omen of my death, or, worse, as the fore-runner of an
attack of mania. I threw myself passionately back in my chair, and
for some moments buried my face in my hands. When I uncovered
my eyes, the apparition was no longer apparent.

My host, however, had in some degree resumed the calmness
of his demeanor, and questioned me very rigorously in respect to
the conformation of the visionary creature. When I had fully satisfied him on this head, he sighed deeply, as if relieved of some intolerable burden, and went on to talk, with what I thought a cruel
calmness, of various points of speculative philosophy, which had
heretofore formed subject of discussion between us. I remember
his insisting very especially (among other things) upon the idea
that the principle source of error in all human investigations lay
in the liability of the understanding to under-rate or to over-value
the importance of an object, through mere mis-admeasurement of
its propinquity. "To estimate properly, for example," he said, "the
influence to be exercised on mankind at large by the thorough dif-
fusion of Democracy, the distance of the epoch at which such dif-
fusion may possibly be accomplished should not fail to form an
item in the estimate. Yet can you tell me one writer on the subject
of government who has ever thought this particular branch of the
subject worthy of discussion at all?"

He here paused for a moment, stepped to a book-case, and
brought forth one of the ordinary synopses of Natural History.
Requesting me then to exchange seats with him, that he might the
better distinguish the fine print of the volume, he took my arm-
chair at the window, and, opening the book, resumed his discourse
very much in the same tone as before.

"But for your exceeding minuteness," he said, "in describing
the monster, I might never have had it in my power to demonstrate
to you what it was. In the first place, let me read to you a schoolboy account of the genus *Sphinx*, of the family Crepuscularia of
the order Lepidoptera, of the class of Insecta—or insects. The account runs thus:

"'Four membranous wings covered with little colored scales of
metallic appearance; mouth forming a rolled proboscis, produced

by an elongation of the jaws, upon the sides of which are found the rudiments of mandibles and downy palpi; the inferior wings retained to the superior by a stiff hair; antennae in the form of an elongated club, prismatic; abdomen pointed. The Death's-headed Sphinx has occasioned much terror among the vulgar, at times, by the melancholy kind of cry which it utters, and the insignia of death which it wears upon its corslet.'"

He here closed the book and leaned forward in the chair, placing himself accurately in the position which I had occupied at the moment of beholding "the monster."

"Ah, here it is," he presently exclaimed— "it is reascending the face of the hill, and a very remarkable looking creature I admit it to be. Still, it is by no means so large or so distant as you imagined it,—for the fact is that, as it wriggles its way up this thread, which some spider has wrought along the window-sash, I find it to be about the sixteenth of an inch in its extreme length, and also about the sixteenth of an inch distant from the pupil of my eye."

The Blue Beetle: A Confession

A. G. Gray, Jr.

Day after day, and night after night did I brood over the discovery which I thought was about to be opened up to me. I had long had a belief in the progressive development of creation; I believed that it was still possible to find the speck—the germ from which I could raise up a perfectly organized living being. I felt a new and strange pleasure in believing that the mystery of creation was now solved—that from the first inorganic atom which had received the force of life all other created beings had slowly, gradually, regularly advanced, up to the period in which I had lived.

The power of creation—the secret of life, was my goal. My belief was, that the force of life might be given to this inorganic atom. My books were those of the alchemists.—With that wild delight I hailed the writings of Albertus Magnus, of Arnold de Villeneuve, Heidenburg of Tritheim, Raymond Lully, and Bernard of Traves. I believed in the alchemists. I struggled through the intricacies of their hidden language: their experiments in search of gold I passed over, wonderful as they were, and strangely as they opened my mind to the real truth, I repeated all their experiments on life force, and substantiated every fact I read. My laboratory was perfectly furnished; my days were spent there, and often entire nights. My mind was absorbed in the great truth I was bringing to light.

The confined air of my laboratory at length affected my health: a change was absolutely necessary. I struggled against the idea of removing for some time and often left my little wife with tears standing in her deep blue eyes, after she had unsuccessfully implored me to leave London for it short while. Dear Annie! And yet I loved her! Heavens to think that I—, but I must proceed with my story as it occurred.

We went to the north of Northumberland to stay with my old friend C—, who had frequently asked us to come on precious occasions. We were received warmly; and, as it was winter time, we had plenty of occupation.

A few brisk runs with the country foxhounds almost made me forget my laboratory. The weather at length changed, first a severe frost with snow, and then to a complete thaw. The dismal north-east wind shrieked through the leafless trees, and drove torrents of sleet splashing against the old-fashioned windows.

Tired of hoping and weary of grumbling, I was driven to take refuge in C—'s library. After a long search for something interesting, I came upon a little brown volume bound with two dingy metal clasps.—On opening its dark and discolored pages, I found that it was written in French manuscript. A hurried glance showed me that the work was on alchemy, a translation from the Arabic. All my former hopes returned in an instant. I pored over the pages of my newly obtained treasure till late on in the evening—heedless of the impatience of my friends, who, after several useless attempts to draw me away, at last left me to my book and self.

The secret, then, was not mine; here, in this old neglected book, I had found a groundwork for my exertions. All the truths I had collected, all the experiments I had made bore me out. I saw what had prevented others, in ancient times, from carrying out their designs. They knew not the life-giving power: the wonders of electricity had not been discovered. Vaguely hinted at and darkly guessed at in their works I saw them groping their way in mist and uncertainty: but I—I was surrounded by the light of science. Wonderful, mysterious truths broke upon my mind. My whole method and plan of operations stood out clearly before me. A restless force urged me to commence my scheme instantly. I must leave for London that very night.

I found my wile and friends retiring to rest. I told them my intention of starting for town immediately. Remonstrance and entreaty were of no avail, and in less than an hour I had reached the train at the neighboring railway station, and was hastening through the stormy night towards London. The train seemed to drag slowly through the darkness, but about noon next day I arrived at my house.

Without rest I commenced my operations; late at night I had nearly completed them, and worn out in body and mind I threw myself on the floor to sleep, lulled by the subdued sound of my furnace, which moaned and muttered like an unhappy spirit.

Early in the morning after a feverish sleep, I rose tired and unrefreshed, and began to complete the last portion of my arrangements. This was to prepare the liquid from which the beings to whom I was to impart life were to spring. On account of the experiments made in my late studies I had all the ingredients ready in my laboratory.

I poured the mixture then carefully into a large silver trough. The liquid was limpid and of a beautiful blue color, probably on account of a salt of copper entering largely into its composition.

And now I prepared my batteries, and soon afterwards the electric agent was applied. To my astonishment no decomposition took place—the liquid remained clear and beautifully blue. Thus it remained for some hours. I hung over it in breathless expectation: the only change apparently being that the color seemed deeper and purer.

Night came on, and the electric fluid still quietly streamed into the liquid. By accident, in adjusting one of the wires, I dashed a few drops from the trough on the floor.—There was a hissing sound as they fell, and as they touched the ground they burst into flame. This I extinguished, and then applied myself to observing closely the contents of the vessel, for I knew that a great change had taken place in their constitution.

I removed the light to a distance, fearing lest it should ignite the vapors which were now rising from the surface. On returning in the dark I found strange flashes of light circling in the interior of the fluid; these gradually became brighter till I was enabled to see every object in the room clearly by their radiance.

Subtle fumes also were arising from the surface. On inhaling these fumes at first I felt faint, but the sensation passed away.—The perfume now was delicious—it was heavenly: I drank it in like nectar. I gazed upon the corruscating surface, and a delicious ecstasy seemed to pervade my whole being: delicious streams of music fell softly on my ears, and shadowy forms of ineffable beauty floated in the air around me. Suddenly an insane desire took possession of me: I longed to seize the silver vessel and quaff the deep blue poison. I stretched out my hands with a cry of joy—and then—

I recovered at last from a fever which kept me insensible for a week. It was some days before I could get any explanation of how I came to be in my own bed-room, with my little wife attending to my every want, her little hands ever busy, and her eyes beaming with love and tenderness.

Gradually the details of my late occupation dawned upon my memory. I imagined I perceived the subtle odor diffusing itself through the chamber, and shuddered as I lay back on my pillow. A feeling of remorse came over me when I thought of my design. I felt as if I had intruded where man should fear to tread, and I felt gratification in thinking that my designs had been frustrated.

One morning, when the physician said that I was able to bear the news, I was told that one of the domestics hearing a scream on that fearful night had forced open the door of the laboratory. A strange overpowering perfume, he said, at first drove him back, but rushing in a second time, he found me lying insensible on the floor.

With breathless eagerness I asked if any of the apparatus in the room had been touched? No, nothing had been touched; the windows had been opened to allow the poisonous vapors to escape, the doors had then been locked and had never been opened since. A weight seemed removed from my mind—I would instantly go down and destroy all that remained of my strange experiment.

I was still too weak: three or four days passed over, and then I was able to go down stairs. With trembling hands and beating heart (why I could not tell) I turned the key and entered the laboratory alone.—Everything remained as I had left it a fortnight before.

There stood the ponderous batteries, long since worked out; there loosely hung the copper connecting wires covered with green rust. The silver trough was tarnished and dim, but everything stood as I had left it.

The interior of the trough was coated with metallic copper, while the solution had almost entirely evaporated: there was still a small quantity of liquid at the bottom, covered with thick, opal-tinted mould.

On looking closely at this mould-covered residue, I noticed a peculiar irregularity in its surface. There were five little heaps or hillocks in regular arrangement—one at each angle of a square, and one in the centre—*exactly like the five-side of a gaming die*. These heaps were of such equal size and uniform shape, that I could not attribute their presence to chance. I suppose that electricity had so acted upon the particles of the solution as to make them take up their present position.

I examined the mould under the microscope, and found it to be a fungus of a peculiar kind, but in removing some more of the mould with a glass rod, I happened to touch one of the little heaps, and found under it a small blue crystal of cubic firm, and under each of the other three angular hillocks I found a similar crystal. On removing the mould from the centre hillock I found what, at first, I thought was a circular mass of the same crystaline substance; but imagine my surprise and horror when I saw the mass begin to struggle among the liquid, and, clearing away the silky needles of the mould, disclose to my view a large scarabaeus of perfect shape and of a deep blue transparent color.

A feeling of terror filled my mind.—Whence had come this strange creature? Whence came the powers with which he stretched out his antennae, drew the blue case-covers from his back, and cleared the mould from his filmy wings? Could this be the result of my researches—my days of toil, my nights of unrest? A beetle! I strove to laugh, but the attempt failed and my heart sank within me with a strange foreboding. At this moment, from the interior of the trough arose a peculiar sound—like the rapid ticking of a clock, although louder, and with a metallic tinkle in it—it was the same sound as that produced by the "death-tick" beetle.

As soon as the sound died away I looked once more at the creature; he was half out of the liquid, and evidently as yet unable to fly. The prominent desire in my mind was to destroy the insect for his unearthly sounds and the strange flashing of his bead-like eyes made me tremble with a vague terror. However, I overcame the feeling, and determined to let him live for a few days.

Early the next morning I visited the laboratory, but on looking into the silver vessel, I was unable to detect the scarabaeus. Puzzled and annoyed, I began to inspect the room, when I suddenly heard the ominous "death-tick," and after a few preliminary flights round the room, the beetle alighted upon the rim of the trough. A ray of sunlight glancing in fell upon him, his color was exquisite—a rich deep cerulean blue, he seemed a living sapphire, and would have been beautiful but for his loathsome form.

I had brought a piece of sugar with me, which I thought might please the taste of my new favorite. I placed it on the bench near— he flew directly towards it and settled upon it; but, as if dissatisfied, a moment afterwards he flew back to the rim of the trough. I heard a low whine at my feet, and looking down, saw my wife's little dog, "Lalette." I threw the rejected sugar towards her, and soon heard her crunching it up in her little jaws. Shortly afterwards I left the room, and as I closed the door, louder than ever I heard the sound of the "death-tick."

I was engaged out of doors during the day, and in the evening my wife's first question was, whether I had seen "Lalette" that day? I then remembered that she had been in the laboratory with me in the morning, and fancying that she must be locked in, I went to the door, and on opening it called her by name. There was no movement or response: but as I called again, something whirred past me in the air and dashed out into the hall. I felt certain that my beetle had escaped. Shutting the door hastily, I rushed back for a light. On reentering the laboratory I could neither see nor hear anything of the beetle; but in the middle of the floor, exactly where I had left her in the morning, poor "Lalette" was lying dead.

Some portions of the sugar were still lying beside her—she had been poisoned. Once more before leaving I sought diligently for the beetle, but no trace was to be found; "Lalette" was a great favorite, and my poor wife was inconsolable. I told her the dog must have picked up some poison in my room; and with promises of a new canine favorite soon her grief calmed down.

All that night an indefinable horror took possession of me. When I thought of that living sapphire being at large in the house, a firm belief possessed me that "Lalette" had been killed by that poisonous insect.

All that night he haunted my dreams; several times I started from slumber, thinking I heard that unearthly death-tick. I determined in my feverish sleeplessness to search every nook and corner of the house on the morrow. I felt at times that my existence, my destiny, was bound up in the life of this hideous insect.

Reproaches seemed spoken to me, in one dream of that long night, that I had created a living poison, and sent it out into the world. I shuddered and awoke. The words seemed burnt upon my brain. Could I ever forget them? Listen!

Next morning I heard that one of the domestics, a young and pretty girl of nineteen years, was ill. Three days afterwards she died. The doctors said it was heart disease. One of them, a sententious old empiric, said the only peculiarity of the case was a strange mark upon the girl's breast. A pang shot through my whole frame. A mark! What mark? What was it like? By a mysterious perception I knew that this mark concerned me. But how? I soon knew. On the cold white breast of the corpse were *five blue spots*, arranged like the spots on the *five side of a die*. Controlling my emotions as best I could, I locked myself in my own room, and, burying my face in my hands, cried, in agony— "Accursed beast! this is thy work; the blood of an innocent being is on my hands!" My brain seemed whirling around, and every attempt to collect my thoughts was in vain. The infernal creature—my creature?— had murdered this young girl, and how knew I where he would stop? One thing was plain; my wife and the whole household must be removed immediately. Seizing a pen, I hurriedly wrote to C—, and explaining, as best I could, the unexpected visit of my wife, I went up to the station and saw her start by the first train to the North. The corpse of the young girl was removed by her friends in the afternoon, and the other servants were despatched to their respective homes.

I was left alone in the house all that long, lonely night. I waited in each room listening for that fearful "death-tick. Never lover waited more anxiously for a loving whisper from loved lip than I for that hideous sound. But, save the hushed murmur of the mighty city, and the clang of the slow hours as they passed, and the beating of me own heart, all was silence. I searched all that night and the next, but no vestige of the loathsome creature could I find. On the fourth day came a letter from my wife. My friend C— was ill; he was sinking fast, and wished to see me.

Locking up my house—not without some dread—I journeyed northward to C—'s house. As I drove up the long avenue in the afternoon, I thought the old mansion had a mournful gloom brooding over it.—My heart was depressed—a presentiment of evil hung about me. I could not cast it off. The tearful face of the servant who admitted me added to my mournful forebodings.

I found C— in bed, dying. Dying!—The first glance showed me that his days were numbered. A sickly smile of welcome played over his features as I approached him but it almost instantly changed for a look of intense suffering. I asked what the particular symptoms of his illness were. The medical man in attendance tried to explain the malady, but left me painfully impressed with the idea that he was entirely ignorant of the disease. I had turned to speak to some of the family who were in the room, when I was startled by a piercing cry of agony from the bed.

C— was sitting up in bed, his wan face was distorted with pain; he was grasping his neck with his white nervous hands.— "My throat is on fire!" he shrieked.— "It burns, it burns! Water! for the love of heaven! a drop of water!" Trembling, I held a tumbler of water to his lips; he had scarcely tasted it than he dashed the glass from my hands to the floor, exclaiming. "Devil! I did not ask for vitriol—give me water—water!" As he said this he tore open the neck of his dressing-gown.—Merciful Heavens! could I believe my eyesight? There was the fatal mark. There seen among the purple distended veins which interlaced like strong cords around his neck—I could see it. *Five blue spots arranged like the five-side of a die!* The room swam before my eyes, and the word "Murderer!", seemed ringing its my ears.

When I recovered, C— was dead. My agitation had been attributed to grief at my friend's death; no one had noticed the cursed mark but myself. The members of the family were absorbed in grief: my wife strove to soothe and solace them: but such work was not for me. I gave myself up to my own frightful reflections.

The creature had then found his way to this remote place; how, I knew not, nor did I ever know. It was enough for me to know that he was there. My oldest, truest friend was dead, and a happy home had been rendered wretched, and through me!—Through this cursed creature of mine.—Why had I not obeyed the first impulse, and killed him as he lay in the mould in the silver trough.

I wandered out into the night; my mind was all in desolate confusion. It was a lovely night—the sky glimmered with stars, and the full moon rose as I walked with uneven steps through the trees. I threw myself on the wet grass and wept like a child. Soon the soft shimmer of the moonlight broke out into full radiance, and bathed the whole country in a flood of beautiful light. The gentleness of the scene after it time impressed me. I became calmer and reflected on my position. "If the creature is here, he must be hunted down." I dare not tell the household: there was guilt and blood on my conscience. They would deem me mad, I thought. Then, again, I thought the excitement of the last few days, together with my late illness, might have produced the effect of an optical illusion—that there was no mark. This conviction strengthened, I turned again to the house.

The servant who opened the door started when he saw my altered appearance, matted hair, and wet disorderly dress. But I asked calmly to be shown to the room where the body of C— was lying. I went in alone. Need I tell the result?—the fearful mark was there, and stood out brightly against the cold white skin.

Every corner of the room I searched, but no trace of the fiendish beast was there.—After some time spent in this vain search I left the room, and gained my wife and her friends below. They were shocked at my strange appearance. I sat apart, moody and silent. A heavy suffocating cloud of presentiment overpowered me—I felt that my cup was not yet filled, I should have to drink it to its bitter—bitter dregs. We separated to retire to rest; but though few of us expected to sleep, no sooner had I laid my head on the pillow than I fell asleep—as dreamless and almost as breathless as that of the corpse in the next chamber. I do not know how long I had slept, when I awoke suddenly with an unaccountable feeling of terror.

How dark the room is getting—put your ear closer to my mouth—I feel faint with speaking; loud—but I must tell you all.

I awoke, and, seemingly, close by my ear—loud and distinct—I heard the death tick! My hands clenched till the nails penetrated the flesh when I knew he was within my reach—close by my ear! Heaven help me if I do not crush the creature now.

The moonbeams poured in through the windows and filled the room with it mysterious light. The rays struck across the pillows of the bed and fell softly on the upturned face of my little wife. She slumbered peacefully; but on her snowy brow, glittering as blue as heaven itself, was the loathsome beetle. With one blow I struck him from her face, and then leaped from the bed. I saw his glittering jewel-like form upon the ground—I seized it and crushed it in my hands—a fierce pain shot up to arm—my blood seemed changed to molten lead. The agony was excruciating, I dropped the vile abortion; he flew from me, and dashing through the glass of the window, disappeared in the moonlight night.

My story is well nigh told. You know—you know how my wife sickened and—died. But listen! you did not see the blue mark upon her white brow.

How dark the room is—and how slowly my heart is beating. Look at this arm—here!—above the elbow, there is the death brand—*five blue spots arranged like the spots on a die.* I have but an hour to live. You know my secret.

Let me rest.

The Strong Spider
Henry Abbey

I
The Chief's Daughter

I was a naturalist, and had crossed the sea
And come to Theodosia, to find
A monstrous spider of which I had heard.
The people of the town wagged doubting heads,
When asked about it; but one day I met
A sturdy fisherman who once had seen
The spider, though he knew not his abode.
He said the spider was as long as he,
And that the woof whereof he wove his web,
Was thick as any cordage on his boat.
At night, belated 'mid the tumuli
That mound the hill-side and the vernal vale,
Like the raised letters of an ancient page
Made for the blind gropers of to-day to read,
He entered a dark tomb, and therein slept,
Until the world, like some round shield upraised,
Splintered the thrown spears of dawn. As he
    woke,
He found himself ensnared in some thick web,
Yet reached his knife, and slowly cut it through;
Then when he stood, a monstrous spider fled.

At this recital on the slanted shore,
Another joined us from the cottage near—
A vine-clad cottage, fit for love's abode.

A lily-croft, with trees, encinctured it;
Like Ahab in his house of ivory
Dining on sweets, the king bee here
Sipped in the snowy lily's palace hall;
And here were yellow lilies strewn about,
As though the place had been the banquet grove
Of Shishak, king of Egypt; for the flowers
Seemed like the cups of gold that Solomon
Wrought for the holy service of the Lord.

"This is my daughter," said the fisherman.
Her head and face were covered with a scarf,
But large dark eyes looked forth, and in their
    depths
I saw a soul all tenderness and truth.

(Often, in dreams, I thought it sweet to die,
And reft of this gross vision, see at last,
As the large soul, quit of the body can,
Another soul set free and purified.)

The modest maid a crimson jacket wore,
And to her knee the broidered skirt hung down;
While 'neath, the Turkish garment was confined
In plaits about the ankles; but her shoes
Revealed the naked insteps of her feet.
I bade her there adieu, upon the shore
Of the clear Bospore. As I wandered back,
I thought much of the spider that I sought;
But more of two dark eyes, that seemed two stars
Which shone down in my heart; while the far
    space
Behind them, pure, but unknown, was the soul.

I thought to test this maiden's charity;
And so, one friendly day, put on a robe
Tattered and soiled with use. As she went by,
I strode abruptly from behind a wall,
And faced her with a face disguised, and held
My hand out while I begged for some small alms.

She gave abundantly from her lean purse,
And with a look of tender pity, passed.
It matters little who it is that asks,
Or whether he deserves the alms or not;
That given with free heart, is given to God,
And not to him who takes.

Day after day,
Henceforth, I strode a coastward way, to meet
The dark-eyed daughter of the fisherman.
Beneath her roof she made my welcome sweet,
And yielded both her hands, and drew the scarf
That veiled the wondrous beauty of her face.
If painter, or if sculptor, in some dream,
Could mingle Faith with Love and Charity,
And give them utterance in one pure face,
I know the face would be a face like hers.
Her eyes were diamond doors of her true soul,
And with their silken latches softly closed,
When, couched beneath his poppy parachute,
Inactive Sleep came by. Her glances seemed
Like gold-winged angels sent from heavenly doors.
Yet she was often sad when I was near.
Once, tarrying late, I told her of my life,
And of the monster I had come to find;
But now, lo! she around my heart had wound
The close web of her love, and held me fast
As any fly caught in a spider's toils.

Clothed in the sackcloth of regret, she said,
She long had wept the past; but for my sake
She now would cast it off, and live for me.

I said that few could exculpate the past
From stormy doing with the ships of hope.

She said it made her sad to think upon
Their present dwindled fortune, and the yoke
Her people chafed their necks in, on the hills.
Her father was a brave Circassian chief;

But here he dwelt disguised, till once again
He could lead on his race, and wound the heel
That ground them to the dust.

              Our hearts made new,
We kissed good-night, and parted. As I went,
A distant hill, all shadow, took new shape,
And seemed a sprawling spider, while two trees
That grew upon it, were his upraised arms
Clutching at two red fire-flies, that were stars.

                    II
               The Spider

With day-break came a knuckle at my door;
I rose, and opened, and upon the porch,
His face like strange death's, and his dark eyes
      wide
With some vague horror, stood the fisherman.
"Come, hasten with me," were his only words.
We ran our best along the barren shore,
And gained his silent cottage. Entering,
He led me to his daughter's vacant couch.
The room had but one window, and the sash
Was raised. I looked out to the ground beneath.
A vine crept up, and with long fingers made
Abode secure upon the cottage side,
And o'er the window threw a leafy scarf.
But what was this, that fastened to the ledge
Trailed to the ground? A glutinous rope
Twisted with five strands. This the fisherman
Saw with new horror, while between white lips
He gasped, "The Spider!"

              What was best to do?
We saw strange foot-prints on the moistened beach,
But these were lost soon in a wooded dell
Where all trace had an end. The long day through
We sought among the tombs, up from the dell;

But unrewarded, when the sun was quenched,
Sat down to weep. So darkness dropped,
And like an awful spider, o'er the earth
Crawled with gaunt legs of shadow. Then our
    homes
We sadly sought, to meet again at morn.

The night was warm, and with my window raised,
I sat and mourned, and wrung my hopeless hands.
No light was in the house. I half reclined—
My back toward the window. Something shut
The puny sheen of starlight from the room.
The Thing, a monstrous shape, was with me there,
And two hard arms were thrown about my waist.
For very terror I was hushed, nor moved
To cast my foe off. I was in the arms
Of the strong spider. As we went, I grew
Glad, for I thought that now I should be brought
To the great spider's web, and there, mayhap,
Learn the sad fate of her I loved so well.
Up a stark cliff we went, then crossed the web
Just as the red moon bloomed upon the hills
And silvered all the Panticapean vale.
The funnel of the web was in the mouth
Of a vast tomb, whose outside, hewn on rock,
Outlined a Gorgon's face with jaws agape—
Some stern Medusa, Stheno, or Euryale,
Changed to the stone that in the elder days
She changed the sons of men who looked on her.
We passed the funnel, entering the tomb.
About my arms the spider threw his cords,
And shackled them. I dared not move, but lay
Upon the smooth stone floor, inured to fear.
I fancied now that I was safe till dawn.
If I could use my hands I then might find
Some weapon of defense, some club, or stone,
And so resist with some small chance for life.
The thought bred strength. I slowly drew my arms
Upon my sides, and, with persistence, gained
Their freedom; though about the wrists, the flesh

Was bruised and harrowed, and my blood made wet
The spider's cord wherewith I had been bound.

The night seemed endless. As it came to dawn,
A faint moan woke an echo in the tomb.
The echo seemed a cry of pity, sent
For solace to the moan. As light grew strong,
I saw, not far from where I had been laid,
A maiden sitting. All her hair set free,
She made of it a pillow as she leaned
Against the painted wall. My heart threw wide
To her my arms, his hospitable doors;
The guest within, at once the doors were shut.

The sun came up, and spread a cloth of gold
Over the sea. We saw the vale beneath,
And there the town, and fancied where, among
The trees upon the shore, her cottage stood;
Then hoped 'gainst hope to enter it again.
Two thousand years ago, this distant sea
Teemed with the thrifty commerce of the world.
When Athens was, and when her scholars cut,
With thoughts of iron, their own deathless names
Into the stone page of fame, this vale beneath
Held a great city. These, its tombs, endure.
There is no better scoff at the parade
And vanity of life, than that a tomb suggests.

While we looked forth on the historic view,
We saw the subtle spider throw his cord
Over an eagle tangled in the web.
The eagle fought, not mildly overcome,
And spread his wings, and darted his sharp beak.
At last the spider caught him by the neck,
With his serrated claws that grew like horns,
And killed him; then plucked the vanquished plumes,
And sucked the warm blood from the sundered ends.
From this we knew the monster brought us here
To serve a hideous banquet, and that one
Must need be near, and see the other slain.

The web was like the sail of some large ship,
And reached forth from the Gorgon's open mouth,
On either side, to boughs of blighted trees.
Birds were caught in it, and about the place
Wherein the spider hid to watch for prey,
Their bones lay bleaching in the sun and rain.
Upon the web the winds laid violent hands,
And tugged at it, but lacked the sinewed strength
To tear it or divorce it from its place.
The rain left on it when the sun came up,
Dyed the vast cloth with all prismatic hues,
And made it glitter like the silken sail
Of Cleopatra's barge.

                We felt quite sure
The eagle's death bequeathed new lease of life.
We cast about at once, in hope to find
Some object for defense. The tomb was strange.
Alone the spider could have known of it.
A rich sarcophagus stood in the midst,
Of deftly inlaid woods, or carved, or bronzed.
Within, a skeleton, its white skull crowned
With gold bestarred with diamonds, chilled my blood.
A bronze lamp, cast to represent the beast
Slain by Bellerophon, the Chimaera,
Was on the floor; and from its lion's mouth
The flame had issued, like the flame of life
That flickered and went out with him gold-crowned.
A target stood near by, and on it clashed
Griffon and stag, adverse as right and wrong.
About, lay cups of onyx set in gold.
On conic jars were bacchanalian scenes,—
Nude chubby Bacchi, grotesque leering fauns,
All linked 'neath vines that grew important grapes;
And in the jars were rings and flowers of gold.
We found twin ear-drops cut from choicest stone,
Metallic mirrors, and a statuette
Of amorous Dido naked to the waist.
Life is a harp, and all its nervous strings,
Touched by the fingers of the fear of death,

Jar with pathetic music. Having found
No trusty implement to bar the way
Of threatening peril, we embraced,
And kissed with silent kisses mixed with tears,
And waited for the end.

　　　　　　　　When no more,
Hope, like an eagle in the mountain air,
Soars in time's future, it mounts up with wings
Toward the unmapped city walled by death.
Thither the eagle of our hope took flight.

The sun was in the zenith. His back
Toward us, crouched the spider, at the mouth
Of our strange prison on the towering cliff.
The spider's shape was full a fathom long.
Two parts it had, the fore part, head and breast;
The hinder part, the trunk. The first was black,
But all the last was covered with short hair,
Yellow and fine. Eight sprawling legs adhered
To his tough breast. Eight eyes were in his head,
Two in the front, and three on either side;
They had no eyelids, and were never closed,
Protected by a strong transparent nail.
His pincers grew between his foremost eyes—
Were toothed like saws, were venomous, and sharp,
With claws on either end. Two arms stretched out
From his mailed shoulders, and with these he caught
His tangled prey, or guided what he spun.
Slowly the monster turned, and glared at us,
Working his arms, and opening his claws,
Then moved toward us fiercely for attack.
We ran to gain the limit of the tomb
Where darkness was; there as we crouched with
　　　dread,
My foot struck some hard substance. In despair
I grasped at it, and with great joy upheld
An ancient sword!—surely, a sharp, bold tooth
To bite the spider. I would sink it deep,
Up to the gum of the crossed guard. Alert,

I sprang upon the monster as he came,
And with one blow cut off his brutish head.
He writhed awhile with pain, but in the end,
Drew up the eight long legs and two thick arms,
And rolling over on his useless back,
Died with a pang.

    So we issued forth,
And the green earth seemed happy to be free,
And glad the sky cloud-frescoed 'gainst the blue.
We sought the sea-side cottage, where the chief
Clasped once again his daughter to his breast.
Down from the hill we fetched the spider slain,
And I to science gave these simple facts:
Spiders have no antennae, therefore rank
Not with the insects. As they breathe with gills
Beneath the body, they possess a heart.

The treasure of the tomb brought wealth to us,
And we who loved were wed one golden day;
And the great Czar hearing our story told,
Sent presents to the bride of silk and pearls.

The Queen of the Bees
Erckmann-Chatrian

"As you go from Motiers-Navers to Boudry, on your way to Neufchatel," said the young professor of botany, "you follow a road between two walls of rocks of immense height; they reach a perpendicular elevation of five or six hundred feet, and are hung with wild plants, the mountain basil (*thymus alpinus*), ferns (*polypodium*), the whortleberry (*vitis idoea*), ground ivy, and other climbing plants producing a wonderful effect.

"The road winds along this defile; it rises, falls, turns, sometimes tolerably level, sometimes broken and abrupt, according to the thousand irregularities of the ground. Grey rocks almost meet in an arch overhead, others stand wide apart, leaving the distant blue visible, and discovering sombre and melancholy-looking depths, and rows of firs as far as the eye could reach.

"The Reuss flows along the bottom, sometimes leaping along in waterfalls, then creeping through thickets, or steaming, foaming, and thundering over precipices, while the echoes prolong the tumult and roar of its torrents in one immense endless hum. Since I left Tubingen the weather had continued fine; but when I reached the summit of this gigantic staircase, about two leagues distant from the little hamlet of Novisaigne, I suddenly noticed great grey clouds begin passing overhead, which soon filled up the defile entirely; this vapour was so dense that it soon penetrated my clothes as a heavy dew would have done.

"Although it was only two in the afternoon, the sky became clouded over as if darkness was coming on; and I foresaw a heavy storm was about to break over my head.

"I consequently began looking about for shelter, and I saw through one of those wide openings which afford you a perspective

30

view of the Alps, about two or three hundred yards distant on the slope leading down to the lake, an ancient-looking grey chalet, moss-covered, with its small round windows and sloping roof loaded with large stones, its stairs outside the house, with a carved rail, and its basket-shaped balcony, on which the Swiss maidens generally hang their snowy linen and scarlet petticoats to dry.

"Precisely as I was looking down, a tall woman in a black cap was folding and collecting the linen which was blowing about in the wind.

"To the left of this building a very large apiary supported on beams, arranged like a balcony, formed a projection above the valley.

"You may easily believe that without the loss of a moment I set off bounding through the heather to seek for shelter from the coming storm, and well it was I lost no time, for I had hardly laid my hand on the handle of the door before the hurricane burst furiously overhead; every gust of wind seemed about to carry the cottage bodily away; but its foundations were strong, and the security of the good people within, by the warmth of their reception, completely reassured me about the probability of any accident.

"The cottage was inhabited by Walter Young, his wife Catherine, and little Roesel, their only daughter.

"I remained three days with them; for the wind, which went down about midnight, had so filled the valley of Neufchatel with mist, that the mountain where I had taken refuge was completely enveloped in it; it was impossible to walk twenty yards from the door without experiencing great difficulty in finding it again.

"Every morning these good people would say, when they saw me buckle on my knapsack— What are you about, Mr. Hennetius? You cannot mean to go yet; you will never arrive anywhere. In the name of Heaven stay here a little longer!'

"And Young would open the door and exclaim—

"'Look there, sir; you must be tired of your life to risk it among these rocks. Why, the dove itself would be troubled to find the ark again in such a mist as this.'

"One glance at the mountain side was enough for me to make up my mind to put my stick back again in the corner.

"Walter Young was a man of the old times. He was nearly sixty; his grand head wore a calm and benevolent expression—a real Apostle's head. His wife, who always wore a black silk cap, pale and thoughtful, resembled him much in disposition. Their two profiles, as I looked

at them defined sharply against the little panes of glass in the
chalet's windows, recalled to may mind those drawings of Albert
Durer the sight of which carried me back to the age of faith and
the patriarchal manners of the fifteenth century. The long brown
rafters of the ceiling, the deal table, the ashen chairs with the
carved backs, the tin drinking-cups, the sideboard with its old-fashioned painted plates and dishes, the crucifix with the Saviour
carved in box on an ebony cross, and the wormeaten clock-case
with its many weights and its porcelain dial, completed the illusion.

"But the face of their little daughter Roesel was still more touching. I think I can see her now, with her flat horsehair cap and watered
black silk ribbons, her trim bodice and broad blue sash down to
her knees, her little white hands crossed in the attitude of a
dreamer, her long fair curls—all that was graceful, slender, and
ethereal in nature. Yes, I can see Roesel now, sitting in a large leath-
ern armchair, close to the blue curtain of the recess at the end of
the room, smiling as she listened and meditated.

"Her sweet face had charmed me from the first moment I saw
her, and I was continually on the point of inquiring why she wore
such an habitually melancholy air, why did she hold her pale face
down so invariably, and why did she never raise her eyes when
spoken to?

"Alas! the poor child had been blind from her birth. "She had
never seen the lake's vast expanse, nor its blue sheet blending so
harmoniously with the sky, the fishermen's boats which ploughed
its surface, the wooded heights which crowned it and cast their quivering reflection on its waters, the rocks covered with moss, the green
Alpine plants in their vivid and brilliant colouring; nor had she
ever watched the sun set behind the glaciers, nor the long shades
of evening draw across the valleys, nor the golden broom, nor the
endless heather—nothing. None of these things had she ever seen;
nothing of what we saw every day from the windows of the chalet.

"'What an ironical commentary on the gifts of Fortune!' thought
I, as I sat looking out of the window at the mist, in expectation of
the sun's appearing once more, 'to be blind in this place! here in
presence of Nature in its sublimest form, of such limitless grandeur! To be blind! Oh, Almighty God, who shall dare to dispute
Thy impenetrable decrees, or who shall venture to murmur at the
severity of Thy justice, even when its weight falls on an innocent

child? But to be thus blind in the presence of Thy grandest creations, of creations which ceaselessly renew our enthusiasm, our love, and our adoration for Thy genius, Thy power, and Thy goodness; of what crime can this poor child have been guilty thus to deserve Thy chastisement?'

"And my reflections continually reverted to this topic.

"I asked myself, too, what compensation Divine pity could make its creature for the deprival of its greatest blessing, and, finding none, I began to doubt its power.

"'Man, in his presumption,' said the royal poet, "dares to glorify himself in his knowledge, and judge the Eternal. But his wisdom is but folly, and his light darkness.'

"On that day one of Nature's great mysteries was revealed to me, doubtless with the purpose of humbling my vanity, and of teaching me that nothing is impossible to God, and that it is in His power only to multiply our senses, and by so doing gratify those who please Him."

Here the young professor took a pinch from his tortoiseshell snuff-box, raised his eyes to the ceiling with a contemplative air, and then, after a short pause, continued in these terms:—

"Does it not often happen to you, ladies, when you are in the country in fine weather in summer, especially after a brief storm, when the air is warm, and the exhalations from the ground filling it with the perfume of thousands of plants, and their sweet scent penetrates and warms you; when the foliage from the trees in the solitary avenues, as well as from the hushes, seems to lean over you as if it sought to take you in its arms and embrace you; when the minutest flowers, the humble daisy, the blue forget-me-not, the convolvulus in the hedgerows raise their heads and follow you with a longing look—does it not happen to you to experience an inexpressible sensation of languor, to sigh for no apparent reason, and even to feel inclined to shed tears, and to ask yourselves, 'Why does this feeling of love oppress me? why do my knees bend under me? whence these tears?'

"Whence indeed, ladies? Why from life, and the thousands of living things which surround you, lean to you, and call to you to stay with them, while they gently murmur, 'We love you; love us, and do not leave us.'

"You can easily imagine, then, the deep enthusiastic feeling and the religious sentiment of a person always in a similar state of ecstasy.

Even if blind, abandoned by his friends, do you think there is nothing to envy in his lot? or that his destiny is not infinitely happier than our own? For my own part I have not the slightest doubt of it.

"But you will, doubtless, say such a condition is impossible—the mind of man would break down under such a load of happiness. And, moreover, whence could such happiness be derived? What organs could transmit, and where could it find, such a sensation of universal life?

"This, ladies, is a question to which I can give you no answer; but I ask you to listen and then judge.

"The very day I arrived at the chalet I had made a singular remark—the blind girl was especially uneasy about the bees.

"While the wind was roaring without Roesel sat with her head on her hands listening attentively.

"'Father,' said she, 'I think at the end of the apiary the third hive on the right is still open. Go and see. The wind blows from the north; all the bees are home; you can shut the hive.'

"And her father having gone out by a side door, when he returned he said— 'It is all right, my child; I have closed the hive.'

"Half an hour afterwards the girl, rousing herself once more from her reverie, murmured— 'There are no more bees about, but under the roof of the apiary there are some waiting; they are in the sixth hive near the door; please go and let them in, father.'

"The old man left the house at once. He was away more than a quarter of an hour; then he came back and told his daughter that everything was as she wished it—the bees had just gone into their hive.

"The child nodded, and replied— 'Thank you, father.'

"Then she seemed to doze again.

"I was standing by the stove, lost in a labyrinth of reflections; how could that poor blind girl know that from such or such a hive there were still some bees absent, or that such a hive had been left open? This seemed inexplicable to me; but having been in the house hardly one hour, I did not feel justified in asking my hosts any questions with regard to their daughter, for it is sometimes painful to talk to people on subjects which interest them very nearly. I concluded that Young gave way to his daughter's fancies in order to induce her to believe she was of some service in the family, and that her forethought protected the bees from several accidents. That seemed the simplest explanation I could imagine, and I thought no more about it.

"About seven we supped on milk and cheese, and when it was time to retire Young led me into a good-sized room on the first floor, with a bed and a few chairs in it, panelled in fir, as is generally the case in the greater number of Swiss châlets. You are only separated from your neighbours by a deal partition, and you can hear every footstep and nearly every word.

"That night I was lulled to sleep by the whistling of the wind and the sound of the rain beating against the window-panes. The next day the wind had gone down and we were enveloped in mist. When I awoke I found my windows quite white, quite padded with mist.

"When I opened my window the valley looked like an immense stove; the tops of a few fir-trees alone showed their outlines against the sky; below, the clouds were in regular layers down to the surface of the lake; everything was calm, motionless, and silent.

"When I went down to the sitting-room I found my hosts seated at tables about to begin breakfast.

"'We have been waiting for you,' cried Young gaily.

"'You must excuse us,' said the mother; 'this is our regular breakfast hour.'

"'Of course, of course; I am obliged to you for not noticing my laziness.'

"Roesel was much more lively than the preceding evening; she had a fresh colour in her cheeks.

"'The wind has gone down,' said she; 'the storm has passed away without doing any harm.'

"'Shall I open the apiary?' asked Young.

"'No, not yet; the bees would lose themselves in this mist. Besides, everything is drenched with rain; the brambles and mosses are full of water; the least puff of wind would drown many of them. We must wait a little while. I know what is the matter: they feel dull, they want to work; they are tormented at the idea of devouring their honey instead of making it. But I cannot afford to lose them. Many of the hives are weak—they would starve in winter. We will see what the weather is like to-morrow.'

"The two old people sat and listened without making any observations.

"About nine the blind girl proposed to go and visit her bees; Young and Catherine followed her, and I did the same, from a very natural feeling of curiosity.

"We passed through the kitchen by a door which opened on to a terrace. Above us was the roof of the apiary; it was of thatch, and from its ledge honey-suckle and wild grapes hung in magnificent festoons. The hives were arranged on three shelves.

"Roesel went from one to the other, patting them, and murmuring—

"'Have a little patience; there is too much mist this morning. Ah! the greedy ones, how they grumble!'

"And we could hear a vague humming inside the hive, which increased in intensity until she had passed.

"That awoke all my curiosity once more. I felt there was some strange mystery which I could not fathom, but what was my surprise, when, as I went into the sitting-room, I heard the blind girl say in a melancholy tone of voice—

"'No, father, I would rather not see at all to-day than lose my eyes. I will sing, I will do something or other to pass the time, never mind what; but I will not let the bees out.'

"While she was speaking in this strange manner I looked at Walter Young, who glanced out of the window and then quietly replied—

"'You are right, child; I think you are right. Besides, there is nothing to see; the valley is quite white. It is not worth looking at.'

"And while I sat astounded at what I heard, the child continued—

"'What lovely weather we had the day before yesterday! Who would have thought that a storm on the lake would have caused all this mist? Now one must fold up its wings and crawl about like a wretched caterpillar.'

"Then again, after a few moments' silence—

"'How I enjoyed myself under the lofty pines on the Grinderwald! How the honey-dew dropped from the sky! It fell from every branch. What a harvest we made, and how sweet the air was on the shores of the lake, and in the rich Tannemath pastures—the green moss, and the sweet-smelling herbs! I sang, I laughed, and we filled our cells with wax and, honey. How delightful to lie everywhere, see everything, to fly humming about the woods, the mountains, and the valleys!'

"There was a fresh silence, while I sat, with mouth and eyes open, listening with the greatest attention, not knowing what to think or what to say.

"'And when the shower came,' she went on, 'how frightened we were! A great humble-bee, sheltered under the same fern as myself, shut his eyes at every flash; a grasshopper had sheltered itself under its great green branches, and some poor little crickets had scrambled up a poppy to save themselves from drowning. But what was most frightful was a nest o warblers quite close to us in a bush. The mother hovered round about us, and the little ones opened their beaks, yellow as far as their windpipes. How frightened we were! Good lord, we were frightened indeed! Thanks be to Heaven, a puff of wind carried us off to the mountain side; and now the vintage is over we must not expect to get out again so soon.'

"On hearing these descriptions of Nature so true, at this worship of day and light, I could no longer entertain the least doubt on the subject.

"'The blind girl sees,' said I to myself; 'she sees through thousands of eyes; the apiary is her life, her soul. Every bee carries a part of her away into space, and then returns drawn to her by thousands of invisible threads. The blind girl penetrates the flowers and the mosses; she revels in their perfume; when the sun shines she is everywhere; in the mountain side, in the valleys, in the forests, as far as her sphere of attraction extends.'

"I sat confounded at this strange magnetic influence, and felt tempted to exclaim—

"'Honour, glory, honour to the power, the wisdom, and the infinite goodness of the Eternal God! For Him nothing is impossible. Every day, every instant of our lives reveals to us His magnificence.'

"While I was lost in these enthusiastic reflections, Roesel addressed me with a quiet smile. "'Sir,' said she.

"'What, my child?'

"'You are very much surprised at me, and you are not the first person who has been so. The rector Hegel, of Neufchatel, and other travellers have been here on purpose to see me: they thought I was blind. You thought so too, did you not?'

"'I did indeed, my dear child, and I thank the Lord that I was mistaken.'

"'Yes,' said she, 'I know you are a good man—I can tell it by your voice. When the sun shines I shall open my eyes to look at you, and when you leave here I will accompany you to the foot of the mountain.'

"Then she began to laugh most artlessly.

"'Yes,' said she, 'you shall have music in your ears, and I will seat myself on your cheek; but you must take care—take care. You must not touch me, or I should sting you. You must promise not to be angry.'

"'I promise you, Roesel, I promise you I will not,' I said with tears in my eyes, 'and, moreover, I promise you never to kill a bee or any other insect except those which do harm.'

"'They are the eyes of the Lord,' she murmured. 'I can only see by my own poor bees, but He has every hive, every ant's nest, every leaf, every blade of grass. He lives, He feels, He loves, He suffers, He does good by means of all these. Oh, Monsieur Hennetius, you are right not to pain the Lord, who loves us so much!'

"Never in my life had I been so moved and affected, and it was a full minute before I could ask her—

"'So, my dear child, you see by your bees; will you explain to me how that is?'

"'I cannot tell, Monsieur Hennetius; it may be because I am so fond of them. When I was quite a little child they adopted me, and they have never once hurt me. At first I liked to sit for hours in the apiary all alone and listen to their humming for hours together. I could see nothing then, everything was dark to me; but insensibly light came upon me. At first I could see the sun a little, when it was very hot, then a little more, with the wild vine and the honey-suckle like a shade over me, then the full light of day. I began to emerge from myself; my spirit went forth with the bees. I could see the mountains, the rocks, the lake, the flowers and mosses, and in the evening, when quite alone, I reflected on these things. I thought how beautiful they were, and when people talked of this and that, of whortleberries, and mulberries, and heaths, I said to myself, "I know what all these things are like—they are black, or brown, or green." I could see them in my mind, and every day I became better acquainted with them, thanks to my dear bees; and therefore I love them dearly, Monsieur Hennetius. If you knew how it grieves me when the time comes for robbing them of their wax and their honey!'

"'I believe you, my child—I believe it does.'

"My delight at this wonderful discovery was boundless.

"Two days longer Roesel entertained me with a description of her impressions. She was acquainted with every flower; every Al-pine plant, and gave me an account of a great number which have

as yet received no botanical names, and which are probably only
to be found in inaccessible situations.

"The poor girl was often much affected when she spoke of her
dear friends, some little flowers.

"'Often and often,' said she, 'I have talked for hours with the
golden broom or the tender blue- eyed forget-me-not, and shared
in their troubles. They all wished to quit the earth and fly about;
they all complained of their being condemned to dry up in the
ground, and of being exposed to wait for days and weeks ere a drop
of dew came to refresh them.'

"And so Roesel used to repeat to me endless conversations of
this sort. It was marvellous! If you only heard her you would be
capable of falling in love with a dogrose, or of feeling a lively sympathy and a profound sentiment of compassion for a violet, its
misfortunes and its silent sufferings.

"What more can I tell you, ladies? It is painful to leave a subject where the soul has so many mysterious emanations; there is
such a field for conjecture; but as everything in this world must
have an end, so must even the pleasantest dreams.

"Early in the morning of the third day of my stay a gentle breeze
began to roll away the mist from off the lake. I could see its folds
become larger every second as the wind drove them along, leaving
one blue corner in the sky, and then another; then the tower of a
village church, some green pinnacles on the tops of the mountains,
then a row of firs, a valley, all the time the immense mass of vapour
slowly floated past us; by ten it had left us behind it, and the great
cloud on the dry peaks of the Chasseron still wore a threatening
aspect; but a last effort of the wind gave it a different direction,
and it disappeared at last in the gorges of Saint-Croix.

"Then the mighty nature of the Alps seemed to me to have
grown young again; the heather, the tall pines, the old chestnut-
trees dripping with dew, shone with vigorous health; there was
something in the view of them joyous, smiling, and serious all at
once. One felt the hand of God was in it all—His eternity.

"I went downstairs lost in thought; Roesel was already in the
apiary. Young opened the door and pointed her out to me sitting
in the shade of the wild vine, with her forehead resting on her
hands, as if in a doze.

"'Be careful,' said he to me, 'not to awake her; her mind is elsewhere; she sleeps; she is wandering about; she is happy.'

"The bees were swarming about by thousands, like a flood of gold over a precipice.

"I looked on at this wonderful sight for some seconds, praying the Lord would continue his love for the poor child.

"Then turning round— 'Master Young,' said I, 'it is time to go.'

"He buckled my knapsack on for me himself, and, put my stick into my hand.

"Mistress Catherine looked on kindly, and they both accompanied me to the threshold of the chalet.

"'Farewell!' said Walter, grasping my hand; 'a pleasant journey; and think of us sometimes!'

"'I can never forget you,' I replied, quite melancholy; 'may your bees flourish, and may Heaven grant you are as happy as you deserve to be!'

"'So be it, M. Hennetius,' said good Dame Catherine; 'amen; a happy journey, and good health to you.'

"I moved off.

"They remained on the terrace until I reached the road.

"Thrice I turned round and waved my cap, and they responded by waving their hands.

"Good people; why cannot we meet with such every day?'

"Little Roesel accompanied me to the foot of the mountain, as she had promised. For a long time her musical hum lightened the fatigue of my journey; I seemed to recognise her in every bee which came buzzing about my ears, and I fancied I could hear her say in a small shrill tone of voice—

"'Courage, M. Hennetius, courage; it is very hot, is it not? Come, let me give you a kiss; don't be afraid; you know we are very good friends.'

"It was only at the end of the valley that she took leave of me, when the sound of the lake drowned her gentle voice; but her idea followed me all through my journey, nor do I think it will ever leave me."

The Crab Spider
Erckmann-Chatrian

The warm mineral waters of Spinbronn, situated in the Hundsrueck, several leagues from Pirmesens, formerly enjoyed a magnificent reputation. All who were afflicted with gout or gravel in Germany repaired thither; the savage aspect of the country did not deter them.

They lodged in pretty cottages at the head of the defile; they bathed in the cascade, which fell in large sheets of foam from the summit of the rocks; they drank one or two decanters of mineral water daily, and the doctor of the place, Daniel Haselnoss, who distributed his prescriptions clad in a great wig and chestnut coat, had an excellent practice.

To-day the waters of Spinbronn figure no longer in the "Codex"; in this poor village one no longer sees anyone but a few miserable woodcutters, and, sad to say, Dr. Haselnoss has left!

All this resulted from a series of very strange catastrophes which lawyer Bremer of Pirmesens told me about the other day.

You should know, Master Frantz (said he), that the spring of Spinbronn issues from a sort of cavern, about five feet high and twelve or fifteen feet wide; the water has a warmth of sixty-seven degrees Centigrade; it is salt. As for the cavern, entirely covered without with moss, ivy, and brushwood, its depth is unknown because the hot exhalations prevent all entrance.

Nevertheless, strangely enough, it was noticed early in the last century that birds of the neighborhood—thrushes, doves, hawks—were engulfed in it in full flight, and it was never known to what mysterious influence to attribute this particular.

In 1801, at the height of the season, owing to some circumstance which is still unexplained, the spring became more abundant, and the bathers, walking below on the greensward, saw a human skeleton as white as snow fall from the cascade.

You may judge, Master Frantz, of the general fright; it was thought naturally that a murder had been committed at Spinbronn in a recent year, and that the body of the victim had been thrown in the spring. But the skeleton weighed no more than a dozen francs, and Haselnoss concluded that it must have sojourned more than three centuries in the sand to have become reduced to such a state of desiccation.

This very plausible reasoning did not prevent a crowd of patrons, wild at the idea of having drunk the saline water, from leaving before the end of the day; those worst afflicted with gout and gravel consoled themselves. But the overflow continuing, all the rubbish, slime, and detritus which the cavern contained was disgorged on the following days; a veritable bone-yard came down from the mountain: skeletons of animals of every kind—of quadrupeds, birds, and reptiles—in short, all that one could conceive as most horrible.

Haselnoss issued a pamphlet demonstrating that all these bones were derived from an antediluvian world: that they were fossil bones, accumulated there in a sort of funnel during the universal flood—that is to say, four thousand years before Christ, and that, consequently, one might consider them as nothing but stones, and that it was needless to be disgusted. But his work had scarcely reassured the gouty when, one fine morning, the corpse of a fox, then that of a hawk with all its feathers, fell from the cascade.

It was impossible to establish that these remains antedated the Flood. Anyway, the disgust was so great that everybody tied up his bundle and went to take the waters elsewhere.

"How infamous!" cried the beautiful ladies— "how horrible! So that's what the virtue of these mineral waters came from! Oh, 'twere better to die of gravel than continue such a remedy!"

At the end of a week there remained at Spinbronn only a big Englishman who had gout in his hands as well as in his feet, who had himself addressed as Sir Thomas Hawerburch, Commodore; and he brought a large retinue, according to the usage of a British subject in a foreign land.

This personage, big and fat, with a florid complexion, but with hands simply knotted with gout, would have drunk skeleton soup if it would have cured his infirmity. He laughed heartily over the desertion of the other sufferers, and installed himself in the prettiest chalet at half price, announcing his design to pass the winter at Spinbronn.

(Here lawyer Bremer slowly absorbed an ample pinch of snuff as if to quicken his reminiscences; he shook his laced ruff with his finger tips and continued:)

Five or six years before the Revolution of 1789, a young doctor of Pirmesens, named Christian Weber, had gone out to San Domingo in the hope of making his fortune. He had actually amassed some hundred thousand francs m the exercise of his profession when the negro revolt broke out.

I need not recall to you the barbarous treatment to which our unfortunate fellow countrymen were subjected at Haiti. Dr. Weber had the good luck to escape the massacre and to save part of his fortune. Then he traveled in South America, and especially in French Guiana. In 1801 he returned to Pirmesens, and established himself at Spinbronn, where Dr. Haselnoss made over his house and defunct practice.

Christian Weber brought with him an old negress called Agatha: a frightful creature, with a flat nose and lips as large as your fist, and her head tied up in three bandanas of razor-edged colors. This poor old woman adored red; she had earrings which hung down to her shoulders, and the mountaineers of Hundsrueck came from six leagues around to stare at her.

As for Dr. Weber, he was a tall, lean man, invariably dressed in a sky-blue coat with codfish tails and deerskin breeches. He wore a hat of flexible straw and boots with bright yellow tops, on the front of which hung two silver tassels. He talked little; his laugh was like a nervous attack, and his gray eyes, usually calm and meditative, shone with singular brilliance at the least sign of contradiction. Every morning he fetched a turn round about the mountain, letting his horse ramble at a venture, whistling forever the same tune, some negro melody or other. Lastly, this rum chap had brought from Haiti a lot of bandboxes filled with queer insects— some black and reddish brown, big as eggs; others little and shimmering like sparks. He seemed to set greater store by them than by his patients, and, from time to time, on coming back from his rides, he brought a quantity of butterflies pinned to his hat brim.

Scarcely was he settled in Haselnoss's vast house when he peopled the back yard with outlandish birds—Barbary geese with scarlet cheeks, Guinea hens, and a white peacock, which perched habitually on the garden wall, and which divided with the negress the admiration of the mountaineers.

If I enter into these details, Master Frantz, it's because they recall my early youth; Dr. Christian found himself to be at the same time my cousin and my tutor, and as early as on his return to Germany he had come to take me and install me in his house at Spinbronn. The black Agatha at first sight inspired me with some fright, and I only got seasoned to that fantastic visage with considerable difficulty; but she was such a good woman—she knew so well how to make spiced patties, she hummed such strange songs in a guttural voice, snapping her fingers and keeping time with a heavy shuffle, that I ended by taking her in fast friendship.

Dr. Weber was naturally thick with Sir Thomas Hawerburch, as representing the only one of his clientele then in evidence, and I was not slow in perceiving that these two eccentrics held long conventicles together. They conversed on mysterious matters, on the transmission of fluids, and indulged in certain odd signs which one or the other had picked up in his voyages—Sir Thomas in the Orient, and my tutor in America. This puzzled me greatly. As children will, I was always lying in wait for what they seemed to want to conceal from me; but despairing in the end of discovering anything, I took the course of questioning Agatha, and the poor old woman, after making me promise to say nothing about it, admitted that my tutor was a sorcerer.

For the rest, Dr. Weber exercised a singular influence over the mind of this negress, and this woman, habitually so gay and forever ready to be amused by nothing, trembled like a leaf when her master's gray eyes chanced to alight on her.

All this, Master Frantz, seems to have no bearing on the springs of Spinbronn. But wait, wait—you shall see by what a singular concourse of circumstances my story is connected with it.

I told you that birds darted into the cavern, and even other and larger creatures. After the final departure of the patrons, some of the old inhabitants of the village recalled that a young girl named Louise Mueller, who lived with her infirm old grandmother in a cottage on the pitch of the slope, had suddenly disappeared half a hundred years before. She had gone out to look for herbs in the forest, and there had never been any more news of her afterwards, except that, three or four days later, some woodcutters who were descending the mountain had found her sickle and her apron a few steps from the cavern.

From that moment it was evident to everyone that the skeleton which had fallen from the cascade, on the subject of which Haselnoss had turned such fine phrases, was no other than that of Louise Mueller. The poor girl had doubtless been drawn into the gulf by the mysterious influence which almost daily overcame weaker beings!

What could this influence be? None knew. But the inhabitants of Spinbronn, superstitious like all mountaineers, maintained that the devil lived in the cavern, and terror spread in the whole region.

Now one afternoon in the middle of the month of July, 1802, my cousin undertook a new classification of the insects in his bandboxes. He had secured several rather curious ones the preceding afternoon. I was with him, holding the lighted candle with one hand and with the other a needle which I heated red-hot.

Sir Thomas, seated, his chair tipped back against the sill of a window, his feet on a stool, watched us work, and smoked his cigar with a dreamy air.

I stood in with Sir Thomas Hawerburch, and I accompanied him every day to the woods in his carriage. He enjoyed hearing me chatter in English, and wished to make of me, as he said, a thorough gentleman.

The butterflies labeled, Dr. Weber at last opened the box of the largest insects, and said:

"Yesterday I secured a magnificent horn beetle, the great *Lucanus cervus* of the oaks of the Hartz. It has this peculiarity— the right claw divides in five branches. It's a rare specimen."

At the same time I offered him the needle, and as he pierced the insect before fixing it on the cork, Sir Thomas, until then impassive, got up, and, drawing near a bandbox, he began to examine the spider crab of Guiana with a feeling of horror which was strikingly portrayed on his fat vermilion face.

"That is certainly," he cried, "the most frightful work of the creation. The mere sight of it—it makes me shudder!"

In truth, a sudden pallor overspread his face.

"Bah!" said my tutor, "all that is only a prejudice from child-hood—one hears his nurse cry out—one is afraid—and the impression sticks. But if you should consider the spider with a strong microscope, you would be astonished at the finish of his members, at their admirable arrangement, and even at their elegance."

"It disgusts me," interrupted the commodore brusquely. "Pouah!"

It had turned over in his fingers.

"Oh! I don't know why," he declared, "spiders have always frozen my blood!"

Dr. Weber began to laugh, and I, who shared the feelings of Sir Thomas, exclaimed:

"Yes, cousin, you ought to take this villainous beast out of the box—it is disgusting—it spoils all the rest."

"Little chump," he said, his eyes sparkling, "what makes you look at it? If you don't like it, go take yourself off somewhere."

Evidently he had taken offense; and Sir Thomas, who was then before the window contemplating the mountain, turned suddenly, took me by the hand, and said to me in a manner full of good will:

"Your tutor, Frantz, sets great store by his spider; we like the trees better—the verdure. Come, let's go for a walk."

"Yes, go," cried the doctor, "and come back for supper at six o'clock."

Then raising his voice:

"No hard feelings, Sir Hawerburch."

The commodore replied laughingly, and we got into the carriage, which was always waiting in front of the door of the house.

Sir Thomas wanted to drive himself and dismissed his servant. He made me sit beside him on the same seat and we started off for Rothalps.

While the carriage was slowly ascending the sandy path, an invincible sadness possessed itself of my spirit. Sir Thomas, on his part, was grave. He perceived my sadness and said:

"You don't like spiders, Frantz, nor do I either. But thank Heaven, there aren't any dangerous ones in this country. The spider crab which your tutor has in his box comes from French Guiana. It inhabits the great, swampy forests filled with warm vapors, with scalding exhalations; this temperature is necessary to its life. Its web, or rather its vast snare, envelops an entire thicket. In it it takes birds as our spiders take flies. But drive these disgusting images from your mind, and drink a swallow of my old Burgundy."

Then turning, he raised the cover of the rear seat, and drew from the straw a sort of gourd from which he poured me a full bumper in a leather goblet.

When I had drunk all my good humor returned and I began to laugh at my fright.

The carriage was drawn by a little Ardennes horse, thin and nervous as a goat, which clambered up the nearly perpendicular path. Thousands of insects hummed in the bushes. At our right, at a hundred paces or more, the somber outskirts of the Rothalp forests extended below us, the profound shades of which, choked with briers and foul brush, showed here and there an opening filled with light. On our left tumbled the stream of Spinbronn, and the more we climbed the more did its silvered sheets, floating in the abyss, grow tinged with azure and redouble their sound of cymbals.

I was captivated by this spectacle. Sir Thomas, leaning back in the seat, his knees as high as his chin, abandoned himself to his habitual reveries, while the horse, laboring with his feet and hanging his head on his chest as a counter-weight to the carriage, held on as if suspended on the flank of the rock. Soon, however, we reached a pitch less steep: the haunt of the roebuck, surrounded by tremulous shadows. I always lost my head, and my eyes too, in an immense perspective. At the apparition of the shadows I turned my head and saw the cavern of Spinbronn close at hand. The encompassing mists were a magnificent green, and the stream which, before falling, extends over a bed of black sand and pebbles, was so clear that one would have thought it frozen if pale vapors did not follow its surface.

The horse had just stopped of his own accord to breathe; Sir Thomas, rising, cast his eye over the countryside.

"How calm everything is!" said he.

Then, after an instant of silence:

"If you weren't here, Frantz, I should certainly bathe in the basin."

"But, Commodore," said I, "why not bathe? I would do well to stroll around in the neighborhood. On the next hill is a great glade filled with wild strawberries. I'll go and pick some. I'll be back in an hour."

"Ha! I should like to, Frantz; it's a good idea. Dr. Weber contends that I drink too much Burgundy. It's necessary to offset wine with mineral water. This little bed of sand pleases me."

Then, having set both feet on the ground, he hitched the horse to the trunk of a little birch and waved his hand as if to say:

"You may go."

I saw him sit down on the moss and draw off his boots. As I moved away he turned and called out:

"In an hour, Frantz."

They were his last words.

An hour later I returned to the spring. The horse, the carriage, and the clothes of Sir Thomas alone met my eyes. The sun was setting. The shadows were getting long. Not a bird's song under the foliage, not the hum of an insect in the tall grass. A silence like death looked down on this solitude! The silence frightened me. I climbed up on the rock which overlooks the cavern; I looked to the right and to the left. Nobody! I called. No answer! The sound of my voice, repeated by the echoes, filled me with fear. Night settled down slowly. A vague sense of horror oppressed me. Suddenly the story of the young girl who had disappeared occurred to me; and I began to descend on the run; but, arriving before the cavern, I stopped, seized with unaccountable terror: in casting a glance in the deep shadows of the spring I had caught sight of two motionless red points. Then I saw long lines wavering in a strange manner in the midst of the darkness, and that at a depth where no human eye had ever penetrated. Fear lent my sight, and all my senses, an unheard-of subtlety of perception. For several seconds I heard very distinctly the evening plaint of a cricket down at the edge of the wood, a dog barking far away, very far in the valley. Then my heart, compressed for an instant by emotion, began to beat furiously and I no longer heard anything!

Then uttering a horrible cry, I fled, abandoning the horse, the carriage. In less than twenty minutes, bounding over the rocks and brush, I reached the threshold of our house, and cried in a stifled voice:

"Run! Run! Sir Hawerburch is dead! Sir Hawerburch is in the cavern—!"

After these words, spoken in the presence of my tutor, of the old woman Agatha, and of two or three people invited in that evening by the doctor, I fainted. I have learned since that during a whole hour I raved deliriously.

The whole village had gone in search of the commodore. Christian Weber hurried them off. At ten o'clock in the evening all the crowd came back, bringing the carriage, and in the carriage the clothes of Sir Hawerburch. They had discovered nothing. It was impossible to take ten steps in the cavern without being suffocated.

During their absence Agatha and I waited, sitting in the chimney corner. I, howling incoherent words of terror; she, with hands crossed on her knees, eyes wide open, going from time to time to the window to see what was taking place, for from the foot of the mountain one could see torches flitting in the woods. One could hear hoarse voices, in the distance, calling to each other in the night.

At the approach of her master, Agatha began to tremble. The doctor entered brusquely, pale, his lips compressed, despair written on his face. A score of woodcutters followed him tumultuously, in great felt hats with wide brims—swarthy visaged—shaking the ash from their torches. Scarcely was he in the hall when my tutor's glittering eyes seemed to look for something. He caught sight of the negress, and without a word having passed between them, the poor woman began to cry:

"No! no! I don't want to!"

"And I wish it," replied the doctor in a hard tone.

One would have said that the negress had been seized by an invincible power. She shuddered from head to foot, and Christian Weber showing her a bench, she sat down with a corpse-like stiffness.

All the bystanders, witnesses of this shocking spectacle, good folk with primitive and crude manners, but full of pious sentiments, made the sign of the cross, and I who knew not then, even by name, of the terrible magnetic power of the will, began to tremble, believing that Agatha was dead.

Christian Weber approached the negress, and making a rapid pass over her forehead:

"Are you there?" said he.

"Yes, master."

"Sir Thomas Hawerburch?"

At these words she shuddered again.

"Do you see him?"

"Yes—yes," she gasped in a strangling voice, "I see him."

"Where is he?"

"Up there—in the back of the cavern—dead!"

"Dead!" said the doctor, "how?"

"The spider—Oh! the spider crab—Oh!—"

"Control your agitation," said the doctor, who was quite pale, "tell us plainly—"

"The spider crab holds him by the throat—he is there—at the back—under the rock—wound round by webs—Ah!"

Christian Weber cast a cold glance toward his assistants, who, crowding around, with their eyes sticking out of their heads, were listening intently, and I heard him murmur:

"It's horrible! horrible!"

Then he resumed:

"You see him?"

"I see him—"

"And the spider—is it big?"

"Oh, master, never—never have I seen such a large one—not even on the banks of the Mocaris—nor in the lowlands of Konanama. It is as large as my head—!"

There was a long silence. All the assistants looked at each other, their faces livid, their hair standing up. Christian Weber alone seemed calm; having passed his hand several times over the negress's forehead, he continued:

"Agatha, tell us how death befell Sir Hawerburch."

"He was bathing in the basin of the spring—the spider saw him from behind, with his bare back. It was hungry, it had fasted for a long time; it saw him with his arms on the water. Suddenly it came out like a flash and placed its fangs around the commodore's neck, and he cried out: 'Oh! oh! my God!' It stung and fled. Sir Hawerburch sank down in the water and died. Then the spider returned and surrounded him with its web, and he floated gently, gently, to the back of the cavern. It drew in on the web. Now he is all black."

The doctor, turning to me, who no longer felt the shock, asked:

"Is it true, Frantz, that the commodore went in bathing?"

"Yes, Cousin Christian."

"At what time?"

"At four o'clock."

"At four o'clock—it was very warm, wasn't it?"

"Oh, yes!"

"It's certainly so," said he, striking his forehead. "The monster could come out without fear—"

He pronounced a few unintelligible words, and then, looking toward the mountaineers:

"My friends," he cried, "that is where this mass of debris came from—of skeletons—which spread terror among the bathers. That is what has ruined you all—it is the spider crab! It is there—hidden in its web—awaiting its prey in the back of the cavern! Who can tell the number of its victims?"

And full of fury, he led the way, shouting:

"Fagots! Fagots!"

The woodcutters followed him, vociferating.

Ten minutes later two large wagons laden with fagots were slowly mounting the slope. A long file of woodcutters, their backs bent double, followed, enveloped in the somber night. My tutor and I walked ahead, leading the horses by their bridles, and the melancholy moon vaguely lighted this funereal march. From time to time the wheels grated. Then the carts, raised by the irregularities of the rocky road, fell again in the track with a heavy jolt.

As we drew near the cavern, on the playground of the roebucks, our cortege halted. The torches were lit, and the crowd advanced toward the gulf. The limpid water, running over the sand, reflected the bluish flame of the resinous torches, the rays of which revealed the tops of the black firs leaning over the rock.

"This is the place to unload," the doctor then said. "It's necessary to block up the mouth of the cavern."

And it was not without a feeling of terror that each undertook the duty of executing his orders. The fagots fell from the top of the loads. A few stakes driven down before the opening of the spring prevented the water from carrying them away.

Toward midnight the mouth of the cavern was completely closed. The water running over spread to both sides on the moss. The top fagots were perfectly dry; then Dr. Weber, supplying himself with a torch, himself lit the fire. The flames ran from twig to twig with an angry crackling, and soon leaped toward the sky, chasing clouds of smoke before them.

It was a strange and savage spectacle, the great pile with trembling shadows lit up in this way.

This cavern poured forth black smoke, unceasingly renewed and disgorged. All around stood the woodcutters, somber, motionless, expectant, their eyes fixed on the opening; and I, although trembling from head to foot in fear, could not tear away my gaze.

It was a good quarter of an hour that we waited, and Dr. Weber was beginning to grow impatient, when a black object, with long hooked claws, appeared suddenly in the shadow and precipitated itself toward the opening.

A cry resounded about the pyre.

The spider, driven back by the live coals, reentered its cave. Then, smothered doubtless by the smoke, it returned to the charge and leaped out into the midst of the flames. Its long legs curled up. It was as large as my head, and of a violet red.

One of the woodcutters, fearing lest it leap clear of the fire, threw his hatchet at it, and with such good aim that on the instant the fire around it was covered with blood. But soon the flames burst out more vigorously over it and consumed the horrible destroyer.

Such, Master Frantz, was the strange event which destroyed the fine reputation which the waters of Spinbronn formerly enjoyed. I can certify the scrupulous precision of my account. But as for giving you an explanation, that would be impossible for me to do. At the same time, allow me to tell you that it does not seem to me absurd to admit that a spider, under the influence of a temperature raised by thermal waters, which affords the same conditions of life and development as the scorching climates of Africa and South America, should attain a fabulous size. It was this same extreme heat which explains the prodigious exuberance of the antediluvian creation!

However that may be, my tutor, judging that it would be impossible after this event to reestablish the waters of Spinbronn, sold the house back to Haselnoss, in order to return to America with his negress and collections. I was sent to board in Strasbourg, where I remained until 1809.

The great political events of the epoch then absorbing the attention of Germany and France explain why the affair I have just told you about passed completely unobserved.

A Moth—Genus Novo

H. G. Wells

Probably you have heard of Hapley—not W. T. Hapley, the son, but the celebrated Hapley, the Hapley of *Periplaneta Hapliia*, Hapley the entomologist.

If so you know at least of the great feud between Hapley and Professor Pawkins, though certain of its consequences may be new to you. For those who have not, a word or two of explanation is necessary, which the idle reader may go over with a glancing eye, if his indolence so incline him.

It is amazing how very widely diffused is the ignorance of such really important matters as this Hapley-Pawkins feud. Those epoch-making controversies, again, that have convulsed the Geological Society are, I verily believe, almost entirely unknown outside the fellowship of that body. I have heard men of fair general education even refer to the great scenes at these meetings as vestry-meeting squabbles. Yet the great hate of the English and Scotch geologists has lasted now half a century, and has "left deep and abundant marks upon the body of the science." And this Hapley-Pawkins business, though perhaps a more personal affair, stirred passions as profound, if not profounder. Your common man has no conception of the zeal that animates a scientific investigator, the fury of contradiction you can arouse in him. It is the *odium theologicum* in a new form. There are men, for instance, who would gladly burn Professor Ray Lankester at Smithfield for his treatment of the Mollusca in the Encyclopaedia. That fantastic extension of the Cephalopods to cover the Pteropods ... But I wander from Hapley and Pawkins.

It began years and years ago, with a revision of the Microlepidoptera (whatever these may be) by Pawkins, in which he extinguished a new species created by Hapley. Hapley, who was always

quarrelsome, replied by a stinging impeachment of the entire classification of Pawkins.[1] Pawkins in his "Rejoinder"[2] suggested that
Hapley's microscope was as defective as his power of observation,
and called him an "irresponsible meddler"—Hapley was not a professor at that time. Hapley in his retort,[3] spoke of "blundering collectors," and described, as if inadvertently, Pawkins' revision as a
"miracle of ineptitude." It was war to the knife. However, it would
scarcely interest the reader to detail how these two great men quar-
relled, and how the split between them widened until from the Microlepidoptera they were at war upon every open question in entomology. There were memorable occasions. At times the Royal Entomological Society meetings resembled nothing so much as the
Chamber of Deputies. On the whole, I fancy Pawkins was nearer
the truth than Hapley. But Hapley was skilful with his rhetoric,
had a turn for ridicule rare in a scientific man, was endowed with
vast energy, and had a fine sense of injury in the matter of the
extinguished species; while Pawkins was a man of dull presence,
prosy of speech, in shape not unlike a water-barrel, over conscien-
tious with testimonials, and suspected of jobbing museum appoint-
ments. So the young men gathered round Hapley and applauded
him. It was a long struggle, vicious from the beginning and growing at last to pitiless antagonism. The successive turns of fortune,
now an advantage to one side and now to another—now Hapley tormented by some success of Pawkins, and now Pawkins outshone by
Hapley, belong rather to the history of entomology than to this story.

But in 1891 Pawkins, whose health had been bad for some time,
published some work upon the "mesoblast" of the Death's Head
Moth. What the mesoblast of the Death's Head Moth may be does
not matter a rap in this story. But the work was far below his usual
standard, and gave Hapley an opening he had coveted for years.
He must have worked night and day to make the most of his advantage.

In an elaborate critique he rent Pawkins to tatters—one can
fancy the man's disordered black hair, and his queer dark eyes

---

[1] "Remarks on a Recent Revision of Microlepidoptera." *Quart. Journ.
Entomological Soc.*, 1863.

[2] "Rejoinder to certain Remarks," etc. *Ibid.* 1864.

[3] "Further Remarks," etc. *Ibid.*

flashing as he went for his antagonist—and Pawkins made a reply, halting, ineffectual, with painful gaps of silence, and yet malignant. There was no mistaking his will to wound Hapley, nor his incapacity to do it. But few of those who heard him—I was absent from that meeting—realised how ill the man was.

Hapley got his opponent down, and meant to finish him. He followed with a simply brutal attack upon Pawkins, in the form of a paper upon the development of moths in general, a paper showing evidence of a most extraordinary amount of mental labour, and yet couched in a violently controversial tone. Violent as it was, an editorial note witnesses that it was modified. It must have covered Pawkins with shame and confusion of face. It left no loophole; it was murderous in argument, and utterly contemptuous in tone; an awful thing for the declining years of a man's career.

The world of entomologists waited breathlessly for the rejoinder from Pawkins. He would try one, for Pawkins had always been game. But when it came it surprised them. For the rejoinder of Pawkins was to catch influenza, proceed to pneumonia, and die.

It was perhaps as effectual a reply as he could make under the circumstances, and largely turned the current of feeling against Hapley. The very people who had most gleefully cheered on those gladiators became serious at the consequence. There could be no reasonable doubt the fret of the defeat had contributed to the death of Pawkins. There was a limit even to scientific controversy, said serious people. Another crushing attack was already in the press and appeared on the day before the funeral. I don't think Hapley exerted himself to stop it. People remembered how Hapley had hounded down his rival, and forgot that rival's defects. Scathing satire reads ill over fresh mould. The thing provoked comment in the daily papers. This it was that made me think that you had probably heard of Hapley and this controversy. But, as I have already remarked, scientific workers live very much in a world of their own; half the people, I dare say, who go along Piccadilly to the Academy every year, could not tell you where the learned societies abide. Many even think that research is a kind of happy-family cage in which all kinds of men lie down together in peace.

In his private thoughts Hapley could not forgive Pawkins for dying. In the first place, it was a mean dodge to escape the absolute pulverisation Hapley had in hand for him, and in the second, it left Hapley's mind with a queer gap in it. For twenty years he had worked hard, sometimes far into the night, and seven days a week, with microscope, scalpel, collecting-net, and pen, and almost entirely with reference to Pawkins. The European reputation he had won had come as an incident in that great antipathy. He had gradually worked up to a climax in this last controversy. It had killed Pawkins, but it had also thrown Hapley out of gear, so to speak, and his doctor advised him to give up work for a time, and rest. So Hapley went down into a quiet village in Kent, and thought day and night of Pawkins, and good things it was now impossible to say about him.

At last Hapley began to realise in what direction the pre-occupation tended. He determined to make a fight for it, and started by trying to read novels. But he could not get his mind off Pawkins, white in the face and making his last speech—every sentence a beautiful opening for Hapley. He turned to fiction—and found it had no grip on him. He read the "Island Nights' Entertainments" until his "sense of causation" was shocked beyond endurance by the Bottle Imp. Then he went to Kipling, and found he "proved nothing," besides being irreverent and vulgar. These scientific people have their limitations. Then unhappily, he tried Besant's "Inner House," and the opening chapter set his mind upon learned societies and Pawkins at once.

So Hapley turned to chess, and found it a little more soothing. He soon mastered the moves and the chief gambits and commoner closing positions, and began to beat the Vicar. But then the cylindrical contours of the opposite king began to resemble Pawkins standing up and gasping ineffectually against check-mate, and Hapley decided to give up chess.

Perhaps the study of some new branch of science would after all be better diversion. The best rest is change of occupation. Hapley determined to plunge at diatoms, and had one of his smaller microscopes and Halibut's monograph sent down from London. He thought that perhaps if he could get up a vigorous quarrel with Halibut, he might be able to begin life afresh and forget Pawkins. And very soon he was hard at work in his habitual strenuous fashion, at these microscopic denizens of the way-side pool.

It was on the third day of the diatoms that Hapley became aware of a novel addition to the local fauna. He was working late at the microscope, and the only light in the room was the brilliant little lamp with the special form of green shade. Like all experienced microscopists, he kept both eyes open. It is the only way to avoid excessive fatigue. One eye was over the instrument, and bright and distinct before that was the circular field of the microscope, across which a brown diatom was slowly moving. With the other eye Hapley saw, as it were, without seeing. He was only dimly conscious of the brass side of the instrument, the illuminated part of the table-cloth, a sheet of notepaper, the foot of the lamp, and the darkened room beyond.

Suddenly his attention drifted from one eye to the other. The table-cloth was of the material called tapestry by shopmen, and rather brightly coloured. The pattern was in gold, with a small amount of crimson and pale blue upon a greyish ground. At one point the pattern seemed displaced, and there was a vibrating movement of the colours at this point.

Hapley suddenly moved his head back and looked with both eyes. His mouth fell open with astonishment.

It was a large moth or butterfly; its wings spread in butterfly fashion!

It was strange it should be in the room at all, for the windows were closed. Strange that it should not have attracted his attention when fluttering to its present position. Strange that it should match the table-cloth. Stranger far that to him, Hapley, the great entomologist, it was altogether unknown. There was no delusion. It was crawling slowly towards the foot of the lamp.

"New Genus, by heavens! And in England!" said Hapley, staring.

Then he suddenly thought of Pawkins. Nothing would have maddened Pawkins more... And Pawkins was dead!

Something about the head and body of the insect became singularly suggestive of Pawkins, just as the chess king had been.

"Confound Pawkins!" said Hapley. "But I must catch this." And looking round him for some means of capturing the moth, he rose slowly out of his chair. Suddenly the insect rose, struck the edge of the lampshade—Hapley heard the "ping"—and vanished into the shadow.

In a moment Hapley had whipped off the shade, so that the whole room was illuminated. The thing had disappeared, but soon his practised eye detected it upon the wall-paper near the door. He went towards it poising the lamp-shade for capture. Before he was within striking distance, however, it had risen and was fluttering round the room. After the fashion of its kind, it flew with sudden starts and turns, seeming to vanish here and reappear there. Once Hapley struck, and missed; then again.

The third time he hit his microscope. The instrument swayed, struck and overturned the lamp, and fell noisily upon the floor. The lamp turned over on the table and, very luckily, went out. Hapley was left in the dark. With a start he felt the strange moth blunder into his face.

It was maddening. He had no lights. If he opened the door of the room the thing would get away. In the darkness he saw Pawkins quite distinctly laughing at him. Pawkins had ever an oily laugh. He swore furiously and stamped his foot on the floor.

There was a timid rapping at the door.

Then it opened, perhaps a foot, and very slowly. The alarmed face of the landlady appeared behind a pink candle flame; she wore a night-cap over her grey hair and had some purple garment over her shoulders. "What was that fearful smash?" she said. "Has anything—" The strange moth appeared fluttering about the chink of the door. "Shut that door!" said Hapley, and suddenly rushed at her.

The door slammed hastily. Hapley was left alone in the dark. Then in the pause he heard his landlady scuttle upstairs, lock her door, and drag something heavy across the room and put against it.

It became evident to Hapley that his conduct and appearance had been strange and alarming. Confound the moth! and Pawkins! However, it was a pity to lose the moth now. He felt his way into the hall and found the matches, after sending his hat down upon the floor with a noise like a drum. With the lighted candle he returned to the sitting-room. No moth was to be seen. Yet once for a moment it seemed that the thing was fluttering round his head. Hapley very suddenly decided to give up the moth and go to bed. But he was excited. All night long his sleep was broken by dreams of the moth, Pawkins, and his landlady. Twice in the night he turned out and soused his head in cold water.

One thing was very clear to him. His landlady could not possibly understand about the strange moth, especially as he had failed to catch it. No one but an entomologist would understand quite how he felt. She was probably frightened at his behaviour, and yet he failed to see how he could explain it. He decided to say nothing further about the events of last night. After breakfast he saw her in her garden, and decided to go out and talk to reassure her. He talked to her about beans and potatoes, bees, caterpillars, and the price of fruit. She replied in her usual manner, but she looked at him a little suspiciously, and kept walking as he walked, so that there was always a bed of flowers, or a row of beans, or something of the sort, between them. After a while he began to feel singularly irritated at this, and to conceal his vexation went indoors and presently went out for a walk.

The moth, or butterfly, trailing an odd flavour of Pawkins with it, kept coming into that walk, though he did his best to keep his mind off it. Once he saw it quite distinctly, with its wings flattened out, upon the old stone wall that runs along the west edge of the park, but going up to it he found it was only two lumps of grey and yellow lichen. "This," said Hapley, "is the reverse of mimicry. Instead of a butterfly looking like a stone, here is a stone looking like a butterfly!" Once something hovered and fluttered round his head, but by an effort of will he drove that impression out of his mind again.

In the afternoon Hapley called upon the Vicar, and argued with him upon theological questions. They sat in the little arbour covered with briar, and smoked as they wrangled. "Look at that moth!" said Hapley, suddenly, pointing to the edge of the wooden table.

"Where?" said the Vicar.

"You don't see a moth on the edge of the table there?" said Hapley.

"Certainly not," said the Vicar.

Hapley was thunderstruck. He gasped. The Vicar was staring at him. Clearly the man saw nothing. "The eye of faith is no better than the eye of science," said Hapley awkwardly.

"I don't see your point," said the Vicar, thinking it was part of the argument.

That night Hapley found the moth crawling over his counterpane. He sat on the edge of the bed in his shirt sleeves and reasoned with himself. Was it pure hallucination? He knew he was slipping, and he battled for his sanity with the same silent energy he had formerly displayed against Pawkins. So persistent is mental habit, that he felt as if it were still a struggle with Pawkins. He was well versed in psychology. He knew that such visual illusions do come as a result of mental strain. But the point was, he did not only see the moth, he had heard it when it touched the edge of the lampshade, and afterwards when it hit against the wall, and he had felt it strike his face in the dark.

He looked at it. It was not at all dreamlike, but perfectly clear and solid-looking in the candle-light. He saw the hairy body, and the short feathery antennae, the jointed legs, even a place where the down was rubbed from the wing. He suddenly felt angry with himself for being afraid of a little insect.

His landlady had got the servant to sleep with her that night, because she was afraid to be alone. In addition she had locked the door, and put the chest of drawers against it. They listened and talked in whispers after they had gone to bed, but nothing occurred to alarm them. About eleven they had ventured to put the candle out, and had both dozed off to sleep. They woke up with a start, and sat up in bed, listening in the darkness.

Then they heard slippered feet going to and fro in Hapley's room. A chair was overturned, and there was a violent dab at the wall. Then a china mantel ornament smashed upon the fender. Suddenly the door of the room opened, and they heard him upon the landing. They clung to one another, listening. He seemed to be dancing upon the staircase. Now he would go down three or four steps quickly, then up again, then hurry down into the hall. They heard the umbrella stand go over, and the fanlight break. Then the bolt shot and the chain rattled. He was opening the door.

They hurried to the window. It was a dim grey night; an almost unbroken sheet of watery cloud was sweeping across the moon, and the hedge and trees in front of the house were black against the pale roadway.

They saw Hapley, looking like a ghost in his shirt and white trousers, running to and fro in the road, and beating the air. Now he would stop, now he would dart very rapidly at something invisible, now he would move upon it with stealthy strides. At last he went out of sight up the road towards the down. Then, while they argued who should go down and lock the door, he returned. He was walking very fast, and he came straight into the house, closed the door carefully, and went quietly up to his bedroom. Then everything was silent.

"Mrs. Colville," said Hapley, calling down the staircase next morning, "I hope I did not alarm you last night."

"You may well ask that!" said Mrs. Colville.

"The fact is, I am a sleep-walker, and the last two nights I have been without my sleeping mixture. There is nothing to be alarmed about, really. I am sorry I made such an ass of myself. I will go over the down to Shoreham, and get some stuff to make me sleep soundly. I ought to have done that yesterday."

But half-way over the down, by the chalk pits, the moth came upon Hapley again. He went on, trying to keep his mind upon chess problems, but it was no good. The thing fluttered into his face, and he struck at it with his hat in self-defence. Then rage, the old rage—the rage he had so often felt against Pawkins—came upon him again. He went on, leaping and striking at the eddying insect. Suddenly he trod on nothing, and fell headlong.

There was a gap in his sensations, and Hapley found himself sitting on the heap of flints in front of the opening of the chalk-pits, with a leg twisted back under him. The strange moth was still fluttering round his head. He struck at it with his hand, and turning his head saw two men approaching him. One was the village doctor. It occurred to Hapley that this was lucky. Then it came into his mind with extraordinary vividness, that no one would ever be able to see the strange moth except himself, and that it behooved him to keep silent about it.

Late that night, however, after his broken leg was set, he was feverish and forgot his self-restraint. He was lying flat on his bed, and he began to run his eyes round the room to see if the moth was still about. He tried not to do this, but it was no good. He soon caught sight of the thing resting close to his hand, by the night-light, on the green table-cloth. The wings quivered. With a sudden wave of anger he smote at it with his fist, and the nurse woke up with a shriek. He had missed it.

"That moth!" he said; and then, "It was fancy. Nothing!"

All the time he could see quite clearly the insect going round the cornice and darting across the room, and he could also see that the nurse saw nothing of it and looked at him strangely. He must keep himself in hand. He knew he was a lost man if he did not keep himself in hand. But as the night waned the fever grew upon him, and the very dread he had of seeing the moth made him see it. About five, just as the dawn was grey, he tried to get out of bed and catch it, though his leg was afire with pain. The nurse had to struggle with him.

On account of this, they tied him down to the bed. At this the moth grew bolder, and once he felt it settle in his hair. Then, because he struck out violently with his arms, they tied these also. At this the moth came and crawled over his face, and Hapley wept, swore, screamed, prayed for them to take it off him, unavailingly.

The doctor was a blockhead, a just-qualified general practitioner, and quite ignorant of mental science. He simply said there was no moth. Had he possessed the wit, he might still, perhaps, have saved Hapley from his fate by entering into his delusion, and covering his face with gauze, as he prayed might be done. But, as I say, the doctor was a blockhead, and until the leg was healed Hapley was kept tied to his bed, and with the imaginary moth crawling over him. It never left him while he was awake and it grew to a monster in his dreams. While he was awake he longed for sleep, and from sleep he awoke screaming.

So now Hapley is spending the remainder of his days in a padded room, worried by a moth that no one else can see. The asylum doctor calls it hallucination; but Hapley, when he is in his easier mood, and can talk, says it is the ghost of Pawkins, and consequently a unique specimen and well worth the trouble of catching.

The Purple Emperor
Robert W. Chambers

Un souvenir heureux est peut-être, sur terre,
Plus vrai que le bonheur.
A. de Musset.

I

The Purple Emperor watched me in silence. I cast again, spinning out six feet more of waterproof silk, and, as the line hissed through the air far across the pool, I saw my three flies fall on the water like drifting thistledown. The Purple Emperor sneered.

"You see," he said, "I am right. There is not a trout in Brittany that will rise to a tailed fly."

"They do in America," I replied.

"Zut! for America!" observed the Purple Emperor.

"And trout take a tailed fly in England," I insisted sharply.

"Now do I care what things or people do in England?" demanded the Purple Emperor.

"You don't care for anything except yourself and your wriggling caterpillars," I said, more annoyed than I had yet been.

The Purple Emperor sniffed. His broad, hairless, sunburnt features bore that obstinate expression which always irritated me. Perhaps the manner in which he wore his hat intensified the irritation, for the flapping brim rested on both ears, and the two little velvet ribbons which hung from the silver buckle in front wiggled and fluttered with every trivial breeze. His cunning eyes and sharp-pointed nose were out of all keeping with his fat red face. When he met my eye, he chuckled.

"I know more about insects than any man in Morbihan—or Finistère either, for that matter," he said.

"The Red Admiral knows as much as you do," retorted.

"He doesn't," replied the Purple Emperor angrily.

"And his collection of butterflies is twice as large as yours," I added, moving down the stream to a spot directly opposite him.

"It is, is it?" sneered the Purple Emperor. "Well, let me tell you, Monsieur Darrel, in all his collection he hasn't a specimen, a single specimen, of that magnificent butterfly, *Apatura Iris*, commonly known as the 'Purple Emperor.'"

"Everybody in Brittany knows that," I said, casting across the sparkling water; "but just because you happen to be the only man who ever captured a 'Purple Emperor' in Morbihan, it—doesn't follow that you are an authority on sea-trout flies. Why do you say that a Breton sea-trout won't touch a tailed fly?"

"It's so," he replied.

"Why? There are plenty of May-flies about the stream."

"Let 'em fly!" snarled the Purple Emperor, "you won't see a trout touch 'em."

My arm was aching, but I grasped my split bamboo more firmly, and, half turning, waded out into the stream and began to whip the ripples at the head of the pool. A great green dragon-fly came drifting by on the summer breeze and hung a moment above the pool, glittering like an emerald.

"There's a chance! Where is your butterfly net?" I called across the stream

"What for? That dragonfly? I've got dozens—*Anax Junius*, Drury, characteristic, anal angle of posterior wings, in male, round; thorax marked with—"

"That will do," I said fiercely. "Can't I point out an insect in the air without this burst erudition? Can you tell me, in simple every-day French, what this little fly is this one, flitting over the eel grass here beside me? See, it has fallen on the water."

"Huh!" sneered the Purple Emperor, "that's a *Linnobia annulus*."

"What's that?" I demanded.

Before he could answer there came a heavy splash in the pool, and the fly disappeared.

"He! he! he!" tittered the Purple Emperor. "Didn't I tell you the fish knew their business? That was a sea-trout. I hope you don't get him."

He gathered up his butterfly net, collecting box, chloroform bottle, and cyanide jar. Then he rose, swung the box over his shoulder, stuffed the poison bottles into the pockets of his silver-buttoned velvet coat, and lighted his pipe. This latter operation was a demoralizing spectacle, for the Purple Emperor, like all Breton peasants, smoked one of those microscopical Breton pipes which requires ten minutes to find, ten minutes to fill, ten minutes to light, and ten seconds to finish. With true Breton stolidity he went through this solemn rite, blew three puffs of smoke into the air, scratched his pointed nose reflectively, and waddled away, calling back an ironical "Au revoir, and bad luck to all Yankees!"

I watched him out of sight, thinking sadly of the young girl whose life he made a hell upon earth—Lys Trevec, his niece. She never admitted it, but we all knew what the black-and-blue marks meant on her soft, round arm, and it made me sick to see the look of fear come into her eyes when the Purple Emperor waddled into the café of the Groix Inn.

It was commonly said that he half-starved her. This she denied. Marie Joseph and 'Fine Lelocard had seen him strike her the day after the Pardon of the Birds because she had liberated three bullfinches which he had limed the day before. I asked Lys if this were true, and she refused to speak to me for the rest of the week. There was nothing to do about it. If the Purple Emperor had not been avaricious, I should never have seen Lys at all, but he could not resist the thirty francs a week which I offered him; and Lys posed for me all day long, happy as a linnet in a pink thorn hedge. Nevertheless, the Purple Emperor hated me, and constantly threatened to send Lys back to her dreary flax-spinning. He was suspicious, too, and when he had gulped down the single glass of cider which proves fatal to the sobriety of most Bretons, he would pound the long, discoloured oaken table and roar curses on me, on Yves Terrec, and on the Red Admiral. We were the three objects in the world which he most hated: me, because I was a foreigner, and didn't care a rap for him and his butterflies; and the Red Admiral, because he was a rival entomologist.

He had other reasons for hating Terrec.

The Red Admiral, a little wizened wretch, with a badly adjusted glass eye and a passion for brandy, took his name from a butterfly which predominated in his collection. This butterfly, commonly known to amateurs as the "Red Admiral," and to entomologists as *Vanessa Atalanta*, had been the occasion of scandal among the entomologists of France and Brittany. For the Red Admiral had taken one of these common insects, dyed it a brilliant yellow by the aid of chemicals, and palmed it off on a credulous collector as a South African species, absolutely unique. The fifty francs which he gained by this rascality were, however, absorbed in a suit for damages brought by the outraged amateur month later; and when he had sat in the Quimperlé jail for a month, he reappeared in the little village of St. Gildas soured, thirsty, and burning for revenge. Of course we named him the Red Admiral, and he accepted the name with suppressed fury.

The Purple Emperor, on the other hand, had gained his imperial title legitimately, for it was an undisputed fact that the only specimen of that beautiful butterfly, *Apatura Iris*, or the Purple Emperor, as it is called by amateurs—the only specimen that had ever been taken in Finistère or in Morbihan—was captured and brought home alive by Joseph Marie Gloanec, ever afterward to be known as the Purple Emperor.

When the capture of this rare butterfly became known the Red Admiral nearly went crazy. Every day for a week he trotted over to the Groix Inn, where the Purple Emperor lived with his niece, and brought his microscope to bear on the rare newly captured butterfly, in hopes of detecting a fraud. But this specimen was genuine, and he leered through his microscope in vain.

"No chemicals there, Admiral," grinned the Purple Emperor; and the Red Admiral chattered with rage.

To the scientific world of Brittany and France the capture of an *Apatura Iris* in Morbihan was of great importance. The Museum of Quimper offered to purchase the butterfly, but the Purple Emperor, though a hoarder of gold, was a monomaniac on butterflies, and he jeered at the Curator of the Museum. From all parts of Brittany and France letters of inquiry and congratulation poured in upon him. The French Academy of Sciences awarded him a prize, and the Paris Entomological Society made him an honorary member. Being a Breton peasant, and a more than commonly pig-headed one at that, these honours did not disturb his equanimity; but when the little hamlet of St. Gildas elected him mayor, and, as is the custom in Brittany under such circumstances, he left his thatched house to take up an official life in the little Groix Inn, his head became completely turned. To be mayor in a village of nearly one hundred and fifty people! It was an empire! So he became unbearable, drinking himself viciously drunk every night of his life, maltreating his niece,

Lys Trevec, like the barbarous old wretch that he was, and driving the Red Admiral nearly frantic with his eternal harping, on the capture of *Apatura Iris*. Of course he refused to tell where he had caught the butterfly. The Red Admiral stalked his footsteps, but in vain.

"He! he! he!" nagged the Purple Emperor, cuddling his chin over a glass of cider; "I saw you sneaking about the St. Gildas spinny yesterday morning. So you think you can find another *Apatura Iris* by running after me? It won't do, Admiral, it won't do, d'ye see?"

The Red Admiral turned yellow with mortification and envy, but the next day he actually took to his bed, for the Purple Emperor had brought home not a butterfly but a live chrysalis, which, if successfully hatched, would become a perfect specimen of the invaluable *Apatura Iris*. This was the last straw. The Red Admiral shut himself up in his little stone cottage, and for weeks now he had been invisible to everybody except 'Fine Lelocard who carried him a loaf of bread and a mullet or langouste every morning.

The withdrawal of the Red Admiral from the society of St. Gildas excited first the derision and finally the suspicion of the Purple Emperor. What deviltry could he be hatching? Was he experimenting with chemicals again, or was he engaged in some deeper plot, the object of which was to discredit the Purple Emperor? Roux, the postman, who carried the mail on foot once a day from Bannalec, a distance of fifteen miles each way, had brought several suspicious letters, bearing English stamps, to the Red Admiral, and the next day the Admiral had been observed at his window grinning up into the sky and rubbing his hands together. A night or two after this apparition the postman left two packages at the Groix Inn for a moment while he ran across the way to drink a glass of cider with me. The Purple Emperor, who was roaming about the café, snooping into everything that did not concern him, came upon the packages and examined the postmarks and addresses. One of the packages was square and heavy, and felt like a book. The other was also square, but very light, and felt like a pasteboard box. They were both addressed to the Red Admiral, and they bore English stamps.

When Roux, the postman, came back, the Purple Emperor tried to pump him, but the poor little postman knew nothing about the contents of the packages, and after he had taken them around the corner to the cottage of the Red Admiral the Purple Emperor ordered a glass of cider, and deliberately fuddled himself until Lys came in and tearfully supported him to his room. Here he became so abusive and brutal that Lys called to me, and I went and settled the trouble without wasting any words. This also the Purple Emperor remembered, and waited his chance to get even with me.

That had happened a week ago, and until to-day he had not deigned to speak to me.

Lys had posed for me all the week, and today being Saturday, and I lazy, we had decided to take a little relaxation, she to visit and gossip with her little black-eyed friend Yvette in the neighbouring hamlet of St. Julien, and I to try the appetites of the Breton trout with the contents of my American fly book.

I had thrashed the stream very conscientiously for three hours, but not a trout had risen to my cast, and I was piqued. I had begun to believe that there were no trout in the St. Gildas stream, and would probably have given up had I not seen the sea trout snap the little fly which the Purple Emperor had named so scientifically. That set me thinking. Probably the Purple Emperor was right, for he certainly was an expert in everything that crawled and wriggled in Brittany. So I matched, from my American fly book, the fly that the sea trout had snapped up, and withdrawing the cast of three, knotted a new leader to the silk and slipped a fly on the loop. It was a queer fly. It was one of those unnameable experiments which fascinate anglers in sporting stores and which generally prove utterly useless. Moreover, it was a tailed fly, but of course I easily remedied that with a stroke of my pen-knife. Then I was all ready, and I stepped out into the hurrying rapids and cast straight as an arrow to the spot where the sea trout had risen. Lightly as a plume the fly settled on the bosom of the pool; then came a startling splash, a gleam of silver, and the line tightened from the vibrating rod-tip to the shrieking reel. Almost instantly I checked the fish, and as he floundered for a moment, making the water boil along his glittering sides, I sprang to the bank again, for I saw that the fish was a heavy one and I should probably be in for a long run down the stream. The five-ounce rod swept in a splendid circle, quivering under the strain. "Oh, for a gaff-hook!" I said aloud, for I was now firmly convinced that I had a salmon to deal with, and no sea trout at all.

Then as I stood, bringing every ounce to bear on the sulking fish, a lithe, slender girl came hurriedly along the opposite bank calling out to me by name.

"Why, Lys!" I said, glancing up for a second, "I thought you were at St. Julien with Yvette."

"Yvette has gone to Bannalec. I went home and found an awful fight going on at the Groix Inn, and I was so frightened that I came to, tell you."

The fish dashed off at that moment, carrying all the line my reel held, and I was compelled to follow him at a jump. Lys, active and graceful as a young deer, in spite of her Pont-Aven sabots, followed along the opposite bank until the fish settled in a deep pool, shook the line savagely once or twice, and then relapsed into the sulks.

"Fight at the Groix Inn?" I called across the water. "What fight?"

"Not exactly fight," quavered Lys, "but the Red Admiral has come out of his house at last, and he and my uncle are drinking together and disputing about butterflies. I never saw my uncle so angry, and the Red Admiral is sneering and grinning. Oh, it is almost wicked to see such a face!"

"But Lys," I said, scarcely able to repress a smile, "your uncle and the Red Admiral are always quarrelling and drinking."

"I know oh, dear me!—but this is different, Monsieur Darrel. The Red Admiral has grown old and fierce since he shut himself up three weeks ago, and—oh, dear! I never saw such a look in my uncle's eyes before. He seemed insane with fury. His eyes—I can't speak of it—and then Terrec came in."

"Oh," I said more gravely, "that was unfortunate. What did the Red Admiral say to his son?"

Lys sat down on a rock among the ferns, and gave me a mutinous glance from her blue eyes.

Yves Terrec, loafer, poacher, and son of Louis Jean Terrec, otherwise the Red Admiral, had been kicked out by his father, and had also been forbidden the village by the Purple Emperor, in his majestic capacity of mayor. Twice the young ruffian had returned: once to rifle the bedroom of the Purple Emperor—an unsuccessful enterprise—and another time to rob his own father. He succeeded in the latter attempt, but was never caught, although he was frequently seen roving about the forests and moors with his gun. He openly menaced the Purple Emperor; vowed that he would marry Lys in spite of all gendarmes in Quimperlé; and these same gendarmes he led many a long chase through brier-filled swamps and over miles of yellow gorse.

What he did to the Purple Emperor—what he intended to do—disquieted me but little; but I worried over his threat concerning Lys. During the last three months this had bothered me a great deal; for when Lys came to St. Gildas from the convent the first thing she captured was my heart. For a long time I had refused to believe that any tie of blood linked this dainty blue-eyed creature with the Purple Emperor. Although she dressed in the velvet-laced bodice and blue petticoat of Finistère, and wore the bewitching white coiffe of St. Gildas, it seemed like a pretty masquerade. To me she was as sweet and as gently bred as many a maiden of the noble Faubourg who danced with her cousins at a Louis XV fête champêtre. So when Lys said that Yves Terrec had returned openly to St. Gildas, I felt that I had better be there also.

"What did Terrec say, Lys?" I asked, watching the line vibrating above the placid pool.

The wild rose colour crept into her cheeks. "Oh," she answered, with a little toss of her chin, "you know what he always says."

"That he will carry you away?"

"Yes."

"In spite of the Purple Emperor, the Red Admiral, and the gendarmes?"

"Yes."

"And what do you say, Lys?"

"I? Oh, nothing."

"Then let me say it for you."

Lys looked at her delicate pointed sabots, the sabots from Pont-Aven, made to order. They fitted her little foot. They were her only luxury.

"Will you let me answer for you, Lys?" I asked.

"You, Monsieur Darrel?"

"Yes. Will you let me give him his answer?"

"Mon Dieu, why should you concern yourself, Monsieur Darrel?"

The fish lay very quiet, but the rod in my hand trembled.

"Because I love you, Lys."

The wild rose colour in her cheeks deepened; she gave a gentle gasp, then hid her curly head in her hands.

"I love you, Lys."

"Do you know what you say?" she stammered.

"Yes, I love you."

She raised her sweet face and looked at me across the pool.

"I love you," she said, while the tears stood like stars in her eyes. "Shall I come over the brook to you?"

II

That night Yves Terrec left the village of St. Gildas vowing vengeance against his father, who refused him shelter.

I can see him now, standing in the road, his bare legs rising like pillars of bronze from his straw-stuffed sabots, his short velvet jacket torn and soiled by exposure and dissipation, and his eyes, fierce, roving, bloodshot—while the Red Admiral squeaked curses on him, and hobbled away into his little stone cottage.

"I will not forget you!" cried Yves Terrec, and stretched out his hand toward his father with a terrible gesture. Then he whipped his gun to his cheek and took a short step forward, but I caught him by the throat before he could fire, and a second later we were rolling in the dust of Bannalec road. I had to hit him a heavy blow behind the ear before he would let go, and then, rising and shaking myself, I dashed his muzzle-loading fowling piece to bits against a wall, and threw his knife into the river. The Purple Emperor was looking on with a queer light in his eyes. It was plain that he was sorry Terrec had not choked me to death.

"He would have killed his father," I said, as I passed him, going toward the Groix Inn.

"That's his business," snarled the Purple Emperor. There was a deadly light in his eyes. For a moment I thought he was going to attack me; but he was merely viciously drunk, so I shoved him out of my way and went to bed, tired and disgusted.

The worst of it was I couldn't sleep, for I feared that the Purple Emperor might begin to abuse Lys. I lay restlessly tossing among the sheets until I could stay there no longer. I did not dress entirely; I merely slipped on a pair of chaussons and sabots, a pair of knickerbockers, a jersey, and a cap. Then, loosely tying a handkerchief about my throat, I went down the worm-eaten stairs and out into the moonlit road. There was a candle flaring in the Purple Emperor's window, but I could not see him.

"He's probably dead drunk," I thought, and looked up at the window where, three years before, I had first seen Lys.

"Asleep, thank Heaven!" I muttered, and wandered out along the road. Passing the small cottage of the Red Admiral, I saw that it was dark, but the door was open. I stepped inside the hedge to shut it, thinking, in case Yves Terrec should be roving about, his father would lose whatever he had left.

Then after fastening the door with a stone, I wandered on through the dazzling Breton moonlight. A nightingale was singing in a willow swamp below, and from the edge of the mere, among the tall swamp grasses, myriads of frogs chanted a bass chorus.

When I returned, the eastern sky was beginning to lighten, and across the meadows on the cliffs, outlined against the paling horizon, I saw a seaweed gatherer going to his work among the curling breakers on the coast. His long rake was balanced on his shoulder, and the sea wind carried his song across the meadows to me:

St. Gildas!
St. Gildas!
  Pray for us,
  Shelter us,
Us who toil in the sea.

Passing the shrine at the entrance of the village took off my cap and knelt in prayer to Our Lady of Faöuet; and if I neglected myself in that prayer, surely I believed Our Lady of Faöuet would be kinder to Lys. It is said that the shrine casts white shadows. I looked, but saw only the moonlight. Then very peacefully I went to bed again, and was only awakened by the clank of sabres and the trample of horses in the road below my window.

"Good gracious!" I thought, "it must be eleven o'clock, for there are the gendarmes from Quimperlé."

I looked at my watch; it was only half-past eight, and as the gendarmes made their rounds every Thursday at eleven, I wondered what had brought them out so early to St. Gildas.

"Of course," I grumbled, rubbing my eyes, "they are after Terrec," and I jumped into my limited bath.

Before I was completely dressed I heard a timid knock, and opening my door, razor in hand, stood astonished and silent. Lys, her blue eyes wide with terror, leaned on the threshold.

"My darling!" I cried, "what on earth is the matter?" But she only clung to me, panting like a wounded sea gull. At last, when I drew her into the room and raised her face to mine, she spoke in a heart-breaking voice:

"Oh, Dick! they are going to arrest you, but I will die before I believe one word of what they say. No, don't ask me," and she began to sob desperately.

When I found that something really serious was the matter, I flung on my coat and cap, and, slipping one arm about her waist, went down the stairs and out into the road. Four gendarmes sat on their horses in front of the café door; beyond them, the entire population of St. Gildas gaped, ten deep.

"Hello, Durand!" I said to the brigadier, "what the devil is this I hear about arresting me?"

"It's true, mon ami," replied Durand with sepulchral sympathy. I looked him over from the tip of his spurred boots to his sulphur-yellow sabre belt, then upward, button by button, to his disconcerted face.

"What for?" I said scornfully. "Don't try any cheap sleuth work on me! Speak up, man, what's the trouble?"

The Emperor, who sat in the doorway staring at me, started to speak, but thought better of it and got up and went into the house. The gendarmes rolled their eyes mysteriously and looked wise.

"Come, Durand," I said impatiently, "what's the charge?"

"Murder," he said in a faint voice.

"What!" I cried incredulously. "Nonsense! Do I look like a murderer? Get off your horse, you stupid, and tell me who's murdered." Durand got down, looking very silly, and came up to me, offering his hand with a propitiatory grin.

"It was the Purple Emperor who denounced you! See, they found your handkerchief at his door—"

"Whose door, for Heaven's sake?" I cried.

"Why, the Red Admiral's!"

"The Red Admiral's? What has he done?"

"Nothing—he's only been murdered."

I could scarcely believe my senses, although they took me over to the little stone cottage and pointed out the blood-spattered room. But the horror of the thing was that the corpse of the murdered man had disappeared, and there only remained a nauseating lake of blood on the stone floor, in the centre of which lay a human hand. There was no doubt as to whom the hand belonged, for everybody who had ever seen the Red Admiral knew that the shrivelled bit of flesh which lay in the thickening blood was the hand of the Red Admiral. To me it looked like the severed claw of some gigantic bird.

"Well," I said, "there's been murder committed. Why don't you do something?"

"What?" asked Durand.

"I don't know. Send for the Commissaire."

"He's at Quimperlé. I telegraphed."

"Then send for a doctor, and find out how long this blood has been coagulating."

"The chemist from Quimperlé is here; he's a doctor."

"What does he say?"

"He says that he doesn't know."

"And who are you going to arrest?" I inquired, turning away from the spectacle on the floor.

"I don't know," said the brigadier solemnly; "you are denounced by the Purple Emperor, because he found your handkerchief at the door when he went out this morning."

"Just like a pig-headed Breton!" I exclaimed thoroughly angry. "Did he not mention Yves Terrec?"

"No."

"Of course not," I said. "He overlooked the fact that Terrec tried to shoot his father last night and that I took away his gun. All that counts for nothing when he finds my handkerchief at the murdered man's door."

"Come into the café," said Durand, much disturbed, "we can talk it over, there. Of course, Monsieur Darrel, I have never had the faintest idea that you were the murderer!"

The four gendarmes and I walked across the road to the Groix Inn and entered the café. It was crowded with Britons, smoking, drinking, and jabbering in half a dozen dialects, all equally unsatisfactory to a civilized ear; and I pushed through the crowd to where little Max Fortin, the chemist of Quimperlé, stood smoking a vile cigar.

"This is a bad business," he said, shaking hands and offering me the mate to his cigar, which I politely declined.

"Now, Monsieur Fortin," I said, "it appears that the Purple Emperor found my handkerchief near the murdered man's door this morning, and so he concludes"—here I glared at the Purple Emperor— "that I am the assassin. I will now ask him a question," and turning on him suddenly, I shouted, "What were you doing at the Red Admiral's door?"

The Purple Emperor started and turned pale, and I pointed at him triumphantly.

"See what a sudden question will do. Look how embarrassed he is, and yet I do not charge him with murder; and I tell you, gentlemen, that man there knows as well as I do who was the murderer of the Red Admiral!"

"I don't!" bawled the Purple Emperor.

"You do," I said. "It was Yves Terrec."

"I don't believe it," he said obstinately, dropping his voice.

"Of course not, being pig-headed."

"I am not pig-headed," he roared again, "but I am mayor of St. Gildas, and I do not believe that Yves Terrec killed his father."

"You saw him try to kill him last night?"

The mayor grunted.

"And you saw what I did."

He grunted again.

"And," I went on, "you heard Yves Terrec threaten to kill his father. You heard him curse the Red Admiral and swear to kill him. Now the father is murdered and his body is gone."

"And your handkerchief?" sneered the Purple Emperor.

"I dropped it of course.

"And the seaweed gatherer who saw you last night lurking about the Red Admiral's cottage," grinned the Purple Emperor.

I was startled at the man's malice.

"That will do," I said. "It is perfectly true that I was walking on the Bannalec road last night, and that I stopped to close the Red Admiral's door, which was ajar, although his light was not burning. After that I went up the road to the Dinez Woods, and then walked over by St. Julien, whence I saw the seaweed gatherer on the cliffs. He was near enough for me to hear what he sang. What of that?"

"What did you do then?"

"Then I stopped at the shrine and said a prayer, and then I went to bed and slept until Brigadier Durand's gendarmes awoke me with their clatter."

"Now, Monsieur Darrel," said the Purple Emperor, lifting a fat finger and shooting a wicked glance at me, "Now, Monsieur Darrel, which did you wear last night on your midnight stroll—sabots or shoes?"

I thought a moment. "Shoes—no, sabots. I just slipped on my chaussons and went out in my sabots."

"Which was it, shoes or sabots?" snarled the Purple Emperor.

"Sabots, you fool."

"Are these your sabots?" he asked, lifting up a wooden shoe with my initials cut on the instep.

"Yes," I replied.

"Then how did this blood come on the other one?" he shouted, and held up a sabot, the mate to the first, on which a drop of blood had spattered.

"I haven't the least idea," I said calmly; but my heart was beating very fast and I was furiously angry.

"You blockhead!" I said, controlling my rage, "I'll make you pay for this when they catch Yves Terrec and convict him. Brigadier Durand, do your duty if you think I am under suspicion. Arrest me, but grant me one favour. Put me in the Red Admiral's cottage, and I'll see whether I can't find some clew that you have overlooked. Of course, I won't disturb anything until the Commissaire arrives. Bah! You all make me very ill."

"He's hardened," observed the Purple Emperor, wagging his head.

"What motive had I to kill the Red Admiral?" I asked them all scornfully. And they all cried:

"None! Yves Terrec is the man!"

Passing out the door I swung around and shook my finger at the Purple Emperor.

"Oh, I'll make you dance for this, my friend," I said; and I followed Brigadier Durand across the street to the cottage of the murdered man.

III

They took me at my word and placed a gendarme with a bared sabre at the gateway by the hedge.

"Give me your parole," said poor Durand, "and I will let you go where you wish." But I refused, and began prowling about the cottage looking for clews. I found lots of things that some people would have considered most important, such as ashes from the Red Admiral's pipe, footprints in a dusty vegetable bin, bottles smelling of Pouldu cider, and dust—oh lots of dust. I was not an expert, only a stupid, everyday amateur; so I defaced the footprints with my thick shooting boots, and I declined to examine the pipe ashes through a microscope, although the Red Admiral's microscope stood on the table close at hand.

At last I found what I had been looking for, some long wisps of straw, curiously depressed and flattened in the middle, and I was certain I had found the evidence that would settle Yves Terrec for the rest of his life. It was plain as the nose on your face. The straws were sabot straws, flattened where the foot had pressed them, and sticking straight out where they projected beyond the sabot. Now nobody in St. Gildas used straw in sabots except a fisherman who lived near St. Julien, and the straw in his sabots was ordinary yellow wheat straw! This straw, or rather these straws, were from the stalks of the red wheat which only grows inland, and which, everybody in St. Gildas knew, Yves Terrec wore in his sabots. I was perfectly satisfied; and when, three hours later, a hoarse shouting from the Bannalec Road brought me to the window, I was not surprised to see Yves Terrec, bloody, dishevelled, hatless, with his strong arms bound behind him, walking with bent head between two mounted gendarmes. The crowd around him swelled every minute, crying: "Parricide! parricide! Death to the murderer!" As he passed my window I saw great clots of mud on his dusty sabots, from the heels of which projected wisps of red wheat straw. Then I walked back into the Red Admiral's study, determined to find what the microscope would show on the wheat straws. I examined each one very carefully, and then, my eyes aching, I rested my chin on my hand and leaned back in the chair. I had not been as fortunate as some detectives, for there was no evidence that the straws had ever been used in a sabot at all. Furthermore, directly across the hallway stood a carved Breton chest, and now I noticed for the first time that, from beneath the closed lid, dozens of similar red wheat straws projected, bent exactly as mine were bent by the lid.

I yawned in disgust. It was apparent that I was not cut out for a detective, and I bitterly pondered over the difference between clews in real life and clews in a detective story. After a while I rose, walked over to the chest and opened the lid. The interior was wadded with the red wheat straws, and on this wadding lay two curious glass jars, two or three small vials, several empty bottles labelled chloroform, a collecting jar of cyanide of potassium, and a book. In a farther corner of the chest were some letters bearing English stamps, and also the torn coverings of two parcels, all from England, and all directed to the Red Admiral under his proper name of "Sieur Louis Jean Terrec, St. Gildas, par Moëlan, Finistère."

All these traps I carried over to the desk, shut the lid of the chest, and sat down to read the letters. They were written in commercial French, evidently by an Englishman.

Freely translated, the contents of the first letter were as follows:

"London, June 12, 1894.

"Dear Monsieur (sic): Your kind favour of the 19th inst. received and contents noted. The latest work on the Lepidoptera of England is Blowzer's *How to catch British Butterflies*, with notes and tables, and an introduction by Sir Thomas Sniffer. The price of this work (in one volume, calf) is £5 or 125 francs of French money. A post-office order will receive our prompt attention. We beg to remain,

"Yours, etc.,

"Fradley & Toomer,

"470 Regent Square, London, S.W."

The next letter was even less interesting. It merely stated that the money had been received and the book would be forwarded. The third engaged my attention, and I shall quote it, the translation being a free one:

"Dear Sir: Your letter of the 1st of July was duly received, and we at once referred it to Mr. Fradley himself. Mr. Fradley being much interested in your question, sent your letter to Professor Schweineri, of the Berlin Entomological Society, whose note Blowzer refers to on page 630, in his How to catch British Butterflies. We have just received an answer from Professor Schweineri, which we translate into French—(see inclosed slip). Professor Schweineri begs to present to you two jars of cythyl, prepared under his own supervision. We forward the same to you. Trusting that you will find everything satisfactory, we remain,

"Yours sincerely,

"Fradley & Toomer.

The inclosed slip read as follows:

"Messrs. Fradley & Toomer,

"Gentlemen: Cythaline, a complex hydrocarbon, was first used by Professor Schnoot, of Antwerp, a year ago. I discovered an analogous formula about the same time and named it cythyl. I have used it with great success everywhere.

It is as certain as a magnet. I beg to present you three small jars, and would be pleased to have you forward two of them to your correspondent in St. Gildas with my compliments. Blowzer's quotation of me on page 630 of his glorious work, *How to catch British Butterflies*, is correct.

> "Yours, etc.
>> "Heinrich Schweineri,
>> P.H.D., D.D., D.S., M.S."

When I had finished this letter I folded it up and put it into my pocket with the others. Then I opened Blowzer's valuable work, *How to catch British Butterflies*, and turned to page 630.

Now, although the Red Admiral could only have acquired the book very recently, and although all the other pages were perfectly clean, this particular page was thumbed black, and heavy pencil marks inclosed a paragraph at the bottom of the page. This the paragraph:

> "Professor Schweineri says: 'Of the two old methods used by collectors for the capture of the swift-winged, high-flying *Apatura Iris*, or Purple Emperor, the first, which was using a long-handled net, proved successful once in a thousand times; and the second, the placing of bait upon the ground, such as decayed meat, dead cats, rats, etc., was not only disagreeable, even for an enthusiastic collector, but also very uncertain. Once in five hundred times would the splendid butterfly leave the tops of his favourite oak trees to circle about the fetid bait offered. I have found cythyl a perfectly sure bait to draw this beautiful butterfly to the ground, where it can be easily captured. An ounce of cythyl placed in a yellow saucer under an oak tree, will draw to it every *Apatura Iris* within a radius of twenty miles. So, if any collector who possesses a little cythyl, even though it be in a sealed bottle in his pocket—if such a collector does not find a single *Apatura Iris* fluttering close about him within an hour, let him be satisfied that the *Apatura Iris* does not inhabit his country.'"

When I had finished reading this note I sat for a long while thinking hard. Then I examined the two jars. They were labelled

"Cythyl." One was full, the other nearly full. "The rest must be on the corpse of the Red Admiral," I thought, "no matter if it is in a corked bottle—"

I took all the things back to the chest, laid them carefully on the straw, and closed the lid. The gendarme sentinel at the gate saluted me respectfully as I crossed over to the Groix Inn. The inn was surrounded by an excited crowd, and the hallway was choked with gendarmes and peasants. On every side they greeted me cordially, announcing that the real murderer was caught; but I pushed by them without a word and ran upstairs to find Lys. She opened her door when I knocked and threw both arms about my neck. I took her to my breast and kissed her. After a moment I asked her if she would obey me no matter what I commanded, and she said she would, with a proud humility that touched me.

"Then go at once to Yvette in St. Julien," I said. "Ask her to harness the dog-cart and drive to the convent in Quimperlé. Wait for me there. Will you do this without questioning me, my darling?"

She raised her face to mine. "Kiss me," she said innocently; the next moment she had vanished.

I walked deliberately into the Purple Emperor's room and peered into the gauze-covered box which held the chrysalis of *Apatura Iris*. It was as I expected. The chrysalis was empty and transparent, and a great crack ran down the middle of its back, but, on the netting inside the box, a magnificent butterfly slowly waved its burnished purple wings; for the chrysalis had given up its silent tenant, the butterfly symbol of immortality. Then a great fear fell upon me. I know now that it was the fear of the Black Priest, but neither then nor for years after did I know that the Black Priest had ever lived on earth. As I bent over the box I heard a confused murmur outside the house which ended in a furious shout of "Parricide!" and I heard the gendarmes ride away behind a wagon which rattled sharply on the flinty highway. I went to the window. In the wagon sat Yves Terrec, bound and wild-eyed, two gendarmes at either side of him, and all around the wagon rode mounted gendarmes whose bared sabres scarcely kept the crowd away.

"Parricide!" they howled. "Let him die!"

I stepped back and opened the gauze-covered box. Very gently but firmly I took the splendid butterfly by its closed fore wings and lifted it unharmed between my thumb and forefinger. Then, holding it concealed behind my back, I went down into the café.

Of all the crowd that had filled it, shouting for the death of Yves Terrec, only three persons remained seated in front of the huge empty fireplace. They were the Brigadier Durand, Max Fortin, the chemist of Quimperlé, and the Purple Emperor. The latter looked abashed when I entered, but I paid no attention to him and walked straight to the chemist.

"Monsieur Fortin," I said, "do you know much about hydrocarbons?"

"They are my specialty," he said astonished.

"Have you ever heard of such thing as cythyl?"

"Schweineri's cythyl? Oh, yes! We use it in perfumery."

"Good!" I said. "Has it an odour?"

"No—and yes. One is always aware of its presence, but nobody can affirm it has an odour. It is curious," he continued, looking at me, "it is very curious you should have asked me that, for all day I have been imagining I detected the presence of cythyl."

"Do you imagine so now?" I asked.

"Yes, more than ever."

I sprang to the front door and tossed out the butterfly. The splendid creature beat the air for a moment, flitted uncertainly hither and thither, and then, to my astonishment, sailed majestically back into the café and alighted on the hearthstone. For a moment I was non-plussed, but when my eyes rested on the Purple Emperor I comprehended in a flash.

"Lift that hearthstone!" I cried to the Brigadier Durand; "pry it up with your scabbard!"

The Purple Emperor suddenly fell forward in his chair, his face ghastly white, his jaw loose with terror.

"What is cythyl?" I shouted, seizing him by the arm; but he plunged heavily from his chair, face downward on the floor, and at the moment a cry from the chemist made me turn. There stood the Brigadier Durand, one hand supporting the hearthstone, one hand raised in horror. There stood Max Fortin, the chemist, rigid with excitement, and below, in the hollow bed where the hearthstone had rested, lay a crushed mass of bleeding human flesh, from the midst of which stared a cheap glass eye. I seized the Purple Emperor and dragged him to his feet.

"Look!" I cried; "look at your old friend, the Red Admiral!" but he only smiled in a vacant way, and rolled his head muttering; "Bait for butterflies! Cythyl! Oh, no, no, no! You can't do it, Admiral, d'ye see. I alone own the Purple Emperor! I alone am the Purple Emperor!"

And the same carriage that bore me to Quimperlé to claim my bride, carried him to Quimper, gagged and bound, a foaming, howling lunatic.

This, then, is the story of the Purple Emperor. I might tell you a pleasanter story if I chose; but concerning the fish that I had hold of, whether it was a salmon, a grilse, or a sea trout, I may not say, because I have promised Lys, and she has promised me, that no power on earth shall wring from our lips the mortifying confession that the fish escaped.

The Messenger
Robert W. Chambers

I

Little gray messenger,
Robed like painted Death,
Your robe is dust.
Whom do you seek
Among lilies and closed buds
    At dusk?

Among lilies and closed buds
    At dusk,
Whom do you seek,
Little gray messenger,
Robed in the awful panoply
Of painted Death?
        R.W.C.

All-wise,
Hast thou seen all there is to see with thy two eyes?
  Dost thou know all there is to know, and so,
        Omniscient,
Darest thou still to say thy brother lies?
        R.W.C.

"The bullet entered here," said Max Fortin, and he placed his middle finger over a smooth hole exactly in the center of the forehead.

I sat down upon a mound of dry seaweed and unslung my fowling piece.

The little chemist cautiously felt the edges of the shot-hole, first with his middle finger, and then with his thumb.

"Let me see the skull again," said I.

Max Fortin picked it up from the sod.

"It's like all the others," he repeated, wiping his glasses on his handkerchief. "I thought you might care to see one of the skulls, so I brought this over from the gravel pit. The men from Bannalec are digging yet. They ought to stop."

"How many skulls are there altogether?" I inquired.

"They found thirty-eight skulls; there are thirty-nine noted in the list. They lie piled up in the gravel pit on the edge of Le Bihan's wheat field. The men are at work yet. Le Bihan is going to stop them."

"Let's go over," said I; and I picked up my gun and started across the cliffs, Portin on one side, Môme on the other.

"Who has the list?" I asked, lighting my pipe. "You say there is a list?"

"The list was found rolled up in a brass cylinder," said the chemist. He added: "You should not smoke here. You know that if a single spark drifted into the wheat—"

"Ah, but I have a cover to my pipe," said I, smiling.

Fortin watched me as I closed the pepper-box arrangement over the glowing bowl of the pipe. Then he continued:

"The list was made out on thick yellow paper; the brass tube has preserved it. It is as fresh to-day as it was in 1760. You shall see it."

"Is that the date?"

"The list is dated 'April, 1760.' The Brigadier Durand has it. It is not written in French."

"Not written in French!" I exclaimed.

"No," replied Fortin solemnly, "it is written in Breton."

"But," I protested, "the Breton language was never written or printed in 1760."

"Except by priests," said the chemist.

"I have heard of but one priest who ever wrote the Breton language," I began.

Fortin stole a glance at my face.

"You mean—the Black Priest?" he asked.

I nodded.

Fortin opened his mouth to speak again, hesitated, and finally shut his teeth obstinately over the wheat stem that he was chewing.

"And the Black Priest?" I suggested encouragingly. But I knew it was useless; for it is easier to move the stars from their courses than to make an obstinate Breton talk. We walked on for a minute or two in silence.

"Where is the Brigadier Durand?" I asked, motioning Môme to come out of the wheat, which he was trampling as though it were heather. As I spoke we came in sight of the farther edge of the wheat field and the dark, wet mass of cliffs beyond.

"Durand is down there—you can see him; he stands just behind the mayor of St. Gildas."

"I see," said I; and we struck straight down, following a sun-baked cattle path across the heather.

When we reached the edge of the wheat field, Le Bihan, the mayor of St. Gildas, called to me, and I tucked my gun under my arm and skirted the wheat to where he stood.

"Thirty-eight skulls," he said in his thin, high-pitched voice; "there is but one more, and I am opposed to further search. I suppose Fortin told you?"

I shook hands with him, and returned the salute of the Brigadier Durand.

"I am opposed to further search," repeated Le Bihan, nervously picking at the mass of silver buttons which covered the front of his velvet and broadcloth jacket like a breastplate of scale armor.

Durand pursed up his lips, twisted his tremendous mustache, and hooked his thumbs in his saber belt.

"As for me," he said, "I am in favor of further search."

"Further search for what—for the thirty-ninth skull?" I asked.

Le Bihan nodded. Durand frowned at the sunlit sea, rocking like a bowl of molten gold from the cliffs to the horizon. I followed his eyes. On the dark glistening cliffs, silhouetted against the glare of the sea, sat a cormorant, black, motionless, its horrible head raised toward heaven.

"Where is that list, Durand?" I asked.

The gendarme rummaged in his despatch pouch and produced a brass cylinder about a foot long. Very gravely he unscrewed the head and dumped out a scroll of thick yellow paper closely covered with writing on both sides. At a nod from Le Bihan he handed me the scroll. But I could make nothing of the coarse writing, now faded to a dull brown.

"Come, come, Le Bihan," I said impatiently, "translate it, won't you? You and Max Fortin make a lot of mystery out of nothing, it seems."

Le Bihan went to the edge of the pit where the three Bannalec men were digging, gave an order or two in Breton, and turned to me.

As I came to the edge of the pit the Bannalec men were removing a square piece of sailcloth from what appeared to be a pile of cobblestones.

"Look!" said Le Bihan shrilly. I looked. The pile below was a heap of skulls. After a moment I clambered down the gravel sides of the pit and walked over to the men of Bannalec. They saluted me gravely, leaning on their picks and shovels, and wiping their sweating faces with sunburned hands.

"How many?" said I in Breton.

"Thirty-eight," they replied.

I glanced around. Beyond the heap of skulls lay two piles of human bones. Beside these was a mound of broken, rusted bits of iron and steel. Looking closer, I saw that this mound was composed of rusty bayonets, saber blades, scythe blades, with here and there a tarnished buckle attached to a bit of leather hard as iron.

I picked up a couple of buttons and a belt plate. The buttons bore the royal arms of England; the belt plate was emblazoned with the English arms and also with the number "27."

"I have heard my grandfather speak of the terrible English regiment, the 27th Foot, which landed and stormed the fort up there," said one of the Bannalec men.

"Oh!" said I; "then these are the bones of English soldiers?"

"Yes," said the men of Bannalec.

Le Bihan was calling to me from the edge of the pit above, and I handed the belt plate and buttons to the men and climbed the side of the excavation.

"Well," said I, trying to prevent Môme from leaping up and licking my face as I emerged from the pit, "I suppose you know what these bones are. What are you going to do with them?"

"There was a man," said Le Bihan angrily, "an Englishman, who passed here in a dog-cart on his way to Quimper about an hour ago, and what do you suppose he wished to do?"

"Buy the relics?" I asked, smiling.

"Exactly—the pig!" piped the mayor of St. Gildas. "Jean Marie Tregunc, who found the bones, was standing there where Max Fortin stands, and do you know what he answered? He spat upon the ground, and said: 'Pig of an Englishman, do you take me for a desecrator of graves?'"

I knew Tregunc, a sober, blue-eyed Breton, who lived from one year's end to the other without being able to afford a single bit of meat for a meal.

"How much did the Englishman offer Tregunc?" I asked.

"Two hundred francs for the skulls alone."

I thought of the relic hunters and the relic buyers on the battle-fields of our civil war.

"Seventeen hundred and sixty is long ago," I said.

"Respect for the dead can never die," said Fortin.

"And the English soldiers came here to kill your fathers and burn your homes," I continued.

"They were murderers and thieves, but—they are dead," said Tregunc, coming up from the beach below, his long sea rake balanced on his dripping jersey.

"How much do you earn every year, Jean Marie?" I asked, turning to shake hands with him.

"Two hundred and twenty francs, monsieur."

"Forty-five dollars a year," I said. "Bah! you are worth more, Jean. Will you take care of my garden for me? My wife wished me to ask you. I think it would be worth one hundred francs a month to you and to me. Come on, Le Bihan—come along, Fortin—and you, Durand. I want somebody to translate that list into French for me."

Tregunc stood gazing at me, his blue eyes dilated.

"You may begin at once," I said, smiling, "if the salary suits you?"

"It suits," said Tregunc, fumbling for his pipe in a silly way that annoyed Le Bihan.

"Then go and begin your work," cried the mayor impatiently; and Tregunc started across the moors toward St. Gildas, taking off his velvet-ribboned cap to me and gripping his sea rake very hard.

"You offer him more than my salary," said the mayor, after a moment's contemplation of his silver buttons.

"Pooh!" said I, "what do you do for your salary except play dominoes with Max Portin at the Groix Inn?"

Le Bihan turned red, but Durand rattled his saber and winked at Max Fortin, and I slipped my arm through the arm of the sulky magistrate, laughing.

"There's a shady spot under the cliff," I said; "come on, Le Bihan, and read me what is in the scroll."

In a few moments we reached the shadow of the cliff, and I threw myself upon the turf, chin on hand, to listen.

The gendarme, Durand, also sat down, twisting his mustache into needlelike points. Fortin leaned against the cliff, polishing his glasses and examining us with vague, near-sighted eyes; and Le Bihan, the mayor, planted himself in our midst, rolling up the scroll and tucking it under his arm.

"First of all," he began in a shrill voice, "I am going to light my pipe, and while lighting it I shall tell you what I have heard about the attack on the fort yonder. My father told me; his father told him."

He jerked his head in the direction of the ruined fort, a small, square stone structure on the sea cliff, now nothing but crumbling walls. Then he slowly produced a tobacco pouch, a bit of flint and tinder, and a long-stemmed pipe fitted with a microscopical bowl of baked clay. To fill such a pipe requires ten minutes' close attention. To smoke it to a finish takes but four puffs. It is very Breton, this Breton pipe. It is the crystallization of everything Breton.

"Go on," said I, lighting a cigarette.

"The fort," said the mayor, "was built by Louis XIV, and was dismantled twice by the English. Louis XV restored it in 1730. In 1760 it was carried by assault by the English. They came across from the island of Groix—three shiploads, and they stormed the fort and sacked St. Julien yonder, and they started to burn St. Gildas—you can see the marks of their bullets on my house yet; but the men of Bannalec and the men of Lorient fell upon them with pike and scythe and blunderbuss, and those who did not run away lie there below in the gravel pit now—thirty-eight of them."

"And the thirty-ninth skull?" I asked, finishing my cigarette.

The mayor had succeeded in filling his pipe, and now he began to put his tobacco pouch away.

"The thirty-ninth skull," he mumbled, holding the pipe stem between his defective teeth— "the thirty-ninth skull is no business of mine. I have told the Bannalec men to cease digging."

"But what is—whose is the missing skull?" I persisted curiously.

The mayor was busy trying to strike a spark to his tinder. Presently he set it aglow, applied it to his pipe, took the prescribed four puffs, knocked the ashes out of the bowl, and gravely replaced the pipe in his pocket.

"The missing skull?" he asked.

"Yes," said I, impatiently.

The mayor slowly unrolled the scroll and began to read, translating from the Breton into French. And this is what he read:

> "On the Cliffs of St. Gildas,
>   April 13, 1760.
> "On this day, by order of the Count of Soisic, general in chief of the Breton forces now lying in Kerselec Forest, the bodies of thirty-eight English soldiers of the 27th, 50th, and 72d regiments of Foot were buried in this spot, together with their arms and equipments."

The mayor paused and glanced at me reflectively.

"Go on, Le Bihan," I said.

"With them," continued the mayor, turning the scroll and reading on the other side, "was buried the body of that vile traitor who betrayed the fort to the English. The manner of his death was as follows: By order of the most noble Count of Soisic, the traitor was first branded upon the forehead with the brand of an arrowhead. The iron burned through the flesh and was pressed heavily so that the brand should even burn into the bone of the skull. The traitor was then led out and bidden to kneel. He admitted having guided the English from the island of Groix. Although a priest and a Frenchman, he had violated his priestly office to aid him in discovering the password to the fort. This password he extorted during confession from a young Breton girl who was in the habit of rowing across from the island of Groix to visit her husband in the fort. When the fort fell, this young girl, crazed by the death of her husband, sought the Count of Soisic and told how the priest had forced her to confess to him all she knew about the fort. The priest was arrested at St. Gildas as he was about to cross the river to Lorient. When arrested he cursed the girl, Marie Trevec—"

"What!" I exclaimed, "Marie Trevec!"

"Marie Trevec," repeated Le Bihan; "the priest cursed Marie Trevec, and all her family and descendants. He was shot as he knelt, having a mask of leather over his face, because the Bretons who composed the squad of execution refused to fire at a priest unless his face was concealed. The priest was l'Abbé Sorgue, commonly known as the Black Priest on account of his dark face and swarthy eyebrows. He was buried with a stake through his heart."

Le Bihan paused, hesitated, looked at me, and handed the manuscript back to Durand. The gendarme took it and slipped it into the brass cylinder.

"So," said I, "the thirty-ninth skull is the skull of the Black Priest."

"Yes," said Fortin. "I hope they won't find it."

"I have forbidden them to proceed," said the mayor querulously. "You heard me, Max Fortin."

I rose and picked up my gun. Môme came and pushed his head into my hand.

"That's a fine dog," observed Durand, also rising.

"Why don't you wish to find his skull?" I asked Le Bihan. "It would be curious to see whether the arrow brand really burned into the bone."

"There is something in that scroll that I didn't read to you," said the mayor grimly. "Do you wish to know what it is?"

"Of course," I replied in surprise.

"Give me the scroll again, Durand," he said; then he read from the bottom: "I, l'Abbé Sorgue, forced to write the above by my executioners, have written it in my own blood; and with it I leave my curse. My curse on St. Gildas, on Marie Trevec, and on her descendants. I will come back to St. Gildas when my remains are disturbed. Woe to that Englishman whom my branded skull shall touch!"

"What rot!" I said. "Do you believe it was really written in his own blood?"

"I am going to test it," said Fortin, "at the request of Monsieur le Maire. I am not anxious for the job, however."

"See," said Le Bihan, holding out the scroll to me, "it is signed, 'L'Abbé Sorgue.'"

I glanced curiously over the paper.

"It must be the Black Priest," I said. "He was the only man who wrote in the Breton language. This is a wonderfully interesting discovery, for now, at last, the mystery of the Black Priest's disappearance is cleared up. You will, of course, send this scroll to Paris, Le Bihan?"

"No," said the mayor obstinately, "it shall be buried in the pit below where the rest of the Black Priest lies."

I looked at him and recognized that argument would be useless. But still I said, "It will be a loss to history, Monsieur Le Bihan."

"All the worse for history, then," said the enlightened Mayor of St. Gildas.

We had sauntered back to the gravel pit while speaking. The men of Bannalec were carrying the bones of the English soldiers toward the St. Gildas cemetery, on the cliffs to the east, where already a knot of white-coiffed women stood in attitudes of prayer; and I saw the somber robe of a priest among the crosses of the little graveyard.

"They were thieves and assassins; they are dead now," muttered Max Fortin.

"Respect the dead," repeated the Mayor of St. Gildas, looking after the Bannalec men.

"It was written in that scroll that Marie Trevec, of Groix Island, was cursed by the priest—she and her descendants," I said, touching Le Bihan on the arm. "There was a Marie Trevec who married an Yves Trevec of St. Gildas—"

"It is the same," said Le Bihan, looking at me obliquely.

"Oh!" said I; "then they were ancestors of my wife."

"Do you fear the curse?" asked Le Bihan.

"What?" I laughed.

"There was the case of the Purple Emperor," said Max Fortin timidly.

Startled for a moment, I faced him, then shrugged my shoulders and kicked at a smooth bit of rock which lay near the edge of the pit, almost embedded in gravel.

"Do you suppose the Purple-Emperor drank himself crazy because he was descended from Marie Trevec?" I asked contemptuously.

"Of course not," said Max Fortin hastily.

"Of course not," piped the mayor. "I only—Hellow! what's that you're kicking?"

"What?" said I, glancing down, at the same time involuntarily giving another kick. The smooth bit of rock dislodged itself and rolled out of the loosened gravel at my feet.

"The thirty-ninth skull!" I exclaimed. "By jingo, it's the noddle of the Black Priest! See! there is the arrowhead branded on the front!"

The mayor stepped back. Max Fortin also retreated. There was a pause, during which I looked at them, and they looked anywhere but at me.

"I don't like it," said the mayor at last, in a husky, high voice. "I don't like it! The scroll says he will come back to St. Gildas when his remains are disturbed. I—I don't like it, Monsieur Darrel—"

"Bosh!" said I; "the poor wicked devil is where he can't get out. For Heaven's sake, Le Bihan, what is this stuff you are talking in the year of grace 1896?"

The mayor gave me a look.

"And he says 'Englishman.' You are an Englishman, Monsieur Darrel," he announced.

"You know better. You know I'm an American."

"It's all the same," said the Mayor of St. Gildas, obstinately.

"No, it isn't!" I answered, much exasperated, and deliberately pushed the skull till it rolled into the bottom of the gravel pit below.

"Cover it up," said I; "bury the scroll with it too, if you insist, but I think you ought to send it to Paris. Don't look so gloomy, Fortin, unless you believe in werewolves and ghosts. Hey! what the—what the devil's the matter with you, anyway? What are you staring at, Le Bihan?"

"Come, come," muttered the mayor in a low, tremulous voice, "it's time we got out of this. Did you see? Did you see, Fortin?"

"I saw," whispered Max Fortin, pallid with fright.

The two men were almost running across the sunny pasture now, and I hastened after them, demanding to know what was the matter.

"Matter!" chattered the mayor, gasping with exasperation and terror. "The skull is rolling up hill again," and he burst into a terrified gallop, Max Fortin followed close behind.

I watched them stampeding across the pasture, then turned toward the gravel pit, mystified, incredulous. The skull was lying on the edge of the pit, exactly where it had been before I pushed it over the edge. For a second I stared at it; a singular chilly feeling crept up my spinal column, and I turned and walked away, sweat starting from the root of every hair on my head. Before I had gone twenty paces the absurdity of the whole thing struck me. I halted, hot with shame and annoyance, and retraced my steps.

There lay the skull.

"I rolled a stone down instead of the skull," I muttered to myself. Then with the butt of my gun I pushed the skull over the edge of the pit and watched it roll to the bottom; and as it struck the bottom of the pit, Môme, my dog, suddenly whipped his tail between his legs, whimpered, and made off across the moor.

"Môme!" I shouted, angry and astonished; but the dog only fled the faster, and I ceased calling from sheer surprise.

"What the mischief is the matter with that dog!" I thought. He had never before played me such a trick.

Mechanically I glanced into the pit, but I could not see the skull. I looked down. The skull lay at my feet again, touching them.

"Good heavens!" I stammered, and struck at it blindly with my gunstock. The ghastly thing flew into the air, whirling over and over, and rolled again down the sides of the pit to the bottom. Breathlessly I stared at it, then, confused and scarcely comprehending, I stepped back from the pit, still facing it, one, ten, twenty paces, my eyes almost starting from my head, as though I expected to see the thing roll up from the bottom of the pit under my very gaze. At last I turned my back to the pit and strode out across the gorse-covered moorland toward my home. As I reached the road that winds from St. Gildas to St. Julien I gave one hasty glance at the pit over my shoulder. The sun shone hot on the sod about the excavation. There was something white and bare and round on the turf at the edge of the pit. It might have been a stone; there were plenty of them lying about.

II

When I entered my garden I saw Môme sprawling on the stone doorstep. He eyed me sideways and flopped his tail.

"Are you not mortified, you idiot dog?" I said, looking about the upper windows for Lys.

Môme rolled over on his back and raised one deprecating forepaw, as though to ward off calamity.

"Don't act as though I was in the habit of beating you to death," I said, disgusted. I had never in my life raised whip to the brute. "But you are a fool dog," I continued. "No, you needn't come to be babied and wept over; Lys can do that, if she insists, but I am ashamed of you, and you can go to the devil."

Môme slunk off into the house, and I followed, mounting directly to my wife's boudoir. It was empty.

"Where has she gone?" I said, looking hard at Môme, who had followed me. "Oh! I see you don't know. Don't pretend you do. Come off that lounge! Do you think Lys wants tan-colored hairs all over her lounge?"

I rang the bell for Catherine and Fine, but they didn't know where "madame" had gone; so I went into my room, bathed, exchanged my somewhat grimy shooting clothes for a suit of warm, soft knickerbockers, and, after lingering some extra moments over my toilet—for I was particular, now that I had married Lys—I went down to the garden and took a chair out under the fig-trees.

"Where can she be?" I wondered, Môme came sneaking out to be comforted, and I forgave him for Lys's sake, whereupon he frisked.

"You bounding cur," said I, "now what on earth started you off across the moor? If you do it again I'll push you along with a charge of dust shot."

As yet I had scarcely dared think about the ghastly hallucination of which I had been a victim, but now I faced it squarely, flushing a little with mortification at the thought of my hasty retreat from the gravel pit.

"To think," I said aloud, "that those old woman's tales of Max Fortin and Le Bihan should have actually made me see what didn't exist at all! I lost my nerve like a schoolboy in a dark bedroom." For I knew now that I had mistaken a round stone for a skull each time, and had pushed a couple of big pebbles into the pit instead of the skull itself.

"By jingo!" said I, "I'm nervous; my liver must be in a devil of a condition if I see such things when I'm awake! Lys will know what to give me."

I felt mortified and irritated and sulky, and thought disgustedly of Le Bihan and Max Fortin.

But after a while I ceased speculating, dismissed the mayor, the chemist, and the skull from my mind, and smoked pensively, watching the sun low dipping in the western ocean. As the twilight fell for a moment over ocean and moorland, a wistful, restless happiness filled my heart, the happiness that all men know—all men who have loved.

Slowly the purple mist crept out over the sea; the cliffs darkened; the forest was shrouded.

Suddenly the sky above burned with the afterglow, and the world was alight again.

Cloud after cloud caught the rose dye; the cliffs were tinted with it; moor and pasture, heather and forest burned and pulsated with the gentle flush. I saw the gulls turning and tossing above the sand bar, their snowy wings tipped with pink; I saw the sea swallows sheering the surface of the still river, stained to its placid depths with warm reflections of the clouds. The twitter of drowsy hedge birds broke out in the stillness; a salmon rolled its shining side above tidewater.

The interminable monotone of the ocean intensified the silence. I sat motionless, holding my breath as one who listens to the first low rumor of an organ. All at once the pure whistle of a nightingale cut the silence, and the first moonbeam silvered the wastes of mist-hung waters.

I raised my head.

Lys stood before me in the garden.

When we had kissed each other, we linked arms and moved up and down the gravel walks, watching the moonbeams sparkle on the sand bar as the tide ebbed and ebbed. The broad beds of white pinks about us were atremble with hovering white moths; the October roses hung all abloom, perfuming the salt wind.

"Sweetheart," I said, "where is Yvonne? Has she promised to spend Christmas with us?"

"Yes, Dick; she drove me down from Plougat this afternoon. She sent her love to you. I am not jealous. What did you shoot?"

"A hare and four partridges. They are in the gun room. I told Catherine not to touch them until you had seen them."

Now I suppose I knew that Lys could not be particularly enthusiastic over game or guns; but she pretended she was, and always scornfully denied that it was for my sake and not for the pure love of sport. So she dragged me off to inspect the rather meager game bag, and she paid me pretty compliments, and gave a little cry of delight and pity as I lifted the enormous hare out of the sack by his ears.

"He'll eat no more of our lettuce," I said attempting to justify the assassination.

"Unhappy little bunny—and what a beauty! O Dick, you are a splendid shot, are you not?"

I evaded the question and hauled out a partridge.

"Poor little dead things'" said Lys in a whisper; "it seems a pity—doesn't it, Dick? But then you are so clever—"

"We'll have them broiled," I said guardedly, "tell Catherine."

Catherine came in to take away the game, and presently 'Fine Lelocard, Lys's maid, announced dinner, and Lys tripped away to her boudoir.

I stood an instant contemplating her blissfully, thinking, "My boy, you're the happiest fellow in the world—you're in love with your wife'"

I walked into the dining-room, beamed at the plates, walked out again; met Tregunc in the hallway, beamed on him; glanced into the kitchen, beamed at Catherine, and went up stairs, still beaming.

Before I could knock at Lys's door it opened, and Lys came hastily out. When she saw me she gave a little cry of relief, and nestled close to my breast.

"There is something peering in at my window," she said.

"What!" I cried angrily.

"A man, I think, disguised as a priest, and he has a mask on. He must have climbed up by the bay tree."

I was down the stairs and out of doors in no time. The moonlit garden was absolutely deserted. Tregunc came up, and together we searched the hedge and shrubbery around the house and out to the road.

"Jean Marie," said I at length, "loose my bulldog—he knows you—and take your supper on the porch where you can watch. My wife says the fellow is disguised as a priest, and wears a mask."

Tregunc showed his white teeth in a smile. "He will not care to venture in here again, I think, Monsieur Darrel."

I went back and found Lys seated quietly at the table.

"The soup is ready, dear," she said. "Don't worry; it was only some foolish lout from Bannalec. No one in St. Gildas or St. Julien would do such a thing."

I was too much exasperated to reply at first, but Lys treated it as a stupid joke, and after a while I began to look at it in that light.

Lys told me about Yvonne, and reminded me of my promise to have Herbert Stuart down to meet her.

"You wicked diplomat!" I protested. "Herbert is in Paris, and hard at work for the Salon."

"Don't you think he might spare a week to flirt with the prettiest girl in Finistere?" inquired Lys innocently.

"Prettiest girl! Not much!" I said.

"Who is, then?" urged Lys.

I laughed a trifle sheepishly.

"I suppose you mean me, Dick," said Lys, coloring up.

"Now I bore you, don't I?"

"Bore me? Ah, no, Dick."

After coffee and cigarettes were served I spoke about Tregunc, and Lys approved.

"Poor Jean! He will be glad, won't he? What a dear fellow you are!"

"Nonsense," said I; "we need a gardener; you said so yourself, Lys."

But Lys leaned over and kissed me, and then bent down and hugged Môme—who whistled through his nose in sentimental appreciation.

"I am a very happy woman," said Lys.

"Môme was a very bad dog to-day," I observed.

"Poor Môme!" said Lys, smiling.

When dinner was over and Môme lay snoring before the blaze—for the October nights are often chilly in Finistere—Lys curled up in the chimney corner with her embroidery, and gave me a swift glance from under her dropping lashes.

"You look like a schoolgirl, Lys," I said teasingly. "I don't believe you are sixteen yet."

She pushed back her heavy burnished hair thoughtfully. Her wrist was as white as surf foam.

"Have we been married four years? I don't believe it," I said.

She gave me another swift glance and touched the embroidery on her knee, smiling faintly.

"I see," said I, also smiling at the embroidered garment. "Do you think it will fit?"

"Fit?" repeated Lys. Then she laughed

"And," I persisted, "are you perfectly sure that you—er—we shall need it?"

"Perfectly," said Lys. A delicate color touched her cheeks and neck. She held up the little garment, all fluffy with misty lace and wrought with quaint embroidery.

"It is very gorgeous," said I; "don't use your eyes too much, dearest. May I smoke a pipe?"

"Of course," she said selecting a skein of pale blue silk.

For a while I sat and smoked in silence, watching her slender fingers among the tinted silks and thread of gold.

Presently she spoke: "What did you say your crest is, Dick?"

"My crest? Oh, something or other rampant on a something or other—"

"Dick!"

"Dearest?"

"Don't be flippant."

"But I really forget. It's an ordinary crest; everybody in New York has them. No family should be without 'em."

"You are disagreeable, Dick. Send Josephine upstairs for my album."

"Are you going to put that crest on the—the—whatever it is?"

"I am; and my own crest, too."

I thought of the Purple Emperor and wondered a little.

"You didn't know I had one, did you?" she smiled.

"What is it?" I replied evasively.

"You shall see. Ring for Josephine."

I rang, and, when 'Fine appeared, Lys gave her some orders in a low voice, and Josephine trotted away, bobbing her white-coiffed head with a "Bien, Madame!"

After a few minutes she returned, bearing a tattered, musty volume, from which the gold and blue had mostly disappeared.

I took the book in my hands and examined the ancient emblazoned covers.

"Lilies!" I exclaimed.

"Fleur-de-lis," said my wife demurely.

"Oh!" said I, astonished, and opened the book.

"You have never before seen this book?" asked Lys, with a touch of malice in her eyes.

"You know I haven't. Hello! What's this? Oho! So there should be a de before Trevec? Lys de Trevec? Then why in the world did the Purple Emperor—"

"Dick!" cried Lys.

"All right," said I. "Shall I read about the Sieur de Trevec who rode to Saladin's tent alone to seek for medicine for St. Louise? Or shall I read about—what is it? Oh, here it is, all down in black and white—about the Marquis de Trevec who drowned himself before Alva's eyes rather than surrender the banner of the fleur-de-lis to Spain? It's all written here. But, dear, how about that soldier named Trevec who was killed in the old fort on the cliff yonder?"

"He dropped the de, and the Trevecs since then have been Republicans," said Lys— "all except me."

"That's quite right," said I; "it is time that we Republicans should agree upon some feudal system. My dear, I drink to the king!" and I raised my wine glass and looked at Lys.

"To the king," said Lys, flushing. She smoothed out the tiny garment on her knees; she touched the glass with her lips; her eyes were very sweet. I drained the glass to the king.

After a silence I said: "I will tell the king stories. His majesty shall be amused."

"His majesty," repeated Lys softly.

"Or hers," I laughed. "Who knows?"

"Who knows?" murmured Lys; with a gentle sigh.

"I know some stories about Jack the Giant-Killer," I announced. "Do you, Lys?"

"I? No, not about a giant-killer, but I know all about the werewolf, and Jeanne-la-Flamme, and the Man in Purple Tatters, and—O dear me, I know lots more."

"You are very wise," said I. "I shall teach his majesty, English."

"And I Breton," cried Lys jealously.

"I shall bring playthings to the king," said I— "big green lizards from the gorse, little gray mullets to swim in glass globes, baby rabbits from the forest of Kerselec—"

"And I," said Lys, "will bring the first primrose, the first branch of aubepine, the first jonquil, to the king—my king."

"Our king," said I; and there was peace in Finistere.

I lay back, idly turning the leaves of the curious old volume.

"I am looking," said I, "for the crest."

"The crest, dear? It is a priest's head with an arrow-shaped mark on the forehead, on a field—"

I sat up and stared at my wife.

"Dick, whatever is the matter?" she smiled. "The story is there in that book. Do you care to read it? No? Shall I tell it to you? Well, then: It happened in the third crusade. There was a monk whom men called the Black Priest. He turned apostate, and sold himself to the enemies of Christ. A Sieur de Trevec burst into the Saracen camp, at the head of only one hundred lances, and carried the Black Priest away out of the very midst of their army."

"So that is how you come by the crest," I said quietly; but I thought of the branded skull in the gravel pit, and wondered.

"Yes," said Lys. "The Sieur de Trevec cut the Black Priest's head off, but first he branded him with an arrow mark on the forehead.

The book says it was a pious action, and the Sieur de Trevec got great merit by it. But I think it was cruel, the branding," she sighed.

"Did you ever hear of any other Black Priest?"

"Yes. There was one in the last century, here in St. Gildas. He cast a white shadow in the sun. He wrote in the Breton language. Chronicles, too, I believe. I never saw them. His name was the same as that of the old chronicler, and of the other priest, Jacques Sorgue. Some said he was a lineal descendant of the traitor. Of course the first Black Priest was bad enough for anything. But if he did have a child, it need not have been the ancestor of the last Jacques Sorgue. They say he was so good he was not allowed to die, but was caught up to heaven one day," added Lys, with believing eyes.

I smiled.

"But he disappeared," persisted Lys.

"I'm afraid his journey was in another direction," I said jestingly, and thoughtlessly told her the story of the morning. I had utterly forgotten the masked man at her window, but before I finished I remembered him fast enough, and realized what I had done as I saw her face whiten.

"Lys," I urged tenderly, "that was only some clumsy clown's trick. You said so yourself. You are not superstitious, my dear?"

Her eyes were on mine. She slowly drew the little gold cross from her bosom and kissed it. But her lips trembled as they pressed the symbol of faith.

III

About nine o'clock the next morning I walked into the Groix Inn and sat down at the long discolored oaken table, nodding good-day to Marianne Bruyere, who in turn bobbed her white coiffe at me.

"My clever Bannalec maid," said I, "what is good for a stirrup-cup at the Groix Inn?"

"Schist?" she inquired in Breton.

"With a dash of red wine, then," I replied.

She brought the delicious Quimperle cider, and I poured a little Bordeaux into it. Marianne watched me with laughing black eyes.

"What makes your cheeks so red, Marianne?" I asked. "Has Jean Marie been here?"

"We are to be married, Monsieur Darrel," she laughed.

"Ah! Since when has Jean Marie Tregunc lost his head?"

"His head? Oh, Monsieur Darrel—his heart, you mean!"

"So I do," said I. "Jean Marie is a practical fellow."

"It is all due to your kindness—" began the girl, but I raised my hand and held up the glass.

"It's due to himself. To your happiness, Marianne"; and I took a hearty draught of the schist. "Now," said I, "tell me where I can find Le Bihan and Max Fortin."

"Monsieur Le Bihan and Monsieur Fortin are above in the broad room. I believe they are examining the Red Admiral's effects."

"To send them to Paris? Oh, I know. May I go up, Marianne?"

"And God go with you," smiled the girl.

When I knocked at the door of the broad room above little Max Fortin opened it. Dust covered his spectacles and nose; his hat, with the tiny velvet ribbons fluttering, was all awry.

"Come in, Monsieur Darrel," he said; "the mayor and I are packing up the effects of the Purple Emperor and of the poor Red Admiral."

"The collections?" I asked, entering the room. "You must be very careful in packing those butterfly cases; the slightest jar might break wings and antennas, you know."

Le Bihan shook hands with me and pointed to the great pile of boxes.

"They're all cork lined," he said, "but Fortin and I are putting felt around each box. The Entomological Society of Paris pays the freight."

The combined collection of the Red Admiral and the Purple Emperor made a magnificent display.

I lifted and inspected case after case set with gorgeous butterflies and moths, each specimen carefully labelled with the name in Latin. There were cases filled with crimson tiger moths all aflame with color; cases devoted to the common yellow butterflies; symphonies in orange and pale yellow; cases of soft gray and dun-colored sphinx moths; and cases of grayish nettle-bed butterflies of the numerous family of *Vanessa*.

All alone in a great case by itself was pinned the purple emperor, the *Apatura Iris*, that fatal specimen that had given the Purple Emperor his name and quietus.

I remembered the butterfly, and stood looking at it with bent eyebrows.

Le Bihan glanced up from the floor where he was nailing down the lid of a box full of cases.

"It is settled, then," said he, "that madame, your wife, gives the Purple Emperor's entire Collection to the city of Paris?"

I nodded.

"Without accepting anything for it?"

"It is a gift," I said.

"Including the purple emperor there in the case? That butterfly is worth a great deal of money," persisted Le Bihan.

"You don't suppose that we would wish to sell that specimen, do you?" I answered a trifle sharply.

"If I were you I should destroy it," said the mayor in his high-pitched voice.

"That would be nonsense," said I, "like your burying the brass cylinder and scroll yesterday."

"It was not nonsense," said Le Bihan doggedly, "and I should prefer not to discuss the subject of the scroll."

I looked at Max Portin, who immediately avoided my eyes.

"You are a pair of superstitious old women," said I, digging my hands into my pockets; "you swallow every nursery tale that is invented."

"What of it?" said Le Bihan sulkily; "there's more truth than lies in most of 'em."

"Oh!" I sneered, "does the Mayor of St. Gildas and St. Julien believe in the loup-garou?"

"No, not in the loup-garou."

"In what, then—Jeanne-la-Flamme?"

"That," said Le Bihan with conviction, "is history."

"The devil it is!" said I; "and perhaps, Monsieur the mayor, your faith in giants is unimpaired?"

"There were giants—everybody knows it," growled Max Fortin.

"And you a chemist!" I observed scornfully.

"Listen, Monsieur Darrel," squeaked Le Bihan; "you know yourself that the Purple Emperor was a scientific man. Now suppose I should tell you that he always refused to include in his collection a Death's Messenger?"

"A what?" I exclaimed.

"You know what I mean—that moth that flies by night; some call it the Death's Head, but in St. Gildas we call it 'Death's Messenger.'"

"Oh!" said I, "you mean that big sphinx moth that is commonly known as the 'death's-head moth.' Why the mischief should the people here call it death's messenger?"

"For hundreds of years it has been known as death's messenger in St. Gildas," said Max Fortin. "Even Froissart speaks of it in his commentaries on Jacques Sorgue's Chronicles. The book is in your library."

"Sorgue? And who was Jacques Sorgue? I never read his book."

"Jacques Sorgue was the son of some unfrocked priest—I forget. It was during the crusades."

"Good Heavens!" I burst out, "I've been hearing of nothing but crusades and priests and death and sorcery ever since I kicked that skull into the gravel pit, and I am tired of it, I tell you frankly. One would think we lived in the dark ages. Do you know what year of our Lord it is, Le Bihan?"

"Eighteen hundred and ninety-six," replied the mayor.

"And yet you two hulking men are afraid of a death's-head moth."

"I don't care to have one fly into the window," said Max Fortin; "it means evil to the house and the people in it."

"God alone knows why he marked one of his creatures with a yellow death's head on the back," observed Le Bihan piously, "but I take it that he meant it as a warning; and I propose to profit by it," he added triumphantly.

"See here, Le Bihan," I said; "by a stretch of imagination one can make out a skull on the thorax of a certain big sphinx moth. What of it?"

"It is a bad thing to touch," said the mayor wagging his head.

"It squeaks when handled," added Max Fortin

"Some creatures squeak all the time," I observed, looking hard at Le Bihan.

"Pigs," added the mayor.

"Yes, and asses," I replied. "Listen, Le Bihan: do you mean to tell me that you saw that skull roll uphill yesterday?"

The mayor shut his mouth tightly and picked up his hammer.

"Don't be obstinate," I said; "I asked you a question."

"And I refuse to answer," snapped Le Bihan. "Fortin saw what I saw; let him talk about it."

I looked searchingly at the little chemist.

"I don't say that I saw it actually roll up out of the pit, all by itself," said Fortin with a shiver, "but—but then, how did it come up out of the pit, if it didn't roll up all by itself?"

"It didn't come up at all; that was a yellow cobblestone that you mistook for the skull again," I replied. "You were nervous, Max."

"A—a very curious cobblestone, Monsieur Darrel," said Fortin.

"I also was a victim to the same hallucination," I continued, "and I regret to say that I took the trouble to roll two innocent cobblestones into the gravel pit, imagining each time that it was the skull I was rolling."

"It was," observed Le Bihan with a morose shrug.

"It just shows," said I, ignoring the mayor's remark, "how easy it is to fix up a train of coincidences so that the result seems to savor of the supernatural. Now, last night my wife imagined that she saw a priest in a mask peer in at her window—"

Fortin and Le Bihan scrambled hastily from their knees, dropping hammer and nails.

"W-h-a-t—what's that?" demanded the mayor.

I repeated what I had said. Max Fortin turned livid.

"My God!" muttered Le Bihan, "the Black Priest is in St. Gildas!"

"D-don't you—you know the old prophecy?" stammered Fortin; "Froissart quotes it from Jacques Sorgue

"'When the Black Priest rises from the dead,
    St. Gildas folk shall shriek in bed;
  When the Black Priest rises from his grave,
    May the good God St. Gildas save!'"

"Aristide Le Bihan," I said angrily, "and you, Max Fortin, I've got enough of this nonsense! Some foolish lout from Bannalec has been in St. Gildas playing tricks to frighten old fools like you. If you have nothing better to talk about than nursery legends I'll wait until you come to your senses. Good-morning." And I walked out, more disturbed than I cared to acknowledge to myself.

The day had become misty and overcast. Heavy, wet clouds hung in the east. I heard the surf thundering against the cliffs, and the gray gulls squealed as they tossed and turned high in the sky. The tide was creeping across the river sands, higher, higher, and I saw the seaweed floating on the beach, and the lancons springing from the foam, silvery threadlike flashes in the gloom. Curlew were flying up the river in twos and threes; the timid sea swallows skimmed across the moors toward some quiet, lonely pool, safe from the coming tempest. In every hedge field birds were gathering, huddling together, twittering restlessly. When I reached the cliffs I sat down, resting my chin on my clenched hands. Already a vast curtain of rain, sweeping across the ocean miles away, hid the island of Groix. To the east, behind the white semaphore on the hills, black clouds crowded up over the horizon. After a little the thunder boomed, dull, distant, and slender skeins of lightning unraveled across the crest of the coming storm. Under the cliff at my feet the surf rushed foaming over the shore, and the lancons jumped and skipped and quivered until they seemed to be but the reflections of the meshed lightning.

I turned to the east. It was raining over Groix, it was raining at Sainte Barbe, it was raining now at the semaphore. High in the storm whirl a few gulls pitched; a nearer cloud trailed veils of rain in its wake; the sky was spattered with lightning; the thunder boomed.

As I rose to go, a cold raindrop fell upon the back of my hand, and another, and yet another on my face. I gave a last glance at the sea, where the waves were bursting into strange white shapes that seemed to fling out menacing arms toward me. Then something moved on the cliff, something black as the black rock it clutched— a filthy cormorant, craning its hideous head at the sky.

Slowly I plodded homeward across the somber moorland, where the gorse stems glimmered with a dull metallic green, and the heather, no longer violet and purple, hung drenched and dun-colored among the dreary rocks. The wet turf creaked under my heavy boots, the black-thorn scraped and grated against knee and elbow. Over all lay a strange light, pallid, ghastly, where the sea spray whirled across the landscape and drove into my face until it grew numb with the cold. In broad bands, rank after rank, billow on billow, the rain burst out across the endless moors, and yet there was no wind to drive it at such a pace.

Lys stood at the door as I turned into the garden, motioning me to hasten; and then for the first time I became conscious that I was soaked to the skin.

"However in the world did you come to stay out when such a storm threatened?" she said. "Oh, you are dripping! Go quickly and change; I have laid your warm underwear on the bed, Dick."

I kissed my wife, and went upstairs to change my dripping clothes for something more comfortable.

When I returned to the morning room there was a driftwood fire on the hearth, and Lys sat in the chimney corner embroidering.

"Catherine tells me that the fishing fleet from Lorient is out. Do you think they are in danger, dear?" asked Lys, raising her blue eyes to mine as I entered.

"There is no wind, and there will be no sea," said I, looking out of the window. Far across the moor I could see the black cliffs looming in the mist.

"How it rains!" murmured Lys; "come to the fire, Dick."

I threw myself on the fur rug, my hands in my pockets, my head on Lys's knees.

"Tell me a story," I said. "I feel like a boy of ten."

Lys raised a finger to her scarlet lips. I always waited for her to do that.

"Will you be very still, then?" she said.

"Still as death."

"Death," echoed a voice, very softly.

"Did you speak, Lys?" I asked, turning so that I could see her face.

"No; did you, Dick?"

"Who said 'death'?" I asked, startled.

"Death," echoed a voice, softly.

I sprang up and looked about. Lys rose too, her needles and embroidery falling to the floor. She seemed about to faint, leaning heavily on me, and I led her to the window and opened it a little way to give her air. As I did so the chain lightning split the zenith, the thunder crashed, and a sheet of rain swept into the room, driving with it something that fluttered—something that flapped, and squeaked, and beat upon the rug with soft, moist wings.

We bent over it together, Lys clinging to me, and we saw that it was a death's-head moth drenched with rain.

The dark day passed slowly as we sat beside the fire, hand in hand, her head against my breast, speaking of sorrow and mystery and death. For Lys believed that there were things on earth that none might understand, things that must be nameless forever and ever, until God rolls up the scroll of life and all is ended. We spoke of hope and fear and faith, and the mystery of the saints; we spoke of the beginning and the end, of the shadow of sin, of omens, and of love. The moth still lay on the floor quivering its somber wings in the warmth of the fire, the skull and ribs clearly etched upon its neck and body.

"If it is a messenger of death to this house," I said, "why should we fear, Lys?"

"Death should be welcome to those who love God," murmured Lys, and she drew the cross from her breast and kissed it.

"The moth might die if I threw it out into the storm," I said after a silence.

"Let it remain," sighed Lys.

Late that night my wife lay sleeping, and I sat beside her bed and read in the Chronicle of Jacques Sorgue. I shaded the candle, but Lys grew restless, and finally I took the book down into the morning room, where the ashes of the fire rustled and whitened on the hearth.

The death's-head moth lay on the rug before the fire where I had left it. At first I thought it was dead, but when I looked closer I saw a lambent fire in its amber eyes. The straight white shadow it cast across the floor wavered as the candle flickered.

The pages of the Chronicle of Jacques Sorgue were damp and sticky; the illuminated gold and blue initials left flakes of azure and gilt where my hand brushed them.

"It is not paper at all; it is thin parchment," I said to myself; and I held the discolored page close to the candle flame and read, translating laboriously:

"I, Jacques Sorgue, saw all these things. And I saw the Black Mass celebrated in the chapel of St. Gildas-on-the-Cliff. And it was said by the Abbé Sorgue, my kinsman: for which deadly sin the apostate priest was seized by the most noble Marquis of Plougastel and by him condemned to be burned with hot irons, until his seared soul quit its body and fly to its master the devil. But when the Black Priest lay in the crypt of Plougastel, his master Satan came at night and set him free, and carried him across land and sea to Mahmoud, which is Soldan or Saladin. And I, Jacques Sorgue, traveling afterward by sea, beheld with my own eyes my kinsman, the Black Priest of St. Gildas, borne along in the air upon a vast black wing, which was the wing of his master Satan. And this was seen also by two men of the crew."

I turned the page. The wings of the moth on the floor began to quiver. I read on and on, my eyes blurring under the shifting candle flame. I read of battles and of saints, and I learned how the Great Soldan made his pact with Satan, and then I came to the Sieur de Trevec, and read how he seized the Black Priest in the midst of Saladin's tents and carried him away and cut off his head, first branding him on the forehead. "And before he suffered," said the

Chronicle, "he cursed the Sieur de Trevec and his descendants, and he said he would surely return to St. Gildas. 'For the violence you do to me, I will do violence to you. For the evil I suffer at your hands, I will work evil on you and your descendants. Woe to your children, Sieur de Trevec!'" There was a whirr, a beating of strong wings, and my candle flashed up as in a sudden breeze. A humming filled the room; the great moth darted hither and thither, beating, buzzing, on ceiling and wall. I flung down my book and stepped forward. Now it lay fluttering upon the window sill, and for a moment I had it under my hand, but the thing squeaked and I shrank back. Then suddenly it darted across the candle flame; the light flared and went out, and at the same moment a shadow moved in the darkness outside. I raised my eyes to the window. A masked face was peering in at me.

Quick as thought I whipped out my revolver and fired every cartridge, but the face advanced beyond the window, the glass melting away before it like mist, and through the smoke of my revolver I saw something creep swiftly into the room. Then I tried to cry out, but the thing was at my throat, and I fell backward among the ashes of the hearth.

When my eyes unclosed I was lying on the hearth, my head among the cold ashes. Slowly I got on my knees, rose painfully, and groped my way to a chair. On the floor lay my revolver, shining in the pale light of early morning. My mind clearing by degrees, I looked, shuddering, at the window. The glass was unbroken. I stooped stiffly, picked up my revolver and opened the cylinder. Every cartridge had been fired. Mechanically I closed the cylinder and placed the revolver in my pocket. The book, the Chronicles of Jacques Sorgue, lay on the table beside me, and as I started to close it I glanced at the page. It was all splashed with rain, and the lettering had run, so that the page was merely a confused blur of gold and red and black. As I stumbled toward the door I cast a fearful glance over my shoulder. The death's-head moth crawled shivering on the rug.

IV

The sun was about three hours high. I must have slept, for I was aroused by the sudden gallop of horses under our window. People were shouting and calling in the road. I sprang up and opened the sash. Le Bihan was there, an image of helplessness, and Max Fortin stood beside him polishing his glasses. Some gendarmes had just arrived from Quimperle, and I could hear them around the corner of the house, stamping, and rattling their sabres and carbines, as they led their horses into my stable.

Lys sat up, murmuring half-sleepy, half-anxious questions.

"I don't know," I answered. "I am going out to see what it means."

"It is like the day they came to arrest you," Lys said, giving me a troubled look. But I kissed her and laughed at her until she smiled too. Then I flung on coat and cap and hurried down the stairs.

The first person I saw standing in the road was the Brigadier Durand.

"Hello!" said I, "have you come to arrest me again? What the devil is all this fuss about, anyway?"

"We were telegraphed for an hour ago," said Durand briskly, "and for a sufficient reason, I think. Look there, Monsieur Darrel!"

He pointed to the ground almost under my feet.

"Good heavens!" I cried, "where did that puddle of blood come from?"

"That's what I want to know, Monsieur Darrel. Max Fortin found it at daybreak. See, it's splashed all over the grass, too. A trail of it leads into your garden, across the flower beds to your very window, the one that opens from the morning room. There is another trail leading from this spot across the road to the cliffs, then to the gravel pit, and thence across the moor to the forest of Kerselec. We are going to mount in a minute and search the bosquets. Will you join us? Bon Dieu! but the fellow bled like an ox. Max Fortin says it's human blood, or I should not have believed it."

The little chemist of Quimperle came up at that moment, rubbing his glasses with a colored handkerchief.

"Yes, it is human blood," he said, "but one thing puzzles me: the corpuscles are yellow. I never saw any human blood before with yellow corpuscles. But your English Doctor Thompson asserts that he has—"

"Well, it's human blood, anyway—isn't it?" insisted Durand, impatiently.

"Ye-es," admitted Max Fortin.

"Then it's my business to trail it," said the big gendarme, and he called his men and gave the order to mount.

"Did you hear anything last night?" asked Durand of me.

"I heard the rain. I wonder the rain did not wash away these traces."

"They must have come after the rain ceased. See this thick splash, how it lies over and weighs down the wet grass blades. Pah!"

It was a heavy, evil-looking clot, and I stepped back from it, my throat closing in disgust.

"My theory," said the brigadier, "is this: Some of those Biribi fishermen, probably the Icelanders, got an extra glass of cognac into their hides and quarreled on the road. Some of them were slashed, and staggered to your house. But there is only one trail, and yet—and yet, how could all that blood come from only one person? Well, the wounded man, let us say, staggered first to your house and then back here, and he wandered off, drunk and dying, God knows where. That's my theory."

"A very good one," said I calmly. "And you are going to trail him?"

"Yes."

"When?"

"At once. Will you come?"

"Not now. I'll gallop over by-and-bye. You are going to the edge of the Kerselec forest?"

"Yes; you will hear us calling. Are you coming, Max Fortin? And you, Le Bihan? Good; take the dog-cart."

The big gendarme tramped around the corner to the stable and presently returned mounted on a strong gray horse, his sabre shone on his saddle; his pale yellow and white facings were spotless. The little crowd of white-coiffed women with their children fell back as Durand touched spurs and clattered away followed by his two troopers. Soon after Le Bihan and Max Fortin also departed in the mayor's dingy dog-cart.

"Are you coming?" piped Le Bihan shrilly.

"In a quarter of an hour," I replied, and went back to the house.

When I opened the door of the morning room the death's-head moth was beating its strong wings against the window. For a second I hesitated, then walked over and opened the sash. The creature fluttered out, whirred over the flower beds a moment, then darted across the moorland toward the sea. I called the servants together and questioned them. Josephine, Catherine, Jean Marie Tregunc, not one of them had heard the slightest disturbance during the night. Then I told Jean Marie to saddle my horse, and while I was speaking Lys came down.

"Dearest," I began, going to her.

"You must tell me everything you know, Dick," she interrupted, looking me earnestly in the face.

"But there is nothing to tell—only a drunken brawl, and some one wounded."

"And you are going to ride—where, Dick?"

"Well, over to the edge of Kerselec forest. Durand and the mayor, and Max Fortin, have gone on, following a—a trail."

"What trail?"

"Some blood."

"Where did they find it?"

"Out in the road there." Lys crossed herself.

"Does it come near our house?"

"Yes."

"How near?"

"It comes up to the morning room window," said I, giving in.

Her hand on my arm grew heavy. "I dreamed last night—"

"So did I—" but I thought of the empty cartridges in my revolver, and stopped.

"I dreamed that you were in great danger, and I could not move hand or foot to save you; but you had your revolver, and I called out to you to fire—"

"I did fire!" I cried excitedly.

"You—you fired?"

I took her in my arms. "My darling," I said "something strange has happened—something that I cannot understand as yet. But, of course, there is an explanation. Last night I thought I fired at the Black Priest."

"Ah!" gasped Lys.

"Is that what you dreamed?"

"Yes, yes, that was it! I begged you to fire—"

"And I did."

Her heart was beating against my breast. I held her close in silence.

"Dick," she said at length, "perhaps you killed the—the thing."

"If it was human I did not miss," I answered grimly. "And it was human," I went on, pulling myself together, ashamed of having so nearly gone to pieces. "Of course it was human! The whole affair is plain enough. Not a drunken brawl, as Durand thinks; it was a drunken lout's practical joke, for which he has suffered. I suppose I must have filled him pretty full of bullets, and he has crawled away to die in Kerselec forest. It's a terrible affair; I'm sorry I fired so hastily; but that idiot Le Bihan and Max Fortin have been working on my nerves till I am as hysterical as a schoolgirl," I ended angrily.

"You fired—but the window glass was not shattered," said Lys in a low voice.

"Well, the window was open, then. And as for the—the rest—I've got nervous indigestion, and a doctor will settle the Black Priest for me, Lys."

I glanced out of the window at Tregunc waiting with my horse at the gate.

"Dearest, I think I had better go to join Durand and the others."

"I will go, too."

"Oh, no!"

"Yes, Dick."

"Don't, Lys."

"I shall suffer every moment you are away."

"The ride is too fatiguing, and we can't tell what unpleasant sight you may come upon. Lys, you don't really think there is anything supernatural in this affair?"

"Dick," she answered gently, "I am a Bretonne." With both arms around my neck, my wife said, "Death is the gift of God. I do not fear it when we are together. But alone—oh, my husband, I should fear a God who could take you away from me!"

We kissed each other soberly, simply, like two children. Then Lys hurried away to change her gown, and I paced up and down the garden waiting for her.

She came, drawing on her slender gauntlets. I swung her into the saddle, gave a hasty order to Jean Marie, and mounted.

Now, to quail under thoughts of terror on a morning like this, with Lys in the saddle beside me, no matter what had happened or might happen was impossible. Moreover, Môme came sneaking after us. I asked Tregunc to catch him, for I was afraid he might be brained by our horses' hoofs if he followed, but the wily puppy dodged and bolted after Lys, who was trotting along the highroad. "Never mind," I thought; "if he's hit he'll live, for he has no brains to lose."

Lys was waiting for me in the road beside the Shrine of Our Lady of St. Gildas when I joined her. She crossed herself, I doffed my cap, then we shook out our bridles and galloped toward the forest of Kerselec.

We said very little as we rode. I always loved to watch Lys in the saddle. Her exquisite figure and lovely face were the incarnation of youth and grace; her curling hair glistened like threaded gold.

Out of the corner of my eye I saw the spoiled puppy Môme come bounding cheerfully alongside, oblivious of our horses' heels. Our road swung close to the cliffs. A filthy cormorant rose from the black rocks and flapped heavily across our path. Lys's horse reared, but she pulled him down, and pointed at the bird with her riding crop.

"I see," said I; "it seems to be going our way. Curious to see a cormorant in a forest, isn't it?"

"It is a bad sign," said Lys. "You know the Morbihan proverb: 'When the cormorant turns from the sea, Death laughs in the forest, and wise woodsmen build boats.'"

"I wish," said I sincerely, "that there were fewer proverbs in Brittany."

We were in sight of the forest now; across the gorse I could see the sparkle of gendarmes' trappings, and the glitter of Le Bihan's silver-buttoned jacket. The hedge was low and we took it without difficulty, and trotted across the moor to where Le Bihan and Durand stood gesticulating

They bowed ceremoniously to Lys as we rode up.

"The trail is horrible—it is a river," said the mayor in his squeaky voice. "Monsieur Darrel, I think perhaps madame would scarcely care to come any nearer."

Lys drew bridle and looked at me.

"It is horrible!" said Durand, walking up beside me; "it looks as though a bleeding regiment had passed this way. The trail winds and winds about here in the thickets; we lose it at times, but we always find it again. I can't understand how one man—no, nor twenty—could bleed like that!"

A halloo, answered by another, sounded from the depths of the forest.

"It's my men; they are following the trail," muttered the brigadier. "God alone knows what is at the end!"

"Shall we gallop back, Lys?" I asked.

"No; let us ride along the western edge of the woods and dismount. The sun is so hot now, and I should like to rest for a moment," she said.

"The western forest is clear of anything disagreeable," said Durand.

"Very well," I answered; "call me, Le Bihan, if you find anything."

Lys wheeled her mare, and I followed across the springy heather, Môme trotting cheerfully in the rear.

We entered the sunny woods about a quarter of a kilometer from where we left Durand. I took Lys from her horse, flung both bridles over a limb, and, giving my wife my arm, aided her to a flat mossy rock which overhung a shallow brook gurgling among the beech trees. Lys sat down and drew off her gauntlets. Môme pushed his head into her lap, received an undeserved caress, and came doubtfully toward me. I was weak enough to condone his offense, but I made him lie down at my feet, greatly to his disgust.

I rested my head on Lys's knees, looking up at the sky through the crossed branches of the trees.

"I suppose I have killed him," I said. "It shocks me terribly, Lys."

"You could not have known, dear. He may have been a robber, and—if—not—did—have you ever fired your revolver since that day four years ago when the Red Admiral's son tried to kill you? But I know you have not."

"No," said I, wondering. "It's a fact, I have not. Why?"

"And don't you remember that I asked you to let me load it for you the day when Yves went off, swearing to kill you and his father?"

"Yes, I do remember. Well?"

"Well, I—I took the cartridges first to St. Gildas chapel and dipped them in holy water. You must not laugh, Dick," said Lys gently, laying her cool hands on my lips.

"Laugh, my darling!"

Overhead the October sky was pale amethyst, and the sunlight burned like orange flame through the yellow leaves of beech and oak. Gnats and midges danced and wavered overhead; a spider dropped from a twig halfway to the ground and hung suspended on the end of his gossamer thread.

"Are you sleepy, dear?" asked Lys, bending over me.

"I am—a little; I scarcely slept two hours last night," I answered.

"You may sleep, if you wish," said Lys, and touched my eyes caressingly.

"Is my head heavy on your knees?"

"No, Dick."

I was already in a half doze; still I heard the brook babbling under the beeches and the humming of forest flies overhead. Presently even these were stilled.

The next thing I knew I was sitting bolt upright, my ears ringing with a scream, and I saw Lys cowering beside me, covering her white face with both hands.

As I sprang to my feet she cried again and clung to my knees. I saw my dog rush growling into a thicket, then I heard him whimper, and he came backing out, whining, ears flat, tail down. I stooped and disengaged Lys's hand.

"Don't go, Dick!" she cried. "O God, it's the Black Priest!"

In a moment I had leaped across the brook and pushed my way into the thicket. It was empty. I stared about me; I scanned every tree trunk, every bush. Suddenly I saw him. He was seated on a fallen log, his head resting in his hands, his rusty black robe gathered around him. For a moment my hair stirred under my cap; sweat started on forehead and cheek bone; then I recovered my reason, and understood that the man was human and was probably wounded to death. Ay, to death; for there at my feet, lay the wet trail of blood, over leaves and stones, down into the little hollow, across to the figure in black resting silently under the trees.

I saw that he could not escape even if he had the strength, for before him, almost at his very feet, lay a deep, shining swamp.

As I stepped forward my foot broke a twig. At the sound the figure started a little, then its head fell forward again. Its face was masked. Walking up to the man, I bade him tell where he was wounded. Durand and the others broke through the thicket at the same moment and hurried to my side.

"Who are you who hide a masked face in a priest's robe?" said the gendarme loudly.

There was no answer.

"See—see the stiff blood all over his robe," muttered Le Bihan to Fortin.

"He will not speak," said I.

"He may be too badly wounded," whispered Le Bihan.

"I saw him raise his head," I said, "my wife saw him creep up here."

Durand stepped forward and touched the figure.

"Speak!" he said.

"Speak!" quavered Fortin.

Durand waited a moment, then with a sudden upward movement he stripped off the mask and threw back the man's head. We were looking into the eye sockets of a skull. Durand stood rigid; the mayor shrieked. The skeleton burst out from its rotting robes and collapsed on the ground before us. From between the staring ribs and the grinning teeth spurted a torrent of black blood, showering the shrinking grasses; then the thing shuddered, and fell over into the black ooze of the bog. Little bubbles of iridescent air appeared from the mud; the bones were slowly engulfed, and, as the last fragments sank out of sight, up from the depths and along the bank crept a creature, shiny, shivering, quivering its wings.

It was a death's-head moth.

I wish I had time to tell you how Lys outgrew superstitions— for she never knew the truth about the affair, and she never will know, since she has promised not to read this book. I wish I might tell you about the king and his coronation, and how the coronation robe fitted. I wish that I were able to write how Yvonne and Herbert Stuart rode to a boar hunt in Quimperle, and how the hounds raced the quarry right through the town, overturning three gendarmes, the notary, and an old woman. But I am becoming garrulous and Lys is calling me to come and hear the king say that he is sleepy. And his highness shall not be kept waiting.

The King's Cradle Song

Seal with a seal of gold
The scroll of a life unrolled;
Swathe him deep in his purple stole;
Ashes of diamonds, crystalled coal,
Drops of gold in each scented fold.

Crimson wings of the Little Death,
Stir his hair with your silken breath;
Flaming wings of sins to be,
Splendid pinions of prophecy,

Smother his eyes with hues and dyes,
While the white moon spins and the winds arise,
And the stars drip through the skies

Wave, O wings of the Little Death!
Seal his sight and stifle his breath,
Cover his breast with the gemmed shroud pressed;
From north to north, from west to west,
    Wave, O wings of the Little Death!
Till the white moon reels in the cracking skies,
    And the ghosts of God arise.

The Captivity of the Professor
A. Lincoln Green

I

Just after I was nominated for the Presidency of the British Association at Glasgow, I determined if possible to obtain some new facts concerning the "agricultural" and the leaf-cutting (or *saüba*) ants of Brazil. The subject I had chosen for my inaugural address was "Recent Advances in Entomology," and I knew that the scientific world would, upon this important occasion, look to me for something more than a mere repetition of comparatively stale matter.

When Reinhardt returned from the Upper Amazons bringing with him such an astonishing collection of insects new to science, he informed me that the southern and more humid part of the La Montana region was extraordinarily prolific in ant-life, and there still remained several hundred square miles among the eastern foothills of the Andes which had never been explored by naturalists.

I therefore determined to visit this region; and (to be brief) crossed the Atlantic, and made a quick and uneventful river journey to Barra, where the Rio Negro joins the Amazons. Barra, as many of my readers will doubtless recollect, is a town made historical by Bates and Wallace, and is situated nearly a thousand miles from the mouth of the great Brazilian river. Here I was fortunate enough to find a small trading steamer which was about to start for the Jurua, a large stream which enters the Amazons from the southward about six hundred miles higher up. In this way I travelled almost as far as Caranary, on the Jurua; where, owing to the dangerous state of the rapids, I was obliged to leave the steamer and proceed by canoe.

Fortunately I was able to obtain a crew of six stalwart river Indians, who agreed to paddle me as far as Cigano. They were, I believe, members of the once prosperous Passé tribe spoken of by Humboldt and Bates; and they not only proved excellent canoemen, but possessed a fair knowledge of Portuguese. At Cigano I was unfortunately compelled to engage another crew of Indians belonging to a lower and more primitive race; for I could not persuade my civilised and docile Passés to accompany me any farther.

At length, by pushing up a tributary stream called the Jagara (which, although wider than the Thames at Kingston, I cannot find marked on any map), I approached an unexplored district not far from the spot where the boundary-lines of Brazil, Bolivia, and Peru all run together. I now found myself among the foothills of the Andes, and in a densely wooded country abounding in new birds, plants, and insects to a bewildering degree. As we advanced the atmosphere became more and more humid, until it was almost as much charged with moisture as a Russian bath. It was no longer possible to keep sugar or salt in a crystalline condition, and even black gunpowder, when exposed to the air, turned to a semi-liquid paste.

Here I procured a number of valuable specimens, and gathered many novel and interesting facts. Although my time was getting rather short, I decided, before returning, to penetrate this fascinating and fruitful region as far as possible. When we had got some fifty miles up the Jagara my crew of Bura Indians (who were yellow-skinned, stolid savages, apparently akin to the Botocudos), although apparently not afraid of hard poling and paddling up the swift shallow stream, or of the heavy work involved by frequent *portages*, showed a strong disinclination to going farther. At length, when I directed them to turn up a narrow creek entering the stream from the westward, they stolidly ignored my wishes, and persisted in keeping the canoe close to the opposite bank, giving me to understand that there was some great and mysterious danger to be feared in the region on the western side of the Jagara. In answer to my demand for particulars, the natives informed me (chiefly by means of the *lingua geral* and Indian sign-language) that they were very much afraid of certain beings of minute size who inhabited this district, and who were in the habit of capturing and holding in cruel bondage any human trespassers on their domain. From the gestures of my crew I gathered that these supposed supernatural beings were somewhat akin to our European fairies or brownies; and the chief spokesman apparently wished me to believe that, although such terrible fellows, they were no bigger than a moderate-sized ant!

Of course I tried to reason these ignorant, superstitious savages out of such a nonsensical belief. In this I was quite unsuccessful; and at length, being irritated by their stupid obstinacy in refusing to do what I wished, I rated them well as cowards, and even resorted to threats of personal chastisement. As this had no effect, beyond making them extremely sullen, I got into the small and light *piragua* which we towed behind our large canoe, and telling the Indians to make a camp and wait for me on the "safe" side of the Jagara, I proceeded to paddle towards the little creek which I had determined to explore.

I am fairly at home in a canoe, and as I was provided with a double "paradox" gun, a sharp and heavy *machete*, a mosquito-net, a good waterproof blanket, and a knapsack containing provisions and other necessaries, I resolved to push up this small tributary of the Jagara as far as I could before sunset, to spend the night on its banks, and to return to the main stream next morning. My chief purpose in doing this was to convince my superstitious and timid crew that there was no real danger to be apprehended in the region I proposed to visit.

I had not gone far up the streamlet before I came to a succession of small cascades, and had to make repeated *portages*; which, owing to the tangled state of the tropic vegetation on both banks, taxed my strength pretty severely.

As I advanced the route became somewhat easier, and the tropical vegetation around me grew more and more luxuriant. In places the whole air seemed full of the most wondrous flowers, of all hues and sizes, pendent like miniature Chinese lanterns from the network of vines and *lianas* crossing the stream overhead, among which hundreds of sparkling humming-birds and glowing multitudes of butterflies continually flitted and hovered.

At length I reached a spot of such extravagant beauty that I rested on my paddle, almost wondering whether I had wandered into dreamland. I was in a clear circular pool at the foot of a magnificent waterfall, and shut in all around by the dense, tropical forest. In front of me festoons of splendid orchids hung from the lacework of creepers which lined both sides of the cascade, while to and fro between them glittering bunches of hummingbirds, of inconceivable brilliancy of hue, darted in front of the white veil of falling water; so that it seemed as if some ambushed *genii* among the flowers on either bank were pelting one another with handfuls of blazing rubies, emeralds, amethysts, opals, and diamonds!

Many of these exquisite winged jewels, especially those with a dazzling topaz lustre on their breasts, came and hovered near me; and I noticed that each had upon its slender bill, or among its delicate head-feathers, a curious white speck or projection, like a fragment of spray from the fall. So entranced was I at the marvellous, fairyland vision before me, that I paid but little attention to this curious fact, and, indeed, the bewildering and incredible loveliness of my surroundings made me lose all count of time as completely as if I had been bemused by haschish.

At length when I approached the shore on the right-hand side of the stream in order to carry my canoe above the waterfall, I was surprised to observe a narrow white pathway in the forest, which came right down to the water's edge. This, together with the surrounding foliage, seemed at first to be thronged with small ants, yet as soon as the prow of the *piragua* grounded, every insect disappeared as if by magic.

I hauled the canoe ashore, and, carrying my gun and other baggage, I strolled up the mysterious path (which was about two feet wide) to see if it led to the stream above the fall. It seemed to be paved with firm white cement, almost as hard as porcelain, and was as smooth and level as a cycle track.

Suddenly, from the forest recesses round about me, there burst forth a chorus of bird- music which made me look at my watch; for I had learned by experience that this was Nature's vesper-song, indicating the near approach of sunset. I had not recovered my surprise at the lateness of the hour when the light began to fade, and I knew that in ten minutes darkness would be upon me. At the moment I had just reached a small opening in the forest, where the white cemented path widened out into a kind of paved circular space about twenty feet in diameter, surrounded by smooth tree trunks and densely tangled foliage. This dry and open spot struck me as a convenient camping-place, so I leaned my gun against a tree, unslung my other burdens, and placed them upon the ground.

Just as I did so, a beetle of the *longicorn* variety, about the size of a common cockroach but of a blood-red colour, darted from a recess among the roots of the tree against which I had leaned my gun, and ran past me across the white open space with astonishing speed. In a trice I snatched up my butterfly-net, for I saw that this beetle was something quite new to science, more especially as its long, reversed antennae, where they met over its back, seemed joined by a white nodular projection. Although I got my net over it more than once, it succeeded in making its escape into the bushes, owing to its marvellous agility.

After the beetle had disappeared, however, I noticed that the odd white excrescence which I had observed upon its back, between its reversed antennae, had become displaced, and was entangled in the green muslin of my net. On looking at this object more closely I was surprised to find that it was an extremely curious ant, quite different from anything I had ever seen before. Its body was white, and had a smooth glistening appearance almost exactly like the surface of a wax vesta, while its head was of a delicate pink, its antennae bright red, and its lustrous compound eyes of a rich violet or purple. This new and most interesting ant (which was evidently neither an *eciton* nor a *saüba*) was about nine millimetres long. Its thin white limbs were peculiarly delicate and fragile in appearance, and presented a marked contrast to those of the common ants of Brazil.

But by far the most extraordinary feature about it was its pink head, which, when compared with its body, appeared to be of enormous dimensions. The light was failing so rapidly that I could not make use of my Coddington lens; but I saw that the cephalic enlargement seemed to be chiefly, or wholly, due to an abnormal development of the anterior ganglion or brain, and not to a mere overgrowth of the mandibles, or of any part of the chitinous helmet, as is commonly the case when the head of an ant seems disproportionately large. Moreover, when I touched it, the skin of this strange, defenceless ant, instead of feeling hard and hornlike, seemed to be almost as soft as that of a human being.

Needless to say I handled so precious a specimen with extreme gentleness and care while I examined it. As it made no attempt to escape, I let it rest upon my open palm, and, so far from appearing terrified at its position, it turned its velvet-like compound eyes towards my face, and seemed to take stock of me in a calm and philosophical manner which was not a little diverting. I now noticed that one of its antennae, which appeared to have been injured at some time, was cocked upwards and backwards, so that it bore a

resemblance to a red feather in a cap. This gave the insect's countenance (and when I use the word "countenance" I speak advisedly,
for its front aspect had something the appearance of a human face
with a bulging overgrown forehead) a peculiarly waggish yet
Mephistophelean look, which, especially when the little creature
seemed to nod its head knowingly in response to a like movement
on my part, was extremely comical.

Every moment the gloomy shadows around me were growing
deeper, and fearing lest my valuable specimen might escape, in
spite of its deficient powers of locomotion, I placed it, together
with a fresh green leaf, in a ventilated celluloid box with a glass
cover. This I enclosed in my aluminum botanical case, taking care
that the metal catch was securely fastened.

It had now become almost dark, and I was extremely tired after
my exertions in ascending the stream; so, after a hasty supper of
biscuits, washed down by a draught of whisky-and-water from my
flask, I stretched my mosquito-tent over its collapsible bamboo
framework and crept into it. After striking a light and finding every
opening secure, I wrapped my waterproof blanket around me,
pillowed my head upon my knapsack, and was soon fast asleep.

II

In spite of the strangeness of my position I slept soundly for
several hours, and dreamed that I was delivering my inaugural
speech before the British Association at Glasgow. This speech, I
may remark, had been occupying my thoughts a good deal during
my journey, and I had not only noted down many telling phrases
which had occurred to me from time to time, but had already
learned by heart an elaborate and impressive peroration.

In my dream I thought I was about to utter this crowning part
of my Presidential Address, when a certain rival entomologist—
who shall be nameless—maliciously changed himself into a red
howler monkey, and set up a series of such hideous and deafening
yells that, although I raised my voice to its very highest pitch, no
one paid the least heed to what I was saying.

Aroused by this distressing nightmare, I shifted my position
somewhat, noticing as I did so that the forest glade was full of brilliant fireflies, and that a continual stream of these tiny lantern-
bearers seemed circling round and round me, so as to form a kind
of halo above the spot where I lay. Oddly enough, this fact brought

comfort to my dream-lacerated feelings (it must be remembered that I was but half awake), and, after watching the mazy curves of light for a short time, I again slept soundly.

When I reawoke my feet felt uncomfortably cold, and on tossing aside my waterproof blanket I found to my surprise that they were naked, although I had lain down in my stout shooting boots and a pair of coarse woollen stockings. Everything near me was drenched with dew, and a tropic morning mist, which clung closely to the ground and bushes, obscured all surrounding objects. As I disengaged myself from the mosquito-curtain, which had somehow become a good deal torn and damaged during the night, the first ray of sunshine gleamed down the forest path by which I had entered the clearing. I now noticed that around my bare feet were a number of very large ants, which were marching to and fro like soldiers on guard. They were bluish-grey in colour, and nearly an inch long, and their enormous jaws, which were shaped like a pair of pincers, looked so formidable that I involuntarily drew up my naked feet. It now became evident that my boots had been totally destroyed during the night, for upon the white ground just beyond my feet were a few shreds of tough sole leather and a litter of brass eyelet holes and rusty iron nails. While I puzzled over this unpleasant fact, the ground-mist grew rapidly thinner under the influence of the warm tropic sunlight, and I suddenly became aware that, with the exception of a clear space on either side of me, the whole arena was thronged with innumerable ants. Unlike the one I had captured, they were mostly dark brown in colour, and extremely active. All of them seemed hurrying to and fro as if engaged in some important business. Fearing lest I had fallen among a marauding army of large *ecitons* which might prove as dangerous as the terrible "Black Leopard" driver ants which I had encountered in Central Africa, I determined to make a hasty retreat to my canoe. But, on glancing round at my belongings, which of course I did not wish to leave behind me, I found that the warrior ants, which I could now see were gigantic representatives of a species all the members of which possess most formidable stings, had drawn closer to my bare feet, and were standing on the alert with their pincers open in a threatening manner. This made me pause, and while I was looking about me, and reckoning my chances of reaching the canoe without getting seriously injured, I noticed a kind of open lane among the busy multitudes of workers.

Along this opening there came a procession of such an extraordinary kind that I thought I must again be dreaming, for it was made up of active longicorn beetles, similar in many respects to the one I had seen the night before, *each of which carried upon its back a tallow-coloured ant with a large pink head, purple eyes, and bright scarlet antennae!*

As this long procession drew near I saw that it had emerged from another white pathway in the forest, nearly at right angles to that by which I had entered the open circle.

I now observed that a tiny rampart, about an inch high, and made of some white earthy substance, had been built completely round me, and that the crowds of dark-coloured ants—which seemed to be composed of three or four quite distinct species— were bringing materials to add to its height.

The cavalier ants (for so henceforth I will call them) rode over this rampart without difficulty, and formed up in a circle just inside; so that I found myself enveloped by a large squadron of these extraordinary, beetle-riding creatures. The ant which had headed the procession now advanced to the guards about my feet as if to confer with them, and, on observing it closely, I saw that one of its conspicuous red antennae was tilted backwards over its head. This made me glance at my aluminum botanical case, where I had bestowed the specimen I had captured the night before. Surely enough, in spite of its secure metal catch, the case was wide open, as also was my celluloid collecting-box.

"Surely," thought I, tugging desperately at my dishevelled forelock, "I must still be asleep and dreaming!"

And indeed, to tell the truth, from that day up to the present moment I have again and again had doubts as to whether my incredible experiences in the tropics were actual, or merely part of some feverish and interminable dream.

I have, I believe, a fair amount of courage; but there was something so strange and disquieting in the methodical tactics of these ants, that I abandoned all thoughts of trying to save my goods, and prepared to make a dash for the river (which was not more than forty yards off), hoping that I might clear the cordon of warriors before they could do me harm.

Vain hope! I had barely braced my muscles to spring up and run for it, when the soldier ants, all acting together as if by word of command, dug their pincers into my unprotected feet and humped their slate-coloured backs as if about to sting. Involuntarily I leaped up, but only to fall back again, writhing and sick with unspeakable agony—agony I can compare with nothing except the fearful and paralysing throes of *angina pectoris*! Although the worst of the pain soon passed off, all my strength and resolution seemed to have ebbed away as utterly as if I had received some mortal wound.

As I lay still, faint and sweating, with my eyes closed, I felt something soft and tremulous gripping my right fore-finger, and, on glancing up, I looked into the round frightened eyes of a small and very lean monkey.

As far as I could tell it was a "brown capuchin" monkey, a kind very commonly seen in Europe. This creature and I seemed to be alone within the tiny rampart, for, to my unspeakable relief, both the warrior ants and the troop of beetle-riders appeared to have withdrawn. A pink-and-white speck on the little capuchin's furry "hood," close to where it joined the wrinkled face, now attracted my attention. It was a cavalier ant. Could it be that this monkey was being ridden, and directed, by one of these marvellous creatures?

He went on tugging nervously at my finger, making a plaintive chirruping noise meanwhile, and every now and then he glanced backwards towards the forest path by which the mounted procession had come. After doing this for several minutes he left me, and ran a little way towards this path, glancing back at me over his shoulder, then returned, and pulled impatiently at the edge of my coat.

As I watched him it became more and more plain that his movements were to a great extent regulated by the tiny ant upon his head; for whenever he turned this insect seemed to sway sideways and tug at the hair, exactly as a stage-driver braces himself when turning an unruly team.

By-and-by, just as it dawned upon me that I was expected to follow the monkey, the little meagre beast gave a kind of chattering screech, and scampered off a few paces, as if in mortal fear of some object behind me. Although evidently wishing to run away, he suddenly stopped, exactly as a shying horse stops when controlled by a strong-armed rider. On following the monkey's terrified gaze, I saw that the dreadful soldier-ants had again crossed the rampart from the rear, and were coming slowly towards me with open jaws. As I rose hastily to my feet, the little capuchin jumped towards me once more, and gave a frantic tug at my trousers. Casting a nervous glance at my enemies, I started to follow him without more ado, and was greatly relieved to find that I could walk. No sooner had I moved forward than a wide lane opened among the throng of working ants, while the squadron of beetle-riders, advancing with extraordinary swiftness, again surrounded me, this time acting as an escort.

One last thought of escape flashed through my mind as soon as I discovered that my most formidable enemies were no longer close to my heels. But no sooner had I turned my head towards the river path than a large blue dragon-fly, which must have been nearly six inches long, swooped downwards from somewhere above, and hovered so near my face as to touch me with its vibrating, iridescent wings. I started with mingled surprise and terror. Seated just behind its head was a pink-and-white cavalier, while on the blue metallic scales of its body three enormous soldier-ants stood in a row, and reached towards me with their pincer-like mandibles.

It was enough! I followed the little monkey submissively along the narrow white path through the forest!

After we had proceeded some fifty yards, we came to an open clearing, which must have been about an acre in extent. It was dotted all over with small white domes about the size of a water-melon, which I afterwards found were the nests of the cavaliers, and certain of their numerous insect servants. These nests were connected by a network of white cemented paths, between which were dense patches of seed-bearing grass (which I afterwards found to be a kind of "ant-rice") about as high as my knees. In the centre of the clearing was a small grove, or orchard, of banana-trees, and when my guide had led me through this, I found on the other side of it what looked like half-a-dozen round white hillocks, but which turned out to be huts built of fine cement. The largest of these was about six feet six inches in height, and the smallest about a yard. The ground about this group of huts was paved like the paths, and quite level, the whole being encircled by a raised edging or rampart about three inches high. My guide stopped close to the largest hut, which had a round hole in the side just large enough for a man to creep through. After standing upright for an instant before this opening, he bobbed down and ran in on all-fours, glancing back at me as he did so, as if to give me a hint to follow his example.

While I stood hesitating, the dragonfly, with its accursed crew, darted round behind me, and I suddenly felt a bump and a buzz against the nape of my neck. With a shudder—and almost a shriek—I dropped down upon my hands and knees, and shuffled through the opening.

As soon as I was inside, and had turned round to make sure that none of the terrible warriors had entered with me, I beheld the little white cavaliers, which were drawn up in a semicircle round the doorway, dismount from their beetles, and advance almost to the entrance of the hut. Here they broke up into groups, and behaved in a manner which irresistibly reminded me of human beings discussing some exciting topic. They waved their antennae at one another, every now and then pointing them towards the hut as if exchanging ideas about my appearance, and the exciting circumstances of my capture.

On the arrival of another body of cavalier-ants, the first comers seemed eager to tell them the news; and my little cock-horned ex-captive, who apparently was playing the part of chief showman, repeatedly led parties of newcomers to the doorway of the hut, and apparently gave them much instructive and amusing information.

One frequent and very odd manoeuvre puzzled me at first a good deal. I noticed, every now and then, that two or three cavaliers, while engaged in animated converse, would suddenly depress their red antennae, hoist their white hindquarters into the air, and flourish their posterior pair of legs in an excited and highly ridiculous fashion. After watching this curious proceeding repeatedly, I arrived at the remarkable conclusion that it amounted to "ant laughter," or, at any rate, was the cavalier-ants' way of expressing applause, or extreme interest, at what they learned.

If this interpretation be correct, my late captive—and, alas! I must add, my future taskmaster—was undoubtedly something of a wag; for no sooner did he jerk his unmutilated antenna towards me, and begin to "talk," than his hearers, with one consent, would all lower their pink heads to the ground, lift their tallowy latter ends on high, and kick convulsively for several seconds.

III

This must have gone on for an hour or more, and as fresh mounted ants were continually arriving, a great crowd of them had meanwhile assembled in front of the hut. By-and-by the monkey, apparently prompted by his rider, who still maintained its seat upon his head, crept out of the doorway. I was about to follow him, when he turned, as if to push me back, and at the same moment the dragon-fly darted down and effectually barred my egress. Shortly afterwards the monkey returned with a couple of ripe bananas, which he placed before me on the clean floor of the hut. Feeling very hungry, I at once began to strip one of the bananas, and this act evidently caused great excitement among the crowd of lookers-on. All their scarlet antennae became motionless, and every pair of purple compound eyes was turned intently towards me. When I devoured the first banana in a couple of bites, there seemed to be a kind of thrill of suppressed excitement among the crowd of spectators, and then every pink head was lowered to the ground, and the whole throng became a mass of pallid abdomens and furiously gesticulating legs.

I had just eaten my second banana when I was startled by a muffled, growling sound, which appeared to come from just behind the hut. Shortly afterwards a huge male jaguar passed across the paved surface in front of me, and disappeared down one of the narrow paths leading into the forest. None of the white ants took any notice of him; but I could distinctly see a blue soldier-bearing dragon-fly hovering above his head. Could it be that a large and formidable beast of prey such as this was kept in captivity by these extraordinary insects? The capuchin monkey did not seem very much upset by the sight of his hereditary foe, although he was evidently somewhat relieved when the jaguar was gone.

The bananas had only served to awaken my hunger, and I was wondering whether I should be obliged to subsist on such unsatisfying fare, when I saw a long procession of large brown workerants swarming over the three-inch rampart. As they came near I noticed that each ant was carrying something in its jaws. The little monkey, again acting as if under direction, ran to one of the neighbouring banana-trees, and tore off a fragment of a leaf about as large as a sheet of foolscap paper. This he placed upon the floor of the hut, just as the leaders of the new procession arrived. During the next ten minutes a continual stream of brown worker-ants (which seemed to belong to several common South American species) entered the hut and deposited their burdens upon the banana-leaf, until the heap must have contained a pound or more of buff-coloured granules, which had very much the appearance of coarse farina made from the root of the manioc. I wondered what this could all mean, and sat staring at the pile upon the leaf for some time after the last of the burden-bearers had departed. Apparently the cavaliers were watching me with close attention, as if questioning what I would do next. At length, again following the example of the little monkey, I took up some of the granules in my hand and tasted them.

What this stuff was I have not the least idea; but I found it not only exceedingly palatable, but very sustaining. The granules were somewhat soft, and of a sweet nutty flavour, which nevertheless reminded me somewhat of truffles. I found that, when I squeezed a handful of them together, they cohered into a mass, or cake, which was much more convenient to eat without any implements than the separate grains. In a short time I had finished the whole supply, and also another banana which was brought me by the little capuchin. By the time my hunger was appeased by the novel and excellent food which I had eaten, the feeling of faintness which I had experienced ever since I had been stung by the soldier-ants had disappeared entirely.

While marvelling at the extraordinary intelligence of the cavalier-ants, which apparently possessed a fair knowledge both as to the quality and the amount of nourishment required by a human being, I began to regard my captivity almost as a joke. I had then not the least doubt that, ere long, I should find some way of outwitting my custodians and of escaping to my canoe.

After seeing me fed, and apparently manifesting no little interest and amusement at the sight, the crowd of beetle-riders dispersed. I noticed, however, that a strong guard of soldier-ants was parading the top of the rampart, and once, when I attempted to put my head out of the doorway, I found the dragon-fly still on guard. My small tutor nestled down against me and went to sleep, and I now noticed that the cavalier-ant no longer occupied its place upon his head.

After being thus left alone for about a couple of hours, a mounted troop, headed by my cock-horned acquaintance, again drew up before the hut. The little ape at once went to the doorway and crouched down, as if making obeisance to its masters, and at the same instant a tiny humming-bird, which seemed to carry two or three cavaliers perched upon its topaz-coloured crest, darted down and settled for a moment on the capuchin's head. As the bird flew off again I noticed that a pink-and-white ant had again taken its position among the hair just above the monkey's forehead.

The little creature now seized my finger again, as if to drag me out of the hut, and this time, having learned that such hints were best obeyed promptly, I followed without demur. The cavaliers rode around me as before on their swiftly running beetles, and that accursed dragon-fly again hovered menacingly just over my head. As we were entering a narrow pathway between two dense walls of vegetation, I was appalled to see a huge jaguar advancing towards me along this very track. Being quite defenceless, my first instinct was to run away; but I had scarcely faced about when the dragon-fly came buzzing against my nose, so that I distinctly felt the points of one of the soldiers' long mandibles.

It will convey some idea as to the unreasoning terror inspired by an attack of these fearful insects when I say that I spun round and faced the jaguar again without an instant's hesitation!

The little monkey had drawn himself close to the edge of the path, but I could see that he was trembling in every limb. The jaguar came to a standstill about six feet from me, then crouched down and snarled. I could easily have blown his brains out, if I had had my "paradox" gun; but, alas! it stood some sixty yards off in the forest. At this moment I felt something nipping my right heel, and on glancing downwards I was startled to find a score or so of soldier-ants close behind me and advancing in a threatening manner. Forgetful of all else, I took a spring into the air, and tumbled right upon the top of the jaguar!

What happened during the next few seconds I could hardly tell. The brute uttered a series of the most awful roars and yells, and I was aware of being rolled about like a football and of receiving a number of cuffs and scratches in various parts of my body. Fortunately the scuffle ended as quickly as it began, and I got up, greatly relieved at finding that I had not been seriously injured. On glancing around I saw the jaguar's tail vanishing into one of the smaller huts, while, for some reason or other, my escort of cavaliers were all tumbling pell-mell off their beetles and standing head-downwards upon the path, while their white hinder extremities, which were hoisted on high, appeared seized with uncontrollable agitation.

After recovering from this strange epileptic seizure, the cavalier-ants remounted, and the poor little monkey, which seemed almost as much shaken as I was by the encounter, again started on in front.

132 INVERTEBRATA ENIGMATICA

By-and-by we came to a cultivated patch of ground where, apparently, the "ant-rice" had recently been cleared away. Half the little rectangular field—which was about forty feet across—had the appearance of having been roughly ploughed up. My attention was now drawn to a number of objects moving slowly across this piece of ground, and I soon saw that they were armadillos. There were six of them, and they seemed to be advancing in line, diligently scratching up the soil with their powerful digging-claws. Just above them hovered several large dragon-flies, each of which apparently carried a cavalier-ant and several armed warriors. No sooner had we reached the scene of operations than the little monkey snatched up a stick, went behind the armadillos, and began to act as if he were digging the ground. Another heavy stick, which appeared to have been gnawed to a sharp point by the chisel-like teeth of a porcupine, coypu, or some other large rodent animal, lay just in front of me, and, as the dragon-fly seemed becoming rather demonstrative, I lost no time in following the monkey's lead.

I soon saw that the little ape only made a mere pretence of working; and, as it was very hot, and I felt somewhat done up and languid after my recent trying experiences, I was tempted to follow his bad example, and take things easily. Our place, it appeared, was just behind the gang of armadillos, and it seemed to be expected of us that we should dig up the ground to a somewhat greater depth. After lazily prodding the soil for a few minutes, my small companion gave a sudden shriek of alarm, scampered back to the place where we had started work, and commenced digging the ground over again with desperate energy. I was wondering what had influenced him, when a topaz hummingbird came whirring towards us, bearing on its back my cock-horned ex-captive and a strong patrol of slate-coloured warriors. It settled on my head for an instant, and when it flew off again I saw that two at least of the big stinging ants had been left behind. My first instinct was to bring my hand to my head and endeavour to brush these horrible creatures away; but a slight admonitory nip made me pause in terror, and give up all thoughts of rebellion. Forthwith, with trembling knees, I joined my fellow-captive, and began to dig away at the ground with all my might.

It was, alas, abundantly plain that our new taskmaster would stand no shirking. He kept his aerial mount humming round our ears all the time, so we dug away as if for our lives, until all the earth scratched up by the armadillos was thoroughly turned over.

Fortunately the soil was very light and loose, and the sky some-what overcast, otherwise the fatigue of digging in such a climate would have nearly killed me.

When we had done, our strict overseer mercifully removed the guards from my head and went sailing away out of sight; and my little companion, who seemed sadly exhausted and depressed, led me to a spring of clear water which broke out in the middle of the banana-grove. After drinking freely, and washing my face and hands, I felt somewhat better both in mind and body, and was able to eat another pile of the granular food, which I found awaiting me in my quarters.

During the remainder of the day, although not allowed to leave the hut, I was left to my own devices, and spent most of my time resting flat upon my back, trying to realise my strange position, and making many plans of escape. I could not help dwelling upon the caustic irony of fate in placing a man who had been acknowl-edged by the whole scientific world as the foremost living author-ity on ants, in such a position as that in which I now found myself.

It was plain that these marvellous cavaliers excelled all other insects in intelligence, to an even greater degree than man excels all his fellow-mammals. Apparently they had not only turned to their own use, and improved upon, practically all the special primi-tive instincts and habits of other ants, but had also greatly enhanced the more valuable qualities (from their own point of view) of most of their domesticated breeds. I had seen amongst their crowds of slaves unusually large and perfect specimens of nearly every spe-cies of ant in South America. Probably these useful varieties had been bred by the cavaliers for many generations, for all appeared to yield them instinctive obedience, and to require scarcely any supervision. The cavaliers had, moreover, succeeded in taming and breeding, for certain special purposes, many other insects, such as the fireflies, dragon-flies, and swift, smooth-running beetles. In addi-tion to this, they seemed to have a good understanding as to the kind of service which such diverse creatures as men, monkeys, ro-dents, armadillos, and humming-birds could render them. Why they kept such a useless beast as a jaguar in captivity was to me at that time a complete puzzle. I was inclined at first to think that they were prompted by scientific motives, or the mere vanity of possession; but afterwards I received ample proof that here, as in most other matters, they had a shrewd eye to business.

As was to be expected—seeing that the mental attributes of all insects must be more akin to their own than those of birds and mammals—they seemed to have obtained a much greater ascendancy over the former than over the latter. Most of their invertebrate servants appeared to do their bidding as a matter of course, without coercion or any special guidance; whereas I and other warm-blooded captives were always treated as stupid or untrustworthy creatures, which required to be strictly watched, restrained, and generally superintended.

At the approach of nightfall I made up my mind to make my escape in the darkness. But, just as the sun began to sink behind the Andes, a large luminous spider, which spun his web with astonishing rapidity, fixed a curtain over the entrance of my hut. On surveying this web carefully, I found that several threads from its outer side stretched upwards to a number of white nodular projections, about as big as a walnut, which I had already observed just above the doorway. Each of these I now found to my disgust to be a hollow guardroom, garrisoned by several big stinging ants, which would, of course, be able to drop down instantly upon any one disturbing the web.

On testing the walls of the hut elsewhere, I found them so firm and solid that there was not the least chance of my breaking through. I afterwards came to the conclusion that the white cement used for building and paving purposes was manufactured by captive hordes of termites which lived underground; but that the actual building operations were performed by true ant-slaves, similar to those I had seen at work in the forest. Be this as it may, both pavements and buildings were as hard as marble, with a fine porcelainlike surface.

I passed a restless night, brooding over my strange position. Although visited every half-hour or so by a night patrol of cavaliers, which, riding upon large fireflies, sailed in through a small opening in the spider's web and did their round with soldier-like precision, I was quite unmolested during the hours of darkness.

Moreover, although mosquitoes seemed both hungry and plentiful in this region, I was quite free from their attacks until the moment when I regained my liberty. This I believe to have been due to the presence of my spider *concierge* or of the soldier-bearing dragon-flies which were always hovering near my head in the daytime—it being a well-known fact in the tropics that all insects of

the gnat tribe give these hereditary foes as wide a berth as possible.

IV

It would be a long and tedious narrative if I were to tell all the
incidents of my captivity in detail; so having described the events
of the first day, I will henceforth record only some of my more
noteworthy experiences among these extraordinary ants.

As a rule, my life was exceedingly monotonous. Every morning, after being fed, I was set to work at something where my height,
strength, and power of using sticks and other tools proved valuable to the ant-community. After several days of digging in the ant-
rice fields, I was employed in clearing out rotten leaf-mould from
some cave-like underground chambers. These had originally been
filled by the *saübas*, or leaf-cutting ants, in the service of the cavaliers, and had evidently formed hotbeds for growing edible fungi.
On this occasion I managed to wound my right hand rather badly
with a splinter, and was extremely apprehensive lest the cock-
horned ant should think I was shirking, and have me severely pun-
ished. But, strange to relate, my master,—for so henceforth I must
call him,—after examining my wound with a good deal of attention, had the splinter plucked out by a soldier-ant (whose forceps-
like jaws seemed made on purpose), and then gave me an hour's
holiday. Afterwards he was kind enough to find me a lighter job;
and for the rest of that day I stood, with a cane in my left hand, as
foreman over a strong excavating gang of armadillos.

Early during my second week, and before despair had completely robbed me of initiative, I thought I saw a chance of escape.
I had noticed that, when the night-guard was set, and before the
first round of the firefly-borne inspectors, some of the big stinging ants would swarm down upon the floor of the hut and clear up
any remains of my supper. Although they usually came cautiously,
and in detachments, they seemed to have such a weakness for the
granular material upon which I was fed, that it occurred to me to
turn the fact to my advantage. For if, during the night, I could once
lure all of them from the doorway, I could make a dash for freedom
before they could do me any hurt. After one or two vain attempts
to entice them *en masse* from their post of duty, I remembered a
time-honoured plan of corrupting military morals which has often
proved effective in the hands of prisoners—and novelists.

I had carefully preserved the contents of my spirit-flask for special emergencies, and one moonless night I determined to see if I could make my guards drunk by saturating some of my granular food with whisky. The scheme succeeded to admiration. No sooner was it dark than a company of soldier-ants climbed down to the floor, and in less than five minutes they were all too tipsy to return. By-and-by the first detachment was followed by a second. These also, after showing some indignation at the disgraceful state of their comrades, sampled my "Ancient Scotch"—and fell likewise into a state of scandalous intoxication. After making quite sure that there were none left guarding the doorway, I lost not a minute in plunging through the tough spider's web, and hurrying towards the river as fast as the darkness would allow.

I believe that all would have gone well if I had not met the firefly patrol just as I crossed the three-inch rampart, about ten yards from the hut. It consisted of about a dozen mounted cavaliers, six of which forthwith accompanied me in my flight, while the rest separated, and darted off hither and thither.

As I hurried along the narrow track the little illuminated riders kept up with me, three on each side of my face. Their vigilance and excitement made them sit up like jockeys, and as they sped along I thought I could see the hind-legs of each cavalier working furiously against its firefly's body, like the spurred heels of a horseman.

Alas! I had barely entered the bush on the farther side of the clearing when I heard some large creature rushing along an adjoining forest-path, and as I emerged into the open space where I was first captured, I found myself confronted by the jaguar! Just then a brilliant firefly came whizzing down the dark narrow glade like a white-hot rifle-bullet, and directly I saw that it carried my redoubtable cock-horned master, I knew that the game was up. Instantly the jaguar, which previously had seemed to hesitate, sprang at me, knocked me down, and rolled me this way and that with his powerful paws. Then he suddenly drew back, like a sheep-dog which had been called off by the shepherd. As soon as I had recovered my breath, I picked myself up and slunk back to my quarters, thoroughly cowed and submissive. The jaguar sniffed at my dilapidated trousers, and growled horribly all the way, and I knew full well that at any moment, if my custodian gave him the order, he would tear me to pieces.

I now no longer speculated why the cavalier-ants kept this enormous jaguar. His business, like that of a sheep-dog or cattle-dog,
was to chase and punish any of his mammalian fellow-servants who
attempted to break away.

It is needless to say that I felt miserably cast down at the result
of this effort to regain my freedom.

Probably no mere verbal statement would bring home to my
readers the disastrous moral consequences of my condition as a
slave among the cavalier-ants. After the startling novelty of my
adventure had worn off, and I had endured several such defeats as
the foregoing, my prevailing mental state was one of frantic and
futile rage at finding all my human strength and intelligence, all
my scientific knowledge and attainments, and all my experience
of life generally, of absolutely no avail, either in helping me to escape, or in preventing my being treated by these imperious insects
"as a horse or a mule which have no understanding."

In the same way, I suppose, a wild elephant finds his vast
strength and natural wisdom, and all the wonderful fund of forest
lore which he has gathered during half a century, entirely value-
less when he is caught and subjugated by men.

Ere long this state of bitter exasperation alternated with fits of
lethargic despair, during which the grosser and more grovelling
animal instincts seemed to be supplanting all other springs of action. Latterly there were times when this shameful lapse into mere
tame-animalism sent me forth to my labour like a working ox,
prompted only by threats of near punishment or by the desire to
fill my belly.

V

On the morning following my failure to escape, I found a large
assembly of cavaliers formed up in a semicircle in front of my dwelling. Inside this semicircle, and placed in a row close to the doorway, were the delinquent guards, still, seemingly, in a state of helpless intoxication. Shortly afterwards a procession of black working ants, headed by an overgrown *saüba* with curiously distorted,
scissor-like jaws, arrived upon the scene. This insect, apparently
after a brief interview with my master—who advanced without dis-
mounting from his high-bred longicorn—ran to each of the pros-
trate criminals in turn and expeditiously nipped off all their heads.
After the executioner had done his duty, some of the dingy worker-

ants carried the carcasses away; and henceforth a double detachment of slate-coloured warriors (which I found to be absolutely incorruptible) occupied the guardrooms at night. The only punishment I myself suffered was a temporary deprivation of my pleasant granular food. For three days I had to subsist upon bananas and about a quart of gritty millet-like seeds, which I found to be nothing like so nourishing as the mysterious provender which I have already described.

I may state here that whenever, in the opinion of my masters, I became obstreperous, this was the result; and latterly, strange to say, the fear of being deprived of my regular diet (of which I had become extremely fond) influenced my behaviour more than anything else.

The cavaliers, as is the way with most ruling castes, seemed to spend a good deal of time in recreation. In this, and in their evident possession of a sense of humour, and of well-developed powers of hearing (concerning which I shall have more to say presently), they differ widely from all other species of ants. Some of my most humiliating experiences were traceable to these facts; for at times I was compelled to shout, sing, and to go through various absurd performances for their pleasure. While I was a comparative novelty the mere sight of me seemed to suffice. They would come and watch me in crowds, and, on the first occasion when I undressed in their presence, the act seemed to afford them a vast deal of amusement, which they manifested in the odd fashion I have already described. After this I frequently had to take off all my ragged clothes at the command of my master when he brought parties of friends to look at me.

An even more abasing experience awaited me somewhat later, when, having chanced to skip and jump about in a somewhat agile manner when my bare feet were threatened by the horrible stinging-ants, I was made to repeat the performance over and over again for the entertainment of the assembled cavaliers. In fact, these diabolical insects taught me to "dance" by almost precisely the same methods that civilised showmen resort to when training performing elephants.

At the end of the first month a great trouble befell me in the tragic death of my poor little fellow-slave and tutor. I fear that my capture by the cavalier-ants proved a sad misfortune to this frail and gentle monkey. He had, I think, been in captivity for a long time, for he understood the ways and wishes of his masters in a wonderful manner. This fact, and his apparent kinship with mankind, probably caused our masters to appoint him as my guide and exemplar (just as a young setter or sheep-dog is set to work with an old one which knows its business), and as the interpreter of their wishes to my crude untutored mind. Hence, unhappily, he was made to do regular work in the fields and elsewhere—which, as any one who understands ape-nature will know, was to him an absolutely intolerable burden. Recognising this, I did my best to spare him whenever possible, and I believe he repaid my good intentions with real gratitude and love.

One sultry morning, when I had a bad headache, I had great difficulty in understanding some new piece of work connected with the dam which the cavaliers had erected to enlarge a forest pool where they kept their tame coypus and capybaras. After trying in many ways to bring the matter within the scope of my comprehension, my poor little schoolmaster seemed worried out of his wits; and at length, in a spasm of frantic rage at my thick-headedness, he flung himself down upon the ground, accidentally squashing the soft-bodied master-ant which was seated upon his head.

It so happened that a large crowd of cavaliers was present at the time, and the sensation caused by this unhappy accident was very great. Both I and the wretched little capuchin were marched forthwith back to our quarters, where we waited, in considerable trepidation, to learn what would happen next.

Half an hour later a great concourse of cavaliers and warriors lined the three-inch rampart, and, as soon as they were in their places, an armed dragon-fly came buzzing into the hut, and drove the trembling monkey out into the open. Here, before my eyes, he was pounced upon and torn to pieces by the jaguar! This act of hateful injustice to my innocent friend and colleague so filled me with unthinking rage that I rushed out, all unarmed as I was, to take vengeance on the executioner. But I had scarcely taken three strides when several dragon-flies with their armed riders dashed at me like hawks, and a second later I was writhing upon the ground in such unspeakable torment that I wished that the jaguar would kill me also!

Henceforth my position was worse than ever; and, owing to the depression I felt at the loss of my only friend and companion, the mental and moral degeneration which I have already spoken of proceeded more rapidly than before.

Next morning, when I received the signal to go forth to my work, a truculent drab soldier-ant, apparently of a different species from any that I had hitherto seen, was placed by my master just above my bald forehead, where he sat, throughout the day, like a mahout upon an elephant, and prodded me viciously with his mandibles when he considered that I was not doing my best.

I think that all of those who know my character will readily understand that I did not sink into a state of idiotic despair without a struggle to retain my manhood and my reason. When alone I would frequently talk to myself, and recite poetry, and even elementary school lessons which I had learned by rote (such as the Latin and Greek declensions and the Multiplication Table), for the sake of reminding myself that I had once been a civilised human being. At times, when brought very low, I would raise my voice and shout as loudly as possible, in order to create a greater impression upon my failing intellect.

On one occasion when I felt very sick and feeble, after three days of punishment diet for insubordination, and almost demented through being unmercifully harassed and bullied by my master, who kept repeating some order which I could not in the least comprehend, I managed to pull myself to the hut-door in sheer desperation, and began bawling my own name at the very top of my voice—adding to it the whole string of degrees and honourable titles which have been conferred upon me by learned bodies all over the civilised world.

This recital, I was astonished to observe, seemed to make quite a sensation among the cavalier-ants, who immediately assembled in great crowds in front of my dwelling, and not only gave me a command to repeat the whole programme, but greeted my most strenuous vocal efforts with epileptic spasms of applause.

I was immediately rewarded by being allowed to sup upon my favourite provender: but, alas! I found that I had established a precedent; and henceforth, if I failed to shout or sing very loudly for some ten minutes after being brought in from the fields, I got nothing but a few handfuls of gritty millet which I could scarcely swallow.

Before long, however, this form of entertainment seemed to pall upon the cavaliers, who, I found, were exceedingly fickle; and I am ashamed to confess that I could not help feeling some chagrin at the waning of my popularity.

VI

On the whole, my physical health remained fairly good, and indeed seemed to improve somewhat as my mind became more clouded; otherwise I could not possibly have stood the heavy work which I was made to do in the fields and the forest. One saving circumstance was that the extreme dampness of this region shortened my hours of labour. It rained nearly every other day, and my masters had a strong objection to being out in the wet. They seemed to know instinctively when rain was coming, and would then hurry me back to my quarters at once, while they themselves took refuge in their little domelike palaces.

Before I sank into a state of complete mental inertia, I felt a strong wish to investigate the internal economy of these "nests." This desire, however, was not gratified until I had practically ceased to take an intelligent interest in my surroundings. One morning, after a hurricane had torn through the neighbouring forest, I was led forth to repair damages, and found that a large branch of a tree had knocked away one side of the round, porcelain mansion inhabited by my cock-horned chief. I could see that the interior was made up of a bewildering labyrinth of chambers, with pearly semi-transparent walls; but otherwise I did not add to my knowledge of my master's domestic economy.

Although I have fallen into the habit of using the masculine gender when speaking of the ant whose special property I seemed to be—chiefly because there was something essentially virile and masterful in the character of this extraordinary insect—I have no reason for believing that all the cavaliers which I saw were not true amazons, as is the case with the active members of other ant communities.

During the last fortnight of my captivity my state of mental hebetude several times gave place to a kind of mild delirium, although I was not conscious of any fever. At such times I would sometimes imagine myself back at Oxford, and would commence discoursing on scientific subjects, under the momentary impression that I was lecturing to my class.

While moping stupidly in my hut one brilliant sunny afternoon after returning from labour, I was surprised to see a considerable number of mounted cavaliers advancing towards me. In their midst was some strange object which I could not at first make out, but which, when the procession drew near, I found to be a small and active rattlesnake, bearing upon its back a score or so of white-bodied ants somewhat different from any that I had seen before.

Although similar in many respects to the cavaliers, these insects evidently belonged to a distinct species or variety, for their enormous, bulging heads were tinted light blue; while their antennae were, for the most part, of a brilliant ultramarine. I soon noticed also that they differed considerably from the cavaliers in manner, being much more restless and excitable. When about two feet from my hut door the whole concourse dismounted; and when the visitors had to some extent satisfied their curiosity as to my appearance, my master, who seemed to be engaged in an animated discussion with one of the visitors (which chanced to have its antennae tinted respectively of an Oxford and Cambridge blue) gave me an order to sing.

By this time I readily understood such commands as this, and had learned by painful experiences that no excuse would be accepted. I therefore without delay put my head out of the opening and shouted "Rule Britannia" at the very top of my voice. I began almost as mechanically as a phonograph, but when I came to the words *"Britons never, never, never shall be slaves!"* I suddenly realised my position, faltered, and broke down.

Upon this my master and his cavalier friends seemed greatly disconcerted, while the blue-headed strangers were so overcome with derisive "laughter" that they all turned head-over-heels and lay kicking helplessly upon their backs.

After a while the discussion was renewed between my master and the ant with Oxford-and-Cambridge antennae; and, while watching them, I felt a sudden conviction that these ill-bred snake-riding ants had come to buy me from the cavaliers. In spite of the misery of my position, I dreaded being handed over to such unprepossessing insects; for, to tell the truth, I had formed a very low opinion of their character. They had nothing of the suavity and ease of manner which distinguished the cavaliers, but rather put me in mind of a lot of vulgar pushing commercials out for a holiday.

By-and-by the two parties seemed to arrive at some agreement, for the cavaliers remounted their swift beetles and escorted their blue-headed visitors (which, when scrambling on to their loathsome conveyance, strongly resembled a gang of rowdy trippers boarding an excursion train) along one of the paths leading into the forest.

VII

Next morning, at daybreak, I found the whole settlement astir, and that a general migration of the cavaliers seemed to be taking place towards the river. After receiving an unusually liberal breakfast I was placed in charge of my drab mahout and taken towards the forest arena where all my troubles began. My master, who hovered round me on an exquisite white humming-bird—which he only rode on state occasions—seemed to be looking me over with a critical eye, and he more than once gave my rider a hint to make me pull myself together, hold up my head, and step out more briskly.

This, perhaps, should have confirmed my previous suspicions that I was being driven to market; but, curiously enough, it had a very different effect upon my mind.

I have already said that I had recently been subject to attacks of mild delirium, during which I quite forgot my present lamentable circumstances, and thought myself back in the post of honour which I had occupied at home. As I strode along the narrow forest pathway, with my shoulders squared and my chin well up, it suddenly seemed to me that I was passing amid a crowd of admiring people at Glasgow while making a dignified approach towards the Presidential Chair. Automatically I began, below my breath, to rehearse parts of the speech which I had prepared for that great occasion.

As soon as I entered the open space, however, the startling novelty of the scene before me brought my mind back from its wanderings. The little arena was thronged with innumerable cavaliers, who not only occupied a high, terraced rampart, which had been erected all around the paved clearing like the tiers of an amphitheatre, but crowded every point of vantage among the leafy walls above. In fact, only the smooth, columnar tree- trunks which encircled the open space, and a few of the larger branches overhead, were left unoccupied. All else was tinted pink and white by the enormous throng of cavaliers, so that the foliage looked like an apple orchard in full blossom.

I had scarcely taken my appointed place in the centre of the ring when a procession appeared through one of the narrow glades in the forest which surpassed anything I had seen before.

A score or more of huge serpents, most of them pythons or anacondas over twenty feet long, came sliding, two or three abreast, into the opening, like trains entering some great London terminus.

Their backs were blue and white with dense crowds of demonstrative (I had almost said "noisy") snake-riders; and these enormous cargoes of excursionists were followed by numerous smaller parties, mounted on rattlesnakes, coral snakes, whip snakes, and nearly every kind of serpent represented in South America.

For a while I seemed to be standing on a small island surrounded by a writhing sea of snakes; yet, knowing well that the whole business was being arranged by my potent masters, I felt scarcely any alarm, but found myself vaguely wondering where room was to be found for this vast influx of visitors; for the open-air theatre seemed crowded to its fullest capacity.

The two leading boa-constrictors wriggled straight to the nearest tree and coiled themselves spirally around it, one above the other, thus making, as it were, a number of galleries for about ten feet up the trunk. Most of the other large pythons followed their example, while all the smaller serpents swarmed up the trees and creepers surrounding the open space, and in a few minutes were arranged in a series of marvellous hanging bridges—all densely crowded with spectators—which completely festooned the forest walls.

I was so much taken up with watching this astounding spectacle that I did not notice certain tamed animals which the snake-riding ants had brought with them until I smelt a most unpleasant smell, and suddenly discovered, close to my side, a gaunt and very large howler monkey. This beast seemed quite undisturbed by my presence, and was sitting at its ease upon the white ground scratching its mangy, rufous flanks in an extremely diligent manner.

I found also that the cavaliers had just brought into the arena two of their best working teams of armadillos; while, sprawling on the ground close beside them, was a miserable three-toed sloth, which had lost half its hair and appeared to be in the last stages of consumption.

Almost before the newcomers were settled in their places I was made to stand on one side, while the armadillos and the sloth, after being placed in the middle of the ring, were carefully inspected by my cock-horned chief and his Oxford-and-Cambridge visitor. It was fairly plain that certain negotiations were in progress, but I could scarcely believe that my masters would be so silly as to swap both their best teams of trained and well-fed armadillos for a moribund, three-toed sloth.

Apparently, however, in commercial matters the cavaliers were no match for the bustling blue-heads; for shortly afterwards the whole herd of armadillos was driven off in the direction from whence the visitors had come, while the wretched sloth, attended by an armed dragon-fly, crawled away, slowly and painfully, towards the cavalier settlement.

On glancing around I noticed that the majority of the ants, which had hitherto shown but little interest in what was going on in the arena, seemed settling down in their places, like a music-hall audience on the announcement of some popular "turn."

I was now led to the centre again, and made to go down on my hands and knees cheek by jowl with the evil-smelling howler, which was about as large as a collie dog. It seemed as if I were about to be bartered away like the armadillos, and the fears which I had felt during the first visit of the snake-riders were now greatly increased, for the starved and neglected condition of their wretched "pets" showed only too plainly that they were far worse masters than cavaliers.

Yet, in spite of the incident which I had just witnessed, I still had some hope that the obvious difference in exchange-value between myself and a sullen and mangy red howler would prove a bar to any such transaction. In this the event showed that I was woefully out of my reckoning, and that in my estimate of my own intrinsic worth I was altogether at sea.

Shortly after my mahout had made me go down on all-fours, side by side with the disgusting monkey, a fresh wave of delirium must have swamped my mind; for I remember declaring this attitude to be an altogether unprecedented one for the delivery of a Presidential Address!

I was partially aroused by a small dragon-fly buzzing against my lips—which was the recognised signal when my master desired me to shout or sing. Still prompted by the insane fancy that I was facing a scientific audience, I at once commenced to recite my carefully prepared oration; and, at the same moment, the brute of a monkey began howling like a whole menagerie of jackals.

It seemed for a while that the hideous nightmare fancy, already spoken of, had become true in fact. In my present waking delirium I thought I was indeed addressing the British Association at Glasgow, and that my most prominent scientific rival was attempting to howl me down.

Those who have been partially under the influence of intoxicating drugs will know that for some time after most of the faculties are overcome, and are wandering in the maddest mazes, there still seems to remain one critical atom of sanity in the innermost mental chamber which is perfectly aware of the real state of the case. In like manner, I knew,—in a sense—where I was; and what (Heaven help me!) I was doing.

Moreover, an electric flash of recollection told me that this was the very day when, had I been able to return, I should be in reality delivering my Presidential Address to the British Association at Glasgow! Yet so transitory was this lucid interval, that I did not cease raising my voice more and more, in order to make my peroration heard above a hideous crescendo of yelps from the obscene beast beside me.

But, alas! the vocal apparatus of a big howler monkey enables him to defy competition from any living thing! My chances could scarcely have been worse if I had backed myself in a roaring match against the eternal thunders of Niagara!

Suddenly my voice cracked under the intolerable strain. I instantly recovered my sober senses, and came to a full stop; while the monkey's triumphant howls rose louder and louder, to a stupendous and deafening *finale*.

At this the cavaliers seemed to be in a state of the utmost consternation (I am inclined to think that there were some heavy bets on the result), while all the blue-heads gave way to unseemly somersaults of laughter. It was only too plain that their scraggy and abominable ape—which had again seated himself upon the ground, and was engaged in strenuous entomological researches among his frowzy red hair—was acknowledged my victor in the contest.

Although sick with shame and fury, I had a momentary feeling of relief at the thought that those keen low-bred snake-riders would now refuse to trade.

But I had soon a new and graver cause for apprehension. My master, whose quivering antennae told of intense irritation and chagrin, suddenly dashed off on his white humming-bird towards the cavaliers' clearing. For a few minutes both I and the vast concourse of spectators waited in suspense; then a sudden "sensation" quivered through the whole assembly. He had been to fetch the jaguar!

On emerging from the forest-path this hideous brute stopped, and stood blinking and licking his jaws on the farther side of the opening. In the meantime an eager debate seemed to have been started among one section of the cavaliers, and several deputations advanced to interview my master.

It seemed to me that a large number of them were pleading for my life; and I noticed that many of these kept pointing their scarlet antennae towards the path leading to the river.

The jaguar began switching his barred tail to and fro against his hollow flanks, and growled more and more impatiently during the debate; while my master flew round from tier to tier on the rampart, and from gallery to gallery among the trees, as if taking the sense of the meeting. I believe that all the brutal snake-riders without exception urged him to let me be killed, but happily he seemed to treat their demonstrations with aristocratic contempt.

By-and-by, during an animated conference with several of the leading cavaliers, he evidently made some amusing proposal which was hailed with general approbation. Soon afterwards my mahout guided me to the very tree against which I had leaned my gun when I camped in this fatal spot. The ant-carrying snakes which encircled this tree hissed horribly as I drew near, but unwound themselves and moved away at my master's special request. I then saw that my double-barrelled "paradox" gun was still where I had placed it, although red with rust and almost hidden by a creeper. My mahout gave me a signal to bend forward, so I seized hold of the muzzle and managed to drag it forth, recollecting as I did so that on landing I had loaded both barrels with some waterproof ball-cartridges which I had had specially prepared before visiting this humid region.

Fortunately the locks, which had been well soused with hot petroleum and wrapped in a greasy cloth, were less corroded than the barrels.

While I was examining the gun my master's white hummingbird settled for a moment upon my forehead, and then hovered in front of my eyes, showing me that my mahout had been taken away. On glancing towards the river, I found that the line of guards had disappeared, and that the path was as clear as when I had first traversed it.

Scarcely had I noted these facts when the jaguar ceased growling and twitching his tail, and came creeping upon his belly across the clearing, with his eyes aflame with the lust for blood.

In another instant I had raised the gun and pulled both triggers. A stunning explosion knocked me backwards against the tree, and a blinding flame leaped right into my face. The choked left barrel had burst just beyond my fingers; but, in spite of all, one bullet had flown true! The jaguar was writhing on his back in the middle of the arena, and besmearing the white porcelain-like pavement with brains and blood from his shattered skull!

For some minutes I stood rooted to the spot, with no more power to plan or move than the forest trees about me; and I think that the sight I then saw impressed me more than anything else during my living nightmare in the forest. In spite of the terrific flash and detonation, and the death-struggles of the enormous jaguar in their very midst, the valiant cavaliers were all standing upon their heads in convulsions of laughter at the episode!

When their spasms had partially subsided, the spell which held me motionless was broken by the sight of a dozen huge soldier-ants, which came charging towards my naked feet from beyond where the jaguar was lying.

Without another thought I wheeled round and bolted down the path like a rabbit.

My little dug-out *piragua* still lay, tight and uninjured, upon the white pathway just above the pool. As I launched it, and pushed off, a white humming-bird suddenly poised itself in front of my face; and alone upon its snowy crest sat my tiny pink-headed master. This marvellous insect seemed to look me straight in the eyes for a few seconds, then he waved his unmutilated antenna in a friendly way, bobbed his Mephistophelean visage, as if bidding me bon voyage, and whirred off into the forest.

I have no recollection as to how I descended the swollen rivulet; but a great shout greeted me as I swept out into the broad Jagara, and I saw several light canoes darting to meet me from the opposite bank. I was too dazed and idiotic to be surprised or to understand the speech of an aged white-haired Indian who took my *piragua* in tow and jabbered eagerly to me in Portuguese as he paddled across the rapid stream.

I was taken to an Indian village amid the forest on the farther bank, where I was nursed with the utmost kindness; but nearly a week passed before I could understand my aged rescuer, although I had acquired a fair knowledge of Portuguese. When I made my first attempt to give some account of my experiences, and told the old Indian about my cock-horned captive, who afterwards became my master, he crossed himself fervently.

"Ah, senhor!" he exclaimed with a shiver, "him I know well. Sixty years ago he was my master also. Ah, he is a great and terrible *piaché*! Surely he is the very devil!"

"What!" I cried, "have you also been a slave among the cavalierants?"

"Yes, senhor," replied he gravely. "When I was a youth they held me in bondage for two months: then they seemed to get tired of me, and gave me scarcely any food; and at last they dismissed me from their service. When your crew of the Buras came to my village and told me that you had ventured into that forbidden country and had not come back, I said, 'They will, perhaps, get tired of him also in about two months. Let us make a camp on the safe side of the Jagara and wait for him.'"

The Valley of the Spiders
H. G. Wells

Towards midday the three pursuers came abruptly round a bend in the torrent bed upon the sight of a very broad and spacious valley. The difficult and winding trench of pebbles along which they had tracked the fugitives for so long expanded to a broad slope, and with a common impulse the three men left the trail, and rode to a low eminence set with olive-dun trees, and there halted, the two others, as became them, a little behind the man with the silver-studded bridle.

For a space they scanned the great expanse below them with eager eyes. It spread remoter and remoter, with only a few clusters of sere thorn bushes here and there, and the dim suggestions of some now waterless ravine to break its desolation of yellow grass. Its purple distances melted at last into the bluish slopes of the further hills—hills it might be of a greener kind—and above them invisibly supported, and seeming indeed to hang in the blue, were the snow-clad summits of mountains—that grew larger and bolder to the north-westward as the sides of the valley drew together. And westward the valley opened until a distant darkness under the sky told where the forests began. But the three men looked neither east nor west, but only steadfastly across the valley.

The gaunt man with the scarred lip was the first to speak. "Nowhere," he said, with a sigh of disappointment in his voice. "But after all, they had a full day's start."

"They don't know we are after them," said the little man on the white horse.

"She would know," said the leader bitterly, as if speaking to himself.

"Even then they can't go fast. They've got no beast but the mule, and all today the girl's foot has been bleeding—"

The man with the silver bridle flashed a quick intensity of rage on him. "Do you think I haven't seen that?" he snarled.

"It helps, anyhow," whispered the little man to himself.

The gaunt man with the scarred lip stared impassively.

"They can't be over the valley, " he said. "If we ride hard—"

He glanced at the white horse and paused.

"Curse all white horses!" said the man with the silver bridle and turned to scan the beast his curse included.

The little man looked down between the melancholy ears of his steed.

"I did my best," he said.

The two others stared again across the valley for a space. The gaunt man passed the back of his hand across the scarred lip.

"Come up!" said the man who owned the silver bridle, suddenly. The little man started and jerked his rein, and the horse hooves of the three made a multitudinous faint pattering upon the withered grass as they turned back towards the trail....

They rode cautiously down the long slope before them, and so came through a waste of prickly twisted bushes and strange dry shapes of horny branches that grew amongst the rocks, into the level below. And there the trail grew faint, for the soil was scanty, and the only herbage was this scorched dead straw that lay upon the ground. Still, by hard scanning, by leaning beside the horse's neck and pausing ever and again, even these white men could contrive to follow after their prey.

There were trodden places, bent and broken blades of the coarse grass, and ever and again the sufficient intimation of a footmark. And once the leader saw a brown smear of blood where the half-caste girl may have trod. And at that under his breath he cursed her for a fool.

The gaunt man checked his leader's tracking, and the little man on the white horse rode behind, a man lost in a dream. They rode one after another, the man with the silver bridle led the way, and they spoke never a word. After a time it came to the little man on the white horse that the world was very still. He started out of his dream. Besides the minute noises of their horses and equipment, the whole great valley kept the brooding quiet of a painted scene.

Before him went his master and his fellow, each intently leaning forward to the left, each impassively moving with the paces of his horse; their shadows went before them—still, noiseless, tapering

attendants; and nearer a crouched cool shape was his own. He
looked about him. What was it had gone? Then he remembered
the reverberation from the banks of the gorge and the perpetual
accompaniment of shifting, jostling pebbles. And, moreover—?
There was no breeze. That was it! What a vast, still place it was, a
monotonous afternoon slumber. And the sky open and blank, except
for a somber veil of haze that had gathered in the upper valley.

He straightened his back, fretted with his bridle, puckered his
lips to whistle, and simply sighed. He turned in his saddle for a
time, and stared at the throat of the mountain gorge out of which
they had come. Blank! Blank slopes on either side, with never a
sign of a decent beast or tree—much less a man. What a land it
was! What a wilderness! He dropped again into his former pose.

It filled him with a momentary pleasure to see a wry stick of
purple black flash out into the form of a snake, and vanish amidst
the brown. After all, the infernal valley was alive. And then, to re-
joice him still more, came a breath across his face, a whisper that
came and went, the faintest inclination of a stiff black-antlered
bush upon a crest, the first intimations of a possible breeze. Idly
he wetted his finger, and held it up.

He pulled up sharply to avoid a collision with the gaunt man,
who had stopped at fault upon the trail. Just at that guilty moment he caught his master's eye looking towards him.

For a time he forced an interest in the tracking. Then, as they
rode on again, he studied his master's shadow and hat and shoulder appearing and disappearing behind the gaunt man's nearer
contours. They had ridden four days out of the very limits of the
world into this desolate place, short of water, with nothing but a
strip of dried meat under their saddles, over rocks and mountains,
where surely none but these fugitives had ever been before—for
that!

And all this was for a girl, a mere willful child! And the man
had whole cityfuls of people to do his basest bidding—girls, women!
Why in the name of passionate folly this one in particular? asked
the little man, and scowled at the world, and licked his parched
lips with a blackened tongue. It was the way of the master, and
that was all he knew. Just because she sought to evade him....

His eye caught a whole row of high-plumed canes bending in
unison, and then the tails of silk that hung before his neck flapped
and fell.

The breeze was growing stronger. Somehow it took the stiff stillness out of things—and that was well.

"Hullo!" said the gaunt man. All three stopped abruptly.

"What?" asked the master. "What?"

"Over there," said the gaunt man, pointing up the valley.

"What?"

"Something coming towards us."

And as he spoke a yellow animal crested a rise and came bearing down upon them. It was a big wild dog, coming before the wind, tongue out, at a steady pace, and running with such an intensity of purpose that he did not seem to see the horsemen he approached. He ran with his nose up, following, it was plain, neither scent nor quarry. As he drew nearer the little man felt for his sword. "He's mad," said the gaunt rider.

"Shout!" said the little man and shouted.

The dog came on. Then when the little man's blade was already out, swerved aside and went panting by them and past. The eyes of the little man followed its flight. "There was no foam," he said. For a space the man with the silver-studded bridle stared up the valley. "Oh, come on!" he cried at last. "What does it matter?" and jerked his horse to movement again.

The little man left the insoluble mystery of a dog that fled from nothing but the wind, and lapsed into profound musings on human character. "Come on!" he whispered to himself. "Why should it be even to one man to say 'Come on!' with that stupendous violence of effect. Always, all his life, the man with the silver bridle has been saying that. If I said it—!" thought the little man. But people marvelled when the master was disobeyed even in the wildest things. This half-caste girl seemed to him, seemed to everyone, mad—blasphemous to most. The little man, by way of comparison, reflected on the gaunt rider with the scarred lip, as stalwart as his master, as brave and, indeed, perhaps braver, and yet for him there was obedience, nothing but to give obedience duly and stoutly....

Certain sensations of the hands and knees called the little man back to more immediate things. He became aware of something. He rode up beside his gaunt fellow. "Do you notice the horses?" he said in an undertone.

The gaunt face looked interrogation.

"They don't like this wind," said the little man, and dropped behind as the man with the silver bridle turned upon him.

"It's all right," said the gaunt-faced man.

They rode on again for a space in silence. The foremost two rode downcast upon the trail, the hindmost man watched the haze that crept down the vastness of the valley, nearer and nearer, and noted how the wind grew in strength moment by moment. Far away on the left he saw a line of dark bulks—wild hog perhaps, galloping down the valley, but of that he said nothing, nor did he remark again upon the uneasiness of the horses.

And then he saw first one and then a second great white ball, a great shining white ball like a gigantic head of thistledown, that drove before the wind athwart the path. These balls soared high in the air, and dropped and rose again and caught for a moment, and hurried on and passed, but at the sight of them the restlessness of the horses increased.

Then presently he saw that more of these drifting globes—and then soon very many more—were hurrying towards him down the valley.

They became aware of a squealing. Athwart the path a huge boar rushed, turning his head but for one instant to glance at them, and then hurtling on down the valley again. And at that, all three stopped and sat in their saddles, staring into the thickening haze that was coming upon them.

"If it were not for this thistledown—" began the leader.

But now a big globe came drifting past within a score of yards of them. It was really not an even sphere at all, but a vast, soft, ragged, filmy thing, a sheet gathered by the corners, an aerial jellyfish, as it were, but rolling over and over as it advanced, and trailing long, cobwebby threads and streamers that floated in its wake.

"It isn't thistledown," said the little man.

"I don't like the stuff," said the gaunt man.

And they looked at one another.

"Curse it!" cried the leader. "The air's full of it up there. If it keeps on at this pace long, it will stop us altogether."

An instinctive feeling, such as lines out a herd of deer at the approach of some ambiguous thing, prompted them to turn their horses to the wind, ride forwards for a few paces, and stare at that advancing multitude of floating masses. They came on before the wind with a sort of smooth swiftness, rising and falling noiselessly, sinking to earth, rebounding high, soaring—all with a perfect unanimity, with a still, deliberate assurance.

Right and left of the horsemen the pioneers of this strange army passed. At one that rolled along the ground, breaking shapelessly and trailing out reluctantly into long grappling ribbons and bands, all three horses began to shy and dance. The master was seized with a sudden, unreasonable impatience. He cursed the drifting globes roundly. "Get on!" he cried; "get on! What do these things matter? How can they matter? Back to the trail!" He fell swearing at his horse and sawed the bit across its mouth.

He shouted aloud with rage. "I will follow that trail, I tell you," he cried. "Where is the trail!"

He gripped the bridle of his prancing horse and searched amidst the grass. A long and clinging thread fell across his face, a gray streamer dropped about his bridle arm, some big, active thing with many legs ran down the hack of his head. He looked up to discover one of those gray masses anchored as it were above him by these things and flapping out ends as a sail flaps when a boat comes about—but noiselessly.

He had an impression of many eyes, of a dense crew of squat bodies, of long, many-jointed limbs hauling at their mooring ropes to bring the thing down upon him. For a space he stared up, reining in his prancing horse with the instinct born of years of horsemanship. Then the flat of a sword smote his back, and a blade flashed overhead and cut the drifting balloon of spider web free, and the whole mass lifted softly and drove clear and away.

"Spiders!" cried the voice of the gaunt man. "The things are full of big spiders! Look, my lord!"

The man with the silver bridle still followed the mass that drove away.

"Look, my lord!"

The master found himself staring down at a red smashed thing on the ground that, in spite of partial obliteration, could still wriggle unavailing legs. Then when the gaunt man pointed to another mass that bore down upon them, he drew his sword hastily. Up the valley now it was like a fog bank torn to rags. He tried to grasp the situation.

"Ride for it!" the little man was shouting. "Ride for it down the valley."

What happened then was like the confusion of a battle. The man with the silver bridle saw the little man go past him slashing furiously at imaginary cobwebs, saw him cannon into the horse of the gaunt man and hurl it and its rider to earth. His own horse went a dozen paces before he could rein it in. Then he looked up to avoid imaginary dangers, and then back again to see a horse rolling on the ground, the gaunt man standing and slashing over it at a rent and fluttering mass of gray that streamed and wrapped about them both. And thick and fast as thistledown on waste land on a windy day in July, the cobweb masses were coming on.

The little man had dismounted, but he dared not release his horse. He was endeavoring to lug the struggling brute back with the strength of one arm, while with the other he slashed aimlessly. The tentacles of a second gray mass had entangled themselves with the struggle, and this second gray mass came to its moorings, and slowly sank.

The master set his teeth, gripped his bridle, lowered his head and spurred his horse forward. The horse on the ground rolled over, there was blood and moving shapes upon the flanks, and the gaunt man suddenly leaving it, ran forward towards his master, perhaps ten paces. His legs were swathed and encumbered with gray; he made ineffectual movements with his sword. Gray streamers waved from him; there was a thin veil of gray across his face. With his left hand he beat at something on his body, and suddenly he stumbled and fell. He struggled to rise, and fell again, and suddenly, horribly, began to howl, "Oh—ohoo, ohooh!"

The master could see the great spiders upon him, and others upon the ground.

As he strove to force his horse nearer to this gesticulating screaming gray object that struggled up and down, there came a clatter of hooves, and the little man, in act of mounting, swordless, balanced on his belly athwart the white horse, and clutching its mane, whirled past. And again a clinging thread of gray gossamer swept across the master's face. All about him and over him, it seemed this drifting, noiseless cobweb circled and drew nearer him....

To the day of his death he never knew just how the event of that moment happened. Did he, indeed, turn his horse, or did it really of its own accord stampede after its fellow? Suffice it that in another second he was galloping full tilt down the valley with his sword whirling furiously overhead. And all about him on the quickening breeze, the spiders' airships, their air bundles and air sheets, seemed to him to hurry in a conscious pursuit.

Clatter, clatter, thud, thud—the man with the silver bridle rode, heedless of his direction, with his fearful face looking up now right, now left, and his sword arm ready to slash. And a few hundred yards ahead of him, with a tail of torn cobweb trailing behind him, rode the little man on the white horse, still but imperfectly in the saddle. The reeds bent before them, the wind blew fresh and strong, over his shoulder the master could see the webs hurrying to overtake....

He was so intent to escape the spiders' webs that only as his horse gathered together for a leap did he realize the ravine ahead. And then realized it only to misunderstand and interfere. He was leaning forward on his horse's neck and sat up and back all too late.

But if in his excitement he had failed to leap, at any rate he had not forgotten how to fall. He was horseman again in mid-air. He came off clear with a mere bruise upon his shoulder, and his horse rolled, kicking spasmodic legs, and lay still. But the master's sword drove its point into the hard soil, and snapped clean across, as though Chance refused him any longer as her Knight, and the splintered end missed his face by an inch or so.

He was on his feet in a moment, breathlessly scanning the onrushing spider webs. For a moment he was minded to run, and then thought of the ravine, and turned back. He ran aside once to dodge one drifting terror, and then he was swiftly clambering down the precipitous sides, hid out of the touch of the gale.

There under the lee of the dry torrent's steeper banks he might crouch, and watch these strange, gray masses pass and pass in safety till the wind fell, and it became possible to escape. And there for a long time he crouched, watching the strange, gray, ragged masses trail their streamers across his narrowed sky.

Once a stray spider fell into the ravine close beside him—a full foot it measured from leg to leg, and its body was half a man's hand—and after he had watched its monstrous alacrity of search and escape for a little while, and tempted it to bite his broken sword, he lifted up his iron heeled boot and smashed it into a pulp. He swore as he did so, and for a time sought up and down for another.

Then presently, when he was surer these spider swarms could not drop into the ravine, he found a place where he could sit down, and sat and fell into deep thought and began after his manner to gnaw his knuckles and bite his nails. And from this he was moved by the coming of the man with the white horse.

He heard him long before he saw him, as a clattering of hooves, stumbling footsteps, and a reassuring voice. Then the little man appeared, a rueful figure, still with a tail of white cobweb trailing behind him. They approached each other without speaking, without salutation. The little man was fatigued and shamed to the pitch of hopeless bitterness, and came to a stop at last, face to face with his seated master. The latter winced a little under his dependent's eye. "Well?" he said at last, with no pretense of authority.

"You left him!"

"My horse bolted."

"I know. So did mine."

He laughed at his master mirthlessly.

"I say my horse bolted," said the man who once had a silver-studded bridle.

"Cowards both," said the little man.

The other gnawed his knuckle through some meditative moments, with his eyes on his inferior.

"Don't call me a coward," he said at length.

"You are a coward like myself."

"A coward possibly. There is a limit beyond which every man must fear. That I have learnt at last. But not like yourself. That is where the difference comes in."

"I never could have dreamt you would have left him. He saved your life two minutes before.... Why are you our lord?"

The master gnawed his knuckles again, and his countenance was dark.

"No man calls me a coward," he said. "No.... A broken sword is better than none.... One spavined white horse cannot be expected to carry two men a four days' journey. I hate white horses, but this time it cannot be helped. You begin to understand me?... I perceive that you are minded, on the strength of what you have seen and fancy, to taint my reputation. It is men of your sort who unmake kings. Besides which—I never liked you."

"My lord!" said the little man.

"No," said the master. "No!"

He stood up sharply as the little man moved. For a minute perhaps they faced one another. Overhead the spiders' balls went driving.

There was a quick movement among the pebbles; a running of feet a cry of despair, a gasp and a blow....

Towards nightfall the wind fell. The sun set in a calm serenity and the man who had once possessed the silver bridle came at last very cautiously and by an easy slope out of the ravine again; but now he led the white horse that once belonged to the little man. He would have gone back to his horse to get his silver-mounted bridle again but he feared night and a quickening breeze might still find him in the valley, and besides he disliked greatly to think he might discover his horse all swathed in cobwebs and perhaps unpleasantly eaten.

And as he thought of those cobwebs and of all the dangers he had been through and the manner in which he had been preserved that day, his hand sought a little reliquary that hung about his neck and he clasped it for a moment with heartfelt gratitude. As he did so his eyes went across the valley.

"I was hot with passion," he said, "and now she has met her reward. They also no doubt—"

And behold! Far away out of the wooded slopes across the valley, but in the clearness of the sunset distinct and unmistakable, he saw a little spire of smoke.

At that his expression of serene resignation changed to an amazed anger. Smoke? He turned the head of the white horse about and hesitated. And as he did so a little rustle of air went through the grass about him. Far away upon some reeds swayed a tattered sheet of gray. He looked at the cobwebs; he looked at the smoke.

"Perhaps after all it is not them," he said at last. But he knew better.

After he had stared at the smoke for some time, he mounted the white horse.

As he rode he picked his way amidst stranded masses of web. For some reason there were many dead spiders on the ground, and those that lived feasted guiltily on their fellow. At the sound of his horse's hooves they fled.

Their time had passed. From the ground without either a wind to carry them or a winding sheet ready these things, for all their poison, could do him no evil.

He flicked with his belt at those he fancied came too near. Once where a number ran together over a bare place, he was minded to dismount and trample them with his boots, but this impulse he overcame. Ever and again he turned in his saddle, and looked back at the smoke.

"Spiders," he muttered over and over again. "Spiders! Well, well.... The next time I must spin a web."

The Ash-Tree
M. R. James

Everyone who has travelled over Eastern England knows the smaller country-houses with which it is studded—the rather dank little buildings, usually in the Italian style, surrounded with parks of some eighty to a hundred acres. For me they have always had a very strong attraction, with the grey paling of split oak, the noble trees, the meres with their reed-beds, and the line of distant woods. Then, I like the pillared portico—perhaps stuck on to a red-brick Queen Anne house which has been faced with stucco to bring it into line with the "Grecian" taste of the end of the eighteenth century; the hall inside, going up to the roof, which hall ought always to be provided with a gallery and a small organ. I like the library, too, where you may find anything from a Psalter of the thirteenth century to a Shakespeare quarto. I like the pictures, of course; and perhaps most of all I like fancying what life in such a house was when it was first built, and in the piping times of landlords' prosperity, and not least now, when, if money is not so plentiful, taste is more varied and life quite as interesting. I wish to have one of these houses, and enough money to keep it together and entertain my friends in it modestly.

But this is a digression. I have to tell you of a curious series of events which happened in such a house as I have tried to describe. It is Castringham Hall in Suffolk. I think a good deal has been done to the building since the period of my story, but the essential features I have sketched are still there—Italian portico, square block of white house, older inside than out, park with fringe of woods, and mere. The one feature that marked out the house from a score of others is gone. As you looked at it from the park, you saw on the right a great old ash-tree growing within half a dozen yards of the wall, and almost or quite touching the building with its branches.

I suppose it had stood there ever since Castringham ceased to be a fortified place, and since the moat was filled in and the Elizabethan dwelling-house built. At any rate, it had well-nigh attained its full dimensions in the year 1690.

In that year the district in which the Hall is situated was the scene of a number of witch-trials. It will be long, I think, before we arrive at a just estimate of the amount of solid reason—if there was any—which lay at the root of the universal fear of witches in old times. Whether the persons accused of this offence really did imagine that they were possessed of unusual power of any kind; or whether they had the will at least, if not the power, of doing mischief to their neighbours; or whether all the confessions, of which there are so many, were extorted by the cruelty of the witch-finders—these are questions which are not, I fancy, yet solved. And the present narrative gives me pause. I cannot altogether sweep it away as mere invention. The reader must judge for himself.

Castringham contributed a victim to the *auto-da-fe*. Mrs. Mothersole was her name, and she differed from the ordinary run of village witches only in being rather better off and in a more influential position. Efforts were made to save her by several reputable farmers of the parish. They did their best to testify to her character, and showed considerable anxiety as to the verdict of the jury.

But what seems to have been fatal to the woman was the evidence of the then proprietor of Castringham Hall—Sir Matthew Fell. He deposed to having watched her on three different occasions from his window, at the full of the moon, gathering sprigs "from the ash-tree near my house". She had climbed into the branches, clad only in her shift, and was cutting off small twigs with a peculiarly curved knife, and as she did so she seemed to be talking to herself. On each occasion Sir Matthew had done his best to capture the woman, but she had always taken alarm at some accidental noise he had made, and all he could see when he got down to the garden was a hare running across the path in the direction of the village.

On the third night he had been at the pains to follow at his best speed, and had gone straight to Mrs. Mothersole's house; but he had had to wait a quarter of an hour battering at her door, and then she had come out very cross, and apparently very sleepy, as if just out of bed; and he had no good explanation to offer of his visit.

Mainly on this evidence, though there was much more of a less striking and unusual kind from other parishioners, Mrs. Mothersole was found guilty and condemned to die. She was hanged a week after the trial, with five or six more unhappy creatures, at Bury St Edmunds.

Sir Matthew Fell, then Deputy-Sheriff, was present at the execution. It was a damp, drizzly March morning when the cart made its way up the rough grass hill outside Northgate, where the gallows stood. The other victims were apathetic or broken down with misery; but Mrs. Mothersole was, as in life so in death, of a very different temper. Her "poysonous Rage", as a reporter of the time puts it, "did so work upon the Bystanders—yea, even upon the Hangman—that it was constantly affirmed of all that saw her that she presented the living Aspect of a mad Divell. Yet she offer'd no Resistance to the Officers of the Law; onely she looked upon those that laid Hands upon her with so direfull and venomous an Aspect that—as one of them afterwards assured me—the meer Thought of it preyed inwardly upon his Mind for six Months after."

However, all that she is reported to have said were the seemingly meaningless words: "There will be guests at the Hall." Which she repeated more than once in an undertone.

Sir Matthew Fell was not unimpressed by the bearing of the woman. He had some talk upon the matter with the Vicar of his parish, with whom he travelled home after the assize business was over. His evidence at the trial had not been very willingly given; he was not specially infected with the witch-finding mania, but he declared, then and afterwards, that he could not give any other account of the matter than that he had given, and that he could not possibly have been mistaken as to what he saw. The whole transaction had been repugnant to him, for he was a man who liked to be on pleasant terms with those about him; but he saw a duty to be done in this business, and he had done it. That seems to have been the gist of his sentiments, and the Vicar applauded it, as any reasonable man must have done.

A few weeks after, when the moon of May was at the full, Vicar and Squire met again in the park, and walked to the Hall together. Lady Fell was with her mother, who was dangerously ill, and Sir Matthew was alone at home; so the Vicar, Mr. Crome, was easily persuaded to take a late supper at the Hall.

Sir Matthew was not very good company this evening. The talk ran chiefly on family and parish matters, and, as luck would have it, Sir Matthew made a memorandum in writing of certain wishes or intentions of his regarding his estates, which afterwards proved exceedingly useful.

When Mr. Crome thought of starting for home, about half past nine o'clock, Sir Matthew and he took a preliminary turn on the gravelled walk at the back of the house. The only incident that struck Mr. Crome was this: they were in sight of the ash-tree which I described as growing near the windows of the building, when Sir Matthew stopped and said:

"What is that that runs up and down the stem of the ash? It is never a squirrel? They will all be in their nests by now."

The Vicar looked and saw the moving creature, but he could make nothing of its colour in the moonlight. The sharp outline, however, seen for an instant, was imprinted on his brain, and he could have sworn, he said, though it sounded foolish, that, squirrel or not, it had more than four legs.

Still, not much was to be made of the momentary vision, and the two men parted. They may have met since then, but it was not for a score of years.

Next day Sir Matthew Fell was not downstairs at six in the morning, as was his custom, nor at seven, nor yet at eight. Hereupon the servants went and knocked at his chamber door. I need not prolong the description of their anxious listenings and renewed batterings on the panels. The door was opened at last from the outside, and they found their master dead and black. So much you have guessed. That there were any marks of violence did not at the moment appear; but the window was open.

One of the men went to fetch the parson, and then by his directions rode on to give notice to the coroner. Mr. Crome himself went as quick as he might to the Hall, and was shown to the room where the dead man lay. He has left some notes among his papers which show how genuine a respect and sorrow was felt for Sir Matthew, and there is also this passage, which I transcribe for the sake of the light it throws upon the course of events, and also upon the common beliefs of the time:

"There was not any the least Trace of an Entrance having been forc'd to the Chamber: but the Casement stood open, as my poor Friend would always have it in this Season. He had his Evening Drink of small Ale in a silver vessel of about a pint measure, and tonight had not drunk it out. This Drink was examined by the Physician from Bury, a Mr. Hodgkins, who could not, however, as he

afterwards declar'd upon his Oath, before the Coroner's quest, discover that any matter of a venomous kind was present in it. For, as
was natural, in the great Swelling and Blackness of the Corpse,
there was talk made among the Neighbours of Poyson. The Body
was very much Disorder'd as it laid in the Bed, being twisted after
so extream a sort as gave too probable Conjecture that my worthy
Friend and Patron had expir'd in great Pain and Agony. And what
is as yet unexplain'd, and to myself the Argument of some Horrid
and Artfull Designe in the Perpetrators of this Barbarous Murther,
was this, that the Women which were entrusted with the laying-
out of the Corpse and washing it, being both sad Pearsons and very
well Respected in their Mournfull Profession, came to me in a great
Pain and Distress both of Mind and Body, saying, what was indeed
confirmed upon the first View, that they had no sooner touch'd
the Breast of the Corpse with their naked Hands than they were
sensible of a more than ordinary violent Smart and Acheing in their
Palms, which, with their whole Forearms, in no long time swell'd
so immoderately, the Pain still continuing, that, as afterwards
proved, during many weeks they were forc'd to lay by the exercise
of their Calling; and yet no mark seen on the Skin.

"Upon hearing this, I sent for the Physician, who was still in
the House, and we made as carefull a Proof as we were able by the
Help of a small Magnifying Lens of Crystal of the condition of the
Skinn on this Part of the Body: but could not detect with the Instru-
ment we had any Matter of Importance beyond a couple of small
Punctures or Pricks, which we then concluded were the Spotts by
which the Poyson might be introduced, remembering that Ring of
Pope Borgia, with other known Specimens of the Horrid Art of the
Italian Poysoners of the last age.

"So much is to be said of the Symptoms seen on the Corpse. As
to what I am to add, it is meerly my own Experiment, and to be left
to Posterity to judge whether there be anything of Value therein.
There was on the Table by the Beddside a Bible of the small size,
in which my Friend—punctuall as in Matters of less Moment, so in
this more weighty one—used nightly, and upon his First Rising, to
read a sett Portion. And I taking it up—not without a Tear duly
paid to him wich from the Study of this poorer Adumbration was
now pass'd to the contemplation of its great Originall—it came into
my Thoughts, as at such moments of Helplessness we are prone to
catch at any the least Glimmer that makes promise of Light, to make

trial of that old and by many accounted Superstitious Practice of
drawing the Sortes; of which a Principall Instance, in the case of
his late Sacred Majesty the Blessed Martyr King Charles and my
Lord Falkland, was now much talked of. I must needs admit that
by my Trial not much Assistance was afforded me: yet, as the Cause
and Origin of these Dreadfull Events may hereafter be search'd out,
I set down the Results, in the case it may be found that they pointed
the true Quarter of the Mischief to a quicker Intelligence than my
own.

"I made, then, three trials, opening the Book and placing my
Finger upon certain Words: which gave in the first these words,
from Luke xiii. 7, Cut it down; in the second, Isaiah xiii. 20, It shall
never be inhabited; and upon the third Experiment, Job xxxix. 30,
Her young ones also suck up blood."

This is all that need be quoted from Mr. Crome's papers. Sir
Matthew Fell was duly coffined and laid into the earth, and his
funeral sermon, preached by Mr. Crome on the following Sunday,
has been printed under the title of "The Unsearchable Way; or,
England's Danger and the Malicious Dealings of Antichrist", it
being the Vicar's view, as well as that most commonly held in the
neighbourhood, that the Squire was the victim of a recrudescence
of the Popish Plot.

His son, Sir Matthew the second, succeeded to the title and estates. And so ends the first act of the Castringham tragedy. It is to
be mentioned, though the fact is not surprising, that the new Baronet did not occupy the room in which his father had died. Nor,
indeed, was it slept in by anyone but an occasional visitor during
the whole of his occupation. He died in 1735, and I do not find that
anything particular marked his reign, save a curiously constant
mortality among his cattle and live-stock in general, which showed
a tendency to increase slightly as time went on.

Those who are interested in the details will find a statistical
account in a letter to the *Gentleman's Magazine* of 1772, which
draws the facts from the Baronet's own papers. He put an end to it
at last by a very simple expedient, that of shutting up all his beasts
in sheds at night, and keeping no sheep in his park. For he had
noticed that nothing was ever attacked that spent the night indoors.
After that the disorder confined itself to wild birds, and beasts of
chase. But as we have no good account of the symptoms, and as
all-night watching was quite unproductive of any clue, I do not

dwell on what the Suffolk farmers called the "Castringham sickness".

The second Sir Matthew died in 1735, as I said, and was duly succeeded by his son, Sir Richard. It was in his time that the great family pew was built out on the north side of the parish church. So large were the Squire's ideas that several of the graves on that unhallowed side of the building had to be disturbed to satisfy his requirements. Among them was that of Mrs. Mothersole, the position of which was accurately known, thanks to a note on a plan of the church and yard, both made by Mr. Crome.

A certain amount of interest was excited in the village when it was known that the famous witch, who was still remembered by a few, was to be exhumed. And the feeling of surprise, and indeed disquiet, was very strong when it was found that, though her coffin was fairly sound and unbroken, there was no trace whatever inside it of body, bones, or dust. Indeed, it is a curious phenomenon, for at the time of her burying no such things were dreamt of as resurrection-men, and it is difficult to conceive any rational motive for stealing a body otherwise than for the uses of the dissecting-room.

The incident revived for a time all the stories of witch-trials and of the exploits of the witches, dormant for forty years, and Sir Richard's orders that the coffin should be burnt were thought by a good many to be rather foolhardy, though they were duly carried out.

Sir Richard was a pestilent innovator, it is certain. Before his time the Hall had been a fine block of the mellowest red brick; but Sir Richard had travelled in Italy and become infected with the Italian taste, and, having more money than his predecessors, he determined to leave an Italian palace where he had found an English house. So stucco and ashlar masked the brick; some indifferent Roman marbles were planted about in the entrance-hall and gardens; a reproduction of the Sibyl's temple at Tivoli was erected on the opposite bank of the mere; and Castringham took on an entirely new, and, I must say, a less engaging, aspect. But it was much admired, and served as a model to a good many of the neighbouring gentry in after-years.

One morning (it was in 1754) Sir Richard woke after a night of discomfort. It had been windy, and his chimney had smoked persistently, and yet it was so cold that he must keep up a fire. Also something had so rattled about the window that no man could get a moment's peace. Further, there was the prospect of several guests of position arriving in the course of the day, who would expect sport of some kind, and the inroads of the distemper (which continued among his game) had been lately so serious that he was afraid for his reputation as a game-preserver. But what really touched him most nearly was the other matter of his sleepless night. He could certainly not sleep in that room again.

That was the chief subject of his meditations at breakfast, and after it he began a systematic examination of the rooms to see which would suit his notions best. It was long before he found one. This had a window with an eastern aspect and that with a northern; this door the servants would be always passing, and he did not like the bedstead in that. No, he must have a room with a western look-out, so that the sun could not wake him early, and it must be out of the way of the business of the house. The housekeeper was at the end of her resources.

"Well, Sir Richard," she said, "you know that there is but the one room like that in the house."

"Which may that be?" said Sir Richard.

"And that is Sir Matthew's—the West Chamber."

"Well, put me in there, for there I'll lie tonight," said her master. "Which way is it? Here, to be sure"; and he hurried off.

"Oh, Sir Richard, but no one has slept there these forty years. The air has hardly been changed since Sir Matthew died there."

Thus she spoke, and rustled after him.

"Come, open the door, Mrs. Chiddock. I'll see the chamber, at least."

So it was opened, and, indeed, the smell was very close and earthy. Sir Richard crossed to the window, and, impatiently, as was his wont, threw the shutters back, and flung open the casement. For this end of the house was one which the alterations had barely touched, grown up as it was with the great ash-tree, and being otherwise concealed from view.

"Air it, Mrs. Chiddock, all today, and move my bed-furniture in in the afternoon. Put the Bishop of Kilmore in my old room."

"Pray, Sir Richard," said a new voice, breaking in on this speech, "might I have the favour of a moment's interview?"

Sir Richard turned round and saw a man in black in the doorway, who bowed.

"I must ask your indulgence for this intrusion, Sir Richard. You will, perhaps, hardly remember me. My name is William Crome, and my grandfather was Vicar in your grandfather's time."

"Well, sir," said Sir Richard, "the name of Crome is always a passport to Castringham. I am glad to renew a friendship of two generations' standing. In what can I serve you? for your hour of calling—and, if I do not mistake you, your bearing—shows you to be in some haste."

"That is no more than the truth, sir. I am riding from Norwich to Bury St Edmunds with what haste I can make, and I have called in on my way to leave with you some papers which we have but just come upon in looking over what my grandfather left at his death. It is thought you may find some matters of family interest in them."

"You are mighty obliging, Mr. Crome, and, if you will be so good as to follow me to the parlour, and drink a glass of wine, we will take a first look at these same papers together. And you, Mrs. Chiddock, as I said, be about airing this chamber.... Yes, it is here my grandfather died.... Yes, the tree, perhaps, does make the place a little dampish.... No; I do not wish to listen to any more. Make no difficulties, I beg. You have your orders—go. Will you follow me, sir?"

They went to the study. The packet which young Mr. Crome had brought—he was then just become a Fellow of Clare Hall in Cambridge, I may say, and subsequently brought out a respectable edition of Polyaenus—contained among other things the notes which the old Vicar had made upon the occasion of Sir Matthew Fell's death. And for the first time Sir Richard was confronted with the enigmatical Sortes Biblicae which you have heard. They amused him a good deal.

"Well," he said, "my grandfather's Bible gave one prudent piece of advice—Cut it down. If that stands for the ash-tree, he may rest assured I shall not neglect it. Such a nest of catarrhs and agues was never seen."

The parlour contained the family books, which, pending the arrival of a collection which Sir Richard had made in Italy, and the building of a proper room to receive them, were not many in number.

Sir Richard looked up from the paper to the bookcase.

"I wonder," says he, "whether the old prophet is there yet? I fancy I see him."

Crossing the room, he took out a dumpy Bible, which, sure enough, bore on the flyleaf the inscription: "To Matthew Fell, from his Loving Godmother, Anne Aldous, 2 September 1659."

"It would be no bad plan to test him again, Mr. Crome. I will wager we get a couple of names in the Chronicles. H'm! what have we here? "Thou shalt seek me in the morning, and I shall not be." Well, well! Your grandfather would have made a fine omen of that, hey? No more prophets for me! They are all in a tale. And now, Mr. Crome, I am infinitely obliged to you for your packet. You will, I fear, be impatient to get on. Pray allow me—another glass."

So with offers of hospitality, which were genuinely meant (for Sir Richard thought well of the young man's address and manner), they parted.

In the afternoon came the guests—the Bishop of Kilmore, Lady Mary Hervey, Sir William Kentfield, etc. Dinner at five, wine, cards, supper, and dispersal to bed.

Next morning Sir Richard is disinclined to take his gun with the rest. He talks with the Bishop of Kilmore. This prelate, unlike a good many of the Irish Bishops of his day, had visited his see, and, indeed, resided there, for some considerable time. This morning, as the two were walking along the terrace and talking over the alterations and improvements in the house, the Bishop said, pointing to the window of the West Room:

"You could never get one of my Irish flock to occupy that room, Sir Richard."

"Why is that, my lord? It is, in fact, my own."

"Well, our Irish peasantry will always have it that it brings the worst of luck to sleep near an ash-tree, and you have a fine growth of ash not two yards from your chamber window. Perhaps," the Bishop went on, with a smile, "it has given you a touch of its quality already, for you do not seem, if I may say it, so much the fresher for your night's rest as your friends would like to see you."

"That, or something else, it is true, cost me my sleep from twelve to four, my lord. But the tree is to come down tomorrow, so I shall not hear much more from it."

"I applaud your determination. It can hardly be wholesome to have the air you breathe strained, as it were, through all that leafage."

"Your lordship is right there, I think. But I had not my window open last night. It was rather the noise that went on—no doubt from the twigs sweeping the glass—that kept me open-eyed."

"I think that can hardly be, Sir Richard. Here—you see it from this point. None of these nearest branches even can touch your casement unless there were a gale, and there was none of that last night. They miss the panes by a foot."

"No, sir, true. What, then, will it be, I wonder, that scratched and rustled so—ay, and covered the dust on my sill with lines and marks?"

At last they agreed that the rats must have come up through the ivy. That was the Bishop's idea, and Sir Richard jumped at it.

So the day passed quietly, and night came, and the party dispersed to their rooms, and wished Sir Richard a better night.

And now we are in his bedroom, with the light out and the Squire in bed. The room is over the kitchen, and the night outside still and warm, so the window stands open.

There is very little light about the bedstead, but there is a strange movement there; it seems as if Sir Richard were moving his head rapidly to and fro with only the slightest possible sound. And now you would guess, so deceptive is the half-darkness, that he had several heads, round and brownish, which move back and forward, even as low as his chest. It is a horrible illusion. Is it nothing more? There! something drops off the bed with a soft plump, like a kitten, and is out of the window in a flash; another—four—and after that there is quiet again.

Thou shall seek me in the morning, and I shall not be.

As with Sir Matthew, so with Sir Richard—dead and black in his bed!

A pale and silent party of guests and servants gathered under the window when the news was known. Italian poisoners, Popish emissaries, infected air—all these and more guesses were hazarded, and the Bishop of Kilmore looked at the tree, in the fork of whose lower boughs a white tom-cat was crouching, looking down the hollow which years had gnawed in the trunk. It was watching something inside the tree with great interest.

Suddenly it got up and craned over the hole. Then a bit of the edge on which it stood gave way, and it went slithering in. Everyone looked up at the noise of the fall.

It is known to most of us that a cat can cry; but few of us have heard, I hope, such a yell as came out of the trunk of the great ash. Two or three screams there were—the witnesses are not sure which—and then a slight and muffled noise of some commotion or struggling was all that came. But Lady Mary Hervey fainted out-right, and the housekeeper stopped her ears and fled till she fell on the terrace.

The Bishop of Kilmore and Sir William Kentfield stayed. Yet even they were daunted, though it was only at the cry of a cat; and Sir William swallowed once or twice before he could say:

"There is something more than we know of in that tree, my lord. I am for an instant search."

And this was agreed upon. A ladder was brought, and one of the gardeners went up, and, looking down the hollow, could detect nothing but a few dim indications of something moving. They got a lantern, and let it down by a rope.

"We must get at the bottom of this. My life upon it, my lord, but the secret of these terrible deaths is there."

Up went the gardener again with the lantern, and let it down the hole cautiously. They saw the yellow light upon his face as he bent over, and saw his face struck with an incredulous terror and loathing before he cried out in a dreadful voice and fell back from the ladder—where, happily, he was caught by two of the men—letting the lantern fall inside the tree.

He was in a dead faint, and it was some time before any word could be got from him.

By then they had something else to look at. The lantern must have broken at the bottom, and the light in it caught upon dry leaves and rubbish that lay there for in a few minutes a dense smoke began to come up, and then flame; and, to be short, the tree was in a blaze.

The bystanders made a ring at some yards' distance, and Sir William and the Bishop sent men to get what weapons and tools they could; for, clearly, whatever might be using the tree as its lair would be forced out by the fire.

So it was. First, at the fork, they saw a round body covered with fire—the size of a man's head—appear very suddenly, then seem to collapse and fall back. This, five or six times; then a similar ball leapt into the air and fell on the grass, where after a moment it lay still. The Bishop went as near as he dared to it, and saw—what but the remains of an enormous spider, veinous and seared! And, as the fire burned lower down, more terrible bodies like this began to break out from the trunk, and it was seen that these were covered with greyish hair.

All that day the ash burned, and until it fell to pieces the men stood about it, and from time to time killed the brutes as they darted out. At last there was a long interval when none appeared, and they cautiously closed in and examined the roots of the tree.

"They found," says the Bishop of Kilmore, "below it a rounded hollow place in the earth, wherein were two or three bodies of these creatures that had plainly been smothered by the smoke; and, what is to me more curious, at the side of this den, against the wall, was crouching the anatomy or skeleton of a human being, with the skin dried upon the bones, having some remains of black hair, which was pronounced by those that examined it to be undoubtedly the body of a woman, and clearly dead for a period of fifty years."

The Great White Moth
Fred M. White

I

The thing savoured of mystery and possible adventure, and
Drenton Denn, Special Commissioner, was ready for the fray. Anything was better than loafing in the forest behind Shaz waiting for
the transports that never seemed to come, in company with
Glasgow, who was engaged in the up-country trade and had just
returned from one of his adventurous expeditions.

"Here is the back door of Central Africa," remarked Glasgow.
"There is no occasion to knock. Will you come in?"

"Got anything fresh on show?" Denn asked.

Glasgow smiled. Not in vain had he taken his life between his
teeth for the last five years. The brawny Scot was burned a deep
copper bronze; his beard was ragged as a goat's.

"I can promise you the sight of a thing or two you have never
seen in your life before," he said. "And this is about the last trip I
shall make through the great forest of Ulu. It has been dangerous
work, but I have done pretty well. What do you think of this?"

From a cowhide bale amongst his stores Glasgow produced a
feather. It was a magnificent white plume, some two feet in length
and of the most perfect texture. It was soft, almost elusive, to the
touch, and as Glasgow shook it out the thing gleamed like a gossamer spray of falling water.

Denn was loud in his admiration.

"My word," he cried, "the finest ostrich tail in the world is a
mere scrubbing-brush compared with this. Got any more?"

"Got ten thousand of them in that bale. Oh, you can laugh.
Though that feather when shaken out covers a small table-cloth,
you can put half-a-dozen of them in your waistcoat pocket easily. See."

The exquisitely beautiful plume was rolled up into a ball no larger than a marble. When shaken out the shimmering gloss and dainty loveliness of its down were absolutely unimpaired.

"Takes eight of them to weigh an ounce," Glasgow went on. "Nothing injures it. I calculate these things will make a sensation in England."

"You can pile up the stamps on that," Denn replied. "I'd give a trifle to see the bird that feather came from."

"Man, that feather came from no bird at all. What kind of creature it belongs to I know no more than the dead. The Ulu natives are on the best of terms with me now; they bring me these feathers, but whence they come I can get no information. My man Chan will do anything for me, but one question touching feathers sends him muttering an incantation to some Obi god and reduces him to sulky silence for the day."

Denn sat up briskly, despite the heat that beat down in waves.

"Bully for you," he said. "I'll come to Ulu with you and I'll see that bird, or whatever it is. This is going to be an adventure after my own heart."

Glasgow was quite agreeable. He little realized the peril and danger his volatile companion was breeding for him, otherwise the cautious Scot would have traversed the forest alone.

"Have you never tried to see the bird?" Denn asked.

"Not I," Glasgow replied. "I came out here for money, and I have made it by leaving the natives alone. There are queer things, evil things, out yonder, and there are bones of white men bleaching in the sun who have sought to know too much. Curiosity doesn't pay yonder."

They started at dawn the next morning, leaving the camp in charge of two trusty natives, and taking Chan, Glasgow's faithful servant, with them. The latter was a fine specimen of his class, yellow of skin and lithe of limb, with hair straight and black as ebony.

It was cooler in the forest, but the track was narrow, and there were many snakes about. Denn could hear them writhing and wriggling in the dry scrub, and caught the sullen flash of scales from time to time. He had no regret for his leather gaiters.

"That chap of yours will get into trouble in a moment," he muttered to Glasgow. "Seems like asking Providence to tread on the tail of one's coat to come through a snake-infested jungle like this with nothing on but a loin-cloth. Hanged if that isn't a cobra."

It was. The wicked head was raised, the hood uplifted to strike at Chan as he strode carelessly on at the head of the procession. Denn felt the hair pricking and bristling on the back of his scalp.

"Look out, you fool!" he yelled. "Don't you know a cobra when you see it?"

Chan turned with a sweet yet pitiful smile. As he did so the cobra struck, and Chan caught him coolly by the throat. The next instant the slimy back was broken and the limp body cast aside.

"Well, I'm dashed!" Denn exclaimed. "But the brute struck you."

The statement was correct. There were two red punctures in the thick of Chan's thigh. Already the limb was commencing to swell. Half an hour at the most and Chan would cease to be. Denn's face was expressive of sickening horror. Glasgow smiled, and Chan showed two glistening rows of teeth in the grin of the man who courts approval successfully.

"No make fuss," he said; "me all lite in minit gone by."

From his loin-cloth he took a tiny brown substance about the shape and hue of a dried bean. This he wetted with his tongue, and proceeded to rub the bean more or less carelessly on the punctures, after which he resumed his onward march with absolute easiness.

"Some fetich, of course," Denn muttered. "But nothing can save him."

Denn resigned himself to melancholy and the development of the tragedy. But, in his own vigorous metaphor, the tragedy didn't develop worth a cent. The hours went on and the camp was fixed for the night, and, like the monks and the friars at Rheims, Chan did not seem one penny the worse. Denn watched Chan with a glassy eye. Pipes once lighted and the native moved out of earshot, Denn began to speak.

"It seems to me you have missed a pretty short cut to fortune," he said. "Chan's got an infallible cure for snake-bites. If you could get hold of the recipe, you could afford to give those feathers away."

"If I could get hold of it. But I can't. All the Ulu natives carry one of those little brown beans; in fact, I have one myself. Chan gave it to me, and he took his life in his hands in so doing, let me tell you. The thing is mixed up in a way with the feathers, and some religious ceremony with a little tin god of sorts tacked on to the end of it. It's a kind of freemasonry. I'd give all I possess to obtain that recipe, but I know when I am well off, and so keep my fingers out of that pie. If you take my advice you will keep this discovery to yourself."

Denn fell back on a policy of silence. As a matter of fact he had not come all this way to see and be dumb. The *New York Post* did not pay him the salary of an ambassador for that. Besides, it was a distinct duty to humanity to obtain that recipe.

A six-bladed knife and a promise of an apocryphal revolver later on shook Chan's dense religious fanaticism to the marrow. Denn was fishing for secrets it was peril to the soul to reveal, and Chan was troubled. Still, Heaven was far off as yet, and the revolver was so near.

"No dare tell," said Chan. "God Gnew make the juice that keep the snake fangs out. God Gnew have the papyrus in um belly and the priests guard it in the temple at Ulu. Every full moon they make more juice in the temple, then um put papyrus back in Gnew belly again."

"Let me have a squint at that show and you shall have a silver watch, Chan."

Chan shivered and his lips grew grey. His bony knees clattered together and his mouth watered.

"Say that again and me kill you," he said, hoarsely. "Big fool white man; he not know what he talk about palaver so."

And Chan flatly refused to say any more. Still, he was clearly shaken to the pith of his soul, and many a longing glance did he cast at the chain Denn had displayed across his canvas shirt. That the poison was getting in its work the astute Yankee knew well. He had quite made up his mind to see that ceremony. Secret rites, freemasonry, and papyrus in the internal economy of a god called Gnew! The smartest "special" on earth was not to be baffled by a fanatical native with no clothes on. Denn said no more till over in the valley towards night on the third day the huts and stockades of Ulu rose in sight.

Denn stood up alongside Chan.

"What about that watch?" he whispered.

Chan's teeth clicked and his lips quivered with a sort of nervous paralysis. His eyes gleamed as a cat's might in the dark. Then he fell to sobbing, and the big tears rolled down his cheeks. It was not a pretty spectacle, and Denn was not without a sense of shame.

"So it's to be," he said. "The question is, when?"

Chan's lips framed rather than said, "Tomorrow afternoon."

II

Glasgow lay in the hut assigned to him with the air of a man who mourns for wasted hours and yet bears the loss of them philosophically.

"No business done to-day," he said. "They've got one of their bobberies on, some fool nonsense or other at the temple which takes place once a month. They're quiet and peaceful chaps as a rule, but when the periodical madness comes on they are apt to be dangerous. It is only by lying low and not evincing the slightest curiosity that I have got on with the Ulus so well."

"I should have pulled all the inside of the business out by this time," said Denn.

"Yes, and by this time you wouldn't have any inside to pull out," Glasgow replied, drily. "I'm going to have a siesta."

A minute later and Glasgow was asleep. Denn crept quietly out of the hut and made his way to the spot where he had arranged to meet Chan. Not a single Ulu was in sight anywhere.

Chan was looking downcast and troubled, with a furious gleam in his eyes that caused Denn to slap his hip-pocket significantly.

"None of your confounded nonsense," he said. "This is a case of no song, no supper. The question is, how are you going to disguise me so that I can watch the circus procession without any chance of being fired out of the show?

"You go as pilgrim," Chan explained, sullenly. "Pilgrim come from beyond Shaz to the shrine of Gnew. Holy things for pilgrims to do like Mahomet fellows down Cairo way say of what call Mecca."

"That's all right. But I don't look like a pilgrim to any considerable extent. What are you going to do with my face?"

Chan proceeded to unfold a long robe made of coloured grasses fashioned like a sack. This he placed over Denn's head, leaving him with two holes wherewith to see. A pair of moccasins of the same material completed his outfit.

"There pilgrim's dress for you," Chan remarked. "Taken from a dead pilgrim, un had cholera. No other one get. Perhaps you die cholera too."

Denn shuddered slightly. A natural desire to tear the flimsy structure in fragments came over him. "There is a drawback to every pleasure," he said, grimly. "What time do the doors open?"

With a swift critical glance at his companion, Chan pointed the way. Up to the present a strange silence had been observed, and no single Ulu could be seen. Then a queer, grotesque figure came forth into the main street of the village and commenced to blow vigorously on a horn.

From the huts, up from the grass, out of the shelter of the forest, men and women seemed to rise as from the dead. The fierce mob, uttering yells and cries, pushed forward. Their gleaming eyes and set faces were eloquent of the frenzy of fanaticism that possessed them.

An ugly crowd—no mistake about that; a crowd drunk with religious fervour, which is a dangerous thing to the scoffer even in civilized climes. No reason to warn Denn that he would be torn limb from limb on the slightest suggestion of his presence.

It was therefore some comfort to him that there were hundreds of pilgrims besides himself. He and Chan were soon in the thick of the stream, and a greasy, evil-smelling stream it proved to be. As the crowd surged along the cries and yells ceased and a strange, strained silence followed. They were eager and yet strangely reluctant, as a man who is compelled to witness an execution. Fear and curiosity were mingled. Denn could hear his companions breathing heavily, like runners who have come far and fast.

Presently the procession arrived at a huge mass of rocks that thrust themselves out from the hillside. Carried on by the living stream, Denn found himself hustled down a flinty gorge and thence through a pair of massive bronze gates, beautifully modelled and finished.

"Well, this beats everything," he muttered. "Now, where on earth do those magnificent gates come from? Nothing finer was ever cast in Greece or Rome. It seems to me I'm going to have value for my money."

The gates closed right up to the rugged arch of the roof. Inside was a huge natural temple, faintly illuminated by a dozen or more windows cut through the living granite. And each one of the windows u as filled with the most delicate bronze tracery.

The place was so vast that there was room and to spare. Denn found a gloomy corner, where he stood with Chan by his side so that he could observe everything without being seen. No previous adventure had been more fascinating than the present one.

Denn's keen eyes took everything in. One surprise tripped over the heels of another so fast that the American grew quite accustomed to the whirl of sensations. He looked down from the roof to the floor at his feet. He saw that he stood ankle-deep in some white feathery substance that glistened purely in the filtered light.

The whole temple was carpeted with the marvellous feather that Glasgow had shown him a day or two before. There were literally hundreds of them, the pilgrims and Ulus trampling them under foot as if they had been grass. As Denn bent for closer inspection Chan grasped his arm.

"Nothing touch; dead certain fool white man," he whispered.

Denn accepted the hint. And, indeed, there was something else to occupy his attention beyond the beautiful feathers. At the back of the temple there stood a gigantic idol of unusually repulsive aspect. In the centre of the forehead was one gigantic eye behind which a lamp had been lighted. The whole thing was grotesque to the last degree.

At the feet of the idol on a platform a mass of priests, or medicine-men, had gathered. They were old and withered, every one of them, and clad from head to foot in some coarse white cloth. On a table at the foot of the idol Denn could see a wicker basket containing a dozen or more cobras in a state of lively indignation.

Then the priests began to sing, grouped in a semi-circle. At first their chant was low and wailing and monotonous, and to Denn's great surprise he recognised it as familiar and Gregorian. A dreamy sensation of having been there and having done it all before came over him.

"Nothing new under the sun," he muttered. "White men must have been here before. Otherwise, how on earth did those gates get here?"

Presently the chant grew louder and more fierce. Up and up it rose until there was one screaming cry of passion and supplication, till finally the rocking, reeling priests prostrated themselves before the altar.

Instantly the whole assemblage did the same. Denn felt himself dragged down by Chan's powerful hand. After the fearful din the silence was strange and almost painful. And yet Denn had never seen anything more thrilling and impressive before.

Denn lay half smothered in those luscious clinging feathers, soft as down and diaphanous as sea-foam, wondering what was going to happen next. He had some dim conception. of the way in which the ceremony pointed. This music was doubtless an incantation and an appeal for mercy from the god. They were waiting before they had courage to proceed.

A quarter of an hour passed, and then the leader of the priests raised his head cautiously. Another and another, till at length they were all on their feet once more. Loud yells of triumph followed.

Slowly, by reason of the weight of his years, the chief priest proceeded to climb up the frame of the great idol. He looked like a white fly on the head of a Sphinx. The action was nothing in itself, apart from the feebleness of the chief performer, and yet it was followed by almost painful silence. Then the arm of the priest was plunged up to the elbow in an orifice in the idol, to emerge a moment later waving a faded strip of parchment.

Instantly the throbbing silence was broken by a manifestation of mad delight. The pilgrims tossed, and rocked, and yelled in a species of intoxicated delirium. Denn knew enough to grasp the meaning of this. The parchment was doubtless the sacred papyrus containing the recipe for the snake cure. Probably these poor folk always gathered there under the impression that some day the great god might destroy the papyrus in a fit of rage.

However, here it was, passed from one priest to another and perused eagerly. Then fires were lighted on the platform, and upon them gourds were placed, and filled with some liquid that caused a great and acrid smoke to rise. Whilst the gourds were boiling and bubbling the priests danced around them with a solemn, stilted step that tried Denn's gravity to the utmost. The absolute wooden stolidity of those around him did not tend to seriousness on the part of the volatile American.

Presently the dance ceased and no further smoke arose from the gourds. The contents of the whole of them were poured into a large brass vessel to which water was added. A big reddish lump like putty was extracted from the brass pot and handed from priest to priest for inspection.

A great burst of triumph followed. The religious function had been eminently successful. Denn felt that the end had come. Then, as he looked about him, he became conscious of the fact that night was coming on. A minute later and it shot down like a blanket on the place.

As if in a paroxysm of fear the whole of the audience made a rush for the gates. Chan plucked at Denn's sleeve.

"Come!" he whispered, hoarsely. "The white dumb devil! Quick!"

Denn eluded the grasp. If there was anything more to be seen he made up his mind to see it. He drew back into a dark corner so that the stream of frantic, perspiring humanity might pass him by and leave him high above the flood.

The flood went roaring on. Denn, by the feeble light in the eye of the idol, watched the stream ebb away. He saw the papyrus restored to the body of the god, and the stuff the priests had made carried away. And he also saw as the pilgrims hurried out that every eye was turned upwards with shuddering fear.

"Something gone wrong with the works," Denn said, sotto voce, "or why should they clear out like that with the darkness? Doubtless the ceremony took more time than usual. If I do happen to come across the white dumb devil I shall have had a pleasant afternoon."

By this time the place was absolutely quiet. Denn felt no uneasiness. Chan, of course, would imagine that he had been swept out with the crowd. Even when Denn discovered that the great bronze gates were fast and that he was a prisoner he felt no fear.

If the worst came to the worst he could remain there for the night and trust to luck to slip out when the temple was open in the morning. That nobody would molest him till dawn he felt certain, for the fear of the darkness had been on priest and layman alike.

Therefore Denn felt at leisure to explore about him as he pleased. It did not take him long to discover that behind the great idol was a huge cavern going right away into the hillside. So far as he could see the whole floor was carpeted with those peerless white feathers. They had been trodden under many a score of grimy feet, and yet they were still as light as thistledown and seemed to shake off corruption as water runs off a rose.

"I never saw anything more exquisitely lovely," said Denn. "I would give a trifle to see the creature they came from. Now, I wonder if this bird or beast lives in the cavern behind me? It looks like it."

It did indeed, for high above Denn's head, where no human being could possibly go, one of the feathers hung on a jagged ledge of rock.

"Extraordinary thing," Denn went on. "It must be a bird, unless there is such a thing as a flying beast. Upon my word, it begins to look like it. If the creature is here I shall most assuredly drop a card on him."

The idol still glared down at Denn. The idea of taking possession of the papyrus instantly possessed him. It might be useless; on the contrary, it might be in a formula known to science. There was just the chance.

As Denn started forward to carry out his intention something seemed to glide by him and brush his cheek softly, gently, as the touch of a mother's hand. And yet the rush of air that followed was as a strong breeze. In the feeble light of the gleaming eye high overhead something darted like a swallow in the twilight. It was vague, ghostly, yet tangible.

Denn forgot all about the papyrus. A treasure was there beyond rubies, but it slipped from the American's mind. The great white shadow swooped down and stood still in the air quivering before Denn's astonished eyes.

What was it? Something greater than an albatross, more massive in the body and wider across the wings, which vibrated so swiftly that their motion was impossible for the eye to follow. Not a bird or a beast, but a great white moth with an eye soft and mournful, and yet so vaguely terrible that Denn stood paralyzed before it.

This, then, was the dumb white devil that Chan had spoken of. But surely the thing was harmless. The soft, mournful eye, the noiseless, snowy wings, pointed to a gentle, timid thing. Yet as it quivered closer and closer to Denn he backed away. He had heard before of a huge moth unseen by any white man's eye, and here it was.

He backed farther and farther away. The thing followed in the same terribly noiseless manner as if it were floating on the air. Denn could see into the soft, mournful grey eye, he could catch a faint perfume like musk, and with a flash the wings were about him.

There was no pressure, no cruel claws cut into the flesh, no serried teeth met in the flesh of the affrighted man. A certain weight bore him to the ground, and then his eyes and throat and ears seemed to be filled with something that seemed like warm snow, exquisite and glowing to the touch and yet soft as satin.

Denn fought it off as best he might. As a matter of fact, he knew quite well that he was being suffocated to death in a mass of feathers. Try as he would he could find no way out of the white sea surrounding him. He gripped for the body, but only succeeded in burying his arm to the shoulders in the tangle of silken plumes. He could hear a heart beating under it all. Still, it was no time for speculation. A little longer of this and Denn's interest in mundane matters would be finished.

He fought and gasped and struggled for breath. His heart was hammering painfully against his ribs, a cold sweat broke out over him. He began to feel himself floating away on a boundless sea towards oblivion. The strong man was growing weak as a little child.

Then, without warning, the white, fluttering mass lifted. Denn, dazed and confused, lay on his back, looking upwards. He saw the cause of this diversion. High over his head he could see, not one of the great moths, but two of them. They were darting round one another in dazzling flashes faster than a swallow cleaves the air, and yet without the slightest noise. Denn crept away to the shadow and made his way on all fours to the gates.

He looked up again. As he did so he saw the two moths come with a flashing wheel and dazzling circle in full contact with each other. For an instant it seemed as if they had burst like two bombs, for a white cloud, growing wider, enveloped them. As the cloud commenced to fall it resolved itself into a shower of feathers,

The moths were fighting a duel. Great as the rain of plumes had been, there was no sign of loss of plumage in either insect. Again and again they came together with the same wheeling motion, and again and again the showers of diaphanous plumes flecked downwards. Then, as they charged once more, one of the moths avoided the other and darted with amazing swiftness into the purple gloom beyond the great idol. A fraction of a second later and the other moth had disappeared also.

Denn crouched there, gasping and panting. Idol, papyrus, the boon to mankind, everything was forgotten in the mad desire to be beyond those bronze gates. Tangible dangers Denn knew and appreciated—dangers he could grapple with and hold on to; but the silent terror of this danger frightened him. Small wonder that the Ulus had fled at the coming of the night.

Doubtless in the caverns beyond were hundreds of those ghostly moths. And they might return to the attack at any time. One was bad enough, but to be beset by a score of them—to be buried under the crushing weight of those white plumes that filled eyes and throat and ears—

Denn cast the thought shuddering from him. The thing was to get away now before danger returned. Still, that was easier said than done. There was no escape save by the great bronze gates, glittering now in the moonlight that bathed the whole place in a silver flood.

Denn looked outside as a prisoner does through his bars. As he did so a figure crept out of the long grass. To Denn's delight he saw the white, fearful, sweat-bedabbled face of Chan.

"White dumb devil not there?" he whispered.

Denn hastened to reassure the other. Chan pressed on one of the ornaments of the great gates, and they slowly yawned open far enough for Denn to step through. There was no further danger now.

"Fool white man no want any more go yonder," said Chan, recovering himself, as the temple was left behind. "Guess you stay there when others gone. White dumb devil stay in, hide in daylight, and only come out at night. Lots um in cavern yonder. You see um?"

Denn responded that he had done so. Then he fell to asking questions. Some years before, he found, the big white moths had come to this temple. More than one priest had been found mysteriously suffocated before the real truth had come to light. Then it was discovered that the big white moths only dared to come out after sundown, and there was consequently no occasion to leave the temple. After dark it was a different matter. Hence the flight of the Ulus and pilgrims at the fall of night, the ceremony having taken longer than usual.

"But where do those moths come from?" Denn asked.

Chan pointed towards the distant hills.

"Over there," he said, "in the valley of caverns. No dare go there after dark. Many mans killed there. Sen um self every times. No go there time some more not for revolver no, not for silver watch."

Denn laughed at the pointed speech. He laid upon Chan's shoulder a hand that still shook slightly.

"No occasion for the hint, my simple savage," he said. "You shall have the best watch and the best revolver that money can procure."

Chan smiled and he sighed. For he was fearful for the anger of the gods, and his soul was heavy within him.

The Green Spider

Sax Rohmer

I find from my notes that Professor Brayme-Skepley's great lecture which was to revolutionize modern medicine should have been
delivered upon the fifteenth of March, and many of Europe's leading scientists were during the preceding week to be seen daily in
the quaint old streets of Barminster—for the entire world of medical science was waiting agog for the revelation of the Brayme-
Skepley treatment.

Many people wondered that Brayme-Skepley should deliver a
lecture so vastly important in old-world Barminster rather than in
London; but he was not a man to be coerced—so the savants, per-
force, came to Barminster.

At twelve, midnight, as nearly as can be ascertained, on the
fourteenth of March the porter in charge of the North Gate—by
which direct admission can be gained to the quadrangle—was
aroused by a loud ringing of his bell.

Hurrying to the door of his little lodge, he was surprised to find
at the gate the gaunt figure of Professor Brayme-Skepley, enveloped in a huge fur coat. He hastened to unlock the wicket and admit
the great scientist.

"I am sorry to trouble you at so late an hour, Jamieson," said
the Professor, "but there are some little preparations which I must
make for tomorrow's lecture. I shall probably be engaged in the
bacteriological laboratory for a couple of hours. You will not mind
turning out with the key?"

He slipped a sovereign into the porter's hand as he spoke, and
Jamieson only too gladly acquiesced.

The fire in the little sitting-room of the lodge was almost extinct, but the man revived it, and, putting on a shovelful of coal,

lighted his pipe, and sat smoking for about an hour. At one o'clock he stepped outside, and glanced across the quadrangle.

The Professor was still working, and, finding the night air chilly, Jamieson was about to turn in again when a light suddenly appeared in the top window of one of those ancient houses in Spindle Lane. The house was the last of the row, and overlooked the bacteriological laboratory.

"That's old Kragg's house," muttered the porter; "but I didn't know anybody lived there since the old man died."

The light was a vague and flickering one, almost like that of a match; and, as he watched, it disappeared again. There was something uncanny about this solitary light in a house which he believed to be uninhabited, so, with a slight shudder, Jamieson returned to the comforts of his fireside.

Curiously enough, I had been reading upon this particular night in Harborne's rooms; and at something like twenty minutes past two I knocked the ashes from my pipe, and was about to depart—when there came a sudden scuffing on the stairs. We both turned just as the door was flung open, and Jamieson, white-faced and wild-eyed, stumbled, breathless, into the room.

"Thank Heaven I've found somebody up!" he gasped. "Yours was the only window with a light!"

'Where's the brandy?' I said, for the man seemed inclined to faint upon the sofa.

A stiff glass of cognac pulled him together somewhat, and, with a little colour returning to his face, but still wild of eye, he burst out:

"Professor Brayme-Skepley has been murdered!"

"Murdered!" echoed Harborne.

"And no mortal hand has done the thing, sir!" continued the frightened man. "Heaven grant I never see the like again!"

"You're raving!" I said with an assumption of severity, for Jamieson's condition verged closely upon that of hysteria. "Try to talk sense. Where is the Professor?"

"In the bacteriological laboratory, sir."

"How long has he been there?"

"Since twelve o'clock!"

I glanced at Harborne in surprise.

"What was he doing there?" enquired the latter.

"He said he had some preparations to make for his lecture."

"Well, get on! Here, have another pull at the brandy. How do you know he's dead?"

"I went to ask him how much longer he was going to be."

"Well?"

"He didn't answer to my knocking, although there was a light burning. The door was locked from the inside, so I got on to the dust-box, and just managed to reach a window-ledge. I pulled myself up far enough to look inside; and then—I dropped down again!"

"But what did you see, man? What did you see?"

"I saw Professor Brayme-Skepley lying dead on the floor among broken jars by an overturned table. There were only two lamps on—those over the table—and his head came just in the circle of light. His body was in shadow."

"What else?"

"Blood! His hair all matted!"

"Come on, Harborne!" I cried, seizing my hat. "You too, Jamieson!"

"For the love of Heaven, gentlemen," gasped the man, grasping us each by an arm, "I couldn't! You haven't heard all!"

"Then get on with it!" said Harborne. "Every second is of importance."

"I ran for the window ladder, gentlemen; and when I came back with it the electric lamps were out!"

"Out?"

"I ran up the ladder, and looked in at the window; and saw—how can I tell you what I saw?"

"Don't maunder!" shouted Harborne. "What was it?"

"It was a thing, sir, like a kind of green spider—only with a body twice the size of that football!"

Harborne and I looked at one another significantly.

"You're a trifle overwrought, Jamieson," I said, laying my hand upon his shoulder. "Stay here until we come back."

The man stared at me.

"You don't believe it," he said tensely; "and you'll go into that place unprepared. But I'll swear on the Book that there was some awful thing not of this earth creeping in the corner of the laboratory!"

Harborne, with his hand on the doorknob, turned undecidedly.

"Which corner, Jamieson?" he enquired.

"The north-west, sir. I just caught one glimpse of it through the opening in the partition."

"How could you see it, since all the lights were out?" Harborne asked.

The porter looked surprised. "That never occurred to me before, sir," he said; "but I think it must have shone—something like the bottles of phosphorus, sir!"

"Come on!" said my friend. And without further ado we ran downstairs into the Square.

A cheerful beam of light from the door of the lodge cut the black shadows of the archway as we approached, and served to show that the panic-stricken porter had left the wicket open. As we hurried through and sprinted across the quadrangle we were met by a cold, damp wind from the direction of the river. The night was intensely dark, and the bacteriological laboratory showed against the driving masses of inky cloud merely as a square patch of blackness.

"Here's the ladder," said Harborne suddenly; and we both paused, undecided how to act.

"Try the door," I suggested.

We rattled the handle of the door, but it was evidently locked, so that for a moment we were in a quandary. Harborne mounted the ladder and peered into the impenetrable shadows of the laboratory, but reported that there was nothing to be seen.

"We must burst the door in," I said; "it hasn't a very heavy lock."

We accordingly applied our shoulders to the door, and gave a vigorous push. The lock yielded perceptibly. I then crashed my heel against the woodwork just over the keyhole, and the door flew open. We immediately detected a most peculiar odour.

"It's the broken bottles," muttered Harborne. "The switch is over against the wall by the bookcase; we must go straight for that."

Cautiously we stepped into the darkness, and at the third or fourth step there was a crackling of glass underfoot. My boot slipped where some sticky substance lay, and I gave an involuntary shudder. A moment later I heard an exclamation of disgust.

"The wall is all wet!" said Harborne.

Then he found the electric buttons, and turned on the lights in rapid succession.

Heavens! How can I describe the picture revealed! Never have I witnessed such a scene of chaos, fearsome in its indications of an incredible struggle.

At first glance the place gave an impression of having been wantonly wrecked by a madman. Scarcely a jar or bottle remained upon the shelves, all being strewn in fragments upon the floor, which was simply swimming in the spilled spirits and preservatives. The door of the case that had contained the specimens of bacilli was wide open, and the glass completely smashed. The priceless contents were presumably to be sought among the hundred and one objects lying in the liquid on the floor.

Most of the books from the shelf were distributed about the place as though they had been employed as missiles, and one huge volume was wedged up under the frosted glass of the skylight in the centre of the roof. In the wood of the partition a lancet was stuck, and a horribly suggestive streak linked it with a red pool upon the floor. A table was overturned, and the two lamps immediately above it were broken. Of Professor Brayme-Skepley there was no sign, but his hat and fur coat hung upon a hook where he had evidently placed them on entering.

For some time we surveyed the scene in silence. Then Harborne spoke.

"What are these marks on the wall?" he said. "They are still wet. And where is the Professor?"

The marks alluded to were a series of impressions in the shape of irregular rings passing from the pool on the floor to the four walls and up the walls to where the shadows of the lamp shades rendered it impossible to follow them. I pulled down a lamp, and turned the shade upwards, whereupon was revealed a thing that caused me a sudden nausea.

The marks extended right to the top of the wall, and could furthermore be distinguished upon the ceiling; and on the framework of the skylight was the reddish-brown impression of a human hand!

"Drop it!" said Harborne huskily. "If we stay here much longer we shall have no pluck left for looking behind the partition."

The northern end of the laboratory is partitioned off to form a narrow apartment, which runs from side to side of the building, but is only some six feet in width. It is lined with shelves whereon are stored the greater part of the materials used in experiments, and is lighted by a square window at the Spindle Lane end, beneath which is a sink. The partition does not run flush up to the western wall, but only to within three feet of it, leaving an opening connecting the storeroom with the laboratory proper. There are two electric lamps in the place, one over the sink, and the other in the centre; but they cannot be turned on from the laboratory, the switch being behind the partition. Consequently the storeroom was in darkness, and, ignorant of what awful thing might be lurking there, we yet, in justice to the missing man, had no alternative but to enter.

Harborne, whose pallor can have been no greater than my own, strode quickly up the laboratory, and passed through the opening in the partition, I following closely behind. I heard the click of the electric switch; but only one lamp became lighted. That over the sink was broken.

We were both, I think, anticipating some gruesome sight; but, singular to relate, the only abnormal circumstance that at first came under our notice was that of the broken lamp. A sudden draught of air, damp and cold, that set the other shade swinging drew our attention to the fact that the window had been pulled right away from its fastenings and lay flat down against the wall. Then Harborne detected the gruesome tracks right along the centre of the floor; and under the window we made a further discovery.

The wall all round the casement was smeared with blood, and the marks of a clutching hand showed in all directions.

"Good heavens!" I muttered; "this is horrible! It looks as though he had been dragged."

There was a queer catch in Harborne's voice as he answered: "We must get out a party to scour the marshes."

"Hark!" I said. "Jamieson has been knocking some of them up. Here they come across the quad."

A moment later an excited group was surveying the strange scene in the laboratory.

"Clear out and get lanterns, you fellows!" shouted Harborne. "His body has been dragged through the window!"

"What's this about a green spider?" called several men.

"Don't ask me!" said my friend. "I am inclined to agree with Jamieson that this is not the doing of a man. We must spread out and examine Spindle Lane and the surrounding country until we find the Professor's body."

During the remainder of that never-to-be-forgotten night a party which grew in number as the hours wore on to dawn scoured the entire countryside for miles round. Towards five o'clock the rain suddenly broke over the marshes, and drenched us all to the skin, so that it was a sorry gathering that returned at daybreak to

Barminster. The local police had taken charge of the laboratory, and urgent messages had been sent off to Scotland Yard; but when the London experts arrived on the scene we had nothing more to tell them than has already been recounted. Harborne, Doctor Davidson, and myself had devoted the whole of our attention to Spindle Lane and the immediate vicinity of the mysterious crime; but our exertions were not rewarded by the smallest discovery.

Such, then, were the extraordinary but inadequate data which were placed in the hands of the London investigators, and upon which they very naturally based a wholly erroneous theory.

This was the condition of affairs upon the night of the 16th, when Harborne suddenly marched into my rooms, and unceremoniously deposited a dripping leather case, bearing the initials J. B. S., in my fender.

"Any news?" I cried, springing up.

"Not likely to be!" he answered. "You might almost think these detectives have assumed all along that they are dealing with a case of the supernatural, and have, in consequence, overlooked certain clues which, had the circumstances been less bizarre, they would have instantly followed up."

"You have some theory, then? What is in this bag?"

There was that in Harborne's manner which I could not altogether fathom as he evasively replied:

"Leaving the bag for a moment, let me just place the facts before you as they really are, and not as they appear to be. I must confess that, last night, I was more than half inclined to agree with the detectives; and it is eminently probable that but for one thing I should now be in complete agreement with the other investigators— who believe that some huge and unknown insect entered the laboratory and bore away the Professor! When I left you and Doctor Davidson yesterday morning I immediately went in search of Jamieson, and found him—three-parts intoxicated. As you have probably heard, he has since become wholly so, and the detectives have utterly failed to extract a sane word from him. In this respect, therefore, I was first in the field; and from him I obtained the one additional clue needed. About one a.m.—an hour after Brayme-Skepley had entered the laboratory—Jamieson came to the door of his lodge, and saw a light in the end house of Spindle Lane."

"But surely the police have questioned all the tenants in Spindle Lane?"

"The end house is empty."

"Have they examined it?"

"Certainly. But they merely did so as a matter of form: they had no particular reason for doing so. As a result they found nothing. What there was to find I had found before their arrival on the scene."

"I am afraid I don't altogether follow."

"Wait a minute. When I extracted from the porter the fact that he had seen a light in this house the entire affair immediately assumed a different aspect. The key to the mystery was in my hands. I went round into Spindle Lane, and surveyed the end house from the front. It was evidently empty, for the ground-floor windows were almost without glass.

"As I did not want to take anyone into my confidence at this stage of the proceedings it was impracticable to apply for the key, but upon passing round to the north I found that there was a back door with three stone steps leading up from the water's edge. I looked about for some means of gaining these steps—for I did not wish to excite attention by getting out a college boat. In the end I jumped for it. I got off badly from the muddy ground, for the rain was coming down in torrents, but, nevertheless, I landed on the bottom step—off which I promptly shot into the river!

"As I was already drenched to the skin this mattered little, and, notwithstanding my condition, a thrill of gratification warmed me on finding the door to be merely latched. Just as a party of six which had been scouring the east valley appeared upon the opposite bank I entered, and shut the door behind me."

"Well—what then?"

"I went up to the room overlooking the laboratory—for, although no one seems to have attached any particular importance to the circumstance, from the window of this room you could, if the laboratory window were bigger, easily spring through."

"And what did you find there?"

"The origin of the mysterious light."

"Which was?"

"A match! Now, you will agree with me that green spiders do not use matches. Inference: That some human being had been in the room on the night of the murder, and had struck a match, which had been observed by Jamieson. There were also certain marks which considerably mystified me at first. On the thick grime of the window ledge—inside—it was evident that a board had rested. That is to say, a board had been, for some reason, placed across the room. The mortar had fallen off the wall in one corner, and here I found on the floor an impression as though a box had stood on end there—evidently to support the other extremity of the board. My next discovery was even more interesting. I found traces of finger marks—which, by the way, I removed before leaving—on the sill and around the inside of the window-frame. Someone had come in by the window!

"But I remembered that, until I opened it to investigate, the window had been closed. Therefore the mysterious visitor had closed it behind him. Since his blood-stained finger marks testified to the state of his hands on entering, how had he opened the window from outside—a somewhat difficult operation—and yet left no traces upon the sash? for there were none. I assumed, by way of argument, that he had opened the window from the inside.

"I had now constructed a hypothetical assassin who had got into the end house in Spindle Lane, entered the bacteriological laboratory, murdered the Professor, returned through the window, and struck a match—for there were traces of blood upon it. Why had he come back to the room, and by what means had he reached the window of the laboratory? It was upon subsequently examining the laboratory (for the local officer in charge, being an acquaintance, raised no objection to my doing so) that two points became clear. First: That the window could never have been opened from outside. Second: The probability that a plank had been placed across—the same plank that had been used for some other mysterious purpose!

"Working, then, upon this theory, it immediately became evident that a plank could only have been placed in position from one of the windows. Here I had an enlightening inspiration. My assassin must have entered the house from the riverside, as I had done! How had he conveyed the plank into the place? A boat! You will mark that this was all pure supposition. Nevertheless, I determined, for the moment, to assume that a plank had been used.

"It was with this idea before me that I made my examination of the laboratory, and the various facts, viewed in this new light, began to assume their proper places. The horrible marks, suggestive of an incredible assailant, which so horrified us when we first observed them, were less inexplicable when regarded as intentional and not accidental! To consider the handmark upon the ceiling, for example, as incidental to a struggle for life, pointed to an opponent possessing attributes usually associated with insects; but it was the easiest thing in the world for a tall man, standing upon a table, to imprint such a mark! This startling revelation, taken in conjunction with the locked door and the impossibility of anyone entering the place from the quadrangle, brought me face to face with a plausible solution of the mystery.

"The elaborate nature of the affair pointed to premeditation, and the fact that the missing man had locked the door was most significant. Who could have known that he would be there upon this particular night, and why had he failed to unlock the door? For you will remember that the key was in the lock. Then, again, how did it come about that his cries for assistance did not arouse the people living in Spindle Lane?

"These ideas carried me to the second stage of my theory, and I assumed that a plank had been placed in position for the purpose of exit from, and not of entrance to, the laboratory! My final conclusion was as follows:

"Professor Brayme-Skepley entered the end house in Spindle Lane from a boat—which he obtained at Long's boathouse—bearing a plank and some kind of box or case. The plank he placed from window to window, the case upon the floor of the house in the Lane. He then returned to his boat, and landed beside the house. Entering the quadrangle, as we know, he went into the laboratory, and locked the door. His next proceeding was to smash everything breakable, wrench the window from its fastenings, and imprint the weird tracks and marks which proved so misleading. The book beneath the skylight and the lancet in the woodwork were the artistic touches of a man of genius. By this time it was close upon one o'clock, and, desirous of ascertaining whether his apparatus for bringing about the spider illusion was ready for instant use, he crawled from window to window. It was his match that Jamieson saw from the lodge door, and had Jamieson been a man of mettle the whole plot must have failed.

"He then, probably, grew very impatient whilst awaiting the coming of Jamieson, but he heard him ultimately, and lay in the light of the lamps as we have heard. All fell out as he had planned. Jamieson climbed on to the dust-box and looked into the laboratory; then he ran for the window ladder, as a reasoning mind would

have easily foreseen he would do. The Professor, during his absence, broke the lamps, climbed along his plank, and pulled it after
him."

I had listened with breathless interest so far, but I now broke
in: "How about the spider?"

"Perfectly simple!" answered Harborne. "Allow me."

He reached down for the leather case and unstrapped it. From
within he took ... a magic lantern!

"What!" I exclaimed. "A magic lantern?"

"With cinematograph attachment! Here, you see, is the film—
not improved by having been in the river. Some kind of South
American spider, is it not?—beautifully coloured and on a black
ground. The plank, supported upon the window-ledge and the upturned case, did duty for a table, and as Jamieson went up the ladder, and surveyed the place from the south-east, this was directed
from the window of the end house across the few intervening yards
of Spindle Lane and through the open laboratory window on to the
north-west corner of the wall.

"The beam from the lens would be hidden by the partition and
only the weird image visible from the porter's point of view—though
had he mounted further up the ladder and glanced over the wall
he must have observed the ray of light across the lane. The familiar illuminated circle, usually associated with such demonstrations,
was ingeniously eliminated by having a transparent photograph
on an opaque ground. The Professor then retreated to the back door
and hauled up his boat by the painter—which he would, of course,
have attached there. He pulled upstream to return his boat and to
sink his apparatus. He was probably already disguised—his fur coat
would have concealed this from Jamieson."

I stared at Harborne in very considerable amazement.

"You are apparently surprised," he said with a smile; "but there
is really nothing very remarkable in it all. I have not bored you
with all the little details that led to the conclusion, nor related how
I suffered a second ducking in leaving the end house; but my solution was no more than a plausible hypothesis until a happy inspiration, born of nothing more palpable than my own imaginings,
led me to search for and find the cinematograph. You are about to
ask where I found it: I answer, in the deep hole above Long's boathouse where Jimmy Baker made his big catch last summer.
Brayme-Skepley, being a man of very high reasoning powers,

would, I argued, deposit it up and not downstream, knowing that the river would be dragged. He would furthermore put it in the hole, so that the current should not carry it below college.

"There are, however, still one or two points that need clearing up. As to the blood, that offered no insurmountable difficulty to a physiologist; and, by Jove!" ... He suddenly plunged his hand into the case.... "This rubber ring from a soda-water bottle, ingeniously mounted upon a cane handle, accounts for the mysterious tracks. The point to which I particularly allude is the object of the Professor's disappearance."

"I think," I said, "that I can offer a suggestion. He found, too late to withdraw, that his famous theory had a flaw in it, and could devise no less elaborate means of hiding the fact and at the same time of so destroying his apparatus as to leave no trace whereby his great reputation could be marred."

"That is my own idea," agreed Harborne. "For which reason I have carefully covered such very few tracks as he left, and have decided that this handsome case, with its tell-tale inscription—J. B. S.—must be destroyed. My conclusions are not for the world, which is at perfect liberty to believe that Professor Brayme-Skepley was carried off by an unclassified aptera!"

And so, somewhere or other, Professor Brayme-Skepley is pursuing his distinguished career under a new name, while Harborne allows the world to persist in its opinion.

The Empire of the Ants
H. G. Wells

I

When Captain Gerilleau received instructions to take his new
gunboat, the *Benjamin Constant*, to Badama on the Batemo arm of
the Guaramadema and there assist the inhabitants against a plague of
ants, he suspected the authorities of mockery. His promotion had been
romantic and irregular, the affections of a prominent Brazilian lady
and the captain's liquid eyes had played a part in the process, and
the *Diario* and *O Futuro* had been lamentably disrespectful in their
comments. He felt he was to give further occasion for disrespect.

He was a Creole, his conceptions of etiquette and discipline
were pure-blooded Portuguese, and it was only to Holroyd, the
Lancashire engineer who had come over with the boat, and as an
exercise in the use of English—his "th" sounds were very uncertain—that he opened his heart.

"It is in effect," he said, "to make me absurd! What can a man
do against ants? Dey come, dey go."

"They say," said Holroyd, "that these don't go. That chap you
said was a Sambo—"

"Zambo;—it is a sort of mixture of blood."

"Sambo. He said the people are going!"

The captain smoked fretfully for a time. "Dese tings 'ave to happen," he said at last. "What is it? Plagues of ants and suchlike as
God wills. Dere was a plague in Trinidad—the little ants that carry
leaves. Orl der orange-trees, all der mangoes! What does it matter? Sometimes ant armies come into your houses—fighting ants;
a different sort. You go and they clean the house. Then you come
back again;—the house is clean, like new! No cockroaches, no fleas,
no jiggers in the floor."

"That Sambo chap," said Holroyd, "says these are a different sort of ant."

The captain shrugged his shoulders, fumed, and gave his attention to a cigarette.

Afterwards he reopened the subject. "My dear 'Olroyd, what am I to do about dese infernal ants?"

The captain reflected. "It is ridiculous," he said. But in the afternoon he put on his full uniform and went ashore, and jars and boxes came back to the ship and subsequently he did. And Holroyd sat on deck in the evening coolness and smoked profoundly and marvelled at Brazil. They were six days up the Amazon, some hundreds of miles from the ocean, and east and west of him there was a horizon like the sea, and to the south nothing but a sand-bank island with some tufts of scrub. The water was always running like a sluice, thick with dirt, animated with crocodiles and hovering birds, and fed by some inexhaustible source of tree trunks; and the waste of it, the headlong waste of it, filled his soul. The town of Alemquer, with its meagre church, its thatched sheds for houses, its discoloured ruins of ampler days, seemed a little thing lost in this wilderness of Nature, a sixpence dropped on Sahara. He was a young man, this was his first sight of the tropics, he came straight from England, where Nature is hedged, ditched, and drained, into the perfection of submission, and he had suddenly discovered the insignificance of man. For six days they had been steaming up from the sea by unfrequented channels; and man had been as rare as a rare butterfly. One saw one day a canoe, another day a distant station, the next no men at all. He began to perceive that man is indeed a rare animal, having but a precarious hold upon this land.

He perceived it more clearly as the days passed, and he made his devious way to the Batemo, in the company of this remarkable commander, who ruled over one big gun, and was forbidden to waste his ammunition. Holroyd was learning Spanish industriously, but he was still in the present tense and substantive stage of speech, and the only other person who had any words of English was a negro stoker, who had them all wrong. The second in command was a Portuguese, da Cunha, who spoke French, but it was a different sort of French from the French Holroyd had learnt in Southport, and their intercourse was confined to politenesses and simple propositions about the weather. And the weather, like everything else in this amazing new world, the weather had no human aspect, and was hot by night and hot by day, and the air steam, even the wind was hot steam, smelling of vegetation in decay: and the alligators and the strange birds, the flies of many sorts and sizes, the beetles, the ants, the snakes and monkeys seemed to wonder what man was doing in an atmosphere that had no gladness in its sunshine and no coolness in its night. To wear clothing was intolerable, but to cast it aside was to scorch by day, and expose an ampler area to the mosquitoes by night; to go on deck by day was to be blinded by glare and to stay below was to suffocate. And in the daytime came certain flies, extremely clever and noxious about one's wrist and ankle. Captain Gerilleau, who was Holroyd's sole distraction from these physical distresses, developed into a formidable bore, telling the simple story of his heart's affections day by day, a string of anonymous women, as if he was telling beads. Sometimes he suggested sport, and they shot at alligators, and at rare intervals they came to human aggregations in the waste of trees, and stayed for a day or so, and drank and sat about, and, one night, danced with Creole girls, who found Holroyd's poor elements of Spanish, without either past tense or future, amply sufficient for their purposes. But these were mere luminous chinks in the long grey passage of the streaming river, up which the throbbing engines beat. A certain liberal heathen deity, in the shape of a demi-john, held seductive court aft, and, it is probable, forward.

But Gerilleau learnt things about the ants, more things and more, at this stopping-place and that, and became interested in his mission.

"Dey are a new sort of ant," he said. "We have got to be—what do you call it?—entomologie? Big. Five centimetres! Some bigger! It is ridiculous. We are like the monkeys—sent to pick insects... But dey are eating up the country."

He burst out indignantly. "Suppose—suddenly, there are complications with Europe. Here am I—soon we shall be above the Rio Negro—and my gun, useless!"

He nursed his knee and mused.

"Dose people who were dere at de dancing place, dey 'ave come down. Dey 'ave lost all they got. De ants come to deir house one afternoon. Everyone run out. You know when de ants come one must—everyone runs out and they go over the house. If you stayed they'd eat you. See? Well, presently dey go back; dey say, 'The ants 'ave gone.' ... De ants 'aven't gone. Dey try to go in—de son, 'e goes in. De ants fight."

"Swarm over him?"

"Bite 'im. Presently he comes out again—screaming and running. He runs past them to the river. See? He gets into de water and drowns de ants—yes." Gerilleau paused, brought his liquid eyes close to Holroyd's face, tapped Holroyd's knee with his knuckle. "That night he dies, just as if he was stung by a snake."

"Poisoned—by the ants?"

"Who knows?" Gerilleau shrugged his shoulders. "Perhaps they bit him badly... When I joined dis service I joined to fight men. Dese things, dese ants, dey come and go. It is no business for men."

After that he talked frequently of the ants to Holroyd, and whenever they chanced to drift against any speck of humanity in that waste of water and sunshine and distant trees, Holroyd's improving knowledge of the language enabled him to recognise the ascendant word *Saüba*, more and more completely dominating the whole.

He perceived the ants were becoming interesting, and the nearer he drew to them the more interesting they became. Gerilleau abandoned his old themes almost suddenly, and the Portuguese lieutenant became a conversational figure; he knew something about the leaf-cutting ant, and expanded his knowledge. Gerilleau sometimes rendered what he had to tell to Holroyd. He told of the little workers that swarm and fight, and the big workers that command and rule, and how these latter always crawled to the neck and how their bites drew blood. He told how they cut leaves and made fungus beds, and how their nests in Caracas are sometimes a hundred yards across. Two days the three men spent disputing whether ants have eyes. The discussion grew dangerously heated on the second afternoon, and Holroyd saved the situation by going ashore in a boat to catch ants and see. He captured various specimens and returned, and some had eyes and some hadn't. Also, they argued, do ants bite or sting?

"Dese ants," said Gerilleau, after collecting information at a rancho, "have big eyes. They don't run about blind—not as most ants do. No! Dey get in corners and watch what you do."

"And they sting?" asked Holroyd.

"Yes. Dey sting. Dere is poison in the sting." He meditated. "I do not see what men can do against ants. Dey come and go."

"But these don't go."

"They will," said Gerilleau.

Past Tamandu there is a long low coast of eighty miles without any population, and then one comes to the confluence of the main river and the Batemo arm like a great lake, and then the forest came nearer, came at last intimately near. The character of the channel changes, snags abound, and the *Benjamin Constant* moored by a cable that night, under the very shadow of dark trees. For the first time for many days came a spell of coolness, and Holroyd and Gerilleau sat late, smoking cigars and enjoying this delicious sensation. Gerilleau's mind was full of ants and what they could do. He decided to sleep at last, and lay down on a mattress on deck, a man hopelessly perplexed, his last words, when he already seemed asleep, were to ask, with a flourish of despair, "What can one do with ants?... De whole thing is absurd."

Holroyd was left to scratch his bitten wrists, and meditate alone.

He sat on the bulwark and listened to the little changes in Gerilleau's breathing until he was fast asleep, and then the ripple and lap of the stream took his mind, and brought back that sense of immensity that had been growing upon him since first he had left Para and come up the river. The monitor showed but one small light, and there was first a little talking forward and then stillness. His eyes went from the dim black outlines of the middle works of the gunboat towards the bank, to the black overwhelming mysteries of forest, lit now and then by a fire-fly, and never still from the murmur of alien and mysterious activities...

It was the inhuman immensity of this land that astonished and oppressed him. He knew the skies were empty of men, the stars were specks in an incredible vastness of space; he knew the ocean was enormous and untamable, but in England he had come to think of the land as man's. In England it is indeed man's, the wild things live by sufferance, grow on lease, everywhere the roads, the fences, and absolute security runs. In an atlas, too, the land is man's, and all coloured to show his claim to it—in vivid contrast to the universal independent blueness of the sea. He had taken it for granted that a day would come when everywhere about the earth, plough and culture, light tramways and good roads, an ordered security, would prevail. But now, he doubted.

This forest was interminable, it had an air of being invincible, and Man seemed at best an infrequent precarious intruder. One travelled for miles, amidst the still, silent struggle of giant trees, of strangulating creepers, of assertive flowers, everywhere the alligator, the turtle, and endless varieties of birds and insects seemed at home, dwelt irreplaceably—but man, man at most held a footing upon resentful clearings, fought weeds, fought beasts and insects for the barest foothold, fell a prey to snake and beast, insect and fever, and was presently carried away. In many places down the river he had been manifestly driven back, this deserted creek or that preserved the name of a *casa*, and here and there ruinous white walls and a shattered tower enforced the lesson. The puma, the jaguar, were more the masters here...

Who were the real masters?

In a few miles of this forest there must be more ants than there are men in the whole world! This seemed to Holroyd a perfectly new idea. In a few thousand years men had emerged from barbarism to a stage of civilisation that made them feel lords of the future and masters of the earth! But what was to prevent the ants evolving also? Such ants as one knew lived in little communities of a few thousand individuals, made no concerted efforts against the greater world. But they had a language, they had an intelligence! Why should things stop at that any more than men had stopped at the barbaric stage? Suppose presently the ants began to store knowledge, just as men had done by means of books and records, use weapons, form great empires, sustain a planned and organised war?

Things came back to him that Gerilleau had gathered about these ants they were approaching. They used a poison like the poison of snakes. They obeyed greater leaders even as the leaf-cutting ants do. They were carnivorous, and where they came they stayed...

The forest was very still. The water lapped incessantly against the side. About the lantern overhead there eddied a noiseless whirl of phantom moths.

Gerilleau stirred in the darkness and sighed. "What can one *do?*" he murmured, and turned over and was still again.

Holroyd was roused from meditations that were becoming sinister by the hum of a mosquito.

II

The next morning Holroyd learnt they were within forty kilometres of Badama, and his interest in the banks intensified.

He came up whenever an opportunity offered to examine his surroundings. He could see no signs of human occupation whatever,
save for a weedy ruin of a house and the green-stained facade of
the long-deserted monastery at Mojû, with a forest tree growing
out of a vacant window space, and great creepers netted across its
vacant portals. Several flights of strange yellow butterflies with
semi-transparent wings crossed the river that morning, and many
alighted on the monitor and were killed by the men. It was towards
afternoon that they came upon the derelict *cuberta*.

She did not at first appear to be derelict; both her sails were
set and hanging slack in the afternoon calm, and there was the figure of a man sitting on the fore planking beside the shipped sweeps.
Another man appeared to be sleeping face downwards on the sort
of longitudinal bridge these big canoes have in the waist. But it
was presently apparent, from the sway of her rudder and the way
she drifted into the course of the gunboat, that something was out
of order with her. Gerilleau surveyed her through a field-glass, and
became interested in the queer darkness of the face of the sitting
man, a red-faced man he seemed, without a nose—crouching he
was rather than sitting, and the longer the captain looked the less
he liked to look at him, and the less able he was to take his glasses
away.

But he did so at last, and went a little way to call up Holroyd.
Then he went back to hail the cuberta. He ailed her again, and so
she drove past him. *Santa Rosa* stood out clearly as her name.

As she came by and into the wake of the monitor, she pitched a
little, and suddenly the figure of the crouching an collapsed as
though all its joints had given way. His hat fell off, his head was
not nice to look at, and his body flopped lax and rolled out of sight
behind the bulwarks.

"Caramba!" cried Gerilleau, and resorted to Holroyd forthwith.

Holroyd was half-way up the companion. "Did you see dat?"
said the captain.

"Dead!" said Holroyd. "Yes. You'd better send a boat aboard.
There's something wrong."

"Did you—by any chance—see his face?"

"What was it like?"

"It was—ugh!—I have no words." And the captain suddenly
turned his back on Holroyd and became an active and strident commander.

The gunboat came about, steamed parallel to the erratic course of the canoe, and dropped the boat with Lieutenant da Cunha and three sailors to board her. Then the curiosity of the captain made him draw up almost alongside as the lieutenant got aboard, so that the whole of the *Santa Rosa*, deck and hold, was visible to Holroyd.

He saw now clearly that the sole crew of the vessel was these two dead men, and though he could not see their faces, he saw by their outstretched hands, which were all of ragged flesh, that they had been subjected to some strange exceptional process of decay. For a moment his attention concentrated on those two enigmatical bundles of dirty clothes and laxly flung limbs, and then his eyes went forward to discover the open hold piled high with trunks and cases, and aft, to where the little cabin gaped inexplicably empty. Then he became aware that the planks of the middle decking were dotted with moving black specks.

His attention was riveted by these specks. They were all walking in directions radiating from the fallen man in a manner—the image came unsought to his mind—like the crowd dispersing from a bull-fight.

He became aware of Gerilleau beside him. "Capo," he said, "have you your glasses? Can you focus as closely as those planks there?"

Gerilleau made an effort, grunted, and handed him the glasses.

There followed a moment of scrutiny. "It's ants," said the Englishman, and handed the focused field-glass back to Gerilleau.

His impression of them was of a crowd of large black ants, very like ordinary ants except for their size, and for the fact that some of the larger of them bore a sort of clothing of grey. But at the time his inspection was too brief for particulars. The head of Lieutenant da Cunha appeared over the side of the cuberta, and a brief colloquy ensued.

"You must go aboard," said Gerilleau.

The lieutenant objected that the boat was full of ants.

"You have your boots," said Gerilleau.

The lieutenant changed the subject. "How did these men die?" he asked.

Captain Gerilleau embarked upon speculations that Holroyd could not follow, and the two men disputed with a certain increasing vehemence. Holroyd took up the field-glass and resumed his scrutiny, first of the ants and then of the dead man amidships.

He has described these ants to me very particularly.

He says they were as large as any ants he has ever seen, black and moving with a steady deliberation very different from the mechanical fussiness of the common ant. About one in twenty was much larger than its fellows, and with an exceptionally large head. These reminded him at once of the master workers who are said to rule over the leaf-cutter ants; like them they seemed to be directing and co-ordinating the general movements. They tilted their bodies back in a manner altogether singular as if they made some use of the fore feet. And he had a curious fancy that he was too far off to verify, that most of these ants of both kinds were wearing accoutrements, had things strapped about their bodies by bright white bands like white metal threads...

He put down the glasses abruptly, realising that the question of discipline between the captain and his subordinate had become acute.

"It is your duty," said the captain, "to go aboard. It is my instructions."

The lieutenant seemed on the verge of refusing. The head of one of the mulatto sailors appeared beside him.

"I believe these men were killed by the ants," said Holroyd abruptly in English.

The captain burst into a rage. He made no answer to Holroyd. "I have commanded you to go aboard," he screamed to his subordinate in Portuguese. "If you do not go aboard forthwith it is mutiny—rank mutiny. Mutiny and cowardice! Where is the courage that should animate us? I will have you in irons, I will have you shot like a dog." He began a torrent of abuse and curses, he danced to and fro. He shook his fists, he behaved as if beside himself with rage, and the lieutenant, white and still, stood looking at him. The crew appeared forward, with amazed faces.

Suddenly, in a pause of this outbreak, the lieutenant came to some heroic decision, saluted, drew himself together and clambered upon the deck of the cuberta.

"Ah!" said Gerilleau, and his mouth shut like a trap. Holroyd saw the ants retreating before da Cunha's boots. The Portuguese walked slowly to the fallen man, stooped down, hesitated, clutched his coat and turned him over. A black swarm of ants rushed out of the clothes, and da Cunha stepped back very quickly and trod two or three times on the deck.

Holroyd put up the glasses. He saw the scattered ants about the invader's feet, and doing what he had never seen ants doing before. They had nothing of the blind movements of the common ant; they were looking at him—as a rallying crowd of men might look at some gigantic monster that had dispersed it.

"How did he die?" the captain shouted.

Holroyd understood the Portuguese to say the body was too much eaten to tell.

"What is there forward?" asked Gerilleau.

The lieutenant walked a few paces, and began his answer in Portuguese. He stopped abruptly and beat off something from his leg. He made some peculiar steps as if he was trying to stamp on something invisible, and went quickly towards the side. Then he controlled himself, turned about, walked deliberately forward to the hold, clambered up to the fore decking, from which the sweeps are worked, stooped for a time over the second man, groaned audibly, and made his way back and aft to the cabin, moving very rigidly. He turned and began a conversation with his captain, cold and respectful in tone on either side, contrasting vividly with the wrath and insult of a few moments before. Holroyd gathered only fragments of its purport.

He reverted to the field-glass, and was surprised to find the ants had vanished from all the exposed surfaces of the deck. He turned towards the shadows beneath the decking, and it seemed to him they were full of watching eyes.

The cuberta, it was agreed, was derelict, but too full of ants to put men aboard to sit and sleep: it must be towed. The lieutenant went forward to take in and adjust the cable, and the men in the boat stood up to be ready to help him. Holroyd's glasses searched the canoe.

He became more and more impressed by the fact that a great if minute and furtive activity was going on. He perceived that a number of gigantic ants—they seemed nearly a couple of inches in length—carrying oddly-shaped burthens for which he could imagine no use—were moving in rushes from one point of obscurity to another. They did not move in columns across the exposed places, but in open, spaced-out lines, oddly suggestive of the rushes of modern infantry advancing under fire. A number were taking cover under the dead man's clothes, and a perfect swarm was gathering along the side over which da Cunha must presently go.

He did not see them actually rush for the lieutenant as he returned, but he has no doubt they did make a concerted rush. Suddenly the lieutenant was shouting and cursing and beating at his
legs. "I'm stung!" he shouted, with a face of hate and accusation
towards Gerilleau.

Then he vanished over the side, dropped into his boat, and
plunged at once into the water. Holroyd heard the splash.

The three men in the boat pulled him out and brought him
aboard, and that night he died.

III

Holroyd and the captain came out of the cabin in which the
swollen and contorted body of the lieutenant lay and stood together
at the stern of the monitor, staring at the sinister vessel they trailed
behind them. It was a close, dark night that had only phantom
flickerings of sheet lightning to illuminate it. The cuberta, a vague
black triangle, rocked about in the steamer's wake, her sails bobbing and flapping, and the black smoke from the funnels, spark-lit
ever and again, streamed over her swaying masts.

Gerilleau's mind was inclined to run on the unkind things the
lieutenant had said in the heat of his last fever.

"He says I murdered 'im," he protested. "It is simply absurd.
Someone 'ad to go aboard. Are we to run away from these confounded ants whenever they show up?"

Holroyd said nothing. He was thinking of a disciplined rush of
little black shapes across bare sunlit planking.

"It was his place to go," harped Gerilleau. "He died in the execution of his duty. What has he to complain of? Murdered!... But
the poor fellow was—what is it?—demented. He was not in his right
mind. The poison swelled him... U'm."

They came to a long silence.

"We will sink that canoe—burn it."

"And then?"

The inquiry irritated Gerilleau. His shoulders went up, his
hands flew out at right angles from his body. "What is one to *do?*"
he said, his voice going up to an angry squeak.

"Anyhow," he broke out vindictively, "every ant in dat cuberta!—
I will burn dem alive!"

Holroyd was not moved to conversation. A distant ululation of
howling monkeys filled the sultry night with foreboding sounds,

and as the gunboat drew near the black mysterious banks this was reinforced by a depressing clamour of frogs.

"What is one to *do?*" the captain repeated after a vast interval, and suddenly becoming active and savage and blasphemous, decided to burn the *Santa Rosa* without further delay. Everyone aboard was pleased by that idea, everyone helped with zest; they pulled in the cable, cut it, and dropped the boat and fired her with tow and kerosene, and soon the cuberta was crackling and flaring merrily amidst the immensities of the tropical night. Holroyd watched the mounting yellow flare against the blackness, and the livid flashes of sheet lightning that came and went above the forest summits, throwing them into momentary silhouette, and his stoker stood behind him watching also.

The stoker was stirred to the depths of his linguistics. "*Saüba* go pop, pop," he said, "Wahaw" and laughed richly.

But Holroyd was thinking that these little creatures on the decked canoe had also eyes and brains.

The whole thing impressed him as incredibly foolish and wrong, but—what was one to *do?* This question came back enormously reinforced on the morrow, when at last the gunboat reached Badama.

This place, with its leaf-thatch-covered houses and sheds, its creeper-invaded sugar-mill, its little jetty of timber and canes, was very still in the morning heat, and showed never a sign of living men. Whatever ants there were at that distance were too small to see.

"All the people have gone," said Gerilleau, "but we will do one thing anyhow. We will 'oot and vissel."

So Holroyd hooted and whistled.

Then the captain fell into a doubting fit of the worst kind. "Dere is one thing we can do," he said presently, "What's that?" said Holroyd.

"'Oot and vissel again."

So they did.

The captain walked his deck and gesticulated to himself. He seemed to have many things on his mind. Fragments of speeches came from his lips. He appeared to be addressing some imaginary public tribunal either in Spanish or Portuguese. Holroyd's improving ear detected something about ammunition. He came out of these preoccupations suddenly into English. "My dear 'Olroyd!" he cried, and broke off with "But what *can* one do?"

They took the boat and the field-glasses, and went close in to examine the place. They made out a number of big ants, whose still postures had a certain effect of watching them, dotted about the edge of the rude embarkation jetty. Gerilleau tried ineffectual pistol shots at these. Holroyd thinks he distinguished curious earthworks running between the nearer houses, that may have been the work of the insect conquerors of those human habitations. The explorers pulled past the jetty, and became aware of a human skeleton wearing a loin cloth, and very bright and clean and shining, lying beyond. They came to a pause regarding this...

"I 'ave all dose lives to consider," said Gerilleau suddenly.

Holroyd turned and stared at the captain, realising slowly that he referred to the unappetising mixture of races that constituted his crew.

"To send a landing party—it is impossible—impossible. They will be poisoned, they will swell, they will swell up and abuse me and die. It is totally impossible... If we land, I must land alone, alone, in thick boots and with my life in my hand. Perhaps I should live. Or again—I might not land. I do not know. I do not know."

Holroyd thought he did, but he said nothing.

"De whole thing," said Gerilleau suddenly, "'as been got up to make me ridiculous. De whole thing!"

They paddled about and regarded the clean white skeleton from various points of view, and then they returned to the gunboat. Then Gerilleau's indecisions became terrible. Steam was got up, and in the afternoon the monitor went on up the river with an air of going to ask somebody something, and by sunset came back again and anchored. A thunderstorm gathered and broke furiously, and then the night became beautifully cool and quiet and everyone slept on deck. Except Gerilleau, who tossed about and muttered. In the dawn he awakened Holroyd.

"Lord!" said Holroyd, "what now?"

"I have decided," said the captain.

"What—to land?" said Holroyd, sitting up brightly.

"No!" said the captain, and was for a time very reserved. "I have decided," he repeated, and Holroyd manifested symptoms of impatience.

"Well,—yes," said the captain, "*I shall fire de big gun!*"

And he did! Heaven knows what the ants thought of it, but he did. He fired it twice with great sternness and ceremony. All the crew had wadding in their ears, and there was an effect of going into action about the whole affair, and first they hit and wrecked the old sugar-mill, and then they smashed the abandoned store behind the jetty. And then Gerilleau experienced the inevitable reaction.

"It is no good," he said to Holroyd; "no good at all. No sort of bally good. We must go back—for instructions. Dere will be de devil of a row about dis ammunition—oh! de devil of a row! You don't know, 'Olroyd..."

He stood regarding the world in infinite perplexity for a space.

"But what else was there to *do?*" he cried.

In the afternoon the monitor started down stream again, and in the evening a landing party took the body of the lieutenant and buried it on the bank upon which the new ants have so far not appeared...

IV

I heard this story in a fragmentary state from Holroyd not three weeks ago.

These new ants have got into his brain, and he has come back to England with the idea, as he says, of "exciting people" about them "before it is too late." He says they threaten British Guiana, which cannot be much over a trifle of a thousand miles from their present sphere of activity, and that the Colonial Office ought to get to work upon them at once. He declaims with great passion: "These are intelligent ants. Just think what that means!"

There can be no doubt they are a serious pest, and that the Brazilian Government is well advised in offering a prize of five hundred pounds for some effectual method of extirpation. It is certain too that since they first appeared in the hills beyond Badama, about three years ago, they have achieved extraordinary conquests. The whole of the south bank of the Batemo River, for nearly sixty miles, they have in their effectual occupation; they have driven men out completely, occupied plantations and settlements, and boarded and captured at least one ship. It is even said they have in some inexplicable way bridged the very considerable Capuarana arm and pushed many miles towards the Amazon itself. There can be little doubt that they are far more reasonable and with a far better social organisation than any previously known ant species; instead of being in dispersed societies they are organised into what is in effect a single nation; but their peculiar and immediate formidableness lies not so much in this as in the intelligent use they make of poison against their larger enemies. It would seem this poison of theirs is closely akin to snake poison, and it is highly probable they actually manufacture it, and that the larger individuals among them carry the needle-like crystals of it in their attacks upon men.

Of course it is extremely difficult to get any detailed information about these new competitors for the sovereignty of the globe. No eye-witnesses of their activity, except for such glimpses as Holroyd's, have survived the encounter. The most extraordinary legends of their prowess and capacity are in circulation in the region of the Upper Amazon, and grow daily as the steady advance of the invader stimulates men's imaginations through their fears. These strange little creatures are credited not only with the use of implements and a knowledge of fire and metals and with organised feats of engineering that stagger our northern minds—unused as we are to such feats as that of the *Saübas* of Rio de Janeiro, who in 1841 drove a tunnel under the Parahyba where it is as wide as the Thames at London Bridge—but with an organised and detailed method of record and communication analogous to our books. So far their action has been a steady progressive settlement, involving the flight or slaughter of every human being in the new areas they invade. They are increasing rapidly in numbers, and Holroyd at least is firmly convinced that they will finally dispossess man over the whole of tropical South America.

And why should they stop at tropical South America?

Well, there they are, anyhow. By 1911 or thereabouts, if they go on as they are going, they ought to strike the Capuarana Extension Railway, and force themselves upon the attention of the European capitalist.

By 1920 they will be half-way down the Amazon. I fix 1950 or '60 at the latest for the discovery of Europe.

The Lace Designers
Don Mark Lemon

When, some years ago, a New York lace house placed on exhibition in its windows a number of original designs in lace, they instantly attracted critical attention because of their exquisite novelty and beauty. Indeed, the metropolitan lace designers had never before seen anything that could compare with them.

"These wonderful patterns," wrote one of the critics, "seem almost a reconciliation of geometry and art, the designs partaking of the exquisite and exact forms of crystalization, while at the same time expressing the freedom of artistic fancy."

This may have seemed excessive praise to some, but the designs were indeed wonderfully fine, and their designer was besieged by interested capital and enthusiastic admirers.

He proved to be a young fellow of twenty-four, who, two years before, had been compelled to give up his trade as a lithographer and go to Arizona in hope of recovering his lost health. He smiled lightly at the outspoken praise accorded his work.

"It is nothing," he said. "I owe everything to my wife, who did the lace work after I procured the designs."

He turned to the young Spanish girl seated near, and his pallid face lit up with ardent love. The beautiful young creature returned the look. Then her eyes fell and she blushed. Unconversant with the language spoken, she yet divined that she was the subject of praise.

"If it hadn't been for my wife," continued the young fellow, "I probably would have thrown these designs away. In fact, I would never have taken up the matter seriously; but since she has worked out my patterns in thread, I see that they are a great thing, and I've already laid my plans. I propose to control the world's lace designs by creating the most original and beautiful patterns, and my resources in that line are, I believe, practically unlimited. But don't give me credit for being an artist. Fact is, I'm not one at all, and I don't wish to take any golden fleeces of honor by sailing under false colors. I am merely an inventor, or rather, a discoverer, and these designs, while not machine work, are not hand work. I propose, however, to keep their nature a secret, that will be passed on to my heirs, and I think," concluded the speaker, more modestly than lamely, "I have a pretty good outlook in this matter."

The designs on exhibition were withdrawn for fear they might be copied before being patented, and their inventor had just signed a contract with a syndicate of lace manufacturers to furnish designs for the syndicate at fabulous prices, when the fine enterprise was wiped out and the new art lost in a sudden, piteous tragedy.

On returning to his home one afternoon, the young designer found his wife's dead body lying across an inner threshold. At first he thought that the beautiful girl had merely fainted, but when he lifted the face he saw that life was extinct and that Repulsiveness inhabited with Death the once lovely form.

"My God," he sobbed, "I left her this morning so beautiful and happy."

He lifted her to a couch and covered up her face, and going into the street begged a passing pedestrian to come and help him.

When they had taken the body away, and before the police arrived, the young designer hurried up to the attic room of the cottage.

It was a small room, rather scantily furnished. Against the south wall was a large, glass-covered case, while beside it was n cabinet filled with bottles. In the center of the room was a table. Set up on this table were several movable stands, each formed of four slender, braced steel uprights, connected at the top by a fine wire, making a rectangle of about eight by twelve inches. The purpose of these stands seemed to be to offer a light, open framework on which lace designs could be worked out in thread. One stand was in use. An exquisite pattern, worked in filmy silk, hung upon it and trembled like a fairy thing.

But the room, sparely furnished as it was, was no place for a man, for a tall, narrow bottle, jarred from a shelf above, perhaps by a heavily closed door, had crashed through the glass that covered the case against the south wall, and by way of the broken pane there had escaped hundreds of little poisonous spiders. They ran and leapt everywhere—across the floor, up the table legs, along the walls and ceiling, against the window panes, and in and out of the half-shut cabinet door, dancing a myriad maze like beams from some scarlet sun.

Seizing a magazine, the young fellow began to kill them. About the room he went, indifferent to the knowledge that their bite would mean death—death such as had come to his once lovely young wife, fearful and immediate. At last he realized that he, too, had been bitten. He had not sought it, yet he had not cared. What mattered it now, anyway? Still about the room he leapt, striking and stamping, till the poison struck at his heart like an arrow, intense and burning, and even after he had fallen he attempted to smash the scurrying, scarlet bodies.

They found him there a few hours later, as he had found his unhappy young wife in the room below—dead and unnatural. It was pitiful, yet it was more wonderful, for over his dead face Something—could it have been one of those little scarlet spiders, made drunk on a secret fluid?—had spun a gossamer web of novel and exquisite design, such as would have become the lace of a royal bride.

The Feather Pillow
Horacio Quiroga

Her entire honeymoon gave her hot and cold shivers. A blond, angelic, and timid young girl, the childhood fancies she had dreamed about being a bride had been chilled by her husband's rough character. She loved him very much, nonetheless, although sometimes she gave a light shudder when, as they returned home through the streets together at night, she cast furtive glances at the impressive stature of her Jordan, who had been silent for an hour. He, for his part, loved her profoundly but never let it be seen.

For three months—they had been married in April—they lived in a special kind of bliss. Doubtless she would have wished less severity in the rigorous sky of love, more expansive and less cautious tenderness, but her husband's impassive manner always restrained her.

The house in which they lived influenced her chills and shuddering to no small degree. The whiteness of the silent patio- friezes, columns, and marble statues - produced the wintry impression of an enchanted palace. Inside, the glacial brilliance of stucco, the completely bare walls, affirmed the sensation of unpleasant coldness. As one crossed from one room to another, the echo of his steps reverberated throughout the house, as if long abandonment had sensitized its resonance.

Alicia passed the autumn in this strange love nest. She had determined, however, to cast a veil over her former dreams and live like a sleeping beauty in the hostile house, trying not to think about anything till her husband arrived each evening.

It is not strange that she grew thin. She had a light attack of influenza that dragged on insidiously for days and days: after that Alicia's health never returned. Finally one afternoon she was able to go into the garden, supported on her husband's arm. She looked around listlessly. Suddenly Jordan, with deep tenderness, ran his hand very slowly over her head, and Alicia instantly burst into sobs, throwing her arms around his neck. For a long time she cried out all the fears she had kept silent, redoubling her weeping at Jordan's slightest caress. Then her sobs subsided, and she stood a long while, her face hidden in the hollow of his neck, not moving or speaking a word.

This was the last day Alicia was well enough to be up. The following day she awakened feeling faint. Jordan's doctor examined her with minute attention, prescribing calm and absolute rest.

"I don't know," he said to Jordan at the street door. "She has a great weakness that I am unable to explain. And with no vomiting, nothing ... if she wakes tomorrow as she did today, call me at once."

When she awakened the following day, Alicia was worse. There was a consultation. It was agreed there was an anemia of incredible progression, completely inexplicable. Alicia had no more fainting spells but she was visibly moving towards death. The lights were lighted all day long in her bedroom, and there was complete silence. Hours went by without the slightest sound. Alicia dozed. Jordan virtually lived in the drawing-room, which was also always lighted. With tireless persistence he paced ceaselessly from one end of the room to the other. The carpet swallowed his steps. At times he entered the bedroom and continued his silent pacing back and forth alongside the bed, stopping for an instant at each end to regard his wife.

Suddenly Alicia began to have hallucinations, vague images, at first seeming to float in the air, then descending to floor level. Her eyes excessively wide, she stared continuously at the carpet on either side of the head of her bed. One night she suddenly focused on one spot. Then she opened her mouth to scream, and pearls of sweat suddenly beaded her nose and lips.

"Jordan! Jordan!" she clamoured, rigid with fright, still staring at the carpet; she looked at him once again; and after a long moment of stupefied confrontation she regained her senses. She smiled and took her husband's hand in hers, caressing it, trembling, for half an hour.

Among her most persistent hallucinations was that of an anthropoid poised on his fingertips on the carpet, staring at her.

The doctors returned, but to no avail. They saw before them a diminishing life, a life bleeding away day by day, hour by hour, absolutely without their knowing why. During the last consultation Alicia lay in a stupor while they took her pulse, passing her inert wrist from one to another. They observed her a long time in silence and then moved into the dining room.

"Phew..." The discouraged chief physician shrugged his shoulders. "It's an inexplicable case. There is little we can do..."

"That's my last hope," Jordan groaned. And he staggered blindly against the table.

Alicia's life was fading away in the subdelirium of anemia, a delirium which grew worse throughout the evening hours but which let up somewhat after dawn. The illness never worsened during the daytime, but each morning she awakened pale as death, almost in a swoon. It seemed only at night that her life drained out of her in new waves of blood. Always when she awakened she had the sensation of lying collapsed in the bed with a million pound weight on top of her. Following the third day of this relapse she left her bed again. She could scarcely move her head. She did not want her bed to be touched, not even to have her bedcovers arranged. Her crepuscular terrors advanced now in the form of monsters that dragged themselves toward the bed and laboriously climbed upon the bedspread.

Then she lost consciousness. The final two days she raved ceaselessly in a weak voice. The lights funereally illuminated the bedroom and drawing room. In the deathly silence of the house the only sound was the monotonous delirium from the bedroom and the dull echoes of Jordan's eternal pacing.

Finally, Alicia died. The servant, when she came in afterward to strip the now empty bed, stared wonderingly for a moment at the pillow.

"Sir!" she called to Jordan in a low voice. "There are stains on the pillow that look like blood."

Jordan approached rapidly and bent over the pillow. Truly, on the case, on both sides of the hollow left by Alicia's head, were two small dark spots.

"They look like punctures," the servant murmured after a moment of motionless observation.

"Hold it up to the light," Jordan told her.

The servant raised the pillow but immediately dropped it and stood staring at it, livid and trembling. Without knowing why, Jordan felt the hair rise on the back of his neck.

"What is it?" he murmured in a hoarse voice.

"It's very heavy," the servant whispered, still trembling

Jordan picked it up; it was extraordinarily heavy. He carried it out of the room, and on the dining room table he ripped open the case and the ticking with a slash. The top feathers floated away, and the servant, her mouth opened wide, gave a scream of horror and covered her face with clenched fists: in the bottom of the pillow case, among the feathers, slowly moving its hairy legs, was a monstrous animal, a living, viscous ball. It was so swollen one could barely make out its mouth.

Night after night, since Alicia had taken to her bed, this abomination had stealthily applied its mouth—its proboscis one might better say—to the girl's temples, sucking her blood. The puncture was scarcely perceptible. The daily plumping of the pillow had doubtlessly at first impeded its progress, but as soon as the girl could no longer move, the suction became vertiginous. In five days, in five nights, the monster had drained Alicia's life away.

These parasites of feathered creatures, diminutive in their habitual environment, reach enormous proportions under certain conditions. Human blood seems particularly favourable to them, and it is not rare to encounter them in feather pillows.

Caterpillars

E. F. Benson

I saw a month or two ago in an Italian paper that the Villa Cascana, in which I once stayed, had been pulled down, and that a manufactory of some sort was in process of erection on its site.

There is therefore no longer any reason for refraining from writing of those things which I myself saw (or imagined I saw) in a certain room and on a certain landing of the villa in question, nor from mentioning the circumstances which followed, which may or may not (according to the opinion of the reader) throw some light on or be somehow connected with this experience.

The Villa Cascana was in all ways but one a perfectly delightful house, yet, if it were standing now, nothing in the world—I use the phrase in its literal sense—would induce me to set foot in it again, for I believe it to have been haunted in a very terrible and practical manner.

Most ghosts, when all is said and done, do not do much harm; they may perhaps terrify, but the person whom they visit usually gets over their visitation. They may on the other hand be entirely friendly and beneficent. But the appearances in the Villa Cascana were not beneficent, and had they made their "visit" in a very slightly different manner, I do not suppose I should have got over it any more than Arthur Inglis did.

The house stood on an ilex-clad hill not far from Sestri di Levante on the Italian Riviera, looking out over the iridescent blues of that enchanted sea, while behind it rose the pale green chestnut woods that climb up the hillsides till they give place to the pines that, black in contrast with them, crown the slopes. All round it the garden in the luxuriance of mid-spring bloomed and was fragrant, and the scent of magnolia and rose, borne on the salt freshness of the winds from the sea, flowed like a stream through the cool vaulted rooms.

On the ground floor a broad pillared loggia ran round three sides of the house, the top of which formed a balcony for certain rooms of the first floor. The main staircase, broad and of grey marble steps, led up from the hall to the landing outside these rooms, which were three in number, namely, two big sitting-rooms and a bedroom arranged en suite. The latter was unoccupied, the sitting-rooms were in use. From these the main staircase was continued to the second floor, where were situated certain bedrooms, one of which I occupied, while from the other side of the first-floor landing some half-dozen steps led to another suite of rooms, where, at the time I am speaking of, Arthur Inglis, the artist, had his bedroom and studio. Thus the landing outside my bedroom at the top of the house commanded both the landing of the first floor and also the steps that led to Inglis' rooms. Jim Stanley and his wife, finally (whose guest I was), occupied rooms in another wing of the house, where also were the servants' quarters.

I arrived just in time for lunch on a brilliant noon of mid-May. The garden was shouting with colour and fragrance, and not less delightful after my broiling walk up from the marina, should have been the coming from the reverberating heat and blaze of the day into the marble coolness of the villa. Only (the reader has my bare word for this, and nothing more), the moment I set foot in the house I felt that something was wrong. This feeling, I may say, was quite vague, though very strong, and I remember that when I saw letters waiting for me on the table in the hall I felt certain that the explanation was here: I was convinced that there was bad news of some sort for me. Yet when I opened them I found no such explanation of my premonition: my correspondents all reeked of prosperity. Yet this clear miscarriage of a presentiment did not dissipate my uneasiness. In that cool fragrant house there was something wrong.

I am at pains to mention this because to the general view it may explain that though I am as a rule so excellent a sleeper that the extinction of my light on getting into bed is apparently contemporaneous with being called on the following morning, I slept very badly on my first night in the Villa Cascana. It may also explain the fact that when I did sleep (if it was indeed in sleep that I saw what I thought I saw) I dreamed in a very vivid and original manner, original, that is to say, in the sense that something that, as far as I knew, had never previously entered into my conscious- ness, usurped it then. But since, in addition to this evil premoni- tion, certain words and events occurring during the rest of the day might have suggested something of what I thought happened that night, it will be well to relate them.

After lunch, then, I went round the house with Mrs. Stanley, and during our tour she referred, it is true, to the unoccupied bed- room on the first floor, which opened out of the room where we had lunched.

"We left that unoccupied," she said, "because Jim and I have a charming bedroom and dressing-room, as you saw, in the wing, and if we used it ourselves we should have to turn the dining-room into a dressing-room and have our meals downstairs. As it is, how- ever, we have our little flat there, Arthur Inglis has his little flat in the other passage; and I remembered (aren't I extraordinary?) that you once said that the higher up you were in a house the better you were pleased. So I put you at the top of the house, instead of giving you that room."

It is true, that a doubt, vague as my uneasy premonition, crossed my mind at this. I did not see why Mrs. Stanley should have explained all this, if there had not been more to explain. I allow, therefore, that the thought that there was something to ex- plain about the unoccupied bedroom was momentarily present to my mind.

The second thing that may have borne on my dream was this.

At dinner the conversation turned for a moment on ghosts. Inglis, with the certainty of conviction, expressed his belief that anybody who could possibly believe in the existence of supernatu- ral phenomena was unworthy of the name of an ass. The subject instantly dropped. As far as I can recollect, nothing else occurred or was said that could bear on what follows.

We all went to bed rather early, and personally I yawned my way upstairs, feeling hideously sleepy. My room was rather hot, and I threw all the windows wide, and from without poured in the white light of the moon, and the love-song of many nightingales. I undressed quickly, and got into bed, but though I had felt so sleepy before, I now felt extremely wide-awake. But I was quite content to be awake: I did not toss or turn, I felt perfectly happy listening to the song and seeing the light. Then, it is possible, I may have gone to sleep, and what follows may have been a dream. I thought, anyhow, that after a time the nightingales ceased singing and the moon sank. I thought also that if, for some unexplained reason, I was going to lie awake all night, I might as well read, and I remembered that I had left a book in which I was interested in the dining-room on the first floor. So I got out of bed, lit a candle, and went downstairs. I went into the room, saw on a side-table the book I had come to look for, and then, simultaneously, saw that the door into the unoccupied bedroom was open. A curious grey light, not of dawn nor of moonshine, came out of it, and I looked in. The bed stood just opposite the door, a big four-poster, hung with tapestry at the head. Then I saw that the greyish light of the bedroom came from the bed, or rather from what was on the bed. For it was covered with great caterpillars, a foot or more in length, which crawled over it. They were faintly luminous, and it was the light from them that showed me the room. Instead of the sucker-feet of ordinary caterpillars they had rows of pincers like crabs, and they moved by grasping what they lay on with their pincers, and then sliding their bodies forward. In colour these dreadful insects were yellowish-grey, and they were covered with irregular lumps and swellings. There must have been hundreds of them, for they formed a sort of writhing, crawling pyramid on the bed. Occasionally one fell off on to the floor, with a soft fleshy thud, and though the floor was of hard concrete, it yielded to the pincer-feet as if it had been putty, and, crawling back, the caterpillar would mount on to the bed again, to rejoin its fearful companions. They appeared to have no faces, so to speak, but at one end of them there was a mouth that opened sideways in respiration.

Then, as I looked, it seemed to me as if they all suddenly became conscious of my presence.

All the mouths, at any rate, were turned in my direction, and next moment they began dropping off the bed with those soft fleshy thuds on to the floor, and wriggling towards me. For one second a paralysis as of a dream was on me, but the next I was running upstairs again to my room, and I remember feeling the cold of the marble steps on my bare feet. I rushed into my bedroom, and slammed the door behind me, and then—I was certainly wide-awake now—I found myself standing by my bed with the sweat of terror pouring from me. The noise of the banged door still rang in my ears. But, as would have been more usual, if this had been mere nightmare, the terror that had been mine when I saw those foul beasts crawling about the bed or dropping softly on to the floor did not cease then. Awake, now, if dreaming before, I did not at all recover from the horror of dream: it did not seem to me that I had dreamed. And until dawn, I sat or stood, not daring to lie down, thinking that every rustle or movement that I heard was the approach of the caterpillars. To them and the claws that bit into the cement the wood of the door was child's play: steel would not keep them out.

But with the sweet and noble return of day the horror vanished: the whisper of wind became benignant again: the nameless fear, whatever it was, was smoothed out and terrified me no longer. Dawn broke, hueless at first; then it grew dove-coloured, then the flaming pageant of light spread over the sky.

The admirable rule of the house was that everybody had breakfast where and when he pleased, and in consequence it was not till lunch-time that I met any of the other members of our party, since I had breakfast on my balcony, and wrote letters and other things till lunch. In fact, I got down to that meal rather late, after the other three had begun. Between my knife and fork there was a small pill-box of cardboard, and as I sat down Inglis spoke.

"Do look at that," he said, "since you are interested in natural history. I found it crawling on my counterpane last night, and I don't know what it is."

I think that before I opened the pill-box I expected something of the sort which I found in it.

Inside it, anyhow, was a small caterpillar, greyish-yellow in colour, with curious bumps and excrescences on its rings. It was extremely active, and hurried round the box, this way and that.

Its feet were unlike the feet of any caterpillar I ever saw: they were like the pincers of a crab. I looked, and shut the lid down again.

"No, I don't know it," I said, "but it looks rather unwholesome. What are you going to do with it?"

"Oh, I shall keep it," said Inglis. "It has begun to spin: I want to see what sort of a moth it turns into."

I opened the box again, and saw that these hurrying movements were indeed the beginning of the spinning of the web of its cocoon. Then Inglis spoke again.

"It has got funny feet, too," he said. "They are like crabs' pincers. What's the Latin for crab?"

"Oh, yes, Cancer. So in case it is unique, let's christen it: 'Cancer Inglisensis.'" Then something happened in my brain, some momentary piecing together of all that I had seen or dreamed. Something in his words seemed to me to throw light on it all, and my own intense horror at the experience of the night before linked itself on to what he had just said. In effect, I took the box and threw it, caterpillar and all, out of the window. There was a gravel path just outside, and beyond it, a fountain playing into a basin. The box fell on to the middle of this.

Inglis laughed.

"So the students of the occult don't like solid facts," he said. "My poor caterpillar!"

The talk went off again at once on to other subjects, and I have only given in detail, as they happened, these trivialities in order to be sure myself that I have recorded everything that could have borne on occult subjects or on the subject of caterpillars. But at the moment when I threw the pill-box into the fountain, I lost my head: my only excuse is that, as is probably plain, the tenant of it was, in miniature, exactly what I had seen crowded on to the bed in the unoccupied room. And though this translation of those phantoms into flesh and blood—or whatever it is that caterpillars are made of—ought perhaps to have relieved the horror of the night, as a matter of fact it did nothing of the kind. It only made the crawling pyramid that covered the bed in the unoccupied room more hideously real.

After lunch we spent a lazy hour or two strolling about the garden or sitting in the loggia, and it must have been about four o'clock when Stanley and I started off to bathe, down the path that led by the fountain into which I had thrown the pill-box. The water was shallow and clear, and at the bottom of it I saw its white remains. The water had disintegrated the cardboard, and it had become no more than a few strips and shreds of sodden paper. The centre of the fountain was a marble Italian Cupid which squirted the water out of a wine-skin held under its arm. And crawling up its leg was the caterpillar. Strange and scarcely credible as it seemed, it must have survived the falling-to-bits of its prison, and made its way to shore, and there it was, out of arm's reach, weaving and waving this way and that as it evolved its cocoon.

Then, as I looked at it, it seemed to me again that, like the caterpillar I had seen last night, it saw me, and breaking out of the threads that surrounded it, it crawled down the marble leg of the Cupid and began swimming like a snake across the water of the fountain towards me. It came with extraordinary speed (the fact of a caterpillar being able to swim was new to me), and in another moment was crawling up the marble lip of the basin. Just then Inglis joined us.

"Why, if it isn't old 'Cancer Inglisensis' again," he said, catching sight of the beast. "What a tearing hurry it is in!"

We were standing side by side on the path, and when the caterpillar had advanced to within about a yard of us, it stopped, and began waving again as if in doubt as to the direction in which it should go. Then it appeared to make up its mind, and crawled on to Inglis' shoe.

"It likes me best," he said, "but I don't really know that I like it. And as it won't drown I think perhaps—"

He shook it off his shoe on to the gravel path and trod on it.

All afternoon the air got heavier and heavier with the Sirocco that was without doubt coming up from the south, and that night again I went up to bed feeling very sleepy; but below my drowsiness, so to speak, there was the consciousness, stronger than before, that there was something wrong in the house, that something dangerous was close at hand. But I fell asleep at once, and—how long after I do not know—either woke or dreamed I awoke, feeling that I must get up at once, or I should be too late. Then (dreaming or awake) I lay and fought this fear, telling myself that I was but the prey of my own nerves disordered by Sirocco or what not, and at the same time quite clearly knowing in another part of my mind, so to speak, that every moment's delay added to the danger. At last this second feeling became irresistible, and I put on coat and trousers and went out of my room on to the landing. And then I saw that I had already delayed too long, and that I was now too late.

The whole of the landing of the first floor below was invisible under the swarm of caterpillars that crawled there. The folding doors into the sitting-room from which opened the bedroom where I had seen them last night were shut, but they were squeezing through the cracks of it and dropping one by one through the keyhole, elongating themselves into mere string as they passed, and growing fat and lumpy again on emerging. Some, as if exploring, were nosing about the steps into the passage at the end of which were Inglis' rooms, others were crawling on the lowest steps of the staircase that led up to where I stood. The landing, however, was completely covered with them: I was cut off. And of the frozen horror that seized me when I saw that I can give no idea in words.

Then at last a general movement began to take place, and they grew thicker on the steps that led to Inglis' room. Gradually, like some hideous tide of flesh, they advanced along the passage, and I saw the foremost, visible by the pale grey luminousness that came from them, reach his door. Again and again I tried to shout and warn him, in terror all the time that they would turn at the sound of my voice and mount my stair instead, but for all my efforts I felt that no sound came from my throat. They crawled along the hinge-crack of his door, passing through as they had done before, and still I stood there, making impotent efforts to shout to him, to bid him escape while there was time.

At last the passage was completely empty: they had all gone, and at that moment I was conscious for the first time of the cold of the marble landing on which I stood barefooted. The dawn was just beginning to break in the Eastern sky.

Six months after I met Mrs. Stanley in a country house in England. We talked on many subjects and at last she said:

"I don't think I have seen you since I got that dreadful news about Arthur Inglis a month ago."

"I haven't heard," said I.

"No? He has got cancer. They don't even advise an operation, for there is no hope of a cure: he is riddled with it, the doctors say."

Now during all these six months I do not think a day had passed on which I had not had in my mind the dreams (or whatever you like to call them) which I had seen in the Villa Cascana.

"It is awful, is it not?" she continued, "and I feel I can't help feeling, that he may have—"

"Caught it at the villa?" I asked.

She looked at me in blank surprise.

"Why did you say that?" she asked. "How did you know?"

Then she told me. In the unoccupied bedroom a year before there had been a fatal case of cancer. She had, of course, taken the best advice and had been told that the utmost dictates of prudence would be obeyed so long as she did not put anybody to sleep in the room, which had also been thoroughly disinfected and newly whitewashed and painted. But—

The Golden Fly

Algernon Blackwood

It fell upon him out of a clear sky just when existence seemed
on its very best behaviour, and he savagely resented the undeserved
affliction of it. Involving him in an atrocious scandal that reflected
directly upon his honour, it destroyed in a moment the erection his
entire life had so laboriously built up—his reputation. In the eyes of
the world he was a broken, discredited man, at the very moment,
moreover, when his most cherished ambitions touched fulfilment.
And the cruelty of it appalled his sense of justice, for it was impossible to vindicate himself without inculpating others who were dearer
to him than life. It seemed more than he could bear; and the grim
course he contemplated—decision itself as yet hung darkly waiting
in the background—appeared the only way of escape that offered.

He had discussed the matter with friends until his brain
whirled. Their sympathy maddened him, with hints of *qui s'excuse
s'accuse,* and he turned at last in desperation to something that
could not answer back. For the first time in his life he turned to
Nature—to that dead, inanimate Nature he had left to poets and
rhapsodising women: 'I must face it alone,' he put it. For the Finger
of God was a phrase without meaning to him, and his entire being
contained no trace of the religious instinct. He was a business man,
honest, selfish, and ambitious; and the collapse of his worldly position was paramount to the collapse of the universe itself—his
universe, at any rate. This 'crumbling of the universe' was the
thought he took out with him. He left the house by the path that
led into solitude, and reached the heathery expanse that formed
one of the breathing-places of the New Forest. There he flung himself down wearily in the shadow of a little pine-copse. And his
crumbled universe lay down with him, for he could not escape it.

Taking the pistol from the hip-pocket where it hurt him, he lay upon his back and watched the clouds. Half stunned, half dazed, he stared into the sky. The perfumed wind played softly on his eyes; he smelt the heather-honey; golden flies hung motionless in the air, like coloured pins fastening the sunshine against the blue curtain of the summer, while dragonflies, like darting shuttles, wove across its pattern their threads of gleaming bronze. He heard the petulant crying of the peewits, and watched their tumbling flight. Below him tinkled a rivulet, its brown water rippling between banks of peaty earth. Everywhere was singing, peace, and careless unconcern.

And this lordly indifference of Nature calmed and soothed him. Neither human pain nor the injustice of man could shift the key of the water, alter the peewits' cry a single tone, nor influence one fraction of an inch those cloudy frigates of vapour that sailed the sky. The earth bulged sunwards as she had bulged for centuries. The power of her steady gait, superbly cairn, breathed everywhere with grandeur—undismayed, unhasting, and supremely confident... And, like the flash of those golden flies, there leaped suddenly upon him this vivid thought: that his world of agony lay neatly buttoned up within the tiny space of his own brain. Outside himself it had no existence at all. His mind contained it—the minute interior he called his heart. From this vaster world about him it lay utterly apart, like deeds in the black boxes of japanned tin he kept at the office, shut off from the universe, huddled in an overcrowded space within his skull.

How this commonplace thought reached him, garbed in such startling novelty, was odd enough; for it seemed as though the fierceness of his pain had burned away something. His thoughts it merely enflamed; but this other thing it consumed. Something that had obscured clear vision shrivelled before it as a piece of paper, eaten up by fire, dwindles down into a thimbleful of unimportant ashes. The thicket of his mind grew half transparent. At the farther end he saw, for the first time—light. The perspective of his inner life, hitherto so enormous, telescoped into the proportions of a miniature. Just as momentous and significant as before, it was somehow abruptly different—seen from another point of view. The suffering had burned up rubbish he himself had piled over the head of a little Fact. Like a point of metal that glows yet will not burn, he discerned in the depths of him the essential shining fact that not all this ruinous conflagration could destroy. And this brilliant, indestructible kernel was—his Innocence. The rest was self-reared rubbish: opinion of the world. He had magnified an atom into a universe....

Pain, as it seemed, had cleared a way for the sublimity of Nature to approach him. The calm old Universe rolled past. The deep, majestic Day gave him a push, as though the shoulder of some star had brushed his own. He had thought his feelings were the world: instead, they were merely his way of looking at it. The actual 'world' was some glorious, unchanging thing he never saw direct. His attitude of mind was but a peephole into it. The choice of his particular peephole, moreover, lay surely within the power of his individual will. The anguish, centred upon so small a point, had seemed to affect the entire spread universe around him, whereas in reality it affected nothing but his attitude of mind towards it. The truism struck him like a blow between the eyes, that a man is what he thinks or feels himself to be. It leaped the barrier between words and meaning. The intellectual concept became a hard-edged fact, because he realised it—for the first time in his very circumscribed life. And this dreadful pain that had made even suicide seem desirable was entirely a fabrication of his own mind. The universe about him rolled on just the same in the majesty of its eternal purpose. His tiny inner world was clouded, but the glory of this stupendous world about him was undimmed, untroubled, unaffected. Even death itself....

With a swift smash of the hand he crushed the golden fly that settled on his knee. The murder was done impulsively, utterly without intention. He watched the little point of gold quiver for a moment among the hairs of the rough tweed; then lie still for ever ... but the scent of heather-honey filled the air as before; the wind passed sighing through the pines; the clouds still sailed their uncharted sea of blue. There lay the whole spread surface of the Forest in the sun. Only the attitude of the golden fly towards it all was gone. A single, tiny point of view had disappeared. Nature passed on calmly and unhasting; she took no note.

Then, with a rush of awe, another thought flashed through him: Nature *had* taken note. There was a difference everywhere. Not a sparrow falleth, he remembered, without God knowing. God was certainly in Nature somewhere. His clumsy senses could not register this difference, yet it was there. His own small world, fed by these senses, was after all the merest little corner of Existence. To the whole of Existence, that included himself, the golden fly, the sun, and all the stars, he must somehow answer for his crime. It was a wanton interference with a sublime and sovereign Purpose that he now divined for the first time. He looked at the wee point of gold lying still and silent in the forest of hairs. He realised the enormity of his act. It could not have been graver had he put out the sun, or the little, insignificant flame of his own existence. He had done a criminal, evil thing, for he had put an end to a certain point of view; had wiped it out; made it impossible. Had the fly been quicker, less easily overwhelmed, or more tenacious of the scrap of universal life it used, Nature would at this instant be richer for its little contribution to the whole of things—to which he himself also belonged. And wherein, he asked himself, did he differ from that fly in the importance, the significance of his contribution to the universe? The soul ...? He had never given the question a single thought; but if the scrap of life he owned was called a soul, why should that point of golden glory not comprise one too? Its minute size, its trivial purpose, its few hours of apparently futile existence ... these formed no true criterion ...!

Similarly, the thought rushed over him, a Hand was being stretched out to crush himself. His pain was the shadow of its approach; anger in his heart, the warning. Unless he were quick enough, adroit and skilled enough, he also would be wiped out, while Nature continued her slow, unhasting way without him. His attitude towards the personal pain was really the test of his ability, of his merit—of his right to survive. Pain teaches, pain develops, pain brings growth: he had heard it since his copybook days. But now he realised it, as again thought leaped the barrier between familiar words and meaning. In his attitude of mind to his catastrophe lay his salvation or his ... death.

In some such confused and blundering fashion, because along unaccustomed channels, the truth charged into him to overwhelm, yet bringing with it an unwonted sense of joy that seemed to break a crust which long had held back—life. Thus tapped, these sources gushed forth and bubbled over, spread about his being, flooded him with hope and courage, above all with—calmness. Nature held forces just as real and living as human sympathy, and equally able to modify the soul. And Nature was always accessible. A sense of huge companionship, denied him by the littleness of his fellowmen, stole sweetly over him It was amazingly uplifting, yet fear came close behind it, as he realised the presumption of his former attitude of cynical indifference. These Powers were aware of his petty insolence, yet had not crushed him.... It was, of course, the awakening of the religious instinct in a man who hitherto had worshipped merely a rather low-grade form of intellect.

And, while the enormous confusion of it shook him, this sense of incommunicable sweetness remained. Bright haunting eyes, with love in them, gazed at him from the blue; and this thing that came so close, stood also far away upon the line of the horizon. It was everywhere. It filled the hollows, but towered over him as well towards the pinnaces of cloud. It was in the sharpness of the peewits' cry, and in the water's murmur. It whispered in the pine-boughs, and blazed in every patch of sunlight. And it was glory, pure and simple. It filled him with a sense of strength for which he could find but one description—Triumph.

And so, first, the anger faded from his mind and crept away. Resentment then slunk after it. Revolt and disappointment also melted, and bitterness gave place to the most marvellous peace the man had ever known. Then came resignation to fill the empty places. Pain, as a means and not an end, had cleared the way, though the accomplishment was like a miracle. But Conversion *is* a miracle. No ordinary pain can bring it. This anguish he understood now in a new relation to life—as something to be taken willingly into himself and dealt with, all regardless of public opinion. What people said and thought was in their world, not in his. It was less than nothing. The pain cultivated dormant tracts. The terror also purged. It disclosed....

He watched the wind, and even the wind brought revelation; for without obstacles in its path it would be silent. He watched the sunshine, and the sunshine taught him too; for without obstacles to fling it back against his eye, he could never see it. He would neither hear the tinkling water nor feel the summer heat unless both one and other overcame some reluctant medium in their pathways. And, similarly with his moral being—his pain resulted from the friction of his personal ambitions against the stress of some noble Power that sought to lift him higher. That Power he could not know direct, but he recognised its strain against him by the resistance it generated in the inertia of his selfishness. His attitude of mind had switched completely round. It was what the preachers termed development through suffering.

Moreover, he had acquired this energy of resistance somehow from the wind and sun and the beauty of a common summer's day. Their peace and strength had passed into himself. Unconsciously on his way home he drew upon it steadily. He tossed the pistol into a pool of water. Nature had healed him; and Nature, should he turn weak again, was always there. It was very wonderful. He wanted to sing....

The Red Spider
H. B. Holt

The Eastern sky had changed from bluest blue, through almost every hue of the rainbow, to cold grey, and the hush of the evening was over the land. On the still night air there came the crooning of a mother as she lulled her little black babe to slumber, and further in the distance, away from the native quarters, could be heard the rattle of traffic. But these signs of a tangible world were unheeded in a little darkening room where two men talked earnestly in a subdued whisper.

"Thou sayest," said one, "that the god within it still lives, and yet no living man has had the evidence of his own eyes that it is so?"

"Even so."

And as the gathering gloom took the world in its mysterious embrace, two tiny lights shown clearly and yet more clearly from the object upon which the two men gazed reverentially, almost fearfully.

"The god is a malignant and vengeful god, thou sayest. Verily, I believe it might be so."

"I tell thee 'tis so, for when these old dry limbs of mine were not yet grown to boyhood's estate, I heard it from the lips of my father."

"But may the god not be departed from this earthly cage many years?"

"Canst look and question thus?"

And the questioner bowed his head convinced. The night was now at hand; the last shadow had become merged in the darkness, and the two small lights shone vividly. The scintillating opalescent gleam was emitted from the eyes of a huge red spider, carved elaborately from a solid piece of wood. It was a triumph even of

Oriental deftness in its minute accuracy, yet hideous loathsome-
ness. The long angular legs were red, the abhorrent body was red, and
from the deep-set eyes, cruel and sinister, and speaking unutterable malice, issued the strange glow which pierced the darkness to
where the two men were seated.

For generations it had been where it now stood, the subject of
half-veneration and awe, for was not the old fakir said to have uttered a terrible warning on parting with it that it should be guarded
as a sacred object, for a horrible curse would fall upon the hands
which stole or broke it?

This, and this alone, was known by the men in the darkened
room, and a hush fell upon them as they gazed. Their Oriental
minds, prone to superstition, filled in the gap, and with reveren-
tial silence they departed from the room, leaving the great red spider to maintain its solitary vigilance in the darkness. The cruel,
sinister eyes shone even more venomously than usual, as they
stared unblinkingly after the disappearing figures.

Dr. Urillia looked back thoughtfully at the disappearing town
as the *Mercedes* slowly panted her way out to the open sea on her
long journey to the white cliffs of England. A lazy scholar, a student of Oriental customs and ideas, he was not contemplating with
pleasure the return to matter-of-fact England, where a negro is a
curiosity and a native tradition mere heathenish rubbish. The
strange beliefs of strange men had a peculiar fascination for him.
He had penetrated far enough to see that there were simpletons
and rogues amongst all classes of men, and he realized the inevitable result. But he had gone further; in his wanderings over the
face of the earth he had seen the unaccountable in more phases
than most people had, and knew that the finite mind of man—puny
man who crawled along the streets with his nose buried in the surroundings or his material mind fixed on politics—had never
grasped half of Nature's secrets. What particularly engrossed his
mind at this moment was an incident which occurred just as the
Mercedes cast off her moorings and swung out to sea. When the
gangways had been cleared and four feet of space separated the
ship from the dock side, a lascar had pushed his way through the
crowd, and with a flying leap landed on the deck. Tripping, he fell
like a log and lay prone with a broken leg. As he fell, a sharp crack,
not unlike the discharging of a pistol, was heard above the throbbing

of the engines and the hurry and scurry which always occurs on the departure of a vessel, and as an indignant officer approached the fallen creature, the latter hastily concealed something in his scanty clothing.

The great steamer had got well under way before the captain heard of the unexpected addition to his human freight, and sooner than lose a few precious minutes, he decided to carry his incapacitated passenger. So the man was carried below, not too gently, and deposited in a spare cabin in the forecastle.

The whole incident had impressed itself vividly on Dr. Urillia's mind, and he felt himself growing interested without a clearly defined reason. When the land had sunk beneath the horizon he made his way leisurely below deck and sought out the maimed lascar, now groaning in a bunk. Not without some deference—for a lascar is often an unpleasant thing to handle—he set the broken limb, and in doing so discovered the thing which the wretched creature had guarded so jealously.

It was the huge image of a red spider, perfect in workmanship, yet with one leg missing, broken off almost close to the scaly body. The doctor shuddered as he handled the repellant thing and placed it on a table. His knowledge of lascars and their temperament forbade him to inquire how it came into the man's possession. Interrogation would be perfectly useless, so he left his patient and strolled on to the deck, where he stared vacantly at the cold, quivering waves through which the *Mercedes* cut her way.

Again the sun was setting. The throb-throb of the engines was the only sound which came to the ears of the dirty lascar as he lay wracked with pain in the semi-darkness. Full consciousness was only just returning, and he moved his hands uneasily, as though searching for something. Suddenly, in spite of the pain in his broken limb, he raised himself on his arm and dived his hands under the coverlet. Still he found not what he sought, and his eyes moved slowly round until they became fixed in terror as they encountered two tiny lights which twinkled and glittered with an evil glow in the darkness. He uttered an inarticulate cry and sank back, with eyes still riveted on the beady lights. Total darkness now reigned in the cabin, save in the direction of the spider. Hungrily, greedily, the two eyes blazed forth their malignant hatred, and as the lascar lay transfixed in terror at the sight, all power to move being gone, the hideous fact was gradually born upon him that he was not alone—that his stolen treasure had an individuality of its own, and one from which he would fain escape. He shut his eyes; the sweat poured from every limb, and his brain reeled. He dared not look again, and fought with the power that told him to gaze back at the glittering object which he felt was drawing nearer and nearer. With a sickening sensation he realized that the something—the wretch knew it could be nothing but the possessor of those awful eyes—had mounted to where he lay and was trailing its long, sinuous legs up his paralyzed body. He would have shrieked aloud as he felt the thing creeping upwards—now it was on his chest—but the power of speech had left him. Shivering with abject terror, he looked cringingly into the baleful, glowing eyes which encountered his but a few inches away. Every fibre of his body he exerted in one last frantic effort to move and cast the hateful thing from him, but he was unable even to close his eyes now, and the spider drew its scaly legs across its face. A sharp, stinging pain on his temple restored his voice, and he uttered a high screech of unspeakable horror—and then remained still.

Dr. Urillia had smoked a last cigar and was just about to turn in for the night when he recollected the lascar and his hideous prize. Perhaps professional instinct, possibly curiosity, urged him to call in and see how his patient had progressed; also he desired to examine a little more closely the red spider which had caused him such an involuntary start. He had heard a weird legend of a red spider, and the thing interested him more and more.

The doctor entered the cabin where he had left the maimed man. He carried a lamp and placed it on a table, a morbid impulse impelling him to turn his gaze to where he had left the red spider. To his surprise it was no longer there. He turned to where the lascar had lain, but stood dumbfounded, for the patient's form had vanished. Dr. Urillia was not a coward; he had held even life itself in his hands many times, not realizing what fear was, but he knew intuitively that this was no matter of mere life and death—an impression was fast gaining a hold in his brain while dread of an unknown danger and fascination fought for mastery in him.

Throwing the coverlet aside he found the lascar's body had disappeared completely, and hidden in the folds of the cloth was a figure he more than half expected to find—a red spider.

He hastily summoned the captain and explained that the lascar was missing. The ship was searched, but no trace was discovered of the man who had so abruptly joined the vessel as it left the dock.

Dr. Urillia was thoughtful as he stared over the side of the ship at the racing waves and the phosphorescent sea. He was puzzled. Every moment conviction forced itself upon him. A man with a broken leg could not have scrambled overboard. And yet the lascar was gone. Moreover, had he been cast overboard, the incident would have been seen. Repressing a shudder, he once more turned in the direction of the cabin, whence the lascar had disappeared. Repugnantly he picked up and closely examined the carved leg of the spider, but after a moment's scrutiny almost dropped the object. There was no longer a missing leg—this was not the same image he had taken from the lascar. The first glance showed that it was redder, the legs were longer and more sinuous, the claws were sharper, and the evil looking body was an inch greater in diameter. This creature's whole form was perfect, nor did a minute examination of the cabin reveal the spider with the missing leg. Dr. Urillia looked with care, but, looking, knew it was hopeless to continue the search.

But he shrugged his shoulders, and for a while stared with morbid curiosity at the red creature.

Then, wrapping it up gingerly in the covering, he conveyed the spider on to the after-deck. He looked round—no one was watching and he dropped the bundle into the silent sea. As it disappeared, his brows contracted. He lighted another cigar, and looked absently at the quivering depth of water. Dr. Urillia had his theory, but it was unpleasant even for a student of Oriental beliefs.

An Egyptian Hornet
Algernon Blackwood

The word has an angry, malignant sound that brings the idea of attack vividly into the mind. There is a vicious sting about it somewhere—even a foreigner, ignorant of the meaning, must feel it. A hornet is wicked; it darts and stabs; it pierces, aiming without provocation for the face and eyes. The name suggests a metallic droning of evil wings, fierce flight, and poisonous assault. Though black and yellow, it sounds scarlet. There is blood in it. A striped tiger of the air in concentrated form! There is no escape—if it attacks.

In Egypt an ordinary bee is the size of an English hornet, but the Egyptian hornet is enormous. It is truly monstrous—an ominous, dying terror. It shares that universal quality of the land of the Sphinx and Pyramids—great size. It is a formidable insect, worse than scorpion or tarantula. The Rev. James Milligan, meeting one for the first time, realized the meaning of another word as well, a word he used prolifically in his eloquent sermons—devil.

One morning in April, when the heat began to bring the insects out, he rose as usual betimes and went across the wide stone corridor to his bath. The desert already glared in through the open windows. The heat would be afflicting later in the day, but at this early hour the cool north wind blew pleasantly down the hotel passages. It was Sunday, and at half-past eight o'clock he would appear to conduct the morning service for the English visitors. The floor of the passage-way was cold beneath his feet in their thin native slippers of bright yellow. He was neither young nor old; his salary was comfortable; he had a competency of his own, without wife or children to absorb it; the dry climate had been recommended to him; and—the big hotel took him in for next to nothing.

And he was thoroughly pleased with himself, for he was a sleek, vain, pompous, well-advertised personality, but mean as a rat. No worries of any kind were on his mind as, carrying sponge and towel, scented soap and a bottle of Scrubb's ammonia, he travelled amiably across the deserted, shining corridor to the bathroom. And nothing went wrong with the Rev. James Milligan until he opened the door, and his eye fell upon a dark, suspicious-looking object clinging to the window-pane in front of him.

And even then, at first, he felt no anxiety or alarm, but merely a natural curiosity to know exactly what it was—this little clot of an odd-shaped, elongated thing that stuck there on the wooden framework six feet before his aquiline nose. He went straight up to it to see—then stopped dead. His heart gave a distinct, unclerical leap. His lips formed themselves into unregenerate shape. He gasped: "Good God! What is it?" For something unholy, something wicked as a secret sin, stuck there before his eyes in the patch of blazing sunshine. He caught his breath.

For a moment he was unable to move, as though the sight half fascinated him. Then, cautiously and very slowly—stealthily, in fact—he withdrew towards the door he had just entered. Fearful of making the smallest sound, he retraced his steps on tiptoe. His yellow slippers shuffled. His dry sponge fell, and bounded till it settled, rolling close beneath the horribly attractive object facing him. From the safety of the open door, with ample space for retreat behind him, he paused and stared. His entire being focused itself in his eyes. It was a hornet that he saw. It hung there, motionless and threatening, between him and the bathroom door.

And at first he merely exclaimed—below his breath— "Good God! It's an Egyptian hornet!"

Being a man with a reputation for decided action, however, he soon recovered himself. He was well schooled in self-control. When people left his church at the beginning of the sermon, no muscle of his face betrayed the wounded vanity and annoyance that burned deep in his heart. But a hornet sitting directly in his path was a very different matter. He realized in a flash that he was poorly clothed—in a word, that he was practically half naked.

From a distance he examined this intrusion of the devil. It was calm and very still. It was wonderfully made, both before and behind. Its wings were folded upon its terrible body. Long, sinuous things, pointed like temptation, barbed as well, stuck out of it.

There was poison, and yet grace, in its exquisite presentment. Its shiny black was beautiful, and the yellow stripes upon its sleek, curved abdomen were like the gleaming ornaments upon some feminine body of the seductive world he preached against. Almost, he saw an abandoned dancer on the stage. And then, swiftly in his impressionable soul, the simile changed, and he saw instead more blunt and aggressive forms of destruction. The well-filled body, tapering to a horrid point, reminded him of those perfect engines of death that reduce hundreds to annihilation unawares—torpedoes, shells, projectiles, crammed with secret, desolating powers. Its wings, its awful, quiet head, its delicate, slim waist, its stripes of brilliant saffron—all these seemed the concentrated prototype of abominations made cleverly by the brain of man, and beautifully painted to disguise their invisible freight of cruel death.

"Bah!" he exclaimed, ashamed of his prolific imagination. "It's only a hornet after all—an insect!" And he contrived a hurried, careful plan. He aimed a towel at it, rolled up into a ball—but did not throw it. He might miss. He remembered that his ankles were unprotected. Instead, he paused again, examining the black and yellow object in safe retirement near the door, as one day he hoped to watch the world in leisurely retirement in the country. It did not move. It was fixed and terrible. It made no sound. Its wings were folded. Not even the black antennae, blunt at the tips like clubs, showed the least stir or tremble. It breathed, however. He watched the rise and fall of the evil body; it breathed air in and out as he himself did. The creature, he realized, had lungs and heart and organs. It had a brain! Its mind was active all this time. It knew it was being watched. It merely waited. Any second, with a whiz of fury, and with perfect accuracy of aim, it might dart at him and strike. If he threw the towel and missed—it certainly would.

There were other occupants of the corridor, however, and a sound of steps approaching gave him the decision to act. He would lose his bath if he hesitated much longer. He felt ashamed of his timidity, though "pusillanimity" was the word thought selected owing to the pulpit vocabulary it was his habit to prefer. He went with extreme caution towards the bathroom door, passing the point of danger so close that his skin turned hot and cold. With one foot gingerly extended, he recovered his sponge. The hornet did not move a muscle. But—it had seen him pass. It merely waited. All dangerous insects had that trick. It knew quite well he was inside;

it knew quite well he must come out a few minutes later; it also knew quite well that he was—naked.

Once inside the little room, he closed the door with exceeding gentleness, lest the vibration might stir the fearful insect to attack. The bath was already filled, and he plunged to his neck with a feeling of comparative security. A window into the outside passage he also closed, so that nothing could possibly come in. And steam soon charged the air and left its blurred deposit on the glass. For ten minutes he could enjoy himself and pretend that he was safe. For ten minutes he did so. He behaved carelessly, as though nothing mattered, and as though all the courage in the world were his. He splashed and soaped and sponged, making a lot of reckless noise. He got out and dried himself. Slowly the steam subsided, the air grew clearer, he put on dressing-gown and slippers. It was time to go out.

Unable to devise any further reason for delay, he opened the door softly half an inch—peeped out—and instantly closed it again with a resounding bang. He had heard a drone of wings. The insect had left its perch and now buzzed upon the floor directly in his path. The air seemed full of stings; he felt stabs all over him; his unprotected portions winced with the expectancy of pain. The beast knew he was coming out, and was waiting for him. In that brief instant he had felt its sting all over him, on his unprotected ankles, on his back, his neck, his cheeks, in his eyes, and on the bald clearing that adorned his Anglican head. Through the closed door he heard the ominous, dull murmur of his striped adversary as it beat its angry wings. Its oiled and wicked sting shot in and out with fury. Its deft legs worked. He saw its tiny waist already writhing with the lust of battle. Ugh! That tiny waist! A moment's steady nerve and he could have severed that cunning body from the directing brain with one swift, well-directed thrust. But his nerve had utterly deserted him.

Human motives, even in the professedly holy, are an involved affair at any time. Just now, in the Rev. James Milligan, they were inextricably mixed. He claims this explanation, at any rate, in excuse of his abominable subsequent behaviour. For, exactly at this moment, when he had decided to admit cowardice by ringing for the Arab servant, a step was audible in the corridor outside, and courage came with it into his disreputable heart. It was the step of the man he cordially "disapproved of," using the pulpit version of "hated and despised." He had overstayed his time, and the bath was in demand by Mr. Mullins. Mr. Mullins invariably followed him at seven-thirty; it was now a quarter to eight. And Mr. Mullins was a wretched drinking man— "a sot."

In a flash the plan was conceived and put into execution. The temptation, of course, was of the devil. Mr. Milligan hid the motive from himself, pretending he hardly recognized it. The plan was what men call a dirty trick; it was also irresistibly seductive. He opened the door, stepped boldly, nose in the air, right over the hideous insect on the floor, and fairly pranced into the outer passage. The brief transit brought a hundred horrible sensations—that the hornet would rise and sting his leg, that it would cling to his dressing-gown and stab his spine, that he would step upon it and die, like Achilles, of a heel exposed. But with these, and conquering them, was one other stronger emotion that robbed the lesser terrors of their potency—that Mr. Mullins would run precisely the same risks five seconds later, unprepared. He heard the gloating insect buzz and scratch the oilcloth. But it was behind him. He was safe!

"Good morning to you, Mr. Mullins," he observed with a gracious smile. "I trust I have not kept you waiting."

"Mornin'!" grunted Mullins sourly in reply, as he passed him with a distinctly hostile and contemptuous air. For Mullins, though depraved, perhaps, was an honest man, abhorring parsons and making no secret of his opinions—whence the bitter feeling.

All men, except those very big ones who are supermen, have something astonishingly despicable in them. The despicable thing in Milligan came uppermost now. He fairly chuckled. He met the snub with a calm, forgiving smile, and continued his shambling gait with what dignity he could towards his bedroom opposite. Then he turned his head to see. His enemy would meet an infuriated hornet—an Egyptian hornet!—and might not notice it. He might step on it. He might not. But he was bound to disturb it, and rouse it to attack. The chances were enormously on the clerical side. And its sting meant death.

"May God forgive me!" ran subconsciously through his mind. And side by side with the repentant prayer ran also a recognition of the tempter's eternal skill: "I hope the devil it will sting him!"

It happened very quickly. The Rev. James Milligan lingered a moment by his door to watch. He saw Mullins, the disgusting

Mullins, step blithely into the bathroom passage; he saw him pause, shrink back, and raise his arm to protect his face. He heard him swear aloud: "What's the d—d thing doing here? Have I really got 'em again?" And then he heard him laugh—a hearty, guffawing laugh of genuine relief— "It's real!"

The moment of revulsion was overwhelming. It filled the churchly heart with anguish and bitter disappointment. For a space he hated the whole race of men.

For the instant Mr. Mullins realized that the insect was not a fiery illusion of his disordered nerves, he went forward without the smallest hesitation. With his towel he knocked down the flying terror. Then he stooped. He gathered up the venomous thing his well-aimed blow had stricken so easily to the floor. He advanced with it, held at arm's length, to the window. He tossed it out carelessly. The Egyptian hornet flew away uninjured, and Mr. Mullins— the Mr. Mullins who drank, gave nothing to the church, attended no services, hated parsons, and proclaimed the fact with enthusiasm—this same Mr. Mullins went to his unearned bath without a scratch. But first he saw his enemy standing in the doorway across the passage, watching him—and understood. That was the awful part of it. Mullins would make a story of it, and the story would go the round of the hotel.

The Rev. James Milligan, however, proved that his reputation for self-control was not undeserved. He conducted morning service half an hour later with an expression of peace upon his handsome face. He conquered all outward sign of inward spiritual vexation; the wicked, he consoled himself, ever flourished like green bay trees. It was notorious that the righteous never have any luck at all! That was bad enough. But what was worse—and the Rev. James Milligan remembered for very long—was the superior ease with which Mullins had relegated both himself and hornet to the same level of comparative insignificance. Mullins ignored them both—which proved that he thought himself superior. Infinitely worse than the sting of any hornet in the world: he really *was* superior.

The Spider
Hans Heinz Ewers

When the student of medicine, Richard Bracquemont, decided to move into room #7 of the small Hotel Stevens, Rue Alfred Stevens (Paris 6), three persons had already hanged themselves from the cross-bar of the window in that room on three successive Fridays.

The first was a Swiss traveling salesman. They found his corpse on Saturday evening. The doctor determined that the death must have occurred between five and six o'clock on Friday afternoon. The corpse hung on a strong hook that had been driven into the window's cross-bar to serve as a hanger for articles of clothing. The window was closed, and the dead man had used the curtain cord as a noose. Since the window was very low, he hung with his knees practically touching the floor—a sign of the great discipline the suicide must have exercised in carrying out his design. Later, it was learned that he was a married man, a father. He had been a man of a continually happy disposition; a man who had achieved a secure place in life. There was not one written word to be found that would have shed light on his suicide ... not even a will. Furthermore, none of his acquaintances could recall hearing anything at all from him that would have permitted anyone to predict his end.

The second case was not much different. The artist, Karl Krause, a high wire cyclist in the nearby Medrano Circus, moved into room #7 two days later. When he did not show up at Friday's performance, the director sent an employee to the hotel. There, he found Krause in the unlocked room hanging from the window cross-bar in circumstances exactly like those of the previous suicide. This death was as perplexing as the first. Krause was popular. He earned a very high salary, and had appeared to enjoy life at its fullest.

Once again, there was no suicide note; no sinister hints. Krause's sole survivor was his mother to whom the son had regularly sent 300 marks on the first of the month.

For Madame Dubonnet, the owner of the small, cheap guesthouse whose clientele was composed almost completely of employees in a nearby Montmartre vaudeville theater, this second curious death in the same room had very unpleasant consequences. Already several of her guests had moved out, and other regular clients had not come back. She appealed for help to her personal friend, the inspector of police of the ninth precinct, who assured her that he would do everything in his power to help her. He pushed zealously ahead not only with the investigation into the grounds for the suicides of the two guests, but he also placed an officer in the mysterious room. This man, Charles-Maria Chaumié, actually volunteered for the task. Chaumié was an old "Marsouin," a marine sergeant with eleven years of service, who had lain so many nights at posts in Tonkin and Annam, and had greeted so many stealthily creeping river pirates with a shot from his rifle that he seemed ideally suited to encounter the "ghost" that everyone on Rue Alfred Stevens was talking about.

From then on, each morning and each evening, Chaumié paid a brief visit to the police station to make his report, which, for the first few days, consisted only of his statement that he had not noticed anything unusual. On Wednesday evening, however, he hinted that he had found a clue. Pressed to say more, he asked to be allowed more time before making any comment, since he was not sure that what he had discovered had any relationship to the two deaths, and he was afraid he might say something that would make him look foolish.

On Thursday, his behavior seemed a bit uncertain, but his mood was noticeably more serious. Still, he had nothing to report. On Friday morning, he came in very excited and spoke, half humorously, half seriously, of the strangely attractive power that his window had. He would not elaborate this notion and said that, in any case, it had nothing to do with the suicides; and that it would be ridiculous of him to say any more. When, on that same Friday, he failed to make his regular evening report, someone went to his room and found him hanging from the cross-bar of the window.

All the circumstances, down to the minutest detail, were the same here as in the previous cases. Chaumié's legs dragged along the ground. The curtain cord had been used for a noose. The window was closed, the door to the room had not been locked and death had occurred at six o'clock. The dead man s mouth was wide open, and his tongue protruded from it.

Chaumié's death, the third in as many weeks in room #7, had the following consequences: all the guests, with the exception of a German high-school teacher in room #16, moved out. The teacher took advantage of the occasion to have his rent reduced by a third. The next day, Mary Garden, the famous Opéra Comique singer, drove up to the Hotel Stevens and paid two hundred francs for the red curtain cord, saying it would bring her luck. The story, small consolation for Madame Dubonnet, got into the papers.

If these events had occurred in summer, in July or August, Madame Dubonnet would have secured three times that price for her cord, but as it was in the middle of a troubled year, with elections, disorders in the Balkans, bank crashes in New York, the visit of the King and Queen of England, the result was that the affaire Rue Alfred Stevens was talked of less than it deserved to be. As for the newspaper accounts, they were brief, being essentially the police reports word for word.

These reports were all that Richard Bracquemont, the medical student, knew of the matter. There was one detail about which he knew nothing because neither the police inspector nor any of the eyewitnesses had mentioned it to the press. It was only later, after what happened to the medical student, that anyone remembered that when the police removed Sergeant Charles-Maria Chaumié's body from the window cross-bar a large black spider crawled from the dead man's open mouth. A hotel porter flicked it away, exclaiming, "Ugh, another of those damned creatures." When in later investigations which concerned themselves mostly with Bracquemont the servant was interrogated, he said that he had seen a similar spider crawling on the Swiss traveling salesman's shoulder when his body was removed from the window cross-bar. But Richard Bracquemont knew nothing of all this.

It was more than two weeks after the last suicide that Bracquemont moved into the room. It was a Sunday. Bracquemont conscientiously recorded everything that happened to him in his journal. That journal now follows.

Monday, February 28

I moved in yesterday evening. I unpacked my two wicker suit-
cases and straightened the room a little. Then I went to bed. I slept
so soundly that it was nine o'clock the next morning before a knock
at my door woke me. It was my hostess, bringing me breakfast herself. One could read her concern for me in the eggs, the bacon and
the superb café au lait she brought me. I washed and dressed, then
smoked a pipe as I watched the servant make up the room.

So, here I am. I know well that the situation may prove dangerous, but I think I may just be the one to solve the problem. If, once
upon a time, Paris was worth a mass (conquest comes at a dearer
rate these days), it is well worth risking my life *pour un si bel enjeu*.
I have at least one chance to win, and I mean to risk it.

As it is, I'm not the only one who has had this notion. Twenty-
seven people have tried for access to the room. Some went to the
police, some went directly to the hotel owner. There were even
three women among the candidates. There was plenty of competition. No doubt the others are poor devils like me.

And yet, it was I who was chosen. Why? Because I was the only
one who hinted that I had some plan—or the semblance of a plan.
Naturally, I was bluffing.

These journal entries are intended for the police. I must say
that it amuses me to tell those gentlemen how neatly I fooled them.
If the Inspector has any sense, he'll say, "Hm. This Bracquemont
is just the man we need." In any case, it doesn't matter what he'll
say. The point is I'm here now, and I take it as a good sign that I've
begun my task by bamboozling the police. I had gone first to Madame Dubonnet, and it was she who sent me to the police. They
put me off for a whole week—as they put off my rivals as well. Most
of them gave up in disgust, having something better to do than
hang around the musty squad room. The Inspector was beginning
to get irritated at my tenacity. At last, he told me I was wasting my
time. That the police had no use for bungling amateurs. "Ah, if
only you had a plan. Then …"

On the spot, I announced that I had such a plan, though naturally I had no such thing. Still, I hinted that my plan was brilliant,
but dangerous, that it might lead to the same end as that which
had overtaken the police officer, Chaumié. Still, I promised to describe it to him if he would give me his word that he would personally put it into effect. He made excuses, claiming he was too busy

but when he asked me to give him at least a hint of my plan, I saw that I had picqued his interest.

I rattled off some nonsense made up of whole cloth. God alone knows where it all came from. I told him that six o'clock of a Friday is an occult hour. It is the last hour of the Jewish week; the hour when Christ disappeared from his tomb and descended into hell. That he would do well to remember that the three suicides had taken place at approximately that hour. That was all I could tell him just then, I said, but I pointed him to *The Revelations of St. John.*

The Inspector assumed the look of a man who understood all that I had been saying, then he asked me to come back that evening.

I returned, precisely on time, and noted a copy of the *New Testament* on the Inspector's desk. I had, in the meantime, been at the *Revelations* myself without however having understood a syllable. Perhaps the Inspector was cleverer than I. Very politely—nay—deferentially, he let me know that, despite my extremely vague intimations, he believed he grasped my line of thought and was ready to expedite my plan in every way.

And here, I must acknowledge that he has indeed been tremendously helpful. It was he who made the arrangement with the owner that I was to have anything I needed so long as I stayed in the room. The Inspector gave me a pistol and a police whistle, and he ordered the officers on the beat to pass through the Rue Alfred Stevens as often as possible, and to watch my window for any signal. Most important of all, he had a desk telephone installed which connects directly with the police station. Since the station is only four minutes away, I see no reason to be afraid.

Wednesday, March 1
Nothing has happened. Not yesterday. Not today.

Madame Dubonnet brought a new curtain cord from another room—the rooms are mostly empty, of course. Madame Dubonnet takes every opportunity to visit me, and each time she brings something with her. I have asked her to tell me again everything that happened here, but I have learned nothing new. She has her own opinion of the suicides. Her view is that the music hall artist, Krause, killed himself because of an unhappy love affair. During the last year that Krause lived in the hotel, a young woman had made frequent visits to him. These visits had stopped, just before his death. As for the Swiss gentleman, Madame Dubonnet confessed herself baffled. On the other hand, the death of the policeman was easy to explain. He had killed himself just to annoy her.

These are sad enough explanations, to be sure, but I let her babble on to take the edge off my boredom.

Thursday, March 3

Still nothing. The Inspector calls twice a day. Each time, I tell him that all is well. Apparently, these words do not reassure him.

I have taken out my medical books and I study, so that my self-imposed confinement will have some purpose.

Friday. March 4

I ate uncommonly well at noon. The landlady brought me half a bottle of champagne. It seemed a meal for a condemned man. Madame Dubonnet looked at me as if I were already three-quarters dead. As she was leaving, she begged me tearfully to come with her, fearing no doubt that I would hang myself "just to annoy her."

I studied the curtain cord once again. Would I hang myself with it? Certainly, I felt little desire to do so. The cord is stiff and rough—not the sort of cord one makes a noose of. One would need to be truly determined before one could imitate the others.

I am seated now at my table. At my left, the telephone. At my right, the revolver. I'm not frightened; but I am curious.

Six o'clock, the same evening

Nothing has happened. I was about to add, "Unfortunately." The fatal hour has come—and has gone, like any six o'clock on any evening. I won't hide the fact that I occasionally felt a certain impulse to go to the window, but for a quite different reason than one might imagine. The Inspector called me at least ten times between five and six o'clock. He was as impatient as I was. Madame Dubonnet, on the other hand, is happy. A week has passed without someone in #7 hanging himself. Marvelous.

Monday, March 7

I have a growing conviction that I will learn nothing; that the previous suicides are related to the circumstances surrounding the lives of the three men. I have asked the Inspector to investigate the cases further, convinced that someone will find their motivations.

As for me, I hope to stay here as long as possible. I may not conquer Paris here, but I live very well and I'm fattening up nicely. I'm also studying hard, and I am making real progress. There is another reason, too, that keeps me here.

Wednesday, March 9
So! I have taken one step more. Clarimonda.

I haven't yet said anything about Clarimonda. It is she who is my "third" reason for staying here. She is also the reason I was tempted to go to the window during the "fateful" hour last Friday. But of course, not to hang myself.

Clarimonda. Why do I call her that? I have no idea what her name is, but it ought to be Clarimonda. When finally I ask her name, I'm sure it will turn out to be Clarimonda. I noticed her almost at once ... in the very first days. She lives across the narrow street; and her window looks right into mine. She sits there, behind her curtains.

I ought to say that she noticed me before I saw her; and that she was obviously interested in me. And no wonder. The whole neighborhood knows I am here, and why. Madame Dubonnet has seen to that.

I am not of a particularly amorous disposition. In fact, my relations with women have been rather meager. When one comes from Verdun to Paris to study medicine, and has hardly money enough for three meals a day, one has something else to think about besides love. I am then not very experienced with women, and I may have begun my adventure with her stupidly. Never mind. It's exciting just the same.

At first, the idea of establishing some relationship with her simply did not occur to me. It was only that, since I was here to make observations, and, since there was nothing in the room to observe, I thought I might as well observe my neighbor—openly, professionally. Anyhow, one can't sit all day long just reading.

Clarimonda, I have concluded, lives alone in the small flat across the way. The flat has three windows, but she sits only before the window that looks into mine. She sits there, spinning on an old-fashioned spindle, such as my grandmother inherited from a great aunt. I had no idea anyone still used such spindles. Clarimonda's spindle is a lovely object. It appears to be made of ivory; and the thread she spins is of an exceptional fineness. She works all day behind her curtains, and stops spinning only as the sun goes down. Since darkness comes abruptly here in this narrow street and in this season of fogs, Clarimonda disappears from her place at five o'clock each evening. I have never seen a light in her flat.

What does Clarimonda look like? I'm not quite sure. Her hair is black and wavy; her face pale. Her nose is short and finely shaped with delicate nostrils that seem to quiver. Her lips, too, are pale: and when she smiles, it seems that her small teeth are as keen as those of some beast of prey. Her eyelashes are long and dark; and her huge dark eyes have an intense glow. I guess all these details more than I know them. It is hard to see clearly through the curtains.

Something else: she always wears a black dress embroidered with a lilac motif; and black gloves, no doubt to protect her hands from the effects of her work. It is a curious sight: her delicate hands moving perpetually, swiftly grasping the thread, pulling it, releasing it, taking it up again; as if one were watching the indefatigable motions of an insect.

Our relationship? For the moment, still very superficial, though it *feels* deeper. It began with a sudden exchange of glances in which each of us noted the other. I must have pleased her, because one day she studied me a while longer, then smiled tentatively. Naturally, I smiled back. In this fashion, two days went by, each of us smiling more frequently with the passage of time. Yet something kept me from greeting her directly.

Until today. This afternoon, I did it. And Clarimonda returned my greeting. It was done subtly enough, to be sure, but I saw her nod.

Thursday, March 10
Yesterday, I sat for a long time over my books, though I can't truthfully say that I studied much. I built castles in the air and dreamed of Clarimonda.

I slept fitfully.

This morning, when I approached my window, Clarimonda was already in her place. I waved, and she nodded back. She laughed and studied me for a long time.

I tried to read, but I felt much too uneasy. Instead, I sat down at my window and gazed at Clarimonda. She too had laid her work aside. Her hands were folded in her lap. I drew my curtain wider with the window cord, so that I might see better. At the same moment, Clarimonda did the same with the curtains at her window. We exchanged smiles.

We must have spent a full hour gazing at each other.

Finally, she took up her spinning.

Saturday, March 12

The days pass. I eat and drink. I sit at the desk. I light my pipe; I look down at my book but I don't read a word, though I try again and again. Then I go to the window where I wave to Clarimonda. She nods. We smile. We stare at each other for hours.

Yesterday afternoon, at six o'clock, I grew anxious. The twilight came early, bringing with it something like anguish. I sat at my desk. I waited until I was invaded by an irresistible need to go to the window—not to hang myself; but just to see Clarimonda. I sprang up and stood beside the curtain where it seemed to me I had never been able to see so clearly, though it was already dark. Clarimonda was spinning, but her eyes looked into mine. I felt myself strangely contented even as I experienced a light sensation of fear.

The telephone rang. It was the Inspector tearing me out of my trance with his idiotic questions. I was furious.

This morning, the Inspector and Madame Dubonnet visited me. She is enchanted with how things are going. I have now lived for two weeks in room #7. The Inspector, however, does not feel he is getting results. I hinted mysteriously that I was on the trail of something most unusual. The jackass took me at my word and fulfilled my dearest wish. I've been allowed to stay in the room for another week. God knows it isn't Madame Dubonnet's cooking or wine-cellar that keeps me here. How quickly one can be sated with such things. No. I want to stay because of the window Madame Dubonnet fears and hates. That beloved window that shows me Clarimonda. I have stared out of my window, trying to discover whether she ever leaves her room, but I've never seen her set foot on the street.

As for me, I have a large, comfortable armchair and a green shade over the lamp whose glow envelopes me in warmth. The Inspector has left me with a huge packet of fine tobacco—and yet I cannot work. I read two or three pages only to discover that I haven't understood a word. My eyes see the letters, but my brain refuses to make any sense of them. Absurd. As if my brain were posted: "No Trespassing." It is as if there were no room in my head for any other thought than the one: Clarimonda. I push my books away; I lean back deeply into my chair. I dream.

Sunday, March 13

This morning I watched a tiny drama while the servant was tidying my room. I was strolling in the corridor when I paused before a small window in which a large garden spider had her web. Madame Dubonnet will not have it removed because she believes spiders bring luck, and she's had enough misfortunes in her house lately. Today, I saw a much smaller spider, a male, moving across the strong threads towards the middle of the web, but when his movements alerted the female, he drew back shyly to the edge of the web from which he made a second attempt to cross it. Finally, the female in the middle appeared attentive to his wooing, and stopped moving. The male tugged at a strand gently, then more strongly till the whole web shook. The female stayed motionless. The male moved quickly forward and the female received him quietly, calmly, giving herself over completely to his embraces. For a long minute, they hung together motionless at the center of the huge web.

Then I saw the male slowly extricating himself, one leg over the other. It was as if he wanted tactfully to leave his companion alone in the dream of love, but as he started away, the female, overwhelmed by a wild life, was after him, hunting him ruthlessly. The male let himself drop from a thread; the female followed, and for a while the lovers hung there, imitating a piece of art. Then they fell to the window-sill where the male, summoning all his strength, tried again to escape. Too late. The female already had him in her powerful grip, and was carrying him back to the center of the web. There, the place that had just served as the couch for their lascivious embraces took on quite another aspect. The lover wriggled, trying to escape from the female's wild embrace, but she was too much for him. It was not long before she had wrapped him completely in her thread, and he was helpless. Then she dug her sharp pincers into his body, and sucked full draughts of her young lover's blood. Finally, she detached herself from the pitiful and unrecognizable shell of his body and threw it out of her web.

So that is what love is like among these creatures. Well for me that I am not a spider.

Monday, March 14

I don't look at my books any longer. I spend my days at the window. When it is dark, Clarimonda is no longer there, but if I close my eyes, I continue to see her.

This journal has become something other than I intended. I've spoken about Madame Dubonnet, about the Inspector; about spiders and about Clarimonda. But I've said nothing about the discoveries I undertook to make. It can't be helped.

Tuesday, March 15

We have invented a strange game, Clarimonda and I. We play it all day long. I greet her; then she greets me. Then I tap my fingers on the windowpanes. The moment she sees me doing that, she too begins tapping. I wave to her; she waves back. I move my lips as if speaking to her; she does the same. I run my hand through my sleep-disheveled hair and instantly her hand is at her forehead. It is a child's game, and we both laugh over it. Actually, she doesn't laugh. She only smiles a gently contained smile. And I smile back in the same way.

The game is not as trivial as it seems. It's not as if we were grossly imitating each other—that would weary us both. Rather, we are communicating with each other. Sometimes, telepathically, it would seem, since Clarimonda follows my movements instantaneously almost before she has had time to see them. I find myself inventing new movements, or new combinations of movements, but each time she repeats them with disconcerting speed. Sometimes. I change the order of the movements to surprise her, making whole series of gestures as rapidly as possible; or I leave out some motions and weave in others, the way children play "Simon Says." What is amazing is that Clarimonda never once makes a mistake, no matter how quickly I change gestures.

That's how I spend my days ... but never for a moment do I feel that I'm killing time. It seems, on the contrary, that never in my life have I been better occupied.

Wednesday. March 16

Isn't it strange that it hasn't occurred to me to put my relationship with Clarimonda on a more serious basis than these endless games. Last night, I thought about this ... I can, of course, put on my hat and coat, walk down two flights of stairs, take five steps across the street and mount two flights to her door which is marked with a small sign that says "Clarimonda." Clarimonda what? I don't know. Something. Then I can knock and ...

Up to this point I imagine everything very clearly, but I cannot see what should happen next. I know that the door opens. But then I stand before it, looking into a dark void. Clarimonda doesn't come. Nothing comes. Nothing is there, only the black, impenetrable dark.

Sometimes, it seems to me that there can be no other Clarimonda but the one I see in the window; the one who plays gesture-games with me. I cannot imagine a Clarimonda wearing a hat, or a dress other than her black dress with the lilac motif. Nor can I imagine a Clarimonda without black gloves. The very notion that I might encounter Clarimonda somewhere in the streets or in a restaurant eating, drinking or chatting is so improbable that it makes me laugh.

Sometimes I ask myself whether I love her. It's impossible to say, since I have never loved before. However, if the feeling that I have for Clarimonda is really—love, then love is something entirely different from anything I have seen among my friends or read about in novels. It is hard for me to be sure of my feelings and harder still to think of anything that doesn't relate to Clarimonda or, what is more important, to our game. Undeniably, it is our game that concerns me. Nothing else—and this is what I understand least of all.

There is no doubt that I am drawn to Clarimonda, but with this attraction there is mingled another feeling, fear. No. That's not it either. Say rather a vague apprehension in the presence of the unknown. And this anxiety has a strangely voluptuous quality so that I am at the same time drawn to her even as I am repelled by her. It is as if I were moving in giant circles around her, sometimes coming close, sometimes retreating ... back and forth, back and forth. Once, I am sure of it, it will happen, and I will join her.

Clarimonda sits at her window and spins her slender, eternally fine thread, making a strange cloth whose purpose I do not understand. I am amazed that she is able to keep from tangling her delicate thread. Hers is surely a remarkable design, containing mythical beasts and strange masks.

Thursday, March 17
I am curiously excited. I don't talk to people any more. I barely say "hello" to Madame Dubonnet or to the servant. I hardly give

myself time to eat. All I can do is sit at the window and play the game with Clarimonda. It is an enthralling game. Overwhelming.

I have the feeling something will happen tomorrow.

Friday, March 18

Yes. Yes. Something will happen today. I tell myself—as loudly as I can—that that's why I am here. And yet, horribly enough, I am afraid. And in the fear that the same thing is going to happen to me as happened to my predecessors, there is strangely mingled another fear: a terror of Clarimonda. And I cannot separate the two fears.

I am frightened. I want to scream.

Six o'clock, evening

I have my hat and coat on. Just a couple of words.

At five o'clock, I was at the end of my strength. I'm perfectly aware now that there is a relationship between my despair and the "sixth hour" that was so significant in the previous weeks. I no longer laugh at the trick I played the Inspector.

I was sitting at the window, trying with all my might to stay in my chair, but the window kept drawing me. I had to resume the game with Clarimonda. And yet, the window horrified me. I saw the others hanging there: the Swiss traveling salesman, fat, with a thick neck and a grey stubbly beard; the thin artist; and the powerful police sergeant. I saw them, one after the other, hanging from the same hook, their mouths open, their tongues sticking out. And then, I saw myself among them.

Oh, this unspeakable fear. It was clear to me that it was provoked as much by Clarimonda as by the cross-bar and the horrible hook. May she pardon me ... but it is the truth. In my terror, I keep seeing the three men hanging there, their legs dragging on the floor.

And yet, the fact is I had not felt the slightest desire to hang myself; nor was I afraid that I would want to do so. No, it was the window I feared; and Clarimonda. I was sure that something horrid was going to happen. Then I was overwhelmed by the need to go to the window—to stand before it. I had to ...

The telephone rang. I picked up the receiver and before I could hear a word, I screamed, "Come. Come at once."

It was as if my shrill cry had in that instant dissipated the shadows from my soul. I grew calm. I wiped the sweat from my forehead.

I drank a glass of water. Then I considered what I should say to the Inspector when he arrived. Finally, I went to the window. I waved and smiled. And Clarimonda too waved and smiled.

Five minutes later, the Inspector was here. I told him that I was getting to the bottom of the matter, but I begged him not to question me just then. That very soon I would be in a position to make important revelations. Strangely enough, though I was lying to him. I myself had the feeling that I was telling the truth. Even now, against my will, I have that same conviction.

The Inspector could not help noticing my agitated state of mind, especially since I apologized for my anguished cry over the telephone. Naturally, I tried to explain it to him, and yet I could not find a single reason to give for it. He said affectionately that there was no need ever to apologize to him; that he was always at my disposal; that that was his duty. It was better that he should come a dozen times to no effect rather than fail to be here when he was needed. He invited me to go out with him for the evening. It would be a distraction for me. It would do me good not to be alone for a while. I accepted the invitation though I was very reluctant to leave the room.

Saturday, March 19

We went to the *Gaieté Rochechouart*, *La Cigale*, and *La Lune Rousse*. The Inspector was right: It was good for me to get out and breathe the fresh air. At first, I had an uncomfortable feeling, as if I were doing something wrong; as if I were a deserter who had turned his back on the flag. But that soon went away. We drank a lot, laughed and chatted. This morning, when I went to my window, Clarimonda gave me what I thought was a look of reproach, though I may only have imagined it. How could she have known that I had gone out last night? In any case, the look lasted only for an instant, then she smiled again.

We played the game all day long.

Sunday, March 20

Only one thing to record: we played the game.

Monday, March 21

We played the game—all day long.

Tuesday, March 22

Yes, the game. We played it again. And nothing else. Nothing at all.

Sometimes I wonder what is happening to me? What is it I want? Where is all this leading? I know the answer: there is nothing else I want except what is happening. *It* is what I want ... what I long for. This only.

Clarimonda and I have spoken with each other in the course of the last few days, but very briefly; scarcely a word. Sometimes we moved our lips, but more often we just looked at each other with deep understanding.

I was right about Clarimonda's reproachful look because I went out with the Inspector last Friday. I asked her to forgive me. I said it was stupid of me, and spiteful to have gone. She forgave me, and I promised never to leave the window again. We kissed, pressing our lips against each of our windowpanes.

Wednesday, March 23

I know now that I love Clarimonda. That she has entered into the very fiber of my being. It may be that the loves of other men are different. But does there exist one head, one ear, one hand that is exactly like hundreds of millions of others? There are always differences, and it must be so with love. My love is strange, I know that, but is it any the less lovely because of that? Besides, my love makes me happy.

If only I were not so frightened. Sometimes my terror slumbers and I forget it for a few moments, then it wakes and does not leave me. The fear is like a poor mouse trying to escape the grip of a powerful serpent. Just wait a bit, poor sad terror. Very soon, the serpent love will devour you.

Thursday, March 24

I have made a discovery: I don't play with Clarimonda. She plays with me.

Last night, thinking as always about our game, I wrote down five new and intricate gesture patterns with which I intended to surprise Clarimonda today. I gave each gesture a number. Then I practiced the series, so I could do the motions as quickly as possible, forwards or backwards. Or sometimes only the even-numbered ones, sometimes the odd. Or the first and the last of the five patterns.

It was tiring work, but it made me happy and seemed to bring Clarimonda closer to me. I practiced for hours until I got all the motions down pat, like clockwork.

This morning, I went to the window. Clarimonda and I greeted each other, then our game began. Back and forth! It was incredible how quickly she understood what was to be done; how she kept pace with me.

There was a knock at the door. It was the servant bringing me my shoes. I took them. On my way back to the window, my eye chanced to fall on the slip of paper on which I had noted my gesture patterns. It was then that I understood: in the game just finished, *I had not made use of a single one of my patterns.*

I reeled back and had to hold on to the chair to keep from falling. It was unbelievable. I read the paper again—and again. It was still true: I had gone through a long series of gestures at the window, and not one of the patterns had been mine.

I had the feeling, once more, that I was standing before Clarimonda's wide open door, through which, though I stared. I could see nothing but a dark void. I knew, too, that if I chose to turn from that door now. I might be saved; and that I still had the power to leave. And yet, I did not leave—because I felt myself at the very edge of the mystery: as if I were holding the secret in my hands. "Paris! You will conquer Paris," I thought. And in that instant, Paris was more powerful than Clarimonda.

I don't think about that any more. Now, I feel only love. Love, and a delicious terror. Still, the moment itself endowed me with strength. I read my notes again, engraving the gestures on my mind. Then I went back to the window only to become aware that *there was not one of my patterns that I wanted to use.* Standing there, it occurred to me to rub the side of my nose; instead I found myself pressing my lips to the windowpane. I tried to drum with my fingers on the window sill; instead, I brushed my fingers through my hair. And so I understood that it was not that Clarimonda did what I did. Rather, my gestures followed her lead and with such lightning rapidity that we seemed to be moving simultaneously. I, who had been so proud because I thought I had been influencing her, I was in fact being influenced by her. Her influence ... so gentle ... so delightful.

I have tried another experiment. I clenched my hands and put them in my pockets firmly intending not to move them one bit.

Clarimonda raised her hand and, smiling at me, made a scolding gesture with her finger. I did not budge, and yet I could feel how my right hand wished to leave my pocket. I shoved my fingers against the lining, but against my will, my hand left the pocket; my arm rose into the air. In my turn, I made a scolding gesture with my finger and smiled. It seemed to me that it was not I who was doing all this. It was a stranger whom I was watching. But, of course, I was mistaken. It was I making the gesture, and the person watching me was the stranger; that very same stranger who, not long ago, was so sure that he was on the edge of a great discovery. In any case, it was not I.

Of what use to me is this discovery? I am here to do Clarimonda's will. Clarimonda, whom I love with an anguished heart.

Friday, March 25

I have cut the telephone cord. I have no wish to be continually disturbed by the idiotic inspector just as the mysterious hour arrives.

God. Why did I write that? Not a word of it is true. It is as if someone else were directing my pen.

But I want to ... want to ... to write the truth here ... though it is costing me great effort. But I want to ... once more ... do what I want.

I have cut the telephone cord ... ah ...

Because I had to ... there it is. Had to ...

We stood at our windows this morning and played the game, which is now different from what it was yesterday. Clarimonda makes a movement and I resist it for as long as I can. Then I give in and do what she wants without further struggle. I can hardly express what a joy it is to be so conquered; to surrender entirely to her will.

We played. All at once, she stood up and walked back into her room, where I could not see her; she was so engulfed by the dark. Then she came back with a desk telephone, like mine, in her hands. She smiled and set the telephone on the window sill, after which she took a knife and cut the cord. Then I carried my telephone to the window where I cut the cord. After that, I returned my phone to its place.

That's how it happened ...

I sit at my desk where I have been drinking tea the servant brought me. He has come for the empty teapot, and I ask him for the time, since my watch isn't running properly. He says it is five fifteen. Five fifteen ...

I know that if I look out of my window, Clarimonda will be there making a gesture that I will have to imitate. I will look just the same. Clarimonda is there, smiling. If only I could turn my eyes away from hers.

Now she parts the curtain. She takes the cord. It is red, just like the cord in my window. She ties a noose and hangs the cord on the hook in the window cross-bar.

She sits down and smiles.

No. Fear is no longer what I feel. Rather, it is a sort of oppressive terror which I would not want to avoid for anything in the world. Its grip is irresistible, profoundly cruel, and voluptuous in its attraction.

I could go to the window, and do what she wants me to do, but I wait. I struggle. I resist though I feel a mounting fascination that becomes more intense each minute.

Here I am once more. Rashly, I went to the window where I did what Clarimonda wanted. I took the cord, tied a noose, and hung it on the hook ...

Now, I want to see nothing else—except to stare at this paper. Because if I look. I know what she will do ... now ... at the sixth hour of the last day of the week. If I see her, I will have to do what she wants. Have to ...

I won't see her ...

I laugh. Loudly. No. I'm not laughing. Something is laughing in me, and I know why. It is because of my "I won't" ...

I won't, and yet I know very well that I have to ... have to look at her. I must ... must ... and then ... all that follows.

If I still wait, it is only to prolong this exquisite torture. Yes, that's it. This breathless anguish is my supreme delight. I write quickly, quickly ... just so I can continue to sit here; so I can attenuate these seconds of pain.

Again, terror. Again. I know that I will look toward her. That I will stand up. That I will hang myself.

That doesn't frighten me. That is beautiful ... even precious.

There is something else. *What will happen afterwards?* I don't know, but since my torment is so delicious. I feel ... feel that something horrible must follow.

Think ... think ... Write something. Anything at all ... to keep from looking toward her ... My name ... Richard Bracquemont. Richard Bracquemont ... Richard Bracquemont ... Richard ...

I can't ... go on. I must ... no ... no ... must look at her ... Richard Bracquemont ... no ... no more ... Richard ... Richard Bracque ...

The inspector of the ninth precinct, after repeated and vain efforts to telephone Richard, arrived at the Hotel Stevens at 6:05. He found the body of the student Richard Bracquemont hanging from the cross-bar of the window in room #7, in the same position as each of his three predecessors.

The expression on the student's face, however, was different, reflecting an appalling fear. Bracquemont's eyes were wide open and bulging from their sockets. His lips were drawn into a *rictus*, and his jaws were clamped together. A huge black spider whose body was dotted with purple spots lay crushed and nearly bitten in two between his teeth.

On the table, there lay the student's journal. The inspector read it and went immediately to investigate the house across the street. What he learned was that the second floor of that building had not been lived in for many months.

Paris 1908

The Eggs of the Silver Moon
Robert W. Chambers

In the new white marble Administration Building at Bronx Park, my private office separated the offices of Dr. Silas Quint and Professor Boomly; and it had been arranged so on purpose, because of the increasingly frequent personal misunderstanding between these two celebrated entomologists. It was very plain to me that a crisis in this quarrel was rapidly approaching.

A bitter animosity had for some months existed on both sides, born of the most intense professional jealousy. They had been friends for years. No unseemly rivalry disturbed this friendship as long as it was merely a question of collecting, preparing, and mounting for exhibition the vast numbers of butterflies and moths which haunt this insectivorous earth. Even their zeal in the eternal hunt for new and undescribed species had not made them enemies.

I am afraid that my suggestion for the construction of a great glass flying-cage for *living* specimens of moths and butterflies started the trouble between these hitherto godly and middle-aged men. That, and the Carnegie Educational Medal were the causes which began this deplorable affair.

Various field collectors, employed by both Quint and Boomly, were always out all over the world foraging for specimens; also, they were constantly returning with spoils from every quarter of the globe.

Now, to secure rare and beautiful living specimens of butterflies and moths for the crystal flying-cage was a serious and delicate job. Such tropical insects could not survive the journey of several months from the wilds of Australia, India, Asia, Africa, or the jungles of South America—nor could semi-tropical species endure the captivity of a few weeks or even days, when captured in the West Indies, Mexico, or Florida. Only our duller-coloured, smaller, and hardier native species tolerated capture and exhibition.

Therefore, the mode of procedure which I suggested was for our field expeditions to obtain males and females of the same species of butterfly or moth, mate them, and, as soon as any female deposited her eggs, place the tiny pearl-like eggs in cold storage to retard their hatching, which normally occurs, in the majority of species, within ten days or two weeks.

This now was the usual mode of procedure followed by the field collectors employed by Dr. Quint and Professor Boomly. And not only were the eggs of various butterflies and moths so packed for transportation, but a sufficient store of their various native food-plants was also preserved, where such food-plants could not be procured in the United States. So when the eggs arrived at Bronx Park, and were hatched there in due time, the young caterpillars had plenty of nourishment ready for them in cold storage.

Might I not, legitimately, have expected the Carnegie Educational Medal for all this? I have never received it. I say this without indignation—even without sorrow. I merely make the statement.

Yet, my system was really a very beautiful system; a tiny batch of eggs would arrive from Ceylon, or Sumatra, or Africa; when taken from cold storage and placed in the herbarium they would presently hatch; the caterpillars were fed with their accustomed food-plant—a few leaves being taken from cold storage every day for them—they would pass through their three or four moulting periods, cease feeding in due time, transform into the chrysalis stage, and finally appear in all the splendour and magnificence of butterfly or moth.

The great glass flying-cage was now alive with superb moths and butterflies, flitting, darting, fluttering among the flowering bushes or feeding along the sandy banks of the brook which flowed through the flying-cage, bordered by thickets of scented flowers. And it was like looking at a meteoric shower of winged jewels, where the huge metallic-blue *Morphos* from South America flapped and sailed, and; the orange and gold and green *Ornithoptera* from Borneo pursued their majestic, bird-like flight—where big, glittering *Papilios* flashed through the bushes or alighted nervously to feed for a few moments on jasmine and phlox, and where the slowly flopping *Heliconians* winged their way amid the denser tangles of tropical vegetation.

Nothing like this flying-cage had ever before been seen in New York; thousands and thousands of men, women, and children thronged the lawn about the flying-cage all day long.

By night, also, the effect was wonderful; the electric lights among the foliage broke out; the great downy-winged moths, which had been asleep all day while the butterflies flitted through the sunshine, now came out to display their crimson or peacock-spotted wings, and the butterflies folded their wings and went to bed for the night.

The public was enchanted, the authorities of the Bronx proud and delighted; all apparently was happiness and harmony. Except that nobody offered me the Carnegie medal.

I was sitting one morning in my office, which, as I have said, separated the offices of Dr. Quint and Professor Boomly, when there came a loud rapping on my door, and, at my invitation, Dr. Quint bustled in—a little, meagre, excitable, near-sighted man with pointed mustaches and a fleck of an imperial smudging his lower lip.

"Last week," he began angrily, "young Jones arrived from Singapore bringing me the eggs of *Erebia astarte*, the great Silver Moon butterfly. Attempts to destroy them have been made. Last night I left them in a breeding-cage on my desk. Has anybody been in there?"

"I don't know," I said. "What has happened?"

"I found an ichneumon fly in the cage yesterday!" he shouted; "and this morning the eggs have either shrunk to half their size or else the eggs of another species have been secretly substituted for them and the Silver Moon eggs stolen! Has he been in there?"

"Who?" I asked, pretending to misunderstand.

"He!" demanded Quint fiercely. "If he has I'll kill him some day."

He meant his one-time friend, Dr. Boomly. Alas!

"For heaven's sake, why are you two perpetually squabbling?" I asked wearily. "You used to be inseparable friends. Why can't you make up?"

"Because I've come to know him. That's why! I have unmasked this—this Borgia—this Machiavelli—this monster of duplicity! Matters are approaching a point where something has got to be done short of murder. I've stood all his envy and jealousy and cheap imputations and hints and contemptible innuendoes that I'm going to—"

He stopped short, glaring at the doorway, which had suddenly been darkened by the vast bulk of Professor Boomly—a figure largely abdominal but majestic—like the massive butt end of an elephant. For the rest, he had a rather insignificant and peevish face and a melancholy mustache that usually looked damp.

"Mr. Smith," he said to me, in his thin, high, sarcastic voice—a voice incongruously at variance with his bulk— "has anybody had the infernal impudence to enter my room and nose about my desk?"

"Yes, *I* have!" replied Quint excitedly. "I've been in your room. What of it? What about it?"

Boomly permitted his heavy-lidded eyes to rest on Quint for a moment, then, turning to me:

"I want a patent lock put on my door. Will you speak to Professor Farrago?"

"I want one put on mine, too!" cried Quint. "I want a lock put on my door which will keep envious, dull-minded, mentally broken-down, impertinent, and fat people out of my office!"

Boomly flushed heavily:

"Fat?" he repeated, glaring at Quint. "Did you say 'fat?'"

"Yes, *fat*—intellectually and corporeally fat! I want that kind of individual kept out. I don't trust them. I'm afraid of them. Their minds are atrophied. They are unmoral, possibly even criminal! I don't want them in my room snooping about to see what I have and what I'm doing. I don't want them to sneak in, eaten up with jealousy and envy, and try to damage the eggs of the Silver Moon butterfly because the honour and glory of hatching them would probably procure for me the Carnegie Educational Medal—"

"Why, you little, dried-up, protoplasmic atom!" burst out Boomly, his face suffused with passion, "Are you insinuating that I have any designs on your batch of eggs?"

"It's my belief," shouted Quint, "that you want that medal yourself, and that you put an ichneumon fly in my breeding-cage in hopes it would sting the eggs of the Silver Moon."

"If you found an ichneumon fly there," retorted Boomly, "you probably hatched it in mistake for a butterfly!" And he burst into a peal of contemptuous laughter, but his little, pig-like eyes under the heavy lids were furious.

"I now believe," said Quint, trembling with rage, "that you have criminally substituted a batch of common *Plexippus* eggs for the Silver Moon eggs I had in my breeding-cage! I believe you are sufficiently abandoned to do it!"

"Ha! Ha!" retorted Boomly scornfully. "I don't believe you ever had anything in your breeding-cage except a few clothes moths and cockroaches!"

Quint began to dance:

"You did take them!" he yelled; "and you left me a bunch of milkweed butterflies' eggs! Give me my eggs or I shall violently assault you!"

"Assault your grandmother!" remarked Boomly, with unscientific brevity. "What do you suppose I want of your ridiculous eggs? Haven't I enough eggs of *Heliconius salome* hatching to give me the Carnegie medal if I want it?"

"The Silver Moon eggs are unique!" cried Quint. "You know it! You know that if they hatch, pupate, and become perfect insects that I shall certainly be awarded—"

"You'll be awarded the Matteawan medal," remarked Boomly with venom.

Quint ran at him with a half-suppressed howl, his momentum carrying him halfway up Professor Boomly's person. Then, losing foothold, he fell to the floor and began to kick in the general direction of Professor Boomly. It was a sorrowful sight to see these two celebrated scientists panting, mauling, scuffling and punching each other around the room, tables and chairs and scrapbaskets flying in every direction, and I mounted on the window-sill horrified, speechless, trying to keep clear of the revolving storm centre.

"Where are my Silver Moon eggs!" screamed Dr. Quint. "Where are my eggs that Jones brought me from Singapore—you entomological robber! You've got 'em somewhere! If you don't give 'em up I'll find means to destroy you!"

"You insignificant pair of maxillary palpi!" bellowed Professor Boomly, galloping after Dr. Quint as he dodged around my desk. "I'll pull off those antennæ you call whiskers if I can get hold of em—"

Dr. Quint's threatened mustaches bristled as he fled before the elephantine charge of Professor Boomly—once again around my desk, then out into the hall, where I heard the door of his office slam, and Boomly, gasping, panting, breathing vengeance outside, and vowing to leave Quint quite whiskerless when he caught him.

It was a painful scene for scientists to figure in or to gaze upon. Profoundly shocked and upset, I locked up the anthropological department offices and went out into the Park, where the sun was shining and a gentle June wind stirred the trees.

Too completely upset to do any more work that day, I wandered about amid the gaily dressed crowds at hazard; sometimes I contemplated the monkeys; sometimes gazed sadly upon the seals. They dashed and splashed and raced round and round their tank, or crawled up on the rocks, craned their wet, sleek necks, and barked—houp! houp! houp!

For luncheon I went over to the Rolling Stone Restaurant. There was a very pretty girl there—an unusually pretty girl—or perhaps it was one of those days on which every girl looked unusually pretty to me. There are such days.

Her voice was exquisite when she spoke. She said:

"We have, today, corned beef hash, fried ham and eggs, liver and bacon—" but let that pass, too.

I took my tea very weak; by that time I learned that her name was Mildred Case; that she had been a private detective employed in a department store, and that her duties had been to nab wealthy ladies who forgot to pay for objects usually discovered in their reticules, bosoms, and sometimes in their stockings.

But the confinement of indoor work had been too much for Mildred Case, and the only out-door job she could find was the position of lady waitress in the rustic Rolling Stone Inn.

She was very, very beautiful, or perhaps it was one of those days—but let that pass, too.

"You are the great Mr. Percy Smith, Curator of the Anthropological Department, are you not?" she asked shyly.

"Yes," I said modestly; and, to slightly rebuke any superfluous pride in me, I paraphrased with becoming humility, pointing upward: "but remember, Mildred, there is One greater than I."

"Mr. Carnegie?" she nodded innocently. That was true, too. I let it go at that.

We chatted: she mentioned Professor Boomly and Dr. Quint, gently deploring the rupture of their friendship. Both gentlemen, in common with the majority of the administration personnel, were daily customers at the Rolling Stone Inn. I usually took my lunch from my boarding-house to my office, being too busy to go out for mere nourishment.

That is why I had hitherto missed Mildred Case.

"Mildred," I said, "I do not believe it can be wholesome for a man to eat sandwiches while taking minute measurements of defunct monkeys. Also, it is not a fragrant pastime. Hereafter I shall lunch here."

"It will be a pleasure to serve you," said that unusually—there I go again! It was an unusually beautiful day in June. Which careful, exact, and scientific statement, I think ought to cover the subject under consideration.

After luncheon I sadly selected a five-cent cigar; and, as I hesitated, lingering over the glass case, undecided still whether to give full rein to this contemplated extravagance, I looked up and found her beautiful grey eyes gazing into mine.

"What gentle thoughts are yours, Mildred?" I said softly.

"The cigar you have selected," she murmured, "is fly-specked."

Deeply touched that this young girl should have cared—that she should have expressed her solicitude so modestly, so sweetly, concerning the maculatory condition of my cigar, I thanked her and purchased, for the same sum, a packet of cigarettes.

That was going somewhat far for me. I had never in all my life even dreamed of smoking a cigarette. To a reserved, thoughtful, and scientific mind there is, about a packet of cigarettes, something undignified, something vaguely frolicsome.

When I paid her for them I felt as though, for the first time in my life, I had let myself go.

Oddly enough, in this uneasy feeling of gaiety and abandon, a curious sensation of exhilaration persisted.

We had quite a merry little contretemps when I tried to light my cigarette and the match went out, and then *she* struck another match, and we both laughed, and *that* match was extinguished by her breath.

Instantly I quoted: "'Her breath was like the new-mown hay—'"

"Mr. Smith!" she said, flushing slightly.

"'Her eyes,'" I quoted, "'were like the stars at even!'"

"You don't mean *my* eyes, do you?"

I took a puff at my unlighted cigarette. It also smelled like recently mown hay. I felt that I was slipping my cables and heading toward an unknown and tempestuous sea.

"What time are you free, Mildred?" I asked, scarcely recognising my own voice in such reckless apropos.

She shyly informed me.

I struck a match, re-lighted my cigarette, and took one puff. That was sufficient: I was adrift. I realised it, trembled internally, took another puff.

"If," said I carelessly, "on your way home you should chance to stroll along the path beyond the path that leads to the path which—"

I paused, checked by her bewildered eyes. We both blushed.

"Which way do you usually go home?" I asked, my ears afire.

She told me. It was a suitably unfrequented path.

So presently I strolled thither; and seated myself under the trees in a bosky dell.

Now, there is a quality in boskiness not inappropriate to romantic thoughts. Boskiness, cigarettes, a soft afternoon in June, the hum of bees, and the distant barking of the seals, all these were delicately blending to inspire in me a bashful sentiment.

A specimen of *Papilio turnus*, di-morphic form, *Glaucus*, alighted near me; I marked its flight with scientific indifference. Yet it is a rare species in Bronx Park.

A mock-orange bush was in snowy bloom behind me; great bunches of wistaria hung over the rock beside me.

The combination of these two exquisite perfumes seemed to make the boskiness more bosky.

There was an unaccustomed and sportive lightness to my step when I rose to meet Mildred, where she came loitering along the shadow-dappled path.

She seemed surprised to see me.

She thought it rather late to sit down, but she seated herself. I talked to her enthusiastically about anthropology. She was so interested that after a while she could scarcely keep still, moving her slim little feet restlessly, biting her pretty lower lip, shifting her position—all certain symptoms of an interest in science which even approached excitement.

Warmed to the heart by her eager and sympathetic interest in the noble science so precious, so dear to me, I took her little hand to soothe and quiet her, realizing that she might become overexcited as I described the pituitary body and why its former functions had become atrophied until the gland itself was nearly obsolete.

So intense her interest had been that she seemed a little tired. I decided to give adequate material support to her spinal process.

It seemed to rest and soothe her. I don't remember that she said anything except: "Mr. *Smith!*" I don't recollect what we were saying when she mentioned me by name rather abruptly.

The afternoon was wonderfully still and calm. The month was June.

After a while—quite a while—some little time in point of accurate fact—she detected the sound of approaching footsteps.

I remember that she was seated at the opposite end of the bench, rather feverishly occupied with her hat and her hair, when young Jones came hastily along the path, caught sight of us, halted, turned violently red—being a shy young man—but instead of taking himself off, he seemed to recover from a momentary paralysis.

"Mr. Smith!" he said sharply. "Professor Boomly has disappeared; there's a pool of blood on his desk; his coat, hat, and waistcoat are lying on the floor, the room is a wreck, and Dr. Quint is in there tearing up the carpet and behaving like a madman. We think he suddenly went insane and murdered Professor Boomly. What is to be done?"

Horrified, I had risen at his first word. And now, as I understood the full purport of his dreadful message, my hair stirred under my hat and I gazed at him, appalled.

"What is to be done?" he demanded. "Shall I telephone for the police?"

"Do you actually believe," I faltered, "that this unfortunate man has murdered Boomly?"

"I don't know. I looked over the transom, but I couldn't see Professor Boomly. Dr. Quint has locked the door."

"And he's tearing up the carpet?"

"Like a lunatic. I didn't want to call in the police until I'd asked you. Such a scandal in Bronx Park would be a frightful thing for us all—" He hesitated, looked around, coldly, it seemed to me, at Mildred Case. "A scandal," he repeated, "is scarcely what might be expected among a harmonious and earnest band of seekers after scientific knowledge. Is it, Mil—Miss Case?"

Now, I don't know why Mildred should have blushed. There was nothing that I could see in this young man's question to embarrass her.

Preoccupied, still confused by the shock of this terrible news, I looked at Jones and at Mildred; and they were staring rather oddly at each other.

I said: "If this affair turns out to be as ghastly as it seems to promise, we'll have to call in a detective. I'll go back immediately "

"Why not take me, also?" asked Mildred Case, quietly.

"What?" I asked, looking at her.

"Why not, Mr. Smith? I was once a private detective."

Surprised at the suggestion, I hesitated.

"If you desire to keep this matter secret—if you wish to have it first investigated privately and quietly—would it not be a good idea to let me use my professional knowledge before you call in the police? Because as soon as the police are summoned all hope of avoiding publicity is at an end."

She spoke so sensibly, so quietly, so modestly, that her offer of assistance deeply impressed me.

As for young Jones, he looked at her steadily in that odd, chilling manner, which finally annoyed me. There was no need of his being snobbish because this very lovely and intelligent young girl happened to be a waitress at the Rolling Stone Inn.

"Come," I said unsteadily, again a prey to terrifying emotions; "let us go to the Administration Building and learn how matters stand. If this affair is as terrible as I fear it to be, science has received the deadliest blow ever dealt it since Cagliostro perished."

As we three strode hastily along the path in the direction of the Administration Building, I took that opportunity to read these two youthful fellow beings a sermon on envy, jealousy, and covetousness.

"See," said I, "to what a miserable condition the desire for notoriety and fame has brought two learned and enthusiastic delvers in the vineyard of endeavor! The mad desire for the Carnegie medal completely turned the hitherto perfectly balanced brains of these devoted disciples of Science. Envy begat envy, jealousy begat jealousy, pride begat pride, hatred begat hatred—"

"It's like that book in the Bible where everybody begat everybody else," said Mildred seriously.

At first I thought she had made an apt and clever remark; but on thinking it over I couldn't quite see its relevancy. I turned and looked into her sweet face. Her eyes were dancing with brilliancy and her sensitive lips quivered. I feared she was near to tears from the reaction of the shock. Had Jones not been walking with us—but let that go, too.

We were now entering the Administration Building, almost running; and as soon as we came to the closed door of Dr. Quint's room, I could hear a commotion inside—desk drawers being pulled out and their contents dumped, curtains being jerked from their rings, an unmistakable sound indicating the ripping up of a carpet—and through all this din the agitated scuffle of footsteps.

I rapped on the door. No notice taken. I rapped and knocked and called in a low, distinct voice.

Suddenly I recollected I had a general pass-key on my ring which unlocked any door in the building. I nodded to Jones and to Mildred to stand aside, then, gently fitting the key, I suddenly pushed out the key which remained on the inside, turned the lock, and flung open the door.

A terrible sight presented itself: Dr. Quint, hair on end, both mustaches pulled out, shirt, cuffs, and white waistcoat smeared with blood, knelt amid the general wreckage on the floor, in the act of ripping up the carpet.

"Doctor!" I cried in a trembling voice. "What have you done to Professor Boomly?"

He paused in his carpet ripping and looked around at us with a terrifying laugh.

"I've settled *him!*" he said. "If you don't want to get all over dust you'd better keep out "

"Quint!" I cried. "Are you crazy?"

"Pretty nearly. Let me alone—"

"Where is Boomly!" I demanded in a tragic voice. "Where is your old friend, Billy Boomly? Where is he, Quint? And what does *that* mean—that pool of blood on the floor? Whose is it?"

"It's Bill's," said Quint, coolly ripping up another breadth of carpet and peering under it.

"What!" I exclaimed. "Do you admit that?"

"Certainly I admit it. I told him I'd terminate him if he meddled with my Silver Moon eggs."

"You mean to say that you shed blood—the blood of your old friend—merely because he meddled with a miserable batch of butterfly's eggs?" I asked, astounded.

"I certainly did shed his blood for just that particular thing! And listen; you're in my way—you're standing on a part of the carpet which I want to tear up. Do you mind moving?"

Such cold-blooded calmness infuriated me. I sprang at Quint, seized him, and shouted to Jones to tie his hands behind him with the blood-soaked handkerchief which lay on the floor.

At first, while Jones and I were engaged in the operation of securing the wretched man, Quint looked at us both as though surprised; then he grew angry and asked us what the devil we were about.

"Those who shed blood must answer for it!" I said solemnly.

"What? What's the matter with you?" he demanded in a rage. "Shed blood? What if I did? What's that to you? Untie this handkerchief, you unmentionable idiot!"

I looked at Jones:

"His mind totters," I said hoarsely.

"What's that!" cried Quint, struggling to get off the chair whither I had pushed him: but with my handkerchief we tied his ankles to the rung of the chair, heedless of his attempts to kick us, and sprang back out of range.

"Now," I said, "what have you done with the poor victim of your fury? Where is he? Where is all that remains of Professor Boomly?"

"Boomly? I don't know where he is. How the devil should I know?"

"Don't lie," I said solemnly.

"Lie! See here, Smith, when I get out of this chair I'll settle you, too—"

"Quint! There is another and more terrible chair which awaits such criminals as you!"

"You old fluff!" he shouted. "I'll knock your head off, too. Do you understand? I'll attend to you as I attended to Boomly—"

"Assassin!" I retorted calmly. "Only an alienist can save you now. In this awful moment—"

A light touch on my arm interrupted me, and, a trifle irritated, as any man might be when checked in the full flow of eloquence, I turned to find Mildred at my elbow.

"Let me talk to him," she said in a quiet voice. "Perhaps I may not irritate him as you seem to."

"Very well," I said. "Jones and I are here as witnesses." And I folded my arms in an attitude not, perhaps, unpicturesque.

"Dr. Quint," said Mildred in her soft, agreeable voice, and actually smiling slightly at the self-confessed murderer, "is it really true that you are guilty of shedding the blood of Professor Boomly?"

"It is," said Quint, coolly.

She seemed rather taken aback at that, but presently recovered her equanimity.

"Why?" she asked gently.

"Because he attempted a most hellish crime!" yelled Quint.

"W-what crime?" she asked faintly.

"I'll tell you. He wanted the Carnegie medal and he knew it would be given to me if I could incubate and hatch my batch of Silver Moon butterfly eggs. He realised well enough that his Heliconian eggs were not as valuable as my Silver Moon eggs. So first he sneaked in here and put an ichneumon fly in my breeding-cage. And next he stole the Silver Moon eggs and left in their place some common *Plexippus* eggs, thinking that because they were very similar I would not notice the substitution.

"I did notice it! I charged him with that cataclysmic outrage. He laughed. We came into personal collision. He chased me into my room."

Panting, breathless with rage at the memory of the morning's defeat which I had witnessed, Quint glared at me for a moment. Then he jerked his head toward Mildred:

"As soon as he went to luncheon—Boomly, I mean—I climbed over that transom and dropped into this room. I had been hunting for ten minutes before I found my Silver Moon eggs hidden under the carpet. So I pocketed them, climbed back over the transom, and went to my room."

He paused dramatically, staring from one to another of us:

"Boomly was there!" he said slowly.

"Where?" asked Mildred with a shudder.

"In my room. He had picked the lock. I told him to get out! He went. I shouted after him that I had recovered the Silver Moon eggs and that I should certainly be awarded the Carnegie medal.

"Then that monster in human form laughed a horrible laugh, avowing himself guilty of a crime still more hideous than the theft of the Silver Moon eggs! Do you know what he had done?"

"W-what?" faltered Mildred.

"He had stolen from cold storage and had concealed the leaves of the Bimba bush, brought from Singapore to feed the Silver Moon caterpillars! *That's* what Boomly had done!

"And my Silver Moon eggs had already begun to hatch!!! And my caterpillars would starve!!!!"

His voice ended in a yell; he struggled on his chair until it nearly upset.

"You lunatic!" I shouted. "Was that a reason for spilling the blood of a human being!"

"It was reason enough for me!"

"Madman!"

"Let me loose! He's hidden those leaves somewhere or other! I've torn this place to pieces looking for them. I've got to find them, I tell you—"

Mildred went to the infuriated entomologist and laid a firm hand on his shoulder:

"Listen," she said: "how do you know that Professor Boomly has not concealed these Bimba leaves on his own person?"

Quint ceased his contortions and gaped at her.

"I never thought of that," he said.

"What have you done with him?" she asked, very pale.

"I tell you, I don't know."

"You must know what you did with him," she insisted.

Quint shook his head impatiently, apparently preoccupied with other thoughts. We stood watching him in silence until he looked up and became conscious of our concentrated gaze.

"My caterpillars are starving," he began violently. "I haven't anything else they'll eat. They feed only on the Bimba leaf. They *won't* eat anything else. It's a well-known fact that they won't. Why, in Johore, where they came from, they'll travel miles over the ground to find a Bimba bush—"

"What!" exclaimed Mildred.

"Certainly—miles! They'd starve sooner than eat anything except Bimba leaves. If there's a bush within twenty miles they'll find it—"

"Wait," said Mildred quietly. "Where are these starving caterpillars?"

"In a glass jar in my pocket—here! What the devil are you doing!" For the girl had dexterously slipped the glass jar from his coat pocket and was holding it up to the light.

Inside it were several dozen tiny, dark caterpillars, some resting disconsolately on the sides of the glass, some hungrily travelling over the bottom in pitiful and hopeless quest of nourishment.

Heedless of the shouts and threats of Dr. Quint, the girl calmly uncorked the jar, took on her slender forefinger a single little caterpillar, replaced the cork, and, kneeling down, gently disengaged the caterpillar. It dropped upon the floor, remained motionless for a moment, then, turning, began to travel rapidly toward the doorway behind us.

"Now," she said, "if poor Professor Boomly really has concealed these Bimba leaves upon his own person, this little caterpillar, according to Dr. Quint, is certain to find those leaves."

Overcome with excitement and admiration for this intelligent and unusually beautiful girl, I seized her hands and congratulated her.

"Murder," said I to the miserable Quint, "will out! This infant caterpillar shall lead us to that dark and secret spot where you had hoped to conceal the horrid evidence of your guilt. Three things have undone you—a caterpillar replete with mysterious instinct, a humble bunch of Bimba leaves, and the marvellous intelligence of this young and lovely girl. Madman, your hour has struck!"

He looked at me in a dazed sort of way, as though astonishment had left him unable to articulate. But I had become tired of his violence and his shouts and yells; so I asked Jones for his handkerchief, and, before Quint knew what I was up to I had tied it over his mouth.

He became a brilliant purple, but all he could utter was a furious humming, buzzing noise.

Meanwhile, Jones had opened the door; the little caterpillar, followed by Mildred and myself, continued to hustle along as though he knew quite well where he was going.

Down the hallway he went in undulating haste, past my door, we all following in silent excitement as we discovered that, parallel to the caterpillar's course, ran a gruesome trail of blood drops.

And when the little creature turned and made straight for the door of Professor Farrago, our revered chief, the excitement among us was terrific.

The caterpillar halted; I gently tried the door; it was open.

Instantly the caterpillar crossed the threshold, wriggling forward at top speed. We followed, peering fearfully around us. Nobody was visible.

Could Quint have dragged his victim here? By Heaven, he had! For the caterpillar was travelling straight under the lounge upon which Professor Farrago was accustomed to repose after luncheon, and, dropping on one knee, I saw a fat foot partly protruding from under the shirred edges of the fringed drapery.

"He's there!" I whispered, in an awed voice to the others. "Courage, Miss Case! Try not to faint."

Jones turned and looked at her with that same odd expression; then he went over to where she stood and coolly passed one arm around her waist.

"Try not to faint, Mildred," he said. "It might muss your hair."

It was a strange thing to say, but I had no time then to analyze it, for I had seized the fat foot which partly protruded from under the sofa, clad in a low-cut congress gaiter and a white sock.

And then *I* nearly fainted, for instead of the dreadful, inert resistance of lifeless clay, the foot wriggled and tried to kick at me.

"Help!" came a thin but muffled voice. "Help! Help, in the name of Heaven!"

"Boomly!" I cried, scarcely believing my ears.

"Take that man away, Smith!" whimpered Boomly. "He's a devil! He'll murder me! He made my nose bleed all over everything!"

"Boomly! You're *not* dead!"

"Yes, I am!" he whined. "I'm dead enough to suit me. Keep that little lunatic off—that's all I ask. He can have his Carnegie medal for all I care, only tie him up somewhere—"

"Professor Boomly!" cried Mildred excitedly. "Have you any Bimba leaves concealed about your person?"

"Yes, I have," he said sulkily. There came a hitch of the fat foot, a heavy scuffling sound, heavy panting, and then, skittering out across the floor came a flat, sealed parcel.

"There you are," he said; "now, let me alone until that fiend has gone home."

"He won't attack you again," I said. "Come out."

But Professor Boomly flatly declined to stir.

I looked at the parcel: it was marked: "Bimba leaves; Johore."

With a sigh of unutterable relief, I picked up the ravenous little caterpillar, placed him on the packet, and turned to go. And didn't.

It is a very sickening fact I have now to record. But to a scientist all facts are sacred, sickening or otherwise.

For what I caught a glimpse of, just outside the door in the hallway, was Jones kissing Mildred Case. And being shyly indemnified for his trouble with a gentle return in kind. Both his arms were around her waist; both her hands rested upon his shoulders; and, as I looked—but let it pass!—let it pass.

Deliberately I fished in my pocket, found my packet of cigarettes, lighted one.

Tobacco diffugiunt mordaces curae et laetificat cor hominis!

The Blue Cockroach
Edward Heron·Allen

Dora was responsible—the Dora who punctuated her name after the manner of the plural of Mouse as affected by Civil Engineers. D.O.R.A. Primarily responsible, that is to say; for this is a story of one of the very few instances of that Ersatz, which devastated Germany during the Late Unpleasantness, but of which our more favoured Nation suffered but few aggressions.

From another point of view perhaps the responsibility lies with Itha and Armorel. They are the imperious nieces of the Professor of Applied Chemistry in the University of Cosmopoli. Itha was twelve at the time, and Armorel eight, but, having no wife to rule him with a rod of iron, the Professor had, by the dire progression of a process for which he was unable to account, gradually become as a slave beneath their ferrule, and in the most meagre days of Dora's sumptuary regulations Itha and Armorel had demanded Bananas.

Well, Bananas were at that moment as Snakes in Iceland—apparently, and many a rebuff did the Professor endure from 'proud young Porters' at Stores whence of old he had been accustomed to supply his nieces' demands.

Of course the Professor ought to have been married. So ought Pamela, but the youth of the Professor had been spent, not only in consuming the midnight oil and other illuminants, but in abstract researches into their nature, composition, and adaptations. He was an acknowledged authority on Coal-tar Products, Inverted Sugars, and their derivatives commercial and prophylactic. Pamela had waited; and she had waited too long. By the time the Professor had become a Member of Council of the Chemical, and a Fellow of the Royal Societies he was a confirmed bachelor, and Pamela had

280

reached the age which used to be labelled in their series of photo-
graphs of Celebrities (female) by the *Strand Magazine* as 'Present
Day.' They corresponded at long, and met at longer, intervals, when
Pamela, growing fragrant with the fire of forgotten suns, like a
Winter Pear, came up from Wiltshire in a spirit of revolt against
the limitations of the Provincial Milliner.

In the meagre days above referred to, Pamela was in town, and
the Professor, rather grudging the expenditure of time involved,
had bidden her to lunch with him at the Imperial. A visit to
Kingsway, in search of chemical glass, had the result that his way
back to the Imperial lay through Covent Garden Market, at that
time a dreary vista of empty windows and derelict packing cases,
where erstwhile the fruits of distant lands had been wont to overflow in polychromatic luxuriance. But in one of the windows lay a
small bunch—a 'hand' they call it—of home-sick and weary Bananas,
and the Professor remembered the grey reproachful eyes of Itha
and Armorel, who could never believe that he could possibly fail
them if he really made an effort.

He went in. An adolescent representative of an Ancient Race—
who had escaped conscription—received him with scarcely inquisitive apathy.

"Are those the only Bananas you have?" asked the Professor.

"And all we are likely to," replied the Merchant elliptically.

"I am in trouble," said the Professor. "I have a little niece who
is eagerly desirous of Bananas—and she is very delicate," he added
as a mendacious afterthought, blushing as he thought of Itha in a
dilapidated Scout uniform perched in the highest branches of a
tree, or careering along the sands 'bareback' on a repatriated Army
remount. "Do you think you could help me?"

The Adolescent Oriental looked him over with a scrutiny which
became, in the end, sympathetic. Perhaps he had a niece—or something and understood.

"Bill!"

A subterranean noise as though the dirty floor were in labour,
and from a square hole in the planks at their feet half a human
being emerged. This was evidently part of Bill—a sinister figure,
midway between Phil Squod and Quilp. A vision of strabismus and
a fustian cap.

"Could you find this gentleman a hand or two of Bananas out
of that case?—you know."

Disappearance of the upper half of Bill, a sound of rending timbers, and presently his reappearance with two 'hands'—beautiful golden Bananas, and the nether portion of his person.

"Beauties," remarked Bill, "come yesterday."

"How much?" enquired the Professor.

When he recovered he saw himself, mentally, a poorer, but a better man. The Merchant was delivering a lecture upon the economics of War, and the iniquities of Dora. And as he turned the 'hand' over, that its excellence might act as an anaesthetic to the operation of extraction, there ran out upon the counter the Blue Cockroach.

Unconsciously the Professor—like the Poet in the Den of the Scarabee—recoiled, but no Scarabee was there to murmur without emotion 'Blatta.' But Bill was there.

"Ah!" said he, "I've seen him before—queer things we get sometimes in the cases—lizards—snakes—and what-not. Once I found a Monkey. Jolly little beggar—he was all right, lived on the fruit. We used to take them to the live-beast place at the end. Shut up now."

"Don't you ever get bitten—or stung?"

"No—we're careful. This fellow's harmless."

It was a most lovely beast. In shape and size identical with the cockroaches which stray among one's brushes on board ship, and architecturally indistinguishable from the larger members of the Kitchen family, the Blue Cockroach was clad in a pure, pale azure, as if a cunning artificer in enamels had fashioned it, and had given to its surface a texture of the finest smooth velvet. Its long antennae waved enquiringly back and forth, its tiny eyes sparkled black with crimson points, and then it began to run. The Professor caught it in his hand as it toppled from the edge of the counter.

It bit him.

A curious sickening little puncture like the nip of an earwig. A sensation of heat, and then of cold that ran all over him, and Bill and the Merchant grew nebulous—and waved about. The Professor had never fainted in his life, but he said to himself: "This is how they must feel." In a moment it was over. He had shaken off the insect, and true to the scientific instinct he took out of his pocket one of the corked tubes he had just acquired, and drove the Blue Cockroach into it.

"One of the fellows at the Museum may like to have it," he said.

The Merchant shrugged his shoulders. A boot-heel, not a corked tube, seemed to him to be the appropriate climax to the Odyssey of the Blue Cockroach. For some inexplicable reason, however, he reduced the price he had quoted from the limits of Chimaera to within the bounds of Extravagance, and the Professor went upon his way, the Bananas in his hand and the Blue Cockroach in his pocket.

A tiny point on his right palm showed where the insect had attacked him, but beyond that the incident was closed.

As he proceeded along Coventry Street the Professor became aware of a great calm—an undefined happiness. He had regarded his appointment with Pamela more in the light of a kindly duty than as an occasion for pleasurable anticipation, but now he suddenly found himself looking forward to their meeting with a keen sense of curiosity and satisfaction. It was too long since they met last. He felt sure she would have come to town sooner had he expressed a wish in that direction in his letters. What a handsome creature she had been when he was a student! What a shame it was that she had never married. The Professor found himself quietly wondering why—if—whether?

"I am fifty-four," said he to himself. But he smiled frowningly—or frowned smilingly.

"She's a wonderful woman!" was his first thought as she rose to greet him from the big chair in the vestibule. Indeed, Pamela seemed younger than he remembered her to have looked a year ago. She seemed to radiate that impression of delicate strength and ultra-feminine self-reliance which constitutes the undefinable charm of many middle-aged spinsters.

Their lunch was delightful. Pamela seemed as though she were starting fresh. The Professor seemed to have shed his professorial armour, and to have become once more a human being. He entertained her with descriptions of his war activities, no longer as of yore skimming over the subject, but letting her into the secret chamber of his ambitions, his aspirations, his work. When a man of the Professor's intellectual eminence exerts himself to charm, the charm is dangerously subtle. An element of flattery pervades the exercise, which is—or should be— irresistible. Pamela did not resist—she had never been called upon to resist, and was not going to begin now. Thirty years fell away, as time wasted in sleep. It is not a disagreeable admission—indeed, there is a curious emotional joy predominant when two people who should have been lovers find themselves saying in their hearts, 'What fools we have been!'

By the time that the arrival of coffee and cigarettes had cleared away the last barriers which had erected themselves upon their voyage of re-discovery, the Professor was virtually identifying Pamela with his life-work.

"It is not all explosives and bacteriology," he confided to her. "I have been at work upon substitutes for sugar, and I have found one which will be a god-send to the people who properly detest saccharine. I have brought here a little tube of my finished article. It has all the sweetening properties of the finest cane sugar. Will you try it?"

Of course she would. If it had been a dangerous poison she would have gladly offered herself as a martyr to Science—his Science.

"You need not be afraid of it. It is not only a wonderful sweetener—it is also a powerful prophylactic. It acts like an atoxyl that would kill with extraordinary rapidity any pathogenic organisms in the system. I look forward to trying it as a remedy for Sleeping Sickness, Yellow Fever—any of the tropical diseases carried by insects which inject death-dealing bacteria—trypanosomes—into our blood by their bites. My dear"—she quivered— "I believe I hold here one of the greatest discoveries that has ever been made in prophylactic medicine!"

They sweetened their coffee—each with a tiny pellucid crystal.

"It is just like real sugar," she said dreamily, "not harsh like saccharine. My dear"—his eyes grew narrower— "I do believe you are right. I am so proud of you." She ended with a little contented sigh which was half a laugh, and looked round the restaurant, which was by this time gradually becoming empty and wondered whether anyone else there looked out upon their worlds with so supreme a sensation of satisfaction and fulfilment as she. What fools they had been!

The Professor also finished his coffee and leaned back in his chair, looking round the room with a sudden sensation of discomfort. He had just thought again of the Blue Cockroach—the reason he had thought of it was that he had suddenly experienced, as it were, a return of the sensation which came over him at the moment it bit him. It was, however, only momentary, though, casually glancing at his hand, it seemed as if the little puncture were more visible than it had been.

And then a remarkable thing happened. He turned again to Pamela and saw her with new—or rather with old—eyes. He found her eyes fastened upon him with a mingled expression of apprehension and curiosity, and as he returned her gaze she blushed vividly. He felt strangely uncomfortable, and without any conscious volition on his part he found himself going rapidly over in his mind their conversation of the previous hour. It was surely waste of time to orate for an hour to this dull but worthy person, upon a subject which could have no interest for her and of which she could not possibly understand a single word. He was dissatisfied with himself, and naturally blamed her vaguely for his dissatisfaction and discomfort.

"Well!" he said, "it has been very pleasant seeing you again, Pamela. We must—er—not let it be so long again—before ..." His stereotyped phrases lost themselves in embarrassed silence.

He asked for the bill. It seemed to him rather excessive. However, just for once...

Pamela had not ceased looking at him. She was puzzled; it seemed to her as if a newly opened door had been quietly but relentlessly shut in her face. The Professor certainly had aged a good deal since she saw him last; she had not noticed it before. An uncomfortable sensation crept over her that she had been expansive beyond warrantable limits with this grave grey man, and she felt a little hot under an impression that she had allowed the conversation to stray beyond what was quite seemly and decorous—at her age. She was rather relieved that he seemed in a hurry to get away. She had all an intelligent woman's horror of an anti-climax.

An hour later she was in the train. At that moment the Professor laid down his pen in his study and looked before him out of the window. The same thought struck both of them simultaneously.

"What fools we were!"

"Now whether there be truth or no in that which the native Priests do aver, I know not, nor may I make more curious enquiry, but if it be indeed the fact that the sting of divers of their Flyes do engender Passions as of Love, Hate, and the like, then the matter is curious and worthy of enquiry, but such as I did make enquiry of did postpone me with shrewd cunning and avoiding answer, nor would they be come at to speak further upon it at that or any other time.'[1]

   [1] "The True Accompt of the Travels into Distant Lands of the learned Doctor Franzelius Bott, wherein many curious Customs and Wisdom of the Inhabitants are truly set down." (Leyden: 1614, p. 117.)

The Gold-Seekers
Al Khanzir

Fertilissimi sunt auri Dardae.

We all know that there are in this world certain places where one cannot reappear, after the lapse of no matter how many years, without running across a friend. Among such places the Yacht Club in Bombay most assuredly rank high, for that eminently comfortable spot means to many Easterners, as it does to me, either civilisation's first foretaste or her last farewell, according to whether ours is a homeward or an outward journey.

Last April I made one of my periodical descents on the Yacht Club. The war was over at last, home leave had been reopened, and I had found myself among the favoured few selected to go with the first batch. Mine had been the very ordinary story of a regimental officer throughout the war—Egypt, Gallipoli, Egypt again, and then Mesopotamia. My battalion had been selected finally to form part of the post-bellum garrison of Assyria, and I had just completed the wearisome journey by desert, river, and sea from Mosul to Bombay.

The boat from Basra had got in only that very morning, and as the leave-boat sailed next day, I had had a busy time. So it was late when I got to the Yacht Club, and I found the big downstairs bar-room already crowded. But most of the crowd were boxwalas, none of whom I happened to have met, and at first I could not see a single face I knew.

However, I had not long to wait for the expected friend, and I could not have asked for a more welcome one; for I had hardly got my drink when the swing-doors opened, and in came dear old Douglas Rowland. Douglas is a political.[1] A certain summer, a few years before the war, had found me shooting in Ladakh, that quaint old Western Tibetan kingdom, now an outlying province of the dominions of His Highness of Jammu and Kashmir. At that time Rowland had been in charge at Leh, the former Tibetan capital, in whose great bazaar the traders of half a continent forgather on their way to India, bringing with them in their pony-packs the brick-tea of China, and the borax and the wool, the musk and the turquoises of Tibet, the carpets of Bokara, and the felts of Kashgar and Yarkand. A bad go of snow-blindness had driven me in to Leh—for treatment by the Moravian Mission doctor there and Rowland had taken me into his charming house and treated me like a brother. Bottled beer and gram-fed mutton in Ladakh—the memory of them lingers still! We had not met since, but it did not take us long to find out that we were both bound for home next day, and to arrange to dine together.

At dinner our knowledge of each other's recent doings was quickly brought up to date.

"After that summer yonu were up shooting in Ladakh," Rowland began, "I stayed on in Leh till the spring of '14. It was a good job and suited me. My summers in Leh were lonely of course, except when fellows like you came up and stopped with me, for the only other white folk were the Moravian missionaries. But after all, the shooting was well worth it, for it is not every one who has his way paid by Government to shoot an *Ovis ammon*. Then, of course, in winter I went down to Kashmir and lived like a Christian amongst my fellow-men, with some of the finest duck-shooting in the world at my door—no, I've no complaints against Leh.

"But early in '14 they transferred me to the Gulf, and then the war came. At first, of course, I applied repeatedly to be allowed to rejoin my old battalion, but I was, it appeared, indispensable, and as a matter of fact the Hun 'agents provocateurs' did keep us quite busy. After a bit I was transferred to Teheran and thence to the South-Eastern Caspian. There I have been sitting in splendid isolation for the last two years at the court of a Kurdish potentate called the Khan of Bujnurd. He's nominally under the Shah, but as a matter of fact he doesn't give two hoots for any one; so I felt a little lonely sometimes, especially when he commenced to discuss with me in a perfectly academic spirit the probable outcome of his cutting off my head. However, he decided against it in the end—I really never quite knew why.

"In normal times it would not have been too bad at Bujnurd, for there is some good fishing near-by—a fish very like the mahseer. Then, too, there are quite a few tigers in the heavy forest by the Caspian—sort of Terai country it is. No, not the long-haired tiger—the ordinary one. But as things were, I had to keep a very close eye on my Khan, to try to head off Pan-Turanian emissaries from Baku and Bolsheviks from Turkestan, so I was too busy for anything of that sort. Yes, I have just come down from there—a longish trek it is, too."

"Talking about those Moravians at Leh," I said, "I wonder what happened to them in the war? Of course they were Huns to a man, so I suppose they were interned, but I must say I think they might have been made exceptions. Mind you, I hold no particular brief for their missionising, for as a matter of fact they probably did not make a convert from one year's end to another,—Buddhists don't proselytise readily. But if they did not save souls, at least they mended bodies: it is the medical side of the Moravian Mission for which the most stiff-necked Buddhist must be thankful, and many a sahib too, who has fallen sick hundreds of miles from other help when shooting in the hills. You remember old Weismann, and what a fine fellow he was? I should like to meet him again, for I often think of that story you told me about him—how he heard that poor Kenway was lying sick over the passes from Leh, and how he went to fetch him, and crossed the Karzong La twice in one day to reach him and bring him in! In December too, wasn't it? Over the Karzong twice in one day in mid-winter—that's some going. And he saved Kenway that time, though he died later actually in Leh. But you were still there then, so of course you know all about it. Weismann must have been vexed that he failed to save him a second time."

"Yes, I was there all right when Kenway died; but Weismann could not well save him then, for to the best of my belief he was himself already dead."

"You don't say so—I never heard of that; but then, of course, one wouldn't, for they don't publish the death of a Moravian padre in the casualty lists. How did it happen, for he was hale and hearty when last I saw him?"

"Well, we must put Weismann down as 'missing, believed killed,' for as far as I know there is none now alive who saw him die; Kenway probably was there, but then Kenway is dead too. It is a very queer story, and at the time it did not seem to me that any good could come of making public all I knew. But with you it is rather different—for you know the country, and you knew the men concerned—so if you care for the story after dinner I'll tell it to you as well as I can. As a matter of fact, there is a letter, too, which Kenway left me; only yesterday I happened on it in my kit just out of Cox's, so I'll fetch it after dinner, as it is quite handy here in my room."

When dinner was finished we went downstairs to the lawn, and choosing two chairs by the balustrade overlooking the harbour, settled down with our cigars. Stretching out his legs and leaning back in his chair, Rowland began—

"You knew Kenway, of course. Only just met him? Oh, well, I knew him well. He was a very remarkable man. He had been in some Highland regiment, but went early on coming into the family place in Dorset. While he was still in the Service he had been a bit of an archaeologist and a great linguist too—was one of the very few fellows in the British Service with a 'Degree of Honour' in Persian. So, when he realised that money was short and that he would find it very hard to scrape along as a county magnate at home, he let his place to a rich American and wandered about the world to indulge his archaeological bent. But in his subaltern days he had been up in Kashmir on leave, and had got so bitten with that country that in after years he was never long away from the Himalaya. He would spend years on end pottering about amongst the Buddhist inscriptions and remains of Western Tibet and Kashmir—a humble follower in the footsteps of Aurel Stein. I met him several times on his wanderings and liked him immensely, for he always struck me as a large, sane, self-reliant individual, differing from the ordinary run one meets, in that, though he had a very healthy liking for the flesh-pots, still he could deny himself for years together in pursuit of his hobbies. He was a very keen sportsman too; but in this the naturalist always came first, and I remember he was one of those most interested in the proposed mammal-survey of the Himalaya that the Duke of B— had in view at one time. With all this, he was one of the best-read men I have ever met, full of all sorts of abstruse knowledge, especially of Asiatic history—which, of course, was a necessary concomitant of his archaeology. In fact, he was at once a man of the world, a savant, and a sportsman—and a most charming companion at all times.

"It was the winter before you were last up in Leh, wasn't it, that Weismann brought in Kenway over the Karzong La? He had a very bad go of enteric, but the Moravians pulled him through, and by the time I reached Leh that spring he was already convalescent. He had originally intended crossing the Karakerum that summer to have a look at the ruins round Khotan, but after his illness he did not feel fit enough to go so far afield. He had found a kindred spirit in Weismann, who was himself, of course, a recognised authority on all sorts of Tibetan lore,—I remember he had been busy for years on a monumental work which he meant to call a 'Corpus Inscriptionum Tibeticarum,' or some such name, if it had ever been finished. Weismann had told Kenway a lot about the remains of an ancient monastery at Spadum in Zanskar, only a few marches from Leh across the Indus, so finally Kenway decided to put off Khotan till later and to spend the summer investigating Spadum.

"I saw nothing of Kenway all summer; but Weismann went over to spend some weeks with him, and on his return came to tell me about the doings at Spadum. It happened to be a busy day, so I'm afraid I did not give the old boy the attention he deserved. However, I gathered that Kenway had roped in a perfect army of the local Zanskaris, and between them they had unearthed buried ruins of very considerable extent and—according to Weismann—of tremendous interest. Kenway was still out in Zanskar when I went back to Kashmir that autumn, and I understood that he intended wintering in Leh to arrange all the material he had collected at Spadum.

"Sure enough, next spring I found him still in Leh, busy with the arrangements for his deferred trip to Khotan; and, somewhat to my surprise, I heard that Weismann was to go with him. I helped them both a good deal with their preparations, and remember being struck with the extent of the 'bandobast' they were making. The Karakorum road to Turkestan is a big enough undertaking certainly, but Kenway was buying horses and mules wholesale and paying fancy prices for the best. Old Mohan Lai, the merchant in the Leh bazaar, was acting as his agent in this. You remember the good old boy, of course? He drank himself to death in the winter of '13, I'm sorry to say, and how they manage now in Leh without him I can't think. Well, in the end they got together as well-found a caravan as ever left Leh. Chiefly Zanskari ponies they had bought—they're much the best; and Kenway had got hold of old Mahommed Mish as caravan-bashi. He couldn't have done better than that, for the old man went with Maloolmson through Tibet in '96, and knew Central Asia like the palm of his hand.

"One evening, just before they were due to start, Kenway came over to dinner with me and brought Weismann with him, and after dinner we settled down by the fire in my study. It was the last time I ever saw them together, and the scene comes back to me very clearly: the dark room, with its flickering firelight dimly revealing Kenway—solid and well-groomed even in his old shooting-suit— lying back reposefully in his arm-chair, in marked contrast to Weismann, lean and cadaverous, with straggling brown beard, who was crouching forward to the blaze and playing nervously with those blue glare-glasses that he never went without.

"I remember telling them then that I expected a long account of their doings when they got back.

"'As a matter of fact,' Kenway replied, 'that is just what I want to talk to you about. Of course Central Asian exploration is always a bit of a risk; but there are some peculiar features about this trip of ours, so, though it may seem rather nonsense to you, we both feel we are in for a pretty big undertaking accompanied by more than the usual danger. For that reason we want somebody to know where we have gone in case we don't turn up again; but if you were to hear our plans now, in your official position yon might feel obliged to put a spoke in our wheel. So here is a letter that I want to give you, but I'm going to ask you not to read it till we have been gone a month. Do you agree?'

"'All right,' I said; 'you can give me the letter, and I promise not to read it for a month, perhaps not then, for as long as you don't ask me to connive with you in infringing the orders of Government you can go anywhere yon please as far as I'm concerned— to Timbuctu and back if you want to. But mind you take care of yourselves all the same; we don't want any regrettable incidents or complications.'

"So Kenway gave me this letter, and shortly after he and Weismann started on their travels. Some time during the summer I opened the letter: here it is, and this is what I read:—

'Dear Rowland,—W. and I have gone, not to Khotan, but into Tibet—as you probably suspected. But what will surprise you is the reason for our going: we have gone for gold. Now, do not be in a hurry to put us down as mere fatuous treasure-hunters, but first let me explain to you the grounds on which we are basing our search.

'Now, has it ever struck you, I wonder, what a prominent place in history the gold of this part of the world has always held? Perhaps you have never thought about it; anyway the subject has always had a fascination for me, and for years I have been tabulating in my mind odd scraps of evidence bearing upon it.

'To begin very far back—the Greek and Roman writers teem with references to the subject. One of the earliest allusions is to be found in Herodotus, as you may remember; and as his account has a very important after-bearing on my story, I shall quote him more or less in full. This is what he says:— "Another kind of Indians live in the land of Paktyika, away towards the North from the rest of the Indians; their manner of living is much the same as that of the Bactrians. These are the most warlike of all the Indians, and it is they who are sent for the gold. For in this country there is a sandy desert, and in this sand there are ants which are smaller than dogs but larger than foxes. ... These ants make for themselves burrows below ground, and in doing so throw up the earth as ants do with us, and in the same manner; they also look exactly like ours. This thrown-up sand contains the gold, and for the sake of this sand the Indians are sent into the desert. ... When the Indians arrive at the place with their leather bags, they fill these with sand and ride away as quickly as possible, for the ants—who have found out what has happened through their sense of smell—are at once after them, and they are exceedingly swift. Thus, if the Indians do not gain a good start before the ants have gathered, none of them would escape" (Herodotus, lib. iii. 98-106).

'Of course it is very generally agreed that the "Indians" to whom Herodotus refers are none other than the Dards. Now we know that in very early times there was a big Aryan migration of Dards up the Indus towards Tibet, indeed here in Ladakh to this day we find pure Dard settlements mingled with the Tibetans of the Indus valley right into Tibet proper, and I think it is almost certain that it was our local Dards whom Herodotus had in his mind. You must admit, then, that his story points to there having been plenty of gold about—whatever its source may have been, and however little you may be prepared to accept his ants.

'After Herodotus we find Magasthenes independently corroborating the story of our local gold, from information he himself derived when ambassador in India; moreover, he too gives most circumstantial evidence about the gold-digging ants.

'Then again Ktesias, the physician, in his "Indika," talks of the gold of the Upper Indus and Western Tibet, and though he does not mention the ants, still he tells us that gold was so plentiful and found in such a readily obtainable form, that the normal methods of washing were here unnecessary.

'Pliny is the last classical authority I shall quote, and his reference is the more remarkable because he mentions our Dards actually by name. I refer to his well-known line—

> "*Fertilissimi sunt auri Dardae,*
> *Setae vero argenti.*"
> —Lib. vi. c. 19.

'So, you see, in his day the Dards were as noted for their gold as the Seths—the hereditary bankers of India—still are for their connection with silver.

'Now, though the above by no means exhausts my list of classic authorities, I think those I have quoted are enough to prove my point. It has always puzzled me to know what the source of all this gold can have been; for where, to-day, is the gold-bearing desert of Herodotus—where the goldfields of Ktesias—why has the glory of the Dards departed? I felt that much more was needed to account for all these than the puny gold-workings on the Upper Indus and the Tibetan mines of Chokkjalung, which are all that remain to-day. Yes, something more was needed—and W. and I think that we have found out what that something is.

'The fame of our gold was not by any means confined to the times of Greeks and Romans,—come to later days and you will find that the traditional riches of Western Tibet have appealed to adventurers throughout history, for when the Tang Dynasty ruled China, in the days of Saxon England, the "Divine Khan" heard of these riches, and sent out his armies in an effort to obtain them. Again, about the time of

Bannockburn, Zulkadar Khan the Tartar and his host perished in the snows of the Tibetan passes on the same quest.
Later, that Emperor of Delhi—the exploits of whose reign
would have put to the blush a Caligula or a Nero—
Muhammad Tughlak, heard the same tale of gold for the
gathering, a thing he was ever peculiarly in need of, and
launched an army of a hundred thousand men, of whom not
a single soul survived. You remember, too, how some eighty
years ago, Zorawar, the Great Captain of the Dogras, conquered Ladakh for his master Gulab Singh of Jammu. But
afterwards, why did he embark on his mad march farther
eastwards—into Tibet in the midst of a Tibetan winter—to
perish miserably for his pains? What was it that befooled
so tried a leader—what was it that lured all these armies to
their doom? Gold—nothing but the lure of gold for the gathering: the lure that has attracted men of all the ages, from
Jason to Dan M'Grew. And still the gold is there—somewhere—waiting for the finding. Spadum has given us our
clue to the finding of it.

'For this is what we found at Spadum. The monastery is
of great antiquity, and was no doubt founded by those disciples sent out by King Asoka to preach the Excellent Law,
after the third great Buddhist Council of Patna, about 250
B.C. Those early missionaries of course were orthodox Buddhists of the Buddhism of the Dards, their converts, and of
the monastery they had founded. But about 1000 A.D., came
an invasion from Central Tibet that broke the power of the
Dards and swept away the Yellow Robe, establishing in its
place the lamaist[2] Buddhism of Lhassa. It was then that
Spadum was destroyed, and its ruins are now almost as completely buried as are the remains of Nineveh, of Asshur, or
of Taxila. Some few rock-carvings there are still visible
above ground; but these are of no special interest, for the
usual religious subjects only are represented—the most
prominent being a typical carving of the Buddhas of the Five
Kalpas seated upon Lotus Thrones, with the Maitreya in his
three-pointed crown presiding as the central figure.

'It was not till we came to excavate the cells below the
monastery that we made our real discoveries, for then we
found a room which must, we think, have been a large hall

of audience, the back wall of which is formed by the face of a huge boulder. As we cleared away the rubbish we discovered this face to be covered with carvings and inscriptions. The topmost carving to be unearthed was an ordinary figure of Buddha seated upon a lotus; but below this there first appeared a long inscription in Brahmi characters of about 150 B.C., and then you can imagine our excitement as the surface yielded inch by inch to our digging, disclosing even more unexpected carvings beneath.

'Instead of the Garudas—mythological birds—or rows of pyramidical chaityas, which were the sort of things we had expected, we found the best example of an early Dard rock-picture I have ever seen, representing five men fighting for their lives against a swarm of small animals that were attacking them. Four of the men were depicted as defending themselves with spears, whilst the fifth was making off with a big bag on his back. As for the attackers, they seemed to have claws something like those of gigantic lobsters, and to be crawling out of holes in the ground; we were quite defeated as to what nature of beast they were meant to be.

'Then Weismann got busy deciphering that Brahmi inscription. Fortunately that is W.'s long suit, as you know, so in a few days he had got the gist of the sentence, the end of which is somewhat defaced. His translation is as follows:— "Hail!—the Jewel in the Lotus. Preserved by the Lord Buddha, the Seekers have returned with much gold. From the Three Lakes, for fifty days fared they out through the land where no man dwells, towards the rising sun. In the Mountains of the Yak's Head many were slain by the Keepers of the Gold ..."

'Now, though at first sight this may seem rather cryptic, still it evidently referred to my old friends the Dard gold-seekers, so I need not tell you how excited I was to find myself brought into touch with them, as it were, first hand. As you will see, too, the inscription gave us our clue to the full meaning of the rock-picture, for soon after, as we were examining it in the light of W.'s translation, all of a sudden Herodotus's old story of the Indians and the ants came back to me, and— "Ants, by Gad!"—I shouted to Weismann, who was so startled that he dropped those blue spectacles of his.

"Ants? Where?" he asked, looking about him. "Why, there, on the rock—the gold-digging ants of Herodotus for a fiver. They're the Keepers of the Gold." "Lieber Gott! I believe you are right," said he, and the more we looked the more certain of it we became.

'You see, as we understood it, the figure of Buddha was a thank-offering erected by the gold-seekers, while the picture below showed the dangers they had faced: and if we were right about the ants, then, as you must admit, the whole carving is a most astonishing corroboration of Herodotus's story. But most important of all, the inscription tells us too where his "desert" lies in which the gold is found.

'We both believe that we have solved that problem. The first part of it is easy: The "Three Lakes" are the Panggong Tso—that string of lakes extending for ninety miles from our border into Tibet, for the Panggong is sometimes so called to this day. Thence the gold-seekers went fifty marches "through the land where no man dwells, towards the rising sun"—that, of course, must mean E.N.E. through the Northern Tibetan Chang, for the Chang has been uninhabited since the beginning of time. But the mention of the "Mountains of the Yak's Head " is the clearest bit of all, for I am certain that these must be that northern spur of the Kuen Lun which Sven Hedin on one of his journeys saw in the far distance. He tells us that, though the La Shung Tartars never penetrated to these mountains on their wanderings, still they know them as the "Buka Magna," or Mountains of the Wild Yak's Head. Now, in country like this, names never change, but are handed down from father to son throughout the ages; they were the same in the days of Fa Hian's pilgrimage as they are to-day. And the Buka Magna are just about fifty marches from the Panggong too. Yes, I am sure we have got it—it was in the Buka Magna that the Dards found their gold; but for a thousand years the Dards have been a broken subject race, the secret of the gold has been lost, and their gold-seeking has become a vague tradition. And since their day, to the best of our belief, not another soul has visited the Buka Magna.

'You know what the Northern Tibetan Chang is like— from the Karakorum to the Ara Tag it is a vast uninhabited upland formed by the ridges and valleys of the Kuen Lun, where the bottom of the lowest valley is sixteen thousand feet above the sea, and the best-found caravan dies off like flies from starvation and exposure. Inhabitants there are none, save for the bands of wandering yak-hunters and gold-seekers who hang upon its outer fringe. And how many explorers have passed through the Northern Chang? Duotreuil de Rhine—Wellby—Sven Hedin; they managed to get through, but they about complete the list, and not one of them went near our Buka Magna. That is still a white spot on the map.

'So the Buka Magna is our goal, and we are both confident that we shall find there that lost Tibetan gold whose fame has made such a stir in history. Weismann pictures a greater Moravian Mission, endowed with ample funds, extending from Khotan to Kashgar. I see myself a man of means, living like a gentleman in the home of my fathers.

'The Indian Government, of course, keeps the Tibetan frontier closed against all Europeans, so I have got Chinese passports for both of us valid for Turkestan, and nominally we are bound for Khotan. We mean to start by the route taken by the old Forsyth Mission to Yakub Beg at Kashgar—that is, we shall start north up the Kugrang Tsampo and over the Karakorum by the Chang Lung La, but when we reach the uninhabited wastes of the Aksai Chin beyond, and no one can stop us any more, then we shall turn due east into Tibet and head for the Buka Magna. By car route it will be a march of some sixty days, so, starting at the beginning of May, if all goes well we should be back in Leh by October. Two months in the Buka Magna should be ample, for we count on finding the gold in some readily obtainable form—probably in very rich alluvial deposits—and we are going well prepared for simple "placer" work. You see, it stands to reason that the Dards travelled very light, and used only the most primitive methods of extraction.

'And the "Keepers of the Gold"—who were they? for that there was some malign influence at work against the gold-seekers I cannot doubt. Were they merely these roving bands of Tangut robbers, ever the scourge of Northern Tibet, or can a race of giant ants in truth exist there after all? That explanation seems beyond belief; and yet, why not? Herodotus, Megasthenes, and the rock-picture of Spadum—there must be some foundation for their tale. Moreover, if you but go into any Dard village to this day, they will tell you twenty tales of gold-digging ants; and folk-lore always stands upon a strong foundation. In that far-off empty land, who can tell that we may not find the ants of Herodotus, living unknown to-day as the okapi and the takin lived till yesterday, and as—some think—the giant sloth still lives in Patagonia? After all, Pliny told us that Hanno of Carthage had found the gorilla two thousand years ago, but—till he was discovered again by Thomas Savage—how many of us were there that credited his existence? I believe that the local conditions on the Tibetan steppes may well have evolved throughout the ages a giant species to prey upon the field-mice, the marmots, and the antelope that every-where abound—a giant race of ants forgotten for a thou-sand years.

'And what a foe such an ant would be. Think of the black ant we know in India, with all his savagery and blind cour-age, and magnify him some thirty times. No animal in the world could stand against him.

'But whoever the Keepers of the Gold may be, or if they do exist, in three months' time at most Weismann and I shall know.'"

Rowland ceased reading. "That is all," said he, "and I really did not know what to make of it, for it seemed the maddest sort of treasure-hunt, and Kenway was the last man I should ever have accused of madness. Old Weismann too, I thought he was above filthy lucre, but then apparently he wanted it only to extend his Mission. In the end I made up my mind to pull their legs properly for them when they came back, and then more or less forgot all about them.

"It must have been about mid-September that the treasure-hunters were recalled very forcibly to my mind. One morning as I was sitting in my office in Leh I was told that a man had just rid-den in with an urgent letter for me. I had him in at once and found that he was a Tibetan from the western end of the Panggong, with a letter from the Governor of Rudok, the adjoining Tibetan province.

I had the letter translated; after the usual compliments, the gist of it was that an unknown European had just been brought in to the Governor at Rudok town. This European had been found desperately ill, wandering alone in Northern Rudok, and the Governor was having him moved towards the Border as carefully as possible; but it was feared that he might die before he reached there, so I was asked to come out myself to meet the party. I could read between the lines that there was something peculiar in the case, and concluded that the local authorities were in mortal dread of the anger of the Devashang—the supreme council of Lhassa—in case the European's death within their jurisdiction should lead to awkward questions from the British Government.

"It immediately struck me that Kenway or Weismann must be the European referred to, for there was no other party out that could possibly have strayed into that part of the world; but if it were either of them, then why was he alone?—it looked bad. I decided to start at once, and as there was no doctor then in Leh, I had to go alone. It took me about a week to the Panggong, and there a guide met me to take me to the sick man, who had been brought to a point some twenty miles away on the south shore of the lake. There I found the usual Tibetan camp and went to the largest of the tents, which, so two or three Tibetan soldiers lounging outside told me, belonged to the Deputy-Governor of Rudok. At that moment a smooth-faced, foxy-looking individual of about thirty appeared from within—it was the Deputy-Governor himself. He ushered me into the tent, where, after the usual ceremonies, I found myself seated on a numdah to discuss the object of my mission with him.

"There and then I took an instinctive dislike to the Deputy-Governor—a sly deprecating ruffian, who, like the late Mr. Kilmansegg of immortal memory, indulged to excess in that horrid trick of 'washing his hands with invisible soap in imperceptible water'—certainly the only use he ever made of either of those commodities. One felt him to be pre-eminently capable of that emotionless cruelty of the yellow man which is incomprehensible to the honest brutality of the Caucasian. He rejoiced apparently in the name of Stag Tsang—the Tiger Lord—but he was altogether so excessively ''umble' that I felt that I had known him since childhood—a Tibetan edition of Uriah Heap to the life.

"I gathered from Uriah that the European was in a tent close by. A few weeks earlier he had appeared—as though dropped from the clouds—on the fringe of the inhabited districts near the Aru Tso, where, by the merest chance, he had been picked up by one of those notorious robbers of Amdo and Nakktsong, ever a thorn in the flesh of authority. This particular robber—by name Tesshi—appears, however, to have been heartily sick of his trade, for he looked on this find of his as a heaven-sent chance to make his peace with the powers-that-be. So he brought the stranger to Rudok as a peace-offering. Alas, poor simple Tesshi—he had reckoned without Uriah, and his well-laid scheme for reformation was to come to nought, for my friend dismissed him with the brief remark, 'His sins were very many, so he died next day.'

"This summary justice, however, in no way helped to elucidate the identity of the stranger, who was in the last stages of collapse from wounds and exhaustion: the Tibetans were completely at a loss, and finally it was decided to send for me. The sick man had since grown steadily worse, and Uriah expected him to die at any moment, so he was heartily glad that I had appeared to relieve him of responsibility.

"The Tibetans escorted me across to the sick man's tent, a small blanket affair close by. Within, on a heap of numdahs and sheepskins, bearded, emaciated, and incredibly filthy, lay the figure of a man. It was Kenway, but a very different Kenway from the man that I remembered. I had to look many times before I was certain of his identity, and could hardly bring myself to believe that this wild-eyed skeleton, seated in filth, was in reality the friend whom I had known. My entry roused him from a stupor, and he greeted me with incoherent babblings. I did what I could to soothe him till the arrival of my men and baggage, and then carried him over to my tent: he weighed no more than a child. There we washed him and put him to bed. We found a terrible open wound in his left leg; all the muscles of the calf had been torn away as though with a pair of giant pincers, and since had shrunk and atrophied. Septicaemia was far advanced, and it was a wonder that he had not died long since. I cleaned the wound, and dressed it as well as I could with corrosive; the Tibetans had been applying compresses of fresh yak's-dung to it. Kenway was delirious the whole time; obviously his only possible chance was complete rest, so there was no choice but to stay where we were.

"Kenway lived for three days without ever once recovering his reason, and during the whole of that time I hardly quitted his bedside. Hour after hour as he tossed in his delirium he talked of all that he had been through. Never shall I forget these days, and the scene is graven on my memory. Through the open tent-door there showed a sweep of bare grey foreshore, stretching down to the waters of the Panggong—those lifeless waters, incredibly blue and bitter as brine—while across the lake, sheer and precipitous, rose the barren brick-red hills of the Southern Changchenmo. Not a movement, save where a wandering dust-devil raised a momentary puff of whirling sand; not a sound from without, save ever and anon the far-off whistling cries of the Tibetan yak-drovers. Tibet, that unkind land of Arctic cold and blinding hail—no matter how she may have flouted us, she yet holds us all in thrall, all who have known her. One and all we cherish the fond hope of returning to her some day, to hear again the wild music of the snow-cock as he sweeps downwards from the crag to greet once more the mighty Father of All Sheep as he stands at gaze upon the brow.

"And, by my side, throughout these days, rose the dry husky whisper of the dying man—hour after hour. Gradually, from his oft-repeated wanderings, I seemed to piece together a coherent tale—the offspring of a fevered brain to be believed or discarded, as you will. This is how it ran:—

'Not a living thing for the last three days—Weismann. Not an antelope—not even a marmot. I don't like it—the whole country's deserted. ...

'And these paths that we keep coming on—hard-beaten narrow paths—they must be game-paths—yet there isn't any game. ...

'My God! Did you hear that cry? Was it a horse or a man? Wake up! Wake up!—Weismann—how damnably dark it is!—and the cold!

'Mahomed! Mahomed! Why doesn't the fellow answer? The men's tent empty and the horses gone? They can't have left us—they can't have!

'All but your horse and mine—it's the end of everything. ...

'Look!—Weismann, look!—that gravel in the shallows—there's gold there—masses of it.

'We've found the gold!—we've found the gold—but what use is it to us now?

'My God!—what's that? Look, there—coming over the rocks above you—the Keepers of the Gold!

'Run! Weismann, run!—back to the horses—faster! man, faster!—Weismann's down—they've got him!—God! how he screams. ...

'I must go back to him—my ice-axe crushes them like paper—faugh!—the yellow matter that squirts out and the sickening smell of musk!—but more keep crowding up—one has got me by the leg—his body's crushed to pulp, but still his pincers hold. ...

'Weismann moves no more—he's dead—a black heaving mass of ravening tearing bodies!

'It will be my turn next—back to the horses!—I must get back—it's my only chance. ...

'But to desert Weismann—the horror of it and the shame— but I could have done no good—he was dead, I swear he was dead—I swear it. ...

"Such were the oft-repeated ravings to which I listened; and on the third day Kenway died. What do I make of it? Well, I hardly know. The Tibetans say that the party must have been lost from starvation in the Chang, and that of course is the rational explanation—or else that they were set upon by Tesshi's gang of robbers and wiped out, all save Kenway. Of course I reported the whole affair to headquarters, giving the Tibetan version and my own suspicions regarding Tesshi. But Kenway and Weismann had entered Tibet against the express orders of Government; so naturally that august body declined to take any action in the matter, and accepted the Tibetan story without question.

"Still, somehow I feel that there is more behind, and that neither of those explanations satisfies me; for sometimes I seem to hear again that husky whisper telling of unbelievable horrors in an unknown land—that whisper to which I listened for three long days beside the Panggong Tso. And a scene rises before me: I see a barren empty land of vast expanses, of rolling shale-slopes and grey rounded hills—the Home of the Winds and the Roof of the World— rising in the north to a culminating gable of massed snows. In the foreground there lies a snow-fed stream, and an icy wind is blowing from the snows. Not a sound breaks the silence, save the hoarse croak of the Tibetan sand-grouse as he wings his way to water; not another living thing moves in the landscape; but over all there broods a sense of sinister expectancy.

"And then, all at once along a path I see a hurrying stream of squat black forms appear, relentless as death and hideous as a nightmare. It is the army of the Keepers going out on a foray.

"And by the stream something white gleams in the sunshine—I know it for the clean-picked skeleton of a man."

[1] The Political Department is India's Diplomatic and Consular Service.

[2] The Tibetan Buddhists adhere to the "Greater Vehicle of the Law" propounded by Kanishka's Fourth Council. The Lamas are of two persuasions—Red Caps and Yellow; but the robe of both these persuasions is red.

The Spectre Spiders
William J. Wintle

The fog hung thickly over London one morning in late autumn. It was not the dense compound of smoke and moisture, pea-souplike in color and pungent to eyes and nose, that is known as a "London peculiar"; but a fairly clean and white mist that arose from the river and lay about the streets and squares in great wisps and wreaths and banks.

The passing crowd shivered and thought of approaching winter; while a few optimistic souls looked upward to the invisible sky and predicted a warm day when the sun had grown in strength. A little child remarked to a companion that it smelled like washing day: and the comparison was not without its point. It was as if the motor machinery of the metropolis had blown off steam in preparation for a fresh start.

People passed one another in the mist like sheeted ghosts and did not speak. Friend failed to recognize friend; or, if he did, he took for granted that the other did not. Apart from the steady rumble of the traffic and the long deep note that the great city gives forth to hearing ears all the day long, the world seemed strangely silent and unfriendly.

Certainly this applied with truth to one member of the passing crowd whose business brought abroad that misty morning when home and the fireside gained an added attraction. Ephraim Goldstein was silent by nature and unfriendly by profession. For him language was an ingenious device for the concealment of thought; and when there was no special reason for such concealment, why should he trouble to speak?

It was not as if people were over desirous to hear him speak. He was naturally unattractive: and where nature had failed to complete

her task, Ephraim had brought it to perfection. A habit of scowl-
ing had effectually removed any trace of amiability that might have
survived the handicap of evil eyes and unpleasing features. When
strangers saw Ephraim for the first time, they looked quickly
around for a pleasant face to act by way of antidote.

We have said that he was unfriendly by profession. But the un-
wary and innocent would never have suspected this from his professional announcements in the personal column of the morning
papers. The gentleman of fortune who was wishful, without security or inquiry, to advance goodly sums of money to his less fortunate fellow creatures on nominal terms and in the most delicate
manner possible, was surely giving the best of all proofs of a soul
entirely immersed in the milk of human kindness.

Yet those who had done business with Ephraim spoke of him
in terms not usual in the drawing room: men of affairs who knew
the world of finance called him a blood-sucking spider, and Scotland Yard had him noted down as emphatically a wrong 'un.
Ephraim was not popular with those who knew him. He had in fact
only one point of character that could be commended. He had never
changed his name to Edward Gordon or even to Edwin Goldsmith:
he was born Ephraim Goldstein—and Ephraim Goldstein he was
content to remain to the end. A rose by any other name smells just
as sweet—but people did not express it quite like that when
Ephraim was under discussion.

He had not always been a gentleman of fortune, nor had he
always been wishful to share his fortune with others. People with
inconveniently long memories recalled a youth of like name who
got into trouble at Whitechapel for selling Kosher fowls judiciously
weighted with sand: and there was also a story about a young man
who manipulated three thimbles and a pea on Epsom Downs.

But why drag in these scandals of the past? In the case of any
man it is unfair to thus search the record of his youth for evidence
against him; and in the case of Ephraim it was quite unnecessary.
He was a perennial plant: however lurid the past, he blossomed
forth afresh every year in renewed vigor and in equally glowing
colors.

How fortune had come to him seemed to be known by no one
save himself; but certainly it had come, for it is difficult to lend
money if you do not possess it. And with its coming Ephraim had
migrated from Whitechapel to Haggerston, then to Kilburn, and

finally to Maida Vale, where he now had his abode. But it must not be supposed that he indulged in either ambition or luxury. He was content with very modest comfort, and lived a simple bachelor existence; but he found a detached villa with some garden behind it more convenient for his purposes than a house in a terrace with an inquisitive neighbor on either side. His visitors came on business and by no means for pleasure: and privacy was as congenial to them as it was to him.

The business that had brought him out on this foggy morning was of an unusual character in that it had nothing to do with money making. It in fact involved spending money to the extent of two guineas now, with a probability of further sums; and he did not at all relish it. Ephraim was on his way to Cavendish Square to consult a noted oculist.

For some weeks past, he had been troubled with a curious affliction of his sight. He was still on the sunny side of fifty, and hitherto he had been very sharp-sighted in more senses than one. But now something seemed to be going wrong. His vision was perfect during the day, and usually through the evening as well; but twice recently he had been bothered with a curious optical delusion. On each occasion he had been sitting quietly reading after dinner, when something had made him uneasy. It was the same sort of disquiet that he always felt if a cat came into the room. So strong had been this feeling that he had sprung out of his chair without quite knowing why he did it; and each time had fancied that a number of shadows streamed forth from his chair and ran across the carpet to the walls, where they vanished. They were evidently nothing but shadows, for he could see the carpet through them; but they were fairly clear and distinct. They seemed to be about the size of a cricket ball. Though he attached no meaning to the coincidence, it was a little odd that on each occasion he had been reluctantly compelled during the day to insist upon his pound of flesh from a client. And when Ephraim insisted, he did not stick at a trifle. But obviously this could have nothing to do with a defect of vision.

The great specialist made a thorough examination of Ephraim's eyes, but could find nothing wrong with them. So he explored further and investigated the state of his patient's nervous and digestive systems; but found that these were perfectly sound.

Then he embarked upon more delicate matters, and sought to learn something of the habits of Ephraim. A bachelor in the forties may be addicted to the cup that cheers and occasionally inebriates as well: he may be fond of the pleasures of the table: he may be attracted by the excitement of gambling: in fact he may do a great many things that a man of his years should not do. The physician was a man of tact and diplomacy. He asked no injudicious questions; but he had the valuable gift of inducing conversation in others. Not for years had Ephraim talked so freely and frankly to any man. The result was that the doctor could find no reason for suggesting that the trouble was due to any kind of dietary or other indiscretion.

So he fell back on the last refuge of the baffled physician. "Rest, my dear Sir," he said; "that is the best prescription. I am happy to say that I find no serious lesion or even functional disturbance; but there is evidence of fatigue affecting the brain and the optic nerve. There is no reason to anticipate any further or more serious trouble; but a wise man always takes precautions. My advice is that you drop all business for a few weeks and spend the time in golf or other out-of-door amusement—say at Cromer or on the Surrey Downs. In that case you may be pretty confident that no further disturbance of this kind will occur."

Ephraim paid his two guineas with a rather wry face. He had the feeling that he was not getting much for his money; still it was reassuring to find that there was nothing the matter. Rest! Rubbish! He was not overworked. Surrey Downs indeed! Hampstead Heath was just as good and a great deal cheaper: he might take a turn there on Sunday mornings. Golf? You would not catch him making a fool of himself in tramping after a ridiculous ball! So he simply went on much the same as before, and hoped that all would be well.

Yet, somehow, things did not seem to be quite right with him. Business was prosperous, if you can speak of business in connection with the pleasant work of sharing your fortune with the less fortunate—always on the most reasonable terms possible. Ephraim would have told you that he lost terribly through the dishonesty of people who died or went abroad or whose expectations did not turn out as well as they should; and yet, in some mysterious way, he had more money to lend than ever. But he was worried.

One evening, after an unusually profitable day, he was sitting in his garden, smoking a cigar that had been given him by a grateful client who was under the mistaken impression that Ephraim's five per cent was to be reckoned per year, whereas it was really per week. It was a good cigar; and the smoker knew how to appreciate good tobacco. He was lying back in a hammock chair, and idly watching the rings of smoke as they rose on the quiet air and floated away.

Then he suddenly started and stared. The rings were behaving in a very odd fashion. They seemed to form themselves into globes of smoke; and from each of them protruded eight waving filaments that turned and bent like the legs of some uncanny creature. And it seemed as if these trailing limbs of smoke turned and reached toward him. It was curious and not altogether pleasant. But it was no case of an optical delusion. The evening light was good, and the thing was seen clearly enough. It must have been the result of some unusual state of the atmosphere at the time.

He was aroused by hearing conversation on the other side of the wall. The occupant of the next-door house was in his garden with a friend, and their talk was of matters horticultural. It did not interest Ephraim, who paid a jobbing gardener the smallest possible amount to keep the place tidy, and concerned himself no further about it. He did not want to hear of the respective virtues of different local seed vendors. But the talk was insistent, and he presently found himself listening against his will. They were talking about spiders; and his neighbor was saying that he had never known such a plague of them or such large-sized specimens. And he went on to say that they all seemed to come over the wall from Ephraim's side! The listener discovered that his cigar had gone out; and he went indoors in disgust.

It was only a few days later when the next thing happened. Ephraim had gone to bed rather earlier than usual, being somewhat tired, but was unable to sleep. For some hours he tossed about wearily and angrily—for he usually slept well—and then came a spell of disturbed and restless slumber. Dream after dream passed through his mind; and somehow they all seemed to have something to do with spiders. He thought that he fought his way through dense jungles of web; he walked on masses of soft and yielding bodies that crushed and squished beneath his tread; multitudinous hairy legs waved to and fro and clung to him; fanged jaws bit him with the sting of fiery fluids; and gleaming eyes were everywhere staring at him with a gaze of unutterable malignancy. He fell, and the webs wrapped him round in an embrace of death; great woolly creatures flung themselves upon him and suffocated him with their foul stink; unspeakable things had him in their ghastly grip; he was sinking in an ocean of unimaginable horror.

He awoke screaming, and sprang out of bed. Something caught him in the face and clung round his head. He groped for the switch and turned on the light. Then he tore off the bandage that blinded him, and found that it was a mass of silky threads like the web that a giant spider might have spun. And, as he got it clear of his eyes, he saw great shadows run up the walls and vanish. They had grown since he saw them first on the carpet; they were now the size of footballs.

Ephraim was appalled by the horror of it. Unrestful sleep and persistent nightmare were bad enough; but here was something worse. The silky wisps that still clung about his head were not such stuff as dreams are made of. He wondered if he was going mad. Was the whole thing a hallucination? Could he pull himself together and shake it off? He tried; but the bits of web that waved from his fingers and face were real enough. No dream spider could have spun them; mere imagination could not have created them. Moreover, he was not a man of imagination. Quite the opposite. He dealt in realities: real estate was the security he preferred.

A stiff glass of brandy and soda pulled him together. He was not addicted to stimulants—it did not pay in his profession—but this was a case that called for special measures. He shook off the obsession, and thought there might be something in the golf suggestion after all. And when a client called during the morning to negotiate a little loan, Ephraim drove a shrewd bargain that surprised even himself.

The next incident that caused considerable disquiet to the gentleman of fortune seems to have occurred about a month later. He was no lover of animals, but he tolerated the presence of a Scots terrier in the house. It occasionally happened that he had large sums of money on the premises—not often, but sometimes it could not be helped—and the alert little dog was a good protection against the intrusive burglar. So he treated the animal as a sort of confidential servant, and was, after his fashion, attached to it. If he did not exactly love it, he at any rate appreciated and valued it. He did not even grudge the veterinarian's charges when it was ill.

At night the terrier had the run of the house, but usually slept on a mat outside Ephraim's door. On this particular occasion Ephraim dreamed that he had fallen over the dog, and that it gave a loud yelp of pain. So vivid was the impression that it woke him, and the cry of the animal seemed to still linger on his ear. It was as if the terrier outside the door had really cried out. He listened, but all was quiet save for a curious clicking and sucking sound that he heard at intervals. It seemed to come from just outside the door; but that could not be, for the dog would have been roused and would have given the alarm if anything was wrong.

So he presently went to sleep again, and did not wake until his usual time for rising. As he dressed, it struck him as unusual that he heard nothing of the dog, which was accustomed to greet the first sounds of movement with a welcoming bark or two. When he opened his door, the terrier lay dead on the mat.

Ephraim was first shocked, then grieved, and next alarmed. He was shocked because it was simply natural to be shocked under the circumstances; he was grieved because it then dawned upon him that he was more Fond of the animal than he could have believed possible; and he was alarmed because he knew that the mysterious death of a watch dog is often the preliminary to a burglary.

He hurried downstairs and made a hasty examination of the doors and windows, and particularly of a safe that was hidden in the wall behind what looked like a solid piece of furniture. But everything was in good order, and there was no sign of any attempt on the premises. Then he went upstairs to remove the body of the dog, wondering the while if it would be worth the expense to have a post mortem. Ephraim disliked mysteries, especially when they happened in the house.

He picked up the dead terrier, and at once met with a bad shock. It was a mere featherweight, and collapsed in his hands! It was little more than a skeleton, rattling loose in a bag of skin. It had been simply sucked dry!

He dropped it in horror, and as he did so he found some silky threads clinging to his hands. And there were threads waving in the air, for one of them twined itself about his head and clung stickily to his face. And then something fell with a soft thud on the floor behind him, and he turned just in time to see a shadow dart to the wall and disappear. He had seen that shadow form before; but it somehow seemed to be less shadowy and more substantial now.

It seems to have been about this time that a rumor circulated in Maida Vale that a monkey had escaped from the Zoological Gardens in Regent's Park and had been seen climbing on Ephraim's house.

It was first seen early in the morning by a milkman, who mentioned it to a policeman, and soon afterward by a housemaid who was cleaning the steps of a house opposite. It was a rather dark and misty morning, which doubtless accounts for a certain vagueness in the descriptions of the animal. But, so far as they went, all the descriptions agreed.

The monkey was described as a very fat specimen, almost like a football in size and rotundity, with very long arms. It was covered with thick, glossy, black hair, and was seen to climb up the front of the house and enter by an open window. The milkman, who was fond of reading, said that he thought it was a spider monkey; but his only reason for this seems to have been some fancied resemblance to a very large spider.

Later in the morning, the policeman called on Ephraim to mention the matter, and to ask if the monkey was still there. His reception was not polite; and he retired in disorder. Then he rang up the Zoological Gardens, but was informed that no monkeys were missing. The incident was duly recorded at the police station, and there it ended, for no more was ever heard of it.

But another occurrence in the following week gave rise to much more talk, especially among the ladies of the neighborhood. The empty skin of a valuable Persian cat was found in the shrubbery of the house next to Ephraim's—empty, that is, except for the bones of the animal. The skin was quite fresh; as it well might be, for the cat had been seen alive the evening before. The mystery formed a nine days' wonder, and was never solved until an even more shocking mystery came to keep it company. The cat's skin had been sucked dry and the local theory was that a stoat or other beast of prey had escaped from the zoo and done the dire deed. But it was proved that no such escape had occurred, and there the matter had to stop.

Although it seems to have no significance, it may be well to place on record a trifling incident that happened a week or two later. A collector for some charitable institution called upon Ephraim under the mistaken impression that he was a person who wanted to get rid of his money. He was speedily undeceived, and was only in the house for a few minutes. But he told his wife afterward that Mr. Goldstein was evidently a great cat fancier, for he had noticed several fine black Persians curled up asleep in the house. But it was curious that they were all in the darkest and most

obscure corners, where they could not be seen very clearly. He had
made some passing reference to them to Mr. Goldstein, who did
not seem to understand him. Indeed he stared at him as if he
thought him the worse for drink!

Another incident at this time was made the subject of remark
among Ephraim's neighbors. For reasons best known to himself,
he had long been in the habit of sleeping with a loaded revolver at
his bedside; and one morning, about daybreak, the sound of a shot
was heard. The police were quickly on the spot and insisted upon
entering the house. Ephraim assured them that the weapon had
been accidentally discharged through being dropped on the floor;
and, after asking to see his gun licence, the police departed.

But what had really happened was much more interesting.
Ephraim had woke up without apparent cause, but with a vague
sense of danger; and was just in time to see a round black body,
covered with a dense coat of hair, climb up the foot of his bed and
make its way cautiously toward his face. It was a gigantic spider;
and its eight gleaming eyes blazed with lambent green light like a
cluster of sinister opals.

He was paralysed with horror; then, summoning all his force
of will, he snatched up the revolver and fired. The flash and the
noise of the report dazed him for a moment; and when he saw
clearly again the spider was gone. He must have hit it, for he fired
point blank; but it had left no sign. It was just as well, for otherwise his tale would not have passed muster with the police. But,
later in the morning, he found a trail of silky threads running across
the carpet from the bed to the wall.

But the end was now very near. Only a few days later, the police
were again in the house. This time they had been called in by the
gardener, who said that he could not make Mr. Goldstein hear when
he knocked at his door, and that he thought he must be ill. The
door was locked, and had to be forced.

What the police found had better not be described. At the funeral, the undertaker's men said that they had never carried a man
who weighed so little for his size.

The Eggs from Lake Tanganyika
Curt Siodmak

Professor Meyer-Maier drew a sharp needle out of the cush-
ion, carefully picked up with the pincers the fly lying in front of
him and stuck it carefully upon a piece of white paper. He looked
over the rim of his glasses, dipped his pen in the ink and wrote
under the specimen:

"*Glossina pulpulis*, specimen from Tsetsefly River. In
the aboriginal language termed *nei-nei*. Usually found on
river courses and lakes in West Africa. Bearer of the malady
Negana (Tse-tse sickness—sleeping sickness.)

He laid down the pen and took up a powerful magnifying glass
for a closer examination. "A horrible creature," he murmured, and
shivered involuntarily. On each side of the head of the flying horror,
there was a monstrous eye surrounded by many sharp lashes and
divided up into a hundred thousand flashing facets. An ugly proboscis thickly studded with curved barbs or hooks grew out of the
lower side of the head. The wings were small and pointed, the legs
armed with thorns, spines and claws. The thorax was muscular,
like that of a prize fighter. The abdomen was thin and looked like
India rubber. It could take in a great quantity of blood and expand
like a balloon. On the whole, the flying horror, resembling a pre-
historic flying dragon, was not very pleasant-looking—Prof. Meyer-
Maier took a pin and transfixed the body of the fly. It seemed to
him that a vicious sheen of light emanated from the eyes and that
the proboscis rolled up. Quickly he picked up the magnifying glass,
but it was an optical illusion—the thing was dead, with all its poison still within its body.

Memories of the Expedition to Africa

With a deep sigh he laid aside pincers and magnifying glass and sank into a deep reverie. The clock struck 12. 1-2-3-4-5, counted Professor Meyer-Maier.

In Udjidji, a village on lake Tanganyika, the natives had told him of gigantic flies inhabiting the interior further north. These monsters were three times as big as giants composing the giant bodyguard of the Prince of Sauggi, who all had to be of at least standard height. Meyer-Maier laughed over this negro fable, but the negroes were obstinate. They refused to follow him to the northern part of Lake Tanganyika. Even Mau-uru, his black servant, who otherwise made an intelligent impression, trembled with excitement and begged to be left out of the expedition—because there enormous flies and bees were to be found,—that let no man approach. They drank the river dry and guarded the valley of the elephants. "The Valley of the Elephants" was a fabled place where the old pachyderms withdrew to die. "It is inexplicable," soliloquized Meyer-Maier, "that no one ever found a dead elephant."

The clock struck 6-7-8.

The natives had come along on the expedition much against their will. Meyer-Maier had trouble to keep the caravan moving up to the day when he found four great, strange looking eggs, larger than ostrich eggs. The negroes were seized with a panic, half of them deserting in the night, in spite of the great distance from the coast. The other half could only be kept there by tremendous efforts. He had to make up his mind finally, to go back, but he secretly put the eggs he had found into his camping chest to solve their riddle.

Now they were here in his Berlin home, in his work-room. He had not found time as yet to examine them, for he had brought much material home to be worked over.

The clock struck 9-10.

Meyer-Maier kept thinking of the ugly head of the tse-tse fly that he had seen through the magnifying glass. A strange thought occurred to him and made him smile. Suppose the stories of the negroes were true and the giant flies—butterflies and beetles as big as elephants did exist! And suppose that they propagated as flies do!—each one laying eighty million eggs a year! He laughed aloud and pictured to himself how such a creature would stalk through the streets.

A Strange Sound and the Hatching of an Egg

He broke off suddenly, in the midst of his laughter. A sound reached his ear, an earsplitting buzzing like that of a thousand flies, a deafening hum, as if a swarm of bees were entering the room; it burst out like a blast of wind through the room and then stopped. Meyer-Maier jerked the door open. Nothing. All was quiet.

"I must relax for a while," said he, and opened the window. He turned on the light and threw back the lid of the big chest, which contained the giant eggs. Suddenly he grew pale as death and staggered back. A creature was crawling out, a creature as big as a police dog—a frightful creature with wings—a muscular body, and six hairy legs with claws. It crept slowly, raised its incandescent head to the light and polished its wings with its hind legs. Faint with fright, Meyer-Maier pressed against the wall with outspread arms. A loud buzzing,—the creature swept across the room, climbed up on the window sill and was gone.

Meyer-Maier came slowly to himself. "My nerves are deceiving me. Did I dream?" he whispered, and dragged himself to the camp-chest. But he became frozen with horror. One egg was broken open. "It breaks out of the shell like a chicken, it does not change into a chrysalis," he thought mechanically. At last his mind cleared and he awoke to the emergency. He sprang to the door, snatched up his revolver, ran downstairs and out into the street. he so no trace of the escaped giant insect. Meyer-Maier looked up into the lighted windows of his home. Suddenly the light became dim. "The other eggs"—like a blow came the thought— "the other eggs too have broken." He raced back up the stairs. A deafening buzzing filled the room. He jacked his door open and fired—once, twice, until the magazine was empty—the room was silent. Through the window he saw three silhouettes sweeping high across the night-sky and disappearing in the direction of the great woods in the West. In the chest there lay the four broken giant eggs.

A Call for His Colleague

Meyer-Maier sank upon a chair. "It's against all logic," he thought, and glanced at the empty revolver in his hand. "My delirium has taken wings and crawled out of the egg. What shall I do? Shall I call the police? They will send me to an alienist! Keep quiet about it? Look for the creature? I'll call up my colleague, Schmidt-Schmitt!" He dragged himself to the telephone and got a connection. Schmidt-Schmitt was at home! "This is Meyer-Maier," sounded a tired voice. "Come over at once!"

"What's the trouble?" asked Schmidt-Schmitt.

"My African giant eggs have burst," lisped Meyer-Maier with a falling voice. "You must come at once!"

"Your nerves are out of order," answered Schmidt-Schmitt. "Have you still got the creatures?"

"They've gone," whispered Meyer-Maier,—he thought he would collapse,— "flew out of the window."

"There, there," laughed Schmidt-Schmitt. "Now, we are getting to the truth—of course they aren't there. Anyhow, I'll come over. Meanwhile take a cognac and put on a cold pack."

"Take your car, and say nothing about what I told you."

Professor Meyer-Maier hung up the receiver.

It was incredible. He pressed his hand to his forehead. If the empty shells were not irrefutable evidence, he would have been inclined to think of hallucinations.

He helped himself to some brandy and after the second glass he felt better. "I wish Professor Schmidt-Schmitt would come. He ought to be here by now. He will have an explanation and will help me to get myself in hand again. The day of ghosts and miracles is long past. But why isn't he here? He ought to have come by this time."

Meyer-Maier looked out of the window. A car came tearing through the dark street and stopped with squeaking brakes in front of Meyer-Maier's residence. A form jumped out like an India rubber ball, ran up the steps, burst into Meyer-Maier's study, and collapsed into a chair.

"How awful," he gasped.

"It seems to me, you are even more excited over it than I," said Professor Meyer-Maier dispiritedly while he watched his shaking friend.

"Absolutely terrible." Professor Schmidt-Schmitt wiped his forehead with a silk handkerchief. "You were not suffering from nerves, you had no hallucinations. Just now I saw a fly-creature as large as a heifer falling upon a horse. The monster grew big and heavy, while the horse collapsed and the fly flew away. I examined the horse. Its veins and arteries were empty. Not a drop of blood was left in the body. The driver fainted with fright and has not come to yet. It is a world catastrophe."

Notifying the Police

"We must notify the police at once."

A quick telephone connection was obtained. The police Lieutenant in charge himself answered.

"This is Professor Meyer-Maier talking! Please believe what I am going to tell you. I am neither drunk nor crazy. Four poisonous gigantic flies, as large as horses are at large in the city. They must be destroyed at all costs."

"What are you trying to do? Kid me?" the lieutenant came back in an angry voice.

"Believe me—for God's sake," yelled Meyer-Maier, reaching the end of his nervous strength.

"Hold the wire." The Lieutenant turned to the desk of the sergeant. "What is up now?"

"A cab driver has been here who says that his horse was killed by a gigantic bird on Karlstraase."

"Get the men of the second platoon ready for immediate action," he ordered the sergeant, and turned back to the telephone. "Hello Professor! Are you still there? Please come over as quickly as possible. What you told me is true. One of these giant insects has been seen."

Professor Meyer-Maier hung up. He loaded his revolver and put a Browning pistol into his colleague's hand. "Is your car still downstairs?"

"Yes, I took the little limousine."

"Excellent—then the monster cannot attack us." They rushed on through the night.

"What can happen now?" inquired Professor Schmidt-Schmitt.

"These giant flies may propagate and multiply in the manner of the housefly. And in that case, due to their strength and poisonous qualities," continued Professor Meyer-Maier, "the whole human race will perish in a few weeks. When they crept from the shell they were as large as dogs. They grew to the size of a horse within an hour. God knows what will happen next. Let us hope and pray that we will be able to find and kill the four flies and destroy the eggs which they have laid in the meantime, within fourteen days."

The car came to a stop in front of the Police Station. A policeman armed with a steel helmet and hand trench bombs swinging from his belt tore open the limousine door. The lieutenant hastened out and conducted the scientists into the station house.

"Any more news?" inquired Meyer-Maier.

"The West Precinct station just called up. One of their patrolmen saw a giant animal fly over the Teutoburger Forest. Luckily we had war tanks near there which immediately set out in search of the creature."

The telephone-bell rang. The lieutenant rushed to the phone. "Central Police Station."

"East Station talking. Report comes from Lake Wieler, that a gigantic fly attacked two motor boats."

"Put small trench mortars on the police-boat and go out on the lake. Shoot when the beast gets near you."

"The door of the Station-House opened and the city commissioner entered. "I have just heard some fabulous stories," he said, and approached the visitors. "Professor Meyer-Maier? Major Fritsch-Wiholf! Can you explain all this?"

"I brought home with me four large eggs from my African expedition, for examination. Tonight these eggs broke open. Four great flies came out—a sort of tse-tse fly, such as is found on Lake Tanganyika. The creatures escaped through the window and we must make every endeavor to kill them at once."

The telephone bell rang as if possessed.

"This is the Central Broadcasting Station. A giant bird has been caught in the high voltage lines. It has fallen down and lies on the street."

"Close the street at once." The major took up the instrument. "Call up the Second Company. Let all four flying companies go off with munition and gasoline for three days. Come with me my friends, we will get at least one of them!"

As armored automobile came tearing along at a frightful speed. "We appreciate your foresight, Major," said Meyer-Maier, as they stepped from the steel-armored machine.

One of the Giant Flies is Electrocuted

Although it was five o'clock in the morning, the square in front of the broadcasting station was black with people. The police kept a space clear in the center, where monstrously large and ugly, lay the dead giant fly. Its wings were burnt, its proboscis extended, while the legs, with their claws, were drawn up against the body. The abdomen was a great ball, full of bright red liquid. "That is certainly the creature that killed the horse," said Schmidt-Schmitt,

and pointed at the thick abdomen. He then walked around the creature. *"Glossina pulpulis*. A monstrous tse-tse fly."

"Will you please send the monster to the zoological laboratory?"
The major nodded assent. The firemen, prepared for service,
pushed poles under the insect and tried to lift it up from the
ground. Out of the air came a droning sound. An airplane squadron dropped out of the clouds and again disappeared. A bright body
with vibrating wings flew across the sky. The airplane dropped on
it. The noise of the machine-guns started. The bright body fell in a
spiral course to the ground. Crying and screaming, the people fled
from the street and crowded into the houses. They couldn't tell
where the insect would fall and they were afraid of their heads.
The street was empty in an instant. The body of the monster fell
directly in front of the armored car and lay there, stiff. In its fall it
carried away a lot of aerial cable and now it lay on the pavement as
if caught in a net, the head torn by the machine gun bullets. It
looked like a strange gleaming cactus.

"Take me to my home, Major," groaned Meyer-Maier. "I can't
stand it any longer. The excitement is too much for me."

In the Hospital

The armored car started noisily into motion. Meyer-Maier fell
from the seat, senseless, upon the floor. When he came to himself,
he lay in a strange bed. His gaze fell upon a ball which swung to
and fro above his face. In his head there was a humming like an
airplane motor. He made no attempt, even to think. His finger
pressed the push-button and he never released it until half-a-dozen
attendants came rushing into the room. One figure stood out in
dark colors, in the group of white-clad interns. It was his colleague,
Schmidt-Schmitt.

"You're awake?" said he, and stepped to his bed. "How are you
feeling?"

"My head is buzzing as if there were a swarm of hornets living
in it. How many hours have I lain here?"

"Hours?" Schmidt-Schmitt dwelt upon the word. "Today is the
fifteenth day that you are lying in Professor Stiebling's sanitarium.
It was a difficult case. You always woke up at meal-times and without saying a word, went to sleep again."

"Fifteen days?" cried Meyer-Maier excitedly. "And the insects?
Have they been killed?"

"I'll tell you the whole story when you are well again," said Schmidt-Schmitt, quieting him. "Lie as you are, quietly—any excitement may hurt you."

"They must not come into the room!" he screamed out to an excited messenger, who breathlessly pulled the door open.

"Professor!—" the man was in deadly fear— "the Central Police station has given out the news that a swarm of giant flies are descending upon the city."

"Barricade all windows at once!"

"You wasted precious time," screamed Meyer-Maier, and jumped out of bed. "Let me go to my house. I must solve the riddle as to how to get at the insects. Don't touch me," he raved. He snatched a coat from the rack, ran out of the house, and jumped into Schmidt-Schmitt's automobile which stood at the gate, and went like the wind, to his home. The door of his house was ajar. He rushed up four flights and in delirious haste rushed into his workroom. The telephone bell rang.

The Danger is Over

Meyer-Maier snatched up the receiver. He got the consoling message from the city police-commissioner: "The danger is over, Professor. Our air-squadron has destroyed the swarm with a cloud of poison-gas. Only two of the insects escaped death. These we have caught in a net and are taking them to the zoological gardens."

"And if they have left eggs behind them?"

"We are going to search the woods systematically and will inject Lysol into any eggs we find. I think that will help," laughed the Major. "Shall I send some of them to you for examination?"

"No," cried Meyer-Maier in fright. "Keep them off my neck."

He set down at his work-table. There seemed a vicious smile on the face of the transfixed dead tse-tse fly. "You frightful ghost," murmured the professor with pallid lips, and threw a book on the insect.

His head was in a daze. He tried his best to think clearly. An axiom of science came to him: if the flies are as large as elephants, they can only propagate as fast as elephants do. They can't have a million young ones, but only a few. "I can't be wrong," he murmured. "I'll look up the confirmation."

He took the telephone and called the city Commissioner. "Major, how many insects were in the swarm?"

"Thirteen. Eleven are dead. The other two will never escape alive. They are fed up with the poison-gas."

"Thank you." Meyer-Maier hung up the receiver. "Very well," he murmured, "now there can be no question of any danger, for each fly can only lay three or four eggs at once,—not a million."

An immense weariness overcame him. He went into his bed-room and fell exhausted on his bed. "It is well that there is a supreme wisdom which controls the laws of nature. Otherwise the world would be subject to the strangest surprises." He thought of the monsters and crept anxiously under the bed-clothes. "I'll entrust Schmidt-Schmitt with the investigation of the creature phenomenon, I simply can't stand further excitement."

And sleep spread the mantel of well-deserved quiet over him.

Mive

Carl Jacobi

Carling's Marsh, some called it, but more often it was known by the name of Mive. Strange name that—Mive. And it was a strange place. Five wild, desolate miles of thick water, green masses of some kind of kelp, and violent vegetable growth. To the east the cypress trees swelled more into prominence, and this district was vaguely designated by the villagers as the Flan. Again a strange name, and again I offer no explanation. A sense of depression, of isolation perhaps, which threatened to crush any buoyancy of feeling possessed by the most hardened traveler, seemed to emanate from this lonely wasteland. Was it any wonder that its observers always told of seeing it at night, before a storm, or in the spent afternoon of a dark and frowning day? And even if they had wandered upon it, say on a bright morning in June, the impression probably would have been the same, for the sun glittering upon the surface of the olive water would have lost its exuberant brilliance and become absorbed in the roily depths below. However, the presence of this huge marsh would have interested no one, had not the east road skirted for a dismal quarter-mile its melancholy shore.

The east road, avoided, being frequently impassable because of high water, was a roundabout connection between the little towns of Twellen and Lamarr. The road seemed to have been irresistibly drawn toward the Mive, for it cut a huge half-moon across the country for seemingly no reason at all. But this arc led through a wilderness of an entirely different aspect from the land surrounding the other trails. Like the rest it started among the hills, climbed the hills, and rambled down the hills, but after passing Echo Lake, that lowering tarn locked in a deep ravine, it straggled up a last hillock and swept down upon a large flat. And as one proceeded, the flat steadily sank lower; it forgot the hills, and the ground, already damp, became sodden and quivering under the feet.

And then looming up almost suddenly—Mive! ... a morass at first, a mere bog, then a jungle of growth repulsive in its overluxuriance, and finally a sea of kelp, an inland Sargasso.

Just why I had chosen the east road for a long walk into the country I don't really know. In fact, my reason for taking such a hike at all was rather vague. The day was certainly anything but ideal; a raw wind whipping in from the south, and a leaden sky typical of early September lent anything but an inviting aspect to those rolling Rentharpian hills, But walk I did, starting out briskly as the inexperienced all do, and gradually slowing down until four o'clock found me plodding almost mechanically along the flat. I dare say every passerby, no matter how many times he frequented the road, always stopped at exactly the same spot I did and suffered the same feeling of awe and depression that came upon me as my eyes fell upon that wild marsh. But instead of hurrying on, instead of quickening my steps in search of the hills again, I for some unaccountable reason that I have always laid to curiosity, left the trail and plunged through oozing fungi to the water's very edge.

A wave of warm humid air, heavy with the odor of growth, swept over me as though I had suddenly opened the door of some monstrous hothouse. Great masses of vines with fat creeping tendrils hung from the cypress trees. Razor-edged reeds, marsh grass, long waving cattails, swamp vegetation of a thousand kinds flourished here with luxuriant abundance. I went on along the shore; the water lapped steadily the sodden earth at my feet, oily-looking water, grim-looking, reflecting a sullen and overcast sky.

There was something fascinating in it all, and while I am not one of those adventurous souls who revel in the unusual, I gave no thought of turning back to the road, but plodded through the soggy, clinging sod, and over rotting logs as though hurrying toward some destination. The very contrast, the voluptuousness of all the growth seemed some mighty lure, and I came to a halt only when gasping for breath from exertion.

For perhaps half an hour I stumbled forward at intervals, and then from the increasing number of cypress trees I saw that I was approaching that district known as the Flan. A large lagoon lay here, stagnant, dark, and entangled among the rip grass and reeds, reeds that rasped against each other in a dry, unpleasant manner like some sleeper constantly clearing his throat.

All the while I had been wondering over the absolute absence of all animate life. With its dank air, its dark appeal, and its wildness, the Eden recesses of the Mive presented a glorious place for all forms of swamp life. And yet not a snake, not a toad, not an insect had I seen. It was rather strange, and I looked curiously about me as I walked.

And then ... and then as if in contradiction to my thoughts it fluttered before me.

With a gasp of amazement I found myself staring at an enormous, a gigantic ebony-black butterfly. Its jet coloring was magnificent, its proportions startling, for from wing tip to wing tip it measured fully fifteen inches. It approached me slowly, and as it did I saw that I was wrong in my classification. It was not a butterfly; neither was it a moth; nor did it seem to belong to the order of the Lepidoptera at all. As large as a bird, its great body came into prominence over the wings, disclosing a huge proboscis, ugly and repulsive.

I suppose it was instinctively that I stretched out my hand to catch the thing as it suddenly drew nearer. My fingers closed over it, but with a frightened whir it tore away, darted high in the air, and fluttered proudly into the undergrowth. An exclamation of disappointment burst from me, and I glanced ruefully at my hand where the prize should have been.

It was then that I became aware that the first two fingers and a part of my palm were lightly coated with a powdery substance that had rubbed off the delicate membrane of the insect's wings. The perspiration of my hand was fast changing this powder into a sticky bluish substance, and I noticed that this gave off a delightfully sweet odor. The odor grew heavier; it changed to a perfume, an incense, luring, exotic, fascinating. It seemed to fill the air, to crowd my lungs, to create an irresistible desire to taste it. I sat down on a log; I tried to fight it off, but like a blanket it enveloped me, tearing down my resistance in a great attraction as magnet to steel. Like a sword it seared its way into my nostrils, and the desire became maddening, irresistible.

At length I could stand it no longer, and I slowly brought my fingers to my lips. A horribly bitter taste that momentarily paralyzed

my entire mouth and throat was the result. It ended in a long cough-
ing spell.

Disgusted at my lack of willpower and at this rather foolish episode, I turned and began to retrace my steps toward the road. A
feeling of nausea and of sluggishness began to seep into me, and I
quickened my pace to get away from the stifling air. But at the same
time I kept watch for a reappearance of that strange butterfly. No
sound now save the washing of the heavy water against the reeds
and the sucking noise of my steps.

I had gone farther than I realized, and I cursed the foolish whim
that had sent me here. As for the butterfly—whom could I make
believe the truth of its size or even of its existence? I had nothing
for proof, and ... I stopped suddenly!

A peculiar formation of vines had attracted my attention—and
yet not vines either. The thing was oval, about five feet in length,
and appeared to be many weavings or coils of some kind of hemp.
It lay fastened securely in a lower crotch of a cypress. One end was
open, and the whole thing was a grayish color like a cocoon ... a
cocoon! An instinctive shudder of horror swept over me as the
meaning of my thoughts struck me with full force.

With a cocoon as large as this, the size of the butterfly would
be enormous. In a flash I saw the reason for the absence of all other
life in the Mive. These butterflies, developed as they were to such
proportions, had evolved into some strange order and become carnivorous. The fifteen-inch butterfly which had so startled me before faded into insignificance in the presence of this cocoon.

I seized a huge stick for defense and hurried on toward the road.
A low muttering of thunder from somewhere off to the west added
to my discomfort. Black threatening clouds, harbingers of an on-
coming storm, were racing in from the horizon, and my spirits fell
even lower with the deepening gloom. The gloom blurred into a
darkness, and I picked my way forward along the shore with more
and more difficulty. Suddenly the mutterings stopped, and there
came that expectant, sultry silence that precedes the breaking of a
storm.

But no storm came. The clouds all moved slowly, lavalike, toward a central formation directly above me, and there they stopped,
became utterly motionless, engraved upon the sky. There was
something ominous about that monstrous cloud bank, and in spite

of the growing feeling of nausea, I watched it pass through a series of strange color metamorphoses, from a black to a greenish black, and from a decided green to a yellow, and from a yellow to a blinding, glaring red.

And then as I looked those clouds gradually opened; a ray of peculiar colorless light pierced through as the aperture enlarged disclosing an enormous vault-shaped cavern cut through the stratus. The whole vision seemed to move nearer, to change from an indistinguishable blur as though magnified a thousand times. And then towers, domes, streets, and walls took form, and these coagulated into a city painted stereoscopically in the sky. I forgot everything and lost myself in a weird panorama of impossible happenings above me.

Crowds, mobs, millions of men clothed in medieval armor of chain mail with high helmets were hurrying on, racing past in an endless procession of confusion. Regiment upon regiment, men and more men, a turbulent sea of marching humanity were fleeing, retreating as if from some horrible enemy!

And then it came, a swarm, a horde of butterflies ... enormous, ebony-black, carnivorous butterflies, approaching a doomed city. They met—the men and that strange form of life. But the defensive army and the gilded city seemed to be swallowed up, to be dissolved under this terrible force of incalculable power. The entire scene began to disintegrate into a mass, a river of molten gray, swirling and revolving like a wheel—a wheel with a hub, a flaming, fantastic, colossal ball of effulgence.

I was mad! My eyes were mad! I screamed in horror, but like Cyprola turned to stone, stood staring at this blasphemy in the heavens.

Again it began to coalesce; again a picture took form, but this time a design, gigantic, magnificent. And there under tremendous proportions with its black wings outspread was the butterfly I had sought to catch. The whole sky was covered by its massive form, a mighty repulsive tapestry.

It disappeared! The thunder mutterings, which had become silenced before, now burst forth without warning in unrestrained simultaneous fury. The clouds suddenly raced back again, erasing outline and detail, devouring the sight, and there was only the blackness, the gloom of a brooding, overcast sky.

With a wild cry, I turned and ran, plunged through the under-brush, my sole thought being to escape from this insane marsh. Vines and creepers lashed at my face as I tore on; knife reeds and swamp grass penetrated my clothing, leaving stinging burns of pain. Streak lightning of blinding brilliance, thunderations like some volcanic upheaval belched forth from the sky. A wind sprang up, and the reeds and long grasses undulated before it like a thou-sand writhing serpents. The sullen water of the Mive was black now and racing in toward the shore in huge waves, and the thun-der above swelled into one stupendous crescendo.

Suddenly I threw myself flat upon the oozing ground and with wild fear wormed my way deep into the undergrowth. It was coming!

A moment later with a loud flapping the giant butterfly raced out of the storm toward me. Scarcely ten feet away I could see its enormous, swordlike proboscis, its repulsive, disgusting body, and I could hear its sucking inhalations of breath. A wave of horror seared its way through my very brain; the pulsations of my heart throbbed at my temples and at my throat, and I continued to stare helplessly at it. *A thing of evil it was, transnormal, bred in a lep-rous, feverish swamp, a hybrid growth from a paludinous place of rot and overluxuriant vegetation.*

But I was well hidden in the reeds. The monstrosity passed on unseeing. In a flash I was up and lunging on again. The crashing reverberations of the storm seemed to pound against me as if try-ing to hold me back. A hundred times I thought I heard that ter-rible flapping of wings behind me, only to discover with a prayer of thanks that I was mistaken. But at last the road! Without stop-ping, without slackening speed, I tore on, away from the Mive, across the quivering flat, and on and on to the hills. I climbed; I stumbled; I ran; my sole thought was to go as far as possible. At length exhaustion swept over me, and I fell gasping to the ground.

It seemed hours that I lay there, motionless, unheeding the driving rain on my back, and yet fully conscious. My brain was wild now. It pawed over the terrible events that had crowded themselves into the past few hours, repictured them, and strove for an answer.

What had happened to me? What had happened to me? And then suddenly I gave an exclamation. I remembered now, fool that I was. The fifteen-inch butterfly that had so startled me near the district of the Flan ... I had tried to catch the thing, and it had escaped, leaving in my hand only a powderish substance that I had

vainly fought off and at last brought to my lips. That was it. What
had happened after that? A feeling of nausea had set in, a great
inward sickness like the immediate effects of a powerful drug. A
strange insect of an unknown order, a thing resembling and yet
differing from all forms of the Lepidoptera, a butterfly and yet not
a butterfly. ... Who knows what internal effect that powder would
have on one? Had I been wandering in a delirium, a delirium caused
by the tasting of that powder from the insect's wings? And if so,
where did the delirium fade into reality? The vision in the sky ... a
vagary of a poisoned brain perhaps, but the monstrosity that had
pursued me and the telltale cocoon ... again the delirium? No, and
again no! That was too real, too horrible, and yet everything was
all so strange and fantastic.

But what master insect was this that could play with a man's
brain at will? What drug, what unknown opiate existed in the membrane of its ebony-black wings?

And I looked back, confused, bewildered, expecting perhaps an
answer. There it lay, far below me, vague and indistinct in the deepening gloom, the black outlines of the cypress trees writhing in
the night wind, silent, brooding, mysterious—the Mive.

The Worm
David H. Keller, M. D.

The miller patted his dog on the head, as he whispered: "We are going to stay here. Our folks, your ancestors and mine, have been here for nearly two hundred years, and queer it would be to leave now because of fear."

The grist mill stood, a solid stone structure, in an isolated Vermont valley. Years ago every day had been a busy one for the mill and the miller, but now only the mill wheel was busy. There was no grist for the mill and no one lived in the valley. Blackberries and hazel grew where once the pastures had been green. The hand of time had passed over the farms and the only folk left were sleeping in the churchyard. A family of squirrels nested in the pulpit, while on the tombstones silent snails left their cryptic messages in silvery streaks. Thompson's Valley was being handed back to nature. Only the old bachelor miller, John Staples, remained. He was too proud and too stubborn to do anything else.

The mill was his home, even as it had served all of his family for a home during the last two hundred years. The first Staples had built it to stay, and it was still as strong as on the day it was finished. There was a basement for the machinery of the mill, the first floor was the place of grinding and storage and the upper two floors served as the Staples' homestead. The building was warm in winter and cool in summer. Times past it had sheltered a dozen Staples at a time; now it provided a home for John Staples and his dog.

He lived there with his books and his memories. He had no friends and desired no associates. Once a year he went to the nearest town and bought supplies of all kinds, paying for them in gold. It was supposed that he was wealthy. Rumor credited him with

330

being a miser. He attended to his own business, asked the world to do the same, and on a winter's evening laughed silently over Burton and Rabalais, while his dog chased rabbits in his heated sleep upon the hearth.

The winter of 1935 was beginning to threaten the valley, but with an abundance of food and wood in the mill, the recluse looked forward to a comfortable period of desuetude. No matter how cold the weather, he was warm and contented. With the inherent ability of his family, he had been able to convert the water power into electricity. When the wheel was frozen, he used the electricity stored in his storage batteries. Every day he puttered around among the machinery which it was his pride to keep in perfect order. He assured the dog that if business ever did come to the mill, he would be ready for it.

It was on Christmas Day of that winter that he first heard the noise. Going down to the basement to see that nothing had been injured by the bitter freeze of the night before, his attention was attracted, even while descending the stone steps, by a peculiar grinding noise, that seemed to come from out of the ground. His ancestors, building for permanency, had not only put in solid foundations, but had paved the entire basement with slate flagstones three feet wide and as many inches thick. Between these the dust of two centuries had gathered and hardened.

Once his feet were on this pavement, Staples found that he could not only hear the noise, but he could also feel the vibrations which accompanied it through the flagstones. Even through his heavy leather boots he could feel the rhythmic pulsations. Pulling off his mittens, he stooped over and put his finger tips on the stone. To his surprise it was warm in spite of the fact that the temperature had been below zero the night before. The vibration was more distinct to his finger tips than it had been to his feet. Puzzled, he threw himself on the slate stone and put his ear to the warm surface.

The sound he now heard made him think of the grinding of the mill stones when he was a boy and the farmers had brought corn to be ground into meal. There had been no corn-meat ground in the mill for fifty years, yet here was the sound of stone scraping slowly and regularly on stone. He could not understand it. In fact it was some time before he tried to explain it. With the habit born of years of solitary thinking, the first collected all the available facts about this noise. He knew that during the long winter evenings he would have time enough to do his thinking.

Going to his sitting room, he secured a walking stick of ash and went back to the cellar. Holding the handle of the cane lightly, he placed the other end on a hundred different spots on the floor, and each time he held it long enough to determine the presence or absence of vibration. To his surprise he found that while it varied in strength, it was present all over the cellar with the exception of the four corners. The maximum intensity was about in the center.

That evening he concentrated on the problem before him. He had been told by his grandfather, that the mill was built on solid rock. As a young men he had helped clean out a well near the mill and recalled, that instead of being dug out of gravel or dirt, it had the appearance of being drilled out of solid granite. There was no difficulty in believing that the earth under the mill was also solid rock. There was no reason for thinking otherwise. Evidently some of these strata of stone had become loose and were slipping and twisting under the mill. The simplest explanation was the most reasonable: it was simply a geological phenomenon. The behavior of the dog, however, was not so easily explained. He had refused to go with his master into the cellar, and now, instead of sleeping in comfort before the fire, he was in an attitude of strained expectancy. He did not bark, or even whine, but crept silently to his master's chair, looking at him anxiously.

The next morning the noise was louder. Staples heard it in his bed, and at first he thought that some bold adventurer had come into the forest and was sawing down a tree. That was what it sounded like; only softer and longer in its rhythm. Buzzzzzz—Buzzzzzzzz—Buzzzzzzzz. The dog, distinctly unhappy, jumped up on the bed and crawled uneasily so he could nuzzle the man's hand.

Through the four legs of the bed, Staples could feel the same vibration that had come to him through the handle of his cane the day before. That made him think. The vibration was now powerful enough to be appreciated, not through a walking stick, but through the walls of the building. The noise could be heard as well on the third floor as in the cellar.

He tried to fancy what it sounded like—not what it was—what it was like. The first idea had been that it resembled a saw going through oak; then came the thought of bees swarming, only these were large bees and millions of them: but finally all he could think of was the grinding of stones in a grist mill, the upper stone against the lower: and now the second was Grrrrrrr—Grrrrrrrrr instead of Bzzzzzzzzz or Hummmmmmm.

That morning he took longer than usual to shave and was more methodical than was his wont in preparing breakfast for himself and the dog. It seemed as though he knew that sometime he would have to go down into the cellar but wanted to postpone it as long as he could. In fact, he finally put on his coat and beaver hat and mittens and walked outdoors before he went to the basement. Followed by the dog, who seemed happy for the. first time in hours, he walked out on the frozen ground and made a circle around the building he called his home. Without knowing it, he was trying to get away from the noise, to go somewhere be could walk without feeling that peculiar tingling.

Finally he went into the mill and started down the steps to the cellar. The dog hesitated on the top step, went down two steps and then jumped back to the top step, where he started to whine. Staples went down the step, but the dog's behavior did not add to his peace of mind. The noise was much louder than it was the day before, and he did not need a cane to detect the vibration—the whole building was shaking. He sat down on the third step from the bottom and thought the problem over before he ventured out on the floor. He was especially interested in an empty barrel which was dancing around the middle of the floor.

The power of the mill-wheel was transferred through a simple series of shafts, cogs and leather belting to the grinding elements on the first floor. All this machinery for transmitting power was in the basement. The actual grinding had been done on the first floor. The weight of all this machinery, as well as of the heavy millstones on the first floor, was carried entirely by the flooring of the basement. The ceiling of the first floor was built on long pine beams which stretched across the entire building and were sunk into the stone walls at either side.

Staples started to walk around on the slate flagstones when he observed something that made him decide to stay on the steps. The floor was beginning to sink in the middle; not much, but enough to cause some of the shafts to separate from the ceiling. The ceiling seemed to sag. He saw that light objects like the empty barrel were congregating at the middle of the cellar. There was not much light but he was easily able to see that the floor was no longer level;

that it was becoming saucer-shaped. The grinding noise grew louder. The steps he sat on were of solid masonry, stoutly connected with and a part of the wall. These shared in the general vibration. The whole building began to sing like a 'cello.

One day he had been to the city and heard an orchestra play. He had been interested in the large violins, especially the one that was so large the player had to stay on his feet to play it. The feeling of the stone step under him reminded him of the notes of this violin the few times it had been played by itself. He sat there. Suddenly he started, realizing that in a few more minutes he would be asleep. He was not frightened but in some dim way he knew that he must not go to sleep—not here. Whistling, he ran up the steps to get his electric torch. With that in his hand, he went back to the steps. Aided by the steady light, he saw that several large sacks had appeared in the floor and that some of the stones, broken loose from their fellows, were moving slowly in a drunken, meaningless way. He looked at his watch. It was only a little after nine.

And then the noise stopped.

No more noise! No more vibration! Just a broken floor and every bit of the machinery of the mill disabled and twisted. In the middle of the floor was a hole where one of the pavement stones had dropped through. Staples carefully walked across and threw the light down this hole. Then he lay down and carefully put himself in such a position that he could look down the hole. He began to sweat. There did not seem to be any bottom!

Back on the solid steps he tried to give that hole its proper value. He could not understand it, but he did not need the whining of the dog to tell him what to do. That door must be closed as soon as possible.

Like a flash the method of doing so came to him. On the floor above he had cement. There were hundreds of grain sacks. Water was plentiful in the mill race. All that day he worked, carefully closing the hole with a great stopper of bags and wire. Then he placed timbers above and finally covered it all with cement, rich cement. Night came and he still worked. Morning came and still he swaggered down the steps, each time with a bag of crushed stone, or cement on his shoulder or with two buckets of water in his hands. At noon the next day the floor was no longer concave but convex. On top of the hole was four feet of timbers, bags and concrete. Then and only then did he go and make some coffee. He drank it, cup after cup, and slept.

The dog stayed on the bed at his feet.

When the man awoke, the sun was streaming in through the windows. It was a new day. Though the fire had long since died out, the room was warm. Such days in Vermont were called weather breeders. Staples listened. There was no sound except the ticking of his clock. Not realizing what he was doing, he knelt by the bed, thanked God for His mercies, jumped into bed again and slept for another twenty-four hours. This time he awoke and listened. There was no note. He was sure that by this time the cement had hardened. This morning he stayed awake and shared a Gargantuan meal with the dog. Then it seemed the proper thing to go to the basement. There was no doubt that the machinery was a wreck but the hole was closed. Satisfied that the trouble was over, he took his gun and dog and went hunting.

When he returned, he did not have to enter the mill to know that the grinding had begun again. Even before he started down the steps he recognized too well the vibration and the sound. This time it was a melody of notes, a harmony of discords, and he realized that the thing, which before had cut through solid rock, was now wearing its way through a cement in which were bags, timbers and pieces of iron. Each of these gave a different tone. Together they all wailed over their dissolution.

Staples saw, even with the first glance, that it would not be long before this cement "cork" would be destroyed. What was there to do next? All that day when hunting, his mind had been dimly working on that problem. Now he had the answer. He could not cork the hole, so he would fill it with water. The walls of the mill were solid, but he could blast a hole through them and turn the mill race into the cellar. The race, fed by the river, took only a part of what it could take, if its level were rapidly lowered. Whatever it was that was breaking down the floor of the mill could be drowned. If it were alive, it could be killed. If it was fire, it could be quenched. There was no use to wait until the hole was again opened. The best plan was to have everything ready. He went back to his kitchen and cooked a meal of ham and eggs. He ate all he could. He boiled a pot of coffee. Then he started to work. The wall reached three feet down below the surface. A charge of powder, heavy enough to break through, would wreck the whole building, so he began to peck at the wall, like a bird pecking at a nut. First a period of drilling and then a little powder and a muffled explosion. A few buckets of loosened rock. Then some more drilling and another explosion. At last he knew that only a few inches of rock lay between the water and the cellar.

All this time there had been a symphony of noises, a dishar- mony of sounds. The constant grinding came from the floor, inter- rupted with the sound of sledge or crowbar, dull explosion of powder and crashing of rock, fragments on the floor. Staples worked with- out stop save to drink his coffee. The dog stood on the upper steps.

Then without warning the whole floor caved in. Staples jumped to the steps. These held. On the first day there had been a hole a few feet wide. Now the opening nearly occupied the entire area of the floor. Staples, nauseated, looked down to the bottom. There, about twenty feet below him, a mass of rocks and timbers churned in a peculiar way, but all gradually disappeared in a second hole, fifteen feet wide. Even as he looked they all disappeared in this median hole.

The opening he had been breaking in the wall was directly across from the steps. There was a charge of powder there but no way of going across to light the fuse. Still there was no time to lose and he had to think fast. Running to the floor above he picked up his rifle and went to the bottom of the steps. He was able to throw the beam from his search light directly into the hole in the wall. Then he shot—once—twice and the third time the explosion told him he had succeeded.

The water started to run into the cellar. Not fast at first but more rapidly as the mud and weeds were cleared out. Finally an eight-inch stream flowed steadily into the bottomless hole. Staples sat on the bottom steps. Soon he had the satisfaction of seeing the water fill the larger hole and then cover the floor, what there was left of it. In another hour he had to leave the lower steps. He went out to the mill race and saw that there was still enough water to fill a hundred such holes. A deep sense of satisfaction filled his weary mind.

And again, after eating, he sought sleep.

When he awoke, he heard the rain angrily tapping at the win- dows with multifingers. The dog was on the woven rug by the side of the bed. He was still restless and seemed pleased to have his master awake. Staples dressed more warmly than usual and spent an extra half hour making pancakes to eat with honey. Sausages and coffee helped assuage his hunger. Then with rubber boots and a heavy raincoat, he went out into the valley. The very first thing that he noticed was the mill race. It was practically empty. The little stream of water at the bottom was pouring into the hole he had blasted into the stone wall hours before. The race had contained eight feet of water. Now barely six inches remained, and the dread came to the man that the hole in the cellar was not only emptying the race but was also draining the little river that for thousands of years had flowed through the valley. It had never gone dry. He hastened over to the dam and his worst fears were realized. Instead of a river, there was simply a streak of mud with cakes of dirty ice, all being washed by the torrent of rain. With relief he thought of the rain. Millions of tons of snow would melt and fill the river. Ultimately the hole would fill and the water would rise again in the mill-race. Still he was uneasy. What if the hole had no bottom?

When he looked into the basement he was little reassured. The water was still going down, though slowly. It was rising in the basement and this meant that it was now running in faster than it was running down.

Leaving his coat and boots on the first floor, he ran up the stone steps to the second floor, built a fire in the living room and started to smoke—and think. The machinery of the mill was in ruins; of course it could be fixed, but as there was no more need of it, the best thing was to leave it alone. He had gold saved by his ancestors. He did not know how much, but he could live on it. Restlessly he reviewed the past week, and, unable to rest, hunted for occupation. The idea of the gold stayed in his mind and the final result was that he again put on his boots and coat and carried the entire treasure to a little dry cave in the woods about a half mile from the mill. Then he came back and started to cook his dinner. He went past the cellar door three times without looking down.

Just as he and the dog had finished eating, he heard a noise. It was a different one this time, more like a saw going through wood, but the rhythm was the same—Hrrrrr—Hrrrrr. He started to go to the cellar but this time he took his rifle, and while the dog went after him, he howled dismally with his tail between his legs, shivering.

As soon as Staples reached the first floor, he felt the vibration. Not only could he feel the vibration, he could see it. It seemed that the center of the floor was being pushed up. Flashlight in hand, he

opened the cellar door. There was no water there now—in fact there
was no cellar left! In front of him was a black wall on which the
light played in undulating waves. It was a wall and it was moving.
He touched it with the end of his rifle. It was hard and yet there
was a give to it. Feeling the rock, he could feel it move. Was it alive?
Could there be a living rock? He could not see around it but he felt
that the bulk of the thing filled the entire cellar and was pressing
against the ceiling. That was it! The thing was boring through the
first floor. It had destroyed and filled the cellar! It had swallowed
the river! Now it was working at the first floor. If this continued,
the mill was doomed. Staples knew that it was a thing alive and *he
had to stop it!!*

He was thankful that all of the steps in the mill were of stone,
fastened and built into the wall. Even though the floor did fall in,
he could still go to the upper rooms. He realized that from now on
the fight had to be waged from the top floors. Going up the steps,
he saw that a small hole had been cut through the oak flooring.
Even as he watched, this grew larger. Trying to remain calm, realizing that only by doing so could he retain his sanity, he sat down
in a chair and timed the rate of enlargement. But there was no need
of using a watch: the hole grew larger—and larger and larger—and
now he began to see the dark hole which had sucked the river dry.
Now it was three feet in diameter—now four feet—now six. It was
working smoothly now—it was not only grinding—*but it was eating.*

Staples began to laugh. He wanted to see what it would do when
the big stone grinders slipped silently down into that maw. That
would be a rare sight. All well enough to swallow a few pavement
stones, but when it came to a twenty ton grinder, that would be a
different kind of a pill. "I hope you choke!" he cried, "Damn you!
whatever you are! I hope you choke!!" The walls hurled back the
echo of his shouts and frightened him into silence. Then the floor
began to tilt and the chair to slide toward the opening. Staples
sprang toward the steps.

"Not yet!" he shrieked. "Not to-day, Elenora! Some other day,
but not to-day!" and then from the safety of the steps, he witnessed
the final destruction of that floor and all in it. The stones slipped
down, the partitions, the beams, and then, as though satisfied with
the work and the food, the Thing dropped down, down, down and
left Staples dizzy on the steps looking into a hole, dark, deep, coldly

bottomless surrounded by the walls of the mill, and below them a circular hole cut out of the solid rock. On one side a little stream of water came through the blasted wall and fell, a tiny waterfall, below. Staples could not hear it splash at the bottom.

Nauseated and vomiting, he crept up the steps to the second floor, where the howling dog was waiting for him. On the floor he lay, sweating and shivering in dumb misery. It took hours for him to change from a frightened animal to a cerebrating god, but ultimately he accomplished even this, cooked some more food, warmed himself and slept.

And while he dreamed, the dog kept sleepless watch at his feet. He awoke the next morning. It was still raining, and Staples knew that the snow was melting on the hills and soon would change the little valley river into a torrent. He wondered whether it was all a dream, but one look at the dog showed him the reality of the last week. He went to the second floor again and cooked breakfast. After he had eaten, he slowly went down the steps. That is, he started to go, but halted at the sight of the hole. The steps had held and ended on a wide stone platform. From there another flight of steps went down to what had once been the cellar. These two flights of steps clinging to the walls had the solid stone mill on one side, but on the inside they faced a chasm, circular in outline and seemingly bottomless; but the man knew there was a bottom and from that pit the Thing had come—and would come again.

That was the horror of it! He was so certain that it would come again. Unless he was able to stop it. How could he? Could he destroy a Thing that was able to bore a thirty foot hole through solid rock, swallow a river and digest grinding stones like so many pills? One thing he was sure of—he could accomplish nothing without knowing more about it. To know more, he had to watch. He determined to cut a hole through the floor. Then he could see the Thing when it came up. He cursed himself for his confidence, but he was sure it would come.

It did. He was on the floor looking into the hole he had sawed through the plank, and he saw it come: but first he heard it. It was a sound full of slithering slidings, wrathful rasping of rock against rock—but, no! That could not be, for this Thing was alive. Could this be rock and move and grind and eat and drink? Then he saw it come into the cellar and finally to the level of the first floor, and then he saw its head and face.

The face looked at the man and Staples was glad that the hole in the floor was as small as it was. There was a central mouth filling half the space: fully fifteen feet in diameter was that mouth; and the sides were ashen gray and quivering. There were no teeth.

That increased the horror: a mouth without teeth, without any visible means of mastication and yet Staples shivered as he thought of what had gone into that mouth, down into that mouth, deep into the recesses of that mouth and disappeared. The circular lip seemed made of scales of steel, and they were washed clean with the water from the race.

On either side of this gigantic mouth was an eye, lidless, browless, pitiless. They were slightly withdrawn into the head so the Thing could bore into rock without injuring them. Staples tried to estimate their size: all he could do was to avoid their baleful gaze. Then even as he watched the mouth closed and the head began a semicircular movement, so many degrees to the right, so many degrees to the left and up—and up—and finally the top touched the bottom of the plank Staples was on and then Hrrrrrr—Hrrrrr and the man knew that it was starting upon the destruction of the second floor. He could not see now as he had been able to see before, but he had an idea that after grinding a while the Thing opened its mouth and swallowed the debris. He looked around the room. Here was where he did his cooking and washing and here was his winter supply of stove wood. A thought came to him.

Working frantically, he pushed the center burner to the middle of the room right over the hole he had cut in the floor. Then he built a fire in it, starting it with a liberal supply of coal-oil. He soon had the stove red hot. Opening the door he again filled the stove with oak and then ran for the steps. He was just in time. The floor, cut through, disappeared into the Thing's maw and with it the redhot stove. Staples yelled in his glee, "A hot pill for you this time, a HOT PILL!"

If the pill did anything, it simply increased the desire of the Thing to destroy, for it kept on till it had bored a hole in this floor equal in size to the holes in the floors below it. Staples saw his food, his furniture, the ancestral relics disappear into the same opening that had consumed the machinery and mill supplies.

On the upper floor the dog howled.

The man slowly went up to the top floor, and joined the dog, who had ceased to howl and began an uneasy whine. There was a stove on this floor, but there was no food. That did not make any difference to Staples: for some reason he was not hungry any more: it did not seem to make any difference—nothing seemed to matter or make any difference any more. Still he had his gun and over fifty cartridges, and he knew that at the last, even a Thing like that would react to bullets in its eye balls—he just knew that nothing could withstand that.

He lit the lamp and paced the floor in a cold, careless mood. One thing he had determined. He said it over and over to himself.

"This is my home. It has been the home of my family for two hundred years. No devil or beast or worm can make me leave it."

He said it again and again. He felt that if he said it often enough, he would believe it, and if he could only believe it, he might make the Worm believe it. He knew now that it was a Worm, just like the night crawlers he had used so often for bait, only much larger. Yes, that was it. A worm like a night crawler, only much larger, in fact, very much larger. That made him laugh—to think how much larger this worm was than the ones he had used for fishing. All through the night he walked the floor and burned the lamp and said, "This is my home. No worm can make me leave it!" Several times he went down the steps, just a few of them, and shouted the message into the pit as though he wanted the Worm to hear and understand, "This is my home! NO WORM CAN MAKE ME LEAVE IT!!"

Morning come. He mounted the ladder that led to the trap door in the roof and opened it. The rain beat in. Still that might be a place of refuge. Crying, he took his Burton and his Rabalais and wrapped them in his rain coat and put them out on the roof, under a box. He took the small pictures of his father and mother and put them with the books. Then in loving kindness he carried the dog up and wrapped him in a woolen blanket. He sat down and waited, and as he did so he recited poetry—anything that came to him, all mixed up, "Come into the garden where there was a man who was so wondrous wise, he jumped into a bramble bush and you're a better man than I am and no one will work for money and the King of Love my Shepherd is"—and on—and then —

He heard the sliding and the slithering rasping and he knew that the Worm had come again. He waited till the Hrrrr-Hrrrrr told that the wooden floor he was on was being attacked and then he went up the ladder. It was his idea to wait till the Thing had made a large opening, large enough so the eyes could be seen and then use the fifty bullets—where they would do the most good. So, on the roof, beside the dog, he waited.

He did not have to wait long. First appeared a little hole and then it grew wider and wider till finally the entire floor and the furniture had dropped into the mouth, and the whole opening, thirty feet wide and more than that, was filled with the head, the closed mouth of which came within a few foot of the roof. By the aid of the light from the trap door, Staples could see the eye on the left side. It made a beautiful bull's eye, a magnificent target for his rifle and he was only a few feet away. He could not miss. Determined to make the most of his last chance to drive his enemy away, he decided to drop down on the creature, walk over to the eye and put the end of the rifle against the eye before he fired. If the first shot worked well, he could retire to the roof and use the other cartridges. He knew that there was some danger—but it was his last hope. After all he knew that when it came to brains he was a man and this thing was only a Worm. He walked over the head. Surely no sensation could go through such massive scales. He even jumped up and down. Meantime the eye kept looking up at the roof. If it saw the man, it made no signs, gave no evidence. Staples pretended to pull the trigger and then made a running jump for the trap door. It was easy. He did it again, and again. Then he sat on the edge of the door and thought.

He suddenly saw what it all meant. Two hundred years before, his ancestors had started grinding at the mill. For over a hundred and fifty years the mill had been run continuously, often day and night. The vibrations had been transmitted downward through the solid rock. Hundreds of feet below the Worm had heard them and felt them and thought it was another Worm. It had started to bore in the direction of the noise. It had taken two hundred years to do it, but it had finished the task, it had found the place where its mate should be. For two hundred years it had slowly worked its way through the primitive rack. Why should it worry over a mill and the things within it? Staples saw then that the mill had been but a slight incident in its life. It was probable that it had not even known it was there—the water, the gristmillstones, the red hot stove, had meant nothing—they had been taken as a part of the day's work. There was only one thing that the Worm was really interested in, but one idea that had reached its consciousness and remained there through two centuries, and that was to find its mate. The eye looked upward.

Staples, at the end, lost courage and decided to fire from a sitting position in the trap door. Taking careful aim, he pulled the trigger. Then he looked carefully to see what damage had resulted. There was none. Either the bullet had gone into the eye and the opening had closed or else it had glanced off. He fired again and again.

Then the mouth opened—wide—wider—until there was nothing under Staples save a yawning void of darkness.

The Worm belched a cloud of black, nauseating vapor. The man, enveloped in the cloud, lost consciousness and fell.

The Mouth closed on him.

On the roof the dog howled.

Vampires of the Desert

A. Hyatt Verrill

When I sailed for Peru, to accept a position as field paleontologist for the International Petroleum Company at their oil fields
near Talara, I little dreamed what amazing experiences and astounding adventures were in store for me.

The life of a paleontologist is not, as a rule, an exciting or adventurous one. In fact, there is scarcely a branch of scientific field work
that promises so little in the way of adventure, peril or thrills. Fossils, interesting as they may be to the trained scientist who studies
them, are not what one might call dangerous game. Neither are
they elusive, shy nor suspicious of human beings. And, aside from
the ordinary and to-be-expected hardships of camp life and field
work, hunting fossils is perhaps the safest and tamest of profes-
sions. And as I was to hunt and study the smallest and most abundant of fossils—namely, diatoms and foraminifera—for the presence of certain species of these minute fossil animals is known to
have a very direct bearing upon petroleum deposits, and as my
hunting ground was in the open desert where there were neither
wild animals nor wild men, and as my entire field of activities was
within sight and sound of the busy oil refineries, the wells, the
pump-houses and the well ordered "camp" or town, the possibility
of any excitement, any danger or anything unusual never occurred
to me. And had anyone suggested such eventualities, I most assuredly would have laughed them to scorn. Yet, so strange is fate and
so whimsical her moods, and so little do we know of the future
that, within a few months after my arrival at Talara, I was to have
some of the most astounding, even incredible experiences that ever
came into the life of any man. Indeed, were it not that the facts are
well known, and that meagre reports of the remarkable occurrence

have already been published in the press, I should hesitate to write of them for fear of being classed as a romancer and as writing fiction in the guise of fact. But I feel that, as precisely the same things may—in fact, probably will—recur again somewhere—even if not in Peru—and many human lives, perhaps entire communities, may be destroyed by such recurrences, the public should be acquainted with all the facts and details of the visitation, and thus should be prepared for its repetition.

But before beginning my story, I wish to disclaim the undue credit that has been accorded me for solving the baffling mystery of those terrible times and for saving the lives of hundreds—probably thousands—of my fellow men and fellow women. Any man with scientific training, a knowledge of zoology and with an interest in the unusual forms of animal and plants life could have done more than I did. It merely chanced that I was on the spot, that my scientific interests had been aroused before the happenings occurred and that I had always taken a deep interest in the botany of the tropics. Never before had this fad been of any real value to me or to anyone else. In the first place I never had visited the tropics and in the second place I made paleontology my life work and confined my studies to invertebrate paleontology at that. Yet I cannot help feeling that my amateurish interest in plant life must have been inspired by the Divinity and for the sole purpose which it later and so fortunately fulfilled.

One thing more I must mention, for it had a very great bearing upon the affair and enabled me to make dedications and to understand matters that otherwise would have been impossible to understand. During my postgraduate course at Yale I was greatly interested in the deep-sea researches of the United States Fish Commission under the direction of Professor Verrill, who was my instructor.

Largely, this was due to the fact that—as is well known,—the ocean's beds are composed mainly of foraminiferous ooze, the accumulated billions of skeletal remains of foraminifera, and that many living species—closely akin to the fossil form—are obtained from great depths. But I soon found, when on the "Albatross" in company with the Professor and his assistants, that one branch of science—or more especially one branch of any one department of science—hinges upon another. Thus to study diatoms intelligently, I was compelled to make a fairly intensive study of other and higher forms of marine life. Such, for example, were the ascidians, or sea cucumbers; the corals and sea-anemones, the sponges, and such forms of life as the hydroids and bryozoans as well as jelly-fish. And had I not thus acquired a fairly comprehensive and accurate knowledge of the life histories and habits of these harmless and interesting marine creatures, I never would have been able to make head or tail of the affair during that nightmarish time at Talara.

Talara, as I have hinted, is situated on that barren, treeless, waterless strip of South America's coastal desert that stretches from the vicinity of Guayaquil in Peru southward to central Chile. It is not, however, a flat or level desert. Rather it consists of desert sandhills rising to rocky hills, equally bare and sterile, and forming an incorporate part of the desert, and which become higher and more numerous as they approach the Andes, into which they merge. In fact, the sand of the desert proper is nothing more or less than the accumulated detritus of those hills, decomposed and washed down through countless ages. Originally—or at least at some remote period—the area was beneath the sea. Hence the presence of fossils of marine organisms. And it was to study these remains, which millions of years ago were beneath the waters of the Pacific, that I was employed by the International Petroleum Company; for, strange as it may appear, some of the largest of the world's known oil deposits are in this desert country of Peru.

For countless centuries this desert has been rainless; in fact, it is a desert merely because of lack of rainfall, and as the sand is impregnated with nitrates, phosphates and potash, it is fertile and capable of producing huge crops of agricultural products when watered or irrigated. Possibly my readers may think that this somewhat lengthy dissertation upon the Peruvian desert is quite unnecessary to my story, but let me assure them that it is most essential, and I request that those who may read this story of the incredible occurrences at Talara will read this portion very carefully. Otherwise it will be practically impossible to secure an intelligent idea of the happenings and their causes and to realize that they were neither miraculous, supernatural nor at all beyond the realms of cause and effect in nature.

Also, I must try the patience of my readers still further by briefly sketching the causes for the rainless, desert condition of this coast. The Humboldt Current, flowing northward from the Antarctic, tempers the normal temperatures of the tropical coasts of the equatorial and subequatorial regions of the west coast of South America and at the same time acts as a condenser for moisture-laden atmosphere that otherwise would reach the coast. Added to this is the fact that the warm, moisture-filled air from the vast Amazonian jungles is covered by the cold Andes heights, and its moisture is then deposited as rain and snow before it passes westward over the Andes.

At Talara, however, the Humboldt Current does not actually wash the coastline. A small, warm water current, known as the Niño or child; flows southward from the Bay of Panama and forces its way between the Humboldt Current and the shore. And the relative size and volume of these two currents vary considerably according to the force and direction of the prevailing winds and because of other causes—very possible seismic disturbances of the sea bed. From the earliest times, as proved by my studies of fossils and by the observations of more eminent scientists, these currents have varied. Often the variation is slight and temporary, but at other times it has been of long duration and very marked. Even a slight variation in either current has a decided effect upon the climate of the Peruvian coastal land. The temperature alters materially, mist and even light rains fall, and with miraculous suddenness vegetation springs up from the bare desert and barren hillsides. Usually the change continues for only a few days or weeks, but in the past ages such changes of currents, climate and the resultant vegetable and animal life obviously—proved by fossil remains—endured for many years.

In fact, one of the first and most interesting discoveries I made was that the desert soil—to a depth of twenty-five feet or more—was in many spots composed of alternate layers or strata of sand, some clear and some containing a large percentage of plant seeds. It was thus evident that alternating periods of dryness and dampness had occurred from the most remote times, and while the proportionate number of strata and their relative depths varied somewhat, there was abundant evidence to show that from the most ancient times there had existed regularly defined and periodic eras of rainfall and lack of rainfall, with the accompanying abundance of vegetation and lack of vegetation. The lower layers of seeds were fossil, but the upper ones were comparatively recent and with so slight a layer of sand superimposed upon them that a heavy rain would unquestionably enable them to germinate and sprout. That this was the case, was in fact proved when in 1924-5, after a comparatively short period of rainy weather, the hills and deserts about Talara—and as far south as Antofogasta, Chile, became covered with a rank semi-jungle as high as a man's waist. Moreover, nearly all of the plants that then appeared were strange to the inhabitants and totally distinct from any found elsewhere in South America. And in examining the seeds which I discovered, I found that—with few exceptions—they were of species, genera and even families entirely new to me.

It was this discovery that again aroused my long-dormant interest in tropical plant life and I was about to try my hand at growing some of the more unusual seeds, when Nature saved me the trouble. A severe earthquake shook the entire west coast of South America, causing a vast amount of damage in southern Chile, raising Juan Fernandez Island several hundred feet above its former level and upraising the sea bed between that island and the coastline for at least two hundred feet. As a result, the greater position of the Humboldt Current was deflected to the west into the Pacific, the warm Niño current increased in size and volume, and heavy rains at once commenced to fall along the coasts of Peru and Chile. Irreparable damage was caused in many localities. Estuaries, fields, villages and even large towns were swept away by floods that came pouring down the ancient dry river beds from the mountains. Buildings of sun-dried adobe, well adapted to the formerly rainless climate, melted and were reduced to mud, and in a few weeks such cities as Piura, Trujillo and others were utterly obliterated.

In Chile the nitrate beds were completely destroyed, many large and prosperous communities were rendered uninhabitable, and even Lima, Peru's capital—being built largely of adobe—suffered losses totaling millions of dollars. Fortunately the capital's more modern buildings and residences were of concrete and remained unaffected, and for similar reasons Talara suffered little. The native shacks and the old churches and government edifices crumbled and vanished, but the majority of the buildings at the port, as well as the mining camps of Negritos and Lobitos, being of wood, concrete or corrugated iron construction, suffered none at all. Neither did the torrential rains cause any appreciable damage to the petroleum industry.

The sand, being washed away, allowed some of the derricks to topple and fall, many pipe-lines were broken and similar small damages resulted, but on the whole the rains appeared more of a blessing than a curse in the district. The climate, although warmer, was less oppressive; the bare desert and hills became almost instantly covered with tender green, and hollows that became filled with water were the resort of flocks of wild geese and ducks that afforded great sport for the employees of the company.

Finding that my paleontological work was seriously—though I hoped only temporarily—interrupted by the rain and the disruption of some of my favorite localities for study, I had an abundance of spare time which I devoted to examining with the greatest interest the plants that had sprung up from the seeds I had discovered. Also, being a keen sportsman, I spent considerable time hunting, both about the pools I have mentioned and in the embryonic jungle that—within two weeks—had become waist-high and almost impenetrably dense. To my surprise and delight I discovered that with very few exceptions the growth was composed of plants which hitherto had been known only in a fossil state. There were many forms of tree ferns, of the horse-tails, of giant lycopodiums and of odd aberrant leguminous plants that—as nearly as I could judge— were the ancestors of our common beans, peas, etc. At first I was greatly amazed to find these supposedly extinct and fossil forms thus growing in abundance, but a short investigation and a little logical reasoning soon convinced me that it was a perfectly normal and easily explicable condition. From the most remote geological times the country had been periodically wet and dry as I have said. Hence plants that for a few years or centuries grew in the district, would have had no time to alter or evolve to higher forms before a rainless period occurred. Thus the earliest types of plant life that had existed in the district had been perpetuated with no great changes from the far-distant geological periods.

Probably on no other spot on earth could such a condition have occurred, and I decided to take advantage of the unique opportunity to write a monograph on the subject, to describe the habits and appearances of the plants, and to secure accurate photographs as well as to preserve specimens for the benefit of science.

It was while doing this that I came upon a small group of the most peculiar shrubs. I say shrubs, though they were not shrubs in the true sense of the word. They were rather more like attenuated and branched tubers, like gigantic, slender and distorted sweet-potatoes growing above ground. The stalks were fleshy but fibrous and very tough. There were no leaves, and the growth, as well as the branching habit, was by means of joints or articulations, one tough olive-colored section budding from another and increasing in size and length until it, too, developed additional joints. When I first found the things, they were quite small—the largest barely a foot in height—but they grew with truly amazing rapidity. In a few days they were as high as my waist and all my interests became centered upon them. I found no others, although every natural surrounding and condition seemed identical with other localities, but, I reasoned, this was not surprising, as the same conditions that had led to the perpetuation of long-extinct species would at the same time have acted to localize each form.

The more I examined the odd growths, the more they puzzled me. In many respects they could not be classified among any of the various botanical genera, families or orders. I prepared sections and examined them under the microscope. I tried all means of identification—but in vain. Oddly enough, they bore many resemblances to the algæ or marine plants, and especially to those natural-history puzzles, the bryozoans and hydroids which seem to form connecting links between the animal and vegetable kingdoms. But who ever heard of a bryozoan or a hydroid growing on land? Still, I reasoned, in the remote periods of the earth's existence there may have been such, for there are land algæ as there are also marine arachnids or spiders. Why not land bryozoans and hydroids?

It was a fascinating thought, but until my strange growths saw fit to flower or seed I could not determine what they were. Hence my elation can be judged—at least by any scientist—when I discovered signs of the plants budding as if about to flower. At this time they were six feet or so in height with main stems as thick as a man's body and most remarkable appearing things. The buds—if buds they were—broke through the outer bark or skin at the terminal joints of the branches, and at the same time I noticed a distinct swelling or enlargement of these joints.

I can best compare the effect to the flowering of cacti. As the buds increased in size—with remarkable rapidity—they gave promise of being even more interesting and stranger than the plants themselves, and also of developing into blooms of great beauty.

There were indications of long delicate petals of brilliant colors, and it was obvious that the flowers would be of truly gigantic size.

But my expectations had fallen far short of the reality, when, on visiting the spot one morning, I found one of the buds had partly opened. I had never seen anything like it or even resembling it. It was not by any means fully developed, and I judged from its appearance that it was a night-blooming plant and that in order to see the flower in its full glory I would be obliged to visit the spot after dark. However it was sufficiently open for me to obtain a good idea of its character, and I examined it with the most intense interest. It appeared semi-transparent, was very fleshy, or I might even say gelatinous, and was coated with a shining, moist, and apparently sticky substance. At the stem or base, for there was no true stem, it was a dark intense purple and bulbous in form. Beyond this purple area was a border or fringe of pure white membranous growth, and beyond this were the innumerable long and multicolored petals—or so I judged them—that were folded or coiled together like the partly opened petals of a gigantic chrysanthemum flower.

In size the strange bloom was nearly four feet in length by three feet in diameter. It had no appreciable odor, and though I was greatly tempted to do so, I forebore touching it for fear of injuring it and preventing it from expanding to its full perfection. Yet, strange as it may seem, there was something about it, despite its beauty of form, its colors and its translucent gelatinous appearance , that was repellent. It was no doubt on account of its bizarre appearance, for I have noted that the human mind naturally recoils from or at least is suspicious of any unusual or strange form of some well-known natural object. Even human freaks have this effect upon the majority of persons, and the flower and the weird growth that bore it were sufficiently unusual and strange to create a vague dislike and even distrust in even my scientific mind.

However, I determined to visit the things after night-fall, and turned my attention to hunting. I returned to my quarters in time for breakfast with a fine bag of ducks and snipe. The rains had now ceased for several days, but the newly formed streams still flowed across the former deserts, and there was sufficient moisture in the soaked earth to keep vegetation going for some time. I mention this, because the cessation of the rains had a very direct bearing upon subsequent events.

It was while I was eating my breakfast that I had a phone call from Lobitos asking me to come over as soon as possible as a new field was being prospected and they wished me to make microscopic examinations of the samples from the test-holes. I was rather disappointed at thus being summoned away, when I had counted upon witnessing the full development of my strange plants, but I comforted myself with the thought that there would be many more flowers, and that I should not be long absent. So, packing my field outfit, I ordered the car and started for Lobitos. The work, I found, would take me much longer than I had expected, and I wondered if I would be able to return before all the remarkable flowers had blossomed and faded. Little did I dream how soon or in what a remarkable manner I should again meet with those puzzling, amazing productions of the unusual plants I had found.

It was on the second day of my stay at Lobitos that news of the murders at Negritos reached us. Two Indian or rather Cholo laborers had been found dead in front of their barracks. Apparently they had been garroted or strangled to death, but there was no clue to the murderer and no known incentive for the crime. Both men had been—as for that matter were all the Peruvian Cholos—quiet, peaceful, hard-working and very inoffensive fellows. Their companions declared that neither had been in a brawl, a discussion, or an argument during the preceding evening or night; no one had heard hard or angry words, and as both bodies still had their week's wages upon them, robbery was discarded as a possible motive for the crime.

But Negritos was terribly stirred up over the tragedy. For years the place had been a model of law and order. There had not been a murder, a robbery, a burglary nor any serious offense committed for fully ten years and the only arrests had been for drunkenness, gambling or petty thefts among the natives and for trespass. And as Negritos and Lobitos were "dry" camps, even drunkenness was very rare. Hence two murders, occurring on one night, and without any known reason, created a great sensation. Moreover, there seemed little doubt that the crimes were committed by some stranger.

The Peruvian Indian or Cholo is not a particularly brave or desperate character. He abhors bloodshed or violence in any form, and neither I nor any of the officials could imagine a docile Cholo deliberately attacking and successfully strangling two men. And why, it was asked, had there been no outcry? It seemed inconceivable that the two men could have been killed so quickly that they could not have cried out. And why did the second victim remain quietly waiting, while his companion was being killed? In fact, the more we discussed it, the more mysterious it became.

"In my opinion," declared Sturgis, the chief engineer, who had had a tremendous amount of experience with the natives, "it's the work of a Chilean or a Colombian. Likely as not those two Cholos had worked somewhere where there'd been Chilenos or Colombians, and had got into some sort of trouble with them—maybe won too much at gambling, or it might have been over a woman. Then this bird drops in here, recognizes the fellows, and evens scores. The only thing that bothers me is why they weren't knifed—that's the Chileno method as a rule—and why they weren't robbed—no such a criminal ever lets a chance of pocketing a few dollars get by him.

"Hmm, in all probability the murderer didn't have time," suggested Henshaw. "He may have been scared off. But how the devil could one man strangle two others?"

"Maybe they weren't strangled," I put in. "I'll bet no one has made an examination to learn if they weren't knocked over the heads first. You see knifing a man isn't always a safe and quiet method of putting him out of the way—he's liable to yell. And it would have been as hard for a man to knife two Cholos without their giving a cry as it would have been to strangle two of than. In my opinion they were knocked senseless and then garroted. And doesn't it seem more like the work of an East Indian or an Oriental than a South American? Aren't there some coolies—Hindus—working up at Porvenir on the railway? And how about those Chinese and Japs at Talara? I'll bet it was one of those fellows."

"Maybe you're right," agreed Sturgis. "I hadn't thought of the Hindus or Chinese. But anyhow, Stevens will round 'em up whoever 'twas; he was chief of police in Manila and he's no slouch, even if this camp has got so darned law-abiding that he's grown fat and lazy."

At this moment the telephone rang, and Henshaw, who answered, turned to me. "You're wanted at Negritos, Barry," he said. "Stevens wants you to help him on this murder case. Says he needs a microscopist and asks if you're not a doctor of sorts—Doctor Samuels is off on leave, and that interne Rogers refuses to conduct a post-mortem unless he has a competent man—biologist or M.D. or anatomist or some kind of an 'ist'—along with him."

I was surprised, of course. But after all it was not surprising. I was the only microscopist available, and I had at one time taken a course in anatomy with the idea of becoming a surgeon. But I was not sorry to leave Lobitos. It was an unpleasant spot at best, and I was wishing I might have a chance to examine my remarkable flowers. Still I could not leave at once, I had to complete my work at Lobitos, for that, after all, was my real job, and taking the 'phone I told Stevens I would go over to Negritos the next morning early. He swore and raved a bit—he was a testy old chap—but I pointed out that I was employed to conduct paleontological studies and not police-court investigations, and that I was answerable only to the New York office. In fact, I grew a bit peeved myself and added as a clincher that I was coming only to oblige him and out of curiosity, and that unless I were requested politely and not ordered, I wouldn't go at all. This quieted him. He apologized, begged me to hurry, and rang off.

Poor old Major Stevens! I was fated never to hear his voice again, never to see his ruddy face grow apopletically purple as he sputtered, fumed and swore. And I and all the others were fated to have the shock of our lives before another twenty-four hours had passed.

I was aroused from a deep sleep by the furious ringing of the 'phone, and lifting the receiver heard an agitated, excited voice. "For God's sake, get back here!" it cried. "This is Merivale speaking. It's terrible—three more men murdered here last night—two women killed at Talara and—when we went to call Major Stevens we found him dead—strangled like the others. We need every white man we can get—there's a fiend incarnate here somewhere. We must find him and stop this thing. And, Barry, bring Henshaw with you."

I was aghast. What did it mean? Seven, no, eight murders within two days—and Major Stevens among them. It seemed incredible. What was the motive? Who wee the murderer? How could he have committed the crimes without detection, when, as I felt sure, the camps had been patrolled and policed after those first two deaths? Of course, the motive for killing Major Stevens was plain. The murderer feared him and took this means of getting him out of the way. But the others—the Cholos. Only on the theory of a homicidal maniac could I explain it. Henshaw and Sturgis were as shocked and horrified as I was, and both agreed that some crazed native must be at the bottom of the killings, unless, as Sturgis suggested, some Oriental had run amuck. But when we reached Negritos in record time, and learned more of the details of the crime, we were at an utter loss.

Merivale was in charge, and though he was a competent enough young chap, and an excellent executive, he was so flabbergasted and upset over the Major's death that he didn't know which way to turn. In fact, he could scarcely give an intelligible account of the events that had occurred, and I found McGovern, the boss driller, far more lucid. He had been a little of everything in his day and at one time had been a New York policeman with a beat in one of the toughest sections of Manhattan's lower East Side.

Major Stevens, knowing of his police record, and cognizant of McGovern's ability to handle men, had sworn him in as a deputy, and had placed him in charge of policing the camp. He was a huge, burly fellow; red-haired, freckle-faced, and was personally acquainted with every man, woman and child in the district. He had known the two Cholos killed on the first night, and he assured me as he said he had assured the Major, that both were the most industrious and law-abiding of natives.

"Sure, Pablo an' Gonzalez was hard-working, dacint lads," he declared. "Didn't I have thim worrkin' over to thoity-two week afore last. Niver the gamblin' nor drinkin' sort, sor, an' peaceful as lambs. Now who the divvil, I'm askin' ya, would have raison for bumpin' of thim two lads off? An' they weren't robbed, neither. No, sor, 'tis not robbery nor a row nor nothin' of that kind that caused it. 'Twas some extr'o'd'nary motive, as ye might say, an' ye'll have to find the motive afore ye find the murderer, if ye ask me. Who do I think it might be? B'gorra, how should I know? And then these others last night. Yes, sor, the camp was lit bright as day and the gang of us patrollin' the place. Sure, there was fourteen of us all gumshoin' about, an' meself wit' three boys on duty fernist the Cholos' quarters. An niver a sound of a foight nor a cry nor nothin'. Thin with the comin' av day loight come a scream from Block Wan, an' another yell from Block Foive, an' wimmen a-runnin' an' me an' the boys beatin' it to find what the trouble was an' all, an' there they be—the three of thim, deader'n busted drills, an' never a mark onto 'em savin' of the red marks about their necks. B'gorra, no' I'm mistook. Wan of thim had marks on his chest an' another on his face like they'd been shot wit' rock salt, if ye know what I mean. An' then off I goes to tell da Major—God rest his soul—and to find him dead by the same token. 'Tis downright unnat'ral, sor. Damned uncanny. An' I don't mind admittin' it's got me goat, sor."

"What about the women killed at Talara?" I asked.

But McGovern had no definite information about them. They had, so it was reported, been found dead, obviously killed, on the desert just outside the town, and as they had been alive and well at a late hour the preceding evening, and had started for their homes on the hillside beyond the cemetery, about eleven, it was certain they had been murdered sometime between that hour and daybreak.

"I'll be damned if I see how a man could kill three Cholos and the Major up here and two women at Talara at the same time," cried Henshaw. "McGovern and his men didn't see a soul on the street or on the road, there was no car out and it's a sure bet the murderer didn't travel by airplane. And everyone swears those three men in Blocks One and Five were not dead at midnight. And there's the Major—he was all right at two o'clock this morning."

"I don't consider that part of the affair as remarkable as the other facts," I told him. "A man could walk to Talara in a couple of hours. But why should the fiend kill five men here and two women there? How did he manage it without being seen or heard by McGovern or his men, and why didn't any one of the five—or rather, eight—cry out? And how did he kill them? I tell you, Henshaw, there's something deep in this that we haven't thought of yet. In my opinion the murdered people have been killed by some means we haven't suspected—that strangling is just a bluff—it's some terrible poison or something of that sort—perhaps administered hours before the men die."

"How about that knocking them on the head theory of yours?" asked Henshaw.

"That might be it if it was not for the Major," I said. "I can't imagine anyone sneaking up on him."

"It would have been easy enough," declared Henshaw. "He was sitting close to his open door and very likely fell asleep. If I were in your place I'd get on with the post-mortem and see if you can find any signs of any injury or of poison. But I don't envy you your job."

"It's not mine," I informed him. "And if you don't look out, I'll call you in to help. We've got to get into this. I'm going to do all I can and Merivale wants me to take charge as senior here. I wish to Heaven old Doctor Daniels were here. Young Rogers is a good doctor—good enough for his routine or hospital work, but he's never made a post-mortem in his life and I know very little about such things. However, I suppose Rogers can find out if there are injuries and if there was poison given. I'm merely going to be present and make microscopic examinations of the stomach contents and blood."

But the results of the post-mortems left us as much in the dark as ever—in fact more puzzled than ever. The Cholos all seemed to have been victims of pernicious anaemia, or to have bled to death, although there were no wounds that would have accounted for any considerable loss of blood. The marks upon their faces and chests that McGovern had mentioned were punctures, but seemed barely to penetrate the skin, and there were no blood stains of any considerable extent upon the men's garments. In two cases there were severe contusions on the heads, but these might have been caused by falling upon the stones. The third man, however, had a small puncture in his jugular vein, and the left eye was injured and appeared as though the eyeball had been pierced and the liquid had run out. Yet there was no blood upon the fellow's clothes. We did not make a post-mortem upon the Major, but externally there were no marks upon his body that seemed adequate to have caused death, aside from the red line about the throat that was present on all the bodies. And, unlike the Cholos, he appeared to have lost little, if any, blood. We got into telephonic communication with the resident doctor at Talara who reported that the dead women bore no marks of violence aside from numerous small punctures on the breasts and backs, which marks he compared to the marks that might have been caused by bird-shot fired from a distance, yet there were no shot in the wounds. Neither did my microscopic examination of the stomach contents, the tissues or the blood reveal the presence of recognizable poison, and Rogers' chemical tests showed no toxic reactions.

Of course all this took time, and it was late in the afternoon when the disagreeable work had been completed. All ordinary work had come to a complete standstill. No one could put his mind on work; the executives and bosses were all too much engrossed with the procession of mysterious tragedies to carry on, and the Cholos had a glorious loaf, apparently quite unmoved and undisturbed by the uncanny fate of their friends and companions. And naturally the camps were in a tremendous state of excitement and nervous tension. The women were frightened almost out of their wits, no children were allowed out of doors, and even in broad daylight everybody acted as if they expected to be struck down by some invisible hand at any moment.

The men too seemed to be filled with superstitious dread. The mere fact that men were murdered—even had there been three times as many—would not have troubled the hard-boiled roughnecks who made up the working force of white men. Most of them had led wild lives. They had been in many a mining camp where human life was held cheap and murders were everyday matters, and the majority of them had been in the World War. A score of men—either native or white—killed in a riot, a strike, a quarrel or a drunken brawl would not have caused them a moment's thought. But the mysterious manner of the eight deaths, the inexplicable reason for the murders, and the fact that there seemed no clues in the murderer filled these tough, case-hardened old-timers with the fear of the supernatural. Indeed, more than one openly expressed his opinion that the men had not been killed by anything human, that some old Incan devil or evil spirit had had a hand in the tragedies, and that the only safe course was for everyone to clear out and stay out.

Of course, the intelligent population scoffed at such ideas. We knew well enough that murders had been committed, and we felt confident that whoever had so far eluded us would be captured if he attempted to repeat his crimes. And we arranged such a complete cordon of guards, sentries and police about the camp—that we felt positive that if the murderer put in an appearance that night he would never escape us.

Looking back upon it now, I can realize how really silly and amateurish our plans were. On the previous evening the murderer had committed his fiendish crimes despite the brilliant illumination of electric lights and the presence of a large force of men, and had escaped unseen. And yet we thought that by darkening the streets, by hiding in the shadows, and by giving orders that no inhabitant was to be on the streets after eleven, that we could apprehend a murderer who had shown such devilish ingenuity in eluding everyone hitherto.

It was a dark, starless night, and only enough lights had been left burning to enable us to see moving figures, should they appear upon the streets.

Fully fifty men were on duty in the camp, and I had also posted a dozen men outside the limits of the camp where they could watch the surrounding desert. These men were carefully hidden, some in the dense shadows of the oil derricks, others behind piles of pipe, and still others back of rocks or other objects. It seemed to us at the time that it would be utterly impossible for any living creature to approach the camp undetected or to make a way through the streets unseen by the armed watchers. Of course there was the chance that the maniac or fiend or whoever he was would not appear, that he had satiated his lust for killing, or that, knowing we were awaiting him, he would keep away until the excitement and watchfulness had died down, or perhaps forever. But we reasoned that he must be a maniac or a drug-fiend and that in such case he would continue his attacks and, moreover, would not reason that he was courting disaster by reappearing.

Nothing had occurred up to midnight. I had gone the rounds several times, all the men reported on duty, thoroughly wide awake, and not a sign of anyone other than the patrols had been seen. One o'clock, two o'clock passed, and then suddenly echoing horribly through the darkness—came a frenzied scream of deadly terror. Instantly, with chills running up and down my back, I dashed in the direction of the cry, and I heard the racing footsteps of half a dozen of my men behind me. But we had not gone fifty yards before we were met by a flying figure rushing madly towards us from the desert. It was McGovern, and never have I seen mad terror and fear so depicted as upon the big Irishman's face. His eyes rolled, his mouth twisted and slobbered, his teeth chattered and his bulky muscular frame shook and trembled like that of a frightened child. He was almost bereft of his senses. He actually clung to me, and he babbled and mumbled incoherently. With the utmost difficulty we finally got him to talk intelligibly. And the tale he told was incredible.

He had been sitting, he declared—interlarding his story with many ejaculations and frequently crossing himself—upon a pile of lumber in the shadow of a newly-erected derrick about one hundred feet beyond the barracks known as Block Seven. He insisted he had been wide awake, that he had felt no fear, and that he had continually turned and peered in all directions. No human being, he declared positively, could have approached him unseen, and yet, suddenly and without sound or warning, something soft, cool and damp had been thrown over his head, almost smothering him; a muscular arm had encircled his neck, fingers had gripped his throat, and he had felt blinded, choked, strangling. Terrified almost to madness, using all his tremendous strength, he had struggled, fought, tried to tear the throttling arm loose, to throw off the smothering thing that had dropped—like a wet blanket as he described it—over his head. For a time it had seemed as if his struggle had no effect. He turned, twisted, tried to reach his adversary's body, but in vain. Then, whether by accident or design he was not certain, he had flung himself down, had rolled in a pool of thick crude oil, and instantly the strangling hand released its grip, the covering over his head had been jerked away, and leaping up, screaming at the top of his lungs, McGovern had turned and raced towards the camp.

Scarcely waiting to hear the end of his amazing tale we dashed forward to the spot where the Irishman had been attacked. But there was no sign of a living thing in the vicinity. In fact, we would have doubted the Irishman's story, would have thought he had dozed off and had dreamed the whole thing, had it not been for the oil smeared over him, the marks where he had struggled from the pool, and the distinct red imprint upon his neck.

For an hour or more we searched the desert, every possible hiding place in it, and were on the point of giving up when a shout from Jackson brought us on the run. He was standing beside a pile of rusty scrap-iron, his eyes staring, and pointing towards a huddled form lying in the shadow. I flashed my electric torch and sprang back with an involuntary cry of shock and amazement. There, limp and lifeless, his rifle still across the knees, was the dead body of Henderson, one of the patrol.

"Mother of God!" cried McGovern who, still shaking and trembling, had kept close by my side. "The divvil got the poor b'y. Glory be, sor, will ye now be after sayin' 'tis anny human sowl as does be doin' the killin's?"

We stared at one another with blank, frightened faces. It was uncanny, incredible. Whoever the murderer might be, he was possessed of almost supernatural powers, it seemed. Silently, unseen, unheard, unsuspected, he had stolen upon Henderson, had killed him before the poor fellow could utter a sound. And death must have been instantaneous; for otherwise, had there been any struggle, the rifle would not have remained across Henderson's knees. The only explanation was that Henderson, unlike McGovern, had been attacked while he slept. And this, I felt sure, proved that Henderson had been killed before McGovern had been attacked, for otherwise he would have been awakened by the big Irishman's frenzied shrieks.

But the amazing, the baffling events of that night were not yet at an end. When, bearing Henderson's body, we returned to the camp, Merivale and Rogers met us with two of the patrol, and at my first glance at their faces I knew that some tragedy had occurred.

"My God, Barry!" exclaimed Rogers. "the watchman at the hospital has been murdered! He couldn't have been dead five minutes when I found him—and you may think me crazy or not—I caught a glimpse of the fiend that killed him. I'm not mad, I don't drink, and I was wide awake, but I swear as I am alive this minute that I saw a dim shadowy form rise from his body and vanish—yes, absolutely vanish in thin air, before my eyes."

"Nonsense!" I ejaculated, striving to steady my voice, for the manifest terror of the two was a bit contagious. "If you saw the man, who was be? What was he like?"

"Man!" cried Rogers. "It wasn't a man. It was a—a—thing—a—a—ghost!"

"Blessed Mary, protect us!" exclaimed McGovern, crossing himself devoutly and pressing close to my side as he glanced furtively into the shadows as if expecting some terrible demon to materialize. "Didn't Oi say 'twas no human sowl that was afther murderin' the b'ys. An' 'twas no man born of woman as fought wit' me' sor."

I forced a laugh. "You were dreaming, Rogers," I declared. "You imagined you saw something. None of us believes in ghosts or supernatural things."

"He was not dreaming," put in Merivale. "I was up when Rogers yelled and I saw it, too. And it wasn't anything human."

I gasped. I could not doubt the statements of two men. The watchman had been killed; both insisted they had seen a thing, some phantasmal object that had vanished. What did it mean? What could the thing—the death-dealing phantom—be? But I did not and do not believe in ghosts nor in anything supernatural. Everything, I have always argued, is explicable by natural causes, and recovering from my first vague feelings of dread and the tingling of my nerves at the uncanniness of the men's stories, I attacked the matter from a common sense point of view.

"Perhaps you both did see something," I agreed. "But if you did, it was no ghost. Even if we believed in ghosts and I do not, and I don't believe either of you do—no one ever heard of a ghost injuring anyone. And the being who has committed these crimes has muscular strength, is flesh and blood. McGovern here was attacked by him, and he can tell you, when he gets over his mad superstitious terror, that it was no ghostly, spiritual, wraith-like thing that he fought with. If it appeared to vanish, it was merely because it slipped out of sight in the darkness. But of course there is a remote—a very remote possibility that it is not a human being. It may be some strange bird of prey, although I have no faith in such a theory. No bird, nor for that matter any animal, strangles men to death. In my own opinion it is some demented Oriental—perhaps a member of the East Indian Thugg clan. The manner in which a cloth is thrown over the victim's head, and the strangling, are both strikingly like the methods of the Thuggs. I believe that what you two saw was the cloth or blanket or poncho that the fellow uses. In all probability, he is nude or nearly so, and therefore almost invisible in the darkness. But the cloth he uses may be light-colored. As he escaped after murdering the watchman, this cloth showed up for an instant before he gathered it up. That would have given the effect you describe, Rogers. And coming as you did from light into darkness, your eyes would have failed to see his form, and moreover, your eyes being attracted by and focused upon the cloth, you would have failed to see his body. Anyhow, we now know the fellow's method. He smothers his victims' cries by his cloth—that is why there has never been a cry nor a scream when men have been attacked—and then strangles them."

"Fine!" exclaimed Merivale with sarcasm. "But how about those punctures? And what's his big idea? And how does he get by the patrols and get away?"

"I don't think the punctures as you call them have anything to do with the case at all," I replied. "How do we know they were not on the bodies of the people previous to their being killed? A lot of these Cholos have sores and eruptions, you know. And maniacs

are notoriously clever in eluding those set to capture them. A naked Hindu or Chinaman can slip through the shadows where no
white man could pass undetected."

"Well, I hope you're right," said Rogers. "I don't believe in spirits any more than you do, Barry. But I'll admit had a bad turn when
I saw that ghostly-looking, cloud-like thing float away from the
watchman's body and vanish. But I expect the excitement is over
for tonight. The cast is beginning to lighten. It's almost morning."

But though the excitement was over for the night, as Rogers
said, the coming of day brought most exciting news to us at
Negritos. Sturgis called up from Lobitos, and my face paled when
he informed me that two men found killed—strangled—at his camp.
Hardly had he finished speaking when Colcord called from Talara
and reported that four murders had been committed there. An hour
or two later our wireless operator picked up a message from the
Grace Liner "Santa Julia" with the astounding news that three persons—two men of the crew and a passenger—had been found dead
upon the ship's deck that morning, and that all appeared to have
been garroted. And, as if that were not enough, we heard from Paita
that there had been a similar killing there.

My brain whirled; I could scarcely believe my senses, and the
others were struck dumb by these incredible reports. How was it
possible that such things could have occurred? How could the
murderer have killed victims in Negritos, Lobitos, Talara—fifty
miles away at Paita—in the same night? And even if it were possible for any human being to have rushed hither and thither over
such an area, there was the incredible fact that he, it, whatever it
was, had struck down victims aboard a steamship twenty miles
from the coast.

Henshaw was the first to break the tense, awed silence. "Damn
it!" he ejaculated. "It's impossible. I'm not superstitious and I'm
willing to admit anything within reason. But this is too much. No
human being could have done this. Either there's a crowd of the
murderers—an organized gang—or else, well, I'm not going to admit
the ghost or spirit theory yet, but if it's not the work of a gang it's
the work of some damn force or power or plague and not anything
human."

"McGovern will assure you it was neither plague nor disease,"
I reminded him. "And," I added, "Rogers and Merivale actually saw
something. Isn't it possible—even if highly improbable—that it is

the work of some new and strange creature—some bird or gigantic bat, some sort of vampire?"

"I'm beginning to think anything's possible," declared Henshaw. "And by the way, it looks as if we'd have to shut down if this keeps on. All my gang at Lobitos have quit and half the Cholos here have cleared out. McGovern tells me he's leaving for Lima this afternoon; the drillers and riggers are ready to quit, and every woman in the camp who can get away is going to leave this damned place by the first ship."

I nodded. "Yes, I know," I replied. "And I can't much blame them. Any murders are bad enough, but with the mysterious and uncanny added as they are here, no one wants to hang around. And no one knows who may be the next victim. Do you know, one thing that puzzles me is why so few of the whites have been attacked. Poor Major Stevens is the only white man killed so far, and the only other one attacked was McGovern."

"You forget those three on the "Julia," he reminded me. "They were all white."

"And there have only been two women killed," put in Merivale.

"I don't see as those facts make any great difference," declared Rogers. "The fact remains that people are killed every night, that beginning with two the first night the—well, murderers—have increased their toll to eleven—if we include McGovern, who escaped by the skin of his teeth—last night. At that rate of progression there should be twenty-five deaths tonight, fifty or sixty tomorrow night and several hundred by Saturday."

"My God!" cried Henshaw, "I hadn't thought of it that way. Why, damn it, Barry, if this goes on everyone will be wiped out in a week!"

I forced a smile. "Provided Rogers' mathematical series of progression continues, there won't be a living man or woman left on earth in a year or so," I remarked. "But we have no reason to assume that the same increase will continue. Put it another way. The murders began here with two, and last night only one was killed here. Possibly the activities of the killers will be devoted to other localities in the future. But to my mind the all-important thing is to find out who or what they are, why they are killing people at random, and how to put a stop to it. It is not the number of deaths, but the fact that there are any; the fact that no one is safe—that is important. As a mere matter of lives lost—why, last year more men were killed by accident right here in Negritos than all those who have been murdered. It's the manner, the cause of death, that makes it so terrible."

"Well, how are we going to get anywhere? And what more can we do than we have done?" demanded Merivale.

"I suggest we put a barbed wire entanglement around the camp," said Rogers. "If the—the thing—gets in through that, we'll know it's not human."

"And flood the whole damned place with search-lights," added Henshaw.

"We'll do both," I agreed. "And if the—well, the murderer—gets in and attacks anyone, we'll be able to see him at any rate."

But—though it sounds utterly incredible and impossible—despite the barbed-wire barrier and the flood of light, another person fell a victim to the mysterious death that night—and this time a white woman, Mrs. Veitch, the schoolteacher, who, throughout the terrifying and exciting times had remained unperturbed and had slept nightly on her sleeping-porch. And from such places as Piura, Salaverry, Trujillo, and Catovia came reports of the same weirdly mysterious deaths.

"I tell you it's a plague or a disease," declared Rogers. "McGovern just imagined he was attacked."

Henshaw snorted. "And didn't you yourself swear you and Merivale saw something?" he asked.

"I did," admitted Rogers, "but I've come to the conclusion we were both deluded. We must have imagined it. If you can suggest anything within reason—other than some virulent disease—that can kill people hundreds of miles apart and can come in here through barbed wire and flood-lights and strike down victims, then I'll admit anything. But every detail is like the effect of some plague—the way it has spread, the unexpected way it strikes, the lack of wounds on the bodies, the condition of the blood of the victims. And those marks or punctures all indicate some terrible, unknown malady."

"One thing I have noticed," observed Henshaw, "is that this whole business has started since that earthquake and the change in the climate. It's only since the rains started and vegetation grew up that these deaths have occurred. That in a way would bear out the plague theory. I don't know, but it's possible that there's some germ in the soil that has been revived and made active by the wet weather."

"On the contrary," I declared, "we had no deaths during the intensely rainy period. All the murders have occurred since the rains stopped and the weather has been dry, and that looks to me as if it had no connection with the rain."

"Hmm, well, we may have a chance to decide upon that," said Henshaw. "It's clouding up and looks and feels like more rain."

He was not mistaken. It began to rain that afternoon; by nightfall it was pouring, and throughout the night it came down in torrents. And not a death occurred, not a murder was reported within the rainy area, although six men were killed and three women murdered about Salaverry and Trujillo, where no rain fell. Of course, as I pointed out, this might have been a coincidence, but when, on the four succeeding nights, it rained and no deaths occurred, and when the rain had extended southward to Chancay and not a murder took place anywhere, we began to feel that the rain had a lot to do with it and that Rogers' theory of the deaths resulting from some disease was the correct hypothesis.

And as days followed days and not a recurrence of the killings was reported, and as the weather continued rainy, we all decided that, regardless of the fact that none could explain it, no scientific or medical solution could be given, yet the mysterious deaths had been brought about by some germ or spore or microbe that was only virulent during dry spells after heavy rains. As Rogers put it: Some unknown deadly germ was bred or developed from a dormant state by the rain, but only became active when the weather was dry. But even he could offer no suggestion to account for the fact that the deaths occurred only during the night.

However, as the plague seemed over, as all were now convinced that there was no human element in the matter, and as the rains seemed likely to continue indefinitely—the Weather Bureau and the meteorological experts agreed that unless another alteration of the ocean's bed took place, the climate would remain permanently wet—those tragic, terror filled nights were almost forgotten. The drillers and riggers, having had no opportunity to sail away, overcame their fears and returned to work; the Cholos drifted back to the camps from the hills, and the women abandoned their packing and preparations for departure and decided to live on at the camps.

Once more I was free to carry on my studies, and one of my first acts was to make a visit to the strange plants I had been so long forced to neglect.

Much to my chagrin I found them wilted, dead, and with only the scars on the back to show where the flowers had been. In vain I searched about, looking for fruit, seeds or even remains of the blooms. But several weeks had passed, the rains had been severe, and decomposition of all dead vegetation was very rapid. I was greatly disappointed, but it could not be helped, and transforming my botanical expedition into a hunt, I started through the jungle in the hopes of securing some quail or pigeons. I had gone perhaps a quarter of a mile when I reached the banks of one of the recently formed streams and, following up this, I came upon a partly decomposed, mushy, gelatinous object lying at the edge of the water. For a moment I thought it the body of some fish or animal, but there was little odor of decaying animal matter emanating from it, and as I bent nearer I discovered that it was the wilted and decaying flower of some unknown plant. Something about it appeared familiar, and suddenly it dawned upon me that it was the blossom of one of my queer shrubs. Quite obviously it had been blown or washed to the stream and had been carried by the current until it had found a resting place on the shore. It was a very poor specimen, but I examined it with great interest. From what I could determine, it differed but little from the flowers I had seen before in their nearly opened bud-form. The purple color had faded to a dingy brown, the white had turned yellow and was discolored, but I could still distinguish the gigantic bulbous calyx, the membranous fringe that encircled the long semi-circular petals, the thread-like filaments that I assumed were stamens, and the fragment of a thick, fleshy, spiny pistil. In full blossom and freshly opened upon its parent stalk, it must have been a gorgeous and truly remarkable sight, I decided; but it was beyond preservation and with a sigh of regret that I would probably never have the opportunity of witnessing the strange plants in bloom, I turned away.

But a few minutes later I came upon another of the decaying flowers. This time, to my amazement, I discovered that the jointed, leafless shoots of new plants were sprouting from the earth about it. Here was a most interesting state of affairs. There were no seeds or fruit but new plants wore germinating from the flower itself, apparently. Still, upon second thought, I realized this was not so remarkable. Many of the Cacti and Bromeliads, I knew, would grow from portions of the stalks, even from the buds or flowers, and I had long before decided that my plants were closely related to if not members of the Cacti or the Bromeliad group. But more than anything else I was greatly elated to know that I might yet have a chance to witness the blooming of the growths. If the rains continued, they would spring up and develop rapidly, and in a fortnight more should bud and blossom. That afternoon I found several more of the old flowers, and in every case new stalks were sprouting up. At that rate, I thought, in a few months the whole mountainside would be covered with the plants, and I imagined what a truly wonderful sight would be presented when they were covered with hundreds, thousands, of the huge, magnificent flowers in full bloom. What a pity they were night-bloomers like the cereus! But even so, a hillside covered with the gigantic white and mauve flowers when viewed by moonlight would be a sight never to be forgotten, and worth coming many miles to view.

Almost daily I visited some of the plants. They grew rapidly, seeming to absorb the remains of the flowers, and to my surprise I found them scattered over a very wide area. And my surprise was increased when, in speaking of them to my friends, Merivale said he had run across one of the growths far out in the area of the former desert, and Sedgwick declared he had been attracted to some of the queer-looking plants when he was more than half way to Lobitos. It seemed incredible that the big flowers could have blown so far, and I could only account for it on the supposition that there had been other plants that I had not located at the beginning of the rainy period.

When, soon after, I saw indications of the nearest plants budding, I became quite excited, and I watched with intense interest as the buds swelled, the flowers developed, and glimpses of the white and purple blooms showed through their rough brownish integument. Finally the time came when I felt that on any night the blooms might open and, fearing that I might miss the sight, for I felt sure the flowers lasted in their full perfection for only one night, I decided to visit the plants that evening. But the rain came down in torrents and when, after half-wading through the water and mud and drenched to the skin, I reached the nearest clump of plants, l found the flowers in exactly the same state as they had been in the day before. Very obviously they would not expand during rainy weather, and cursing myself for an idiot—for I should have known that this would be the case and that few night-blooming flowers open except in fine weather—I returned to camp, deciding to await dry weather before again going tramping off on such another wild-goose chase.

But I was doomed to bitter disappointment once more. I was unexpectedly summoned to a new oil field being prospected at Langosta Bay, and as luck would have it, dry weather commenced almost as soon as I left. Langosta, being quite out of the world and a mere prospecting camp in the desert—for owing to some freaky wind current or its location this area had not altered in climate like the rest of the coast—no news of the outer world reached us except when—once a fortnight—Lima-Guayaquil plane dropped in on us with mail and newspapers.

Hence it was two weeks after my arrival at Langosta before we had any news of our friends at Negritos and Talara. And when the Ford tri-motored plane came gliding down and we received our letters and the papers, we found them filled with most amazing and fearful tales. Everywhere during the past week, men, women, children and even domestic animals had fallen victims to the baffling, mysterious death that stalked abroad at night and struck down silently, instantly. More than fifty had been killed in and about Talara; as many more had succumbed from the plague at Negritos, for by this time everyone was agreed that it was some terrible, unknown malady. Nineteen out of the total population of four hundred had died at Lobitos. Several of the native villages in the hills had been completely wiped out, and scores had been killed at Paita, at Salaverry, about Trujillo and back in the hills about Piura. A few deaths had even been reported from as far south as Casma and as far north as Tumbes, but the center appeared to be about Talara and Negritos, and a theory was advanced that the germs of the deadly, terrible disease were brought up by the drilling or by the oil. Work had completely ceased at the camps. Nearly all the Cholos and most of the whites had left the stricken district, but finding a rigid quarantine in force at Lima and in all other parts, the poor frightened inhabitants had been forced to return to their homes, where they were living in a state of terror almost impossible to describe.

Doctors and specialists were being rushed from the States and the Canal Zone to the locality with orders to make a thorough investigation and to locate the death-dealing germs, and the International Petroleum Company had employed the most eminent specialists at enormous salaries and with offers of veritable fortunes in the form of rewards to anyone who could discover a way of checking the inroads of this new menace to the entire population of the country.

The first to arrive had been Doctor Heinrich, the noted German biologist, who had been in Guayaquil making an intensive study of tropical fungus diseases of the skin. He had dashed to Talara by plane and had at once plunged into the problem with his customary energy and thoroughness.

But his first reports somewhat amused me, despite the seriousness of the situation. The deaths, he announced, were the result of some malady that attacked the respiratory organs, the effect being to smother the victim. This primary effect was followed almost instantly by a high fever, a constriction of the throat muscles, and the consequent rupture of small blood vessels. The germs, which he felt sure entered the system through the almost invisible openings in the skin, caused, as a third and final effect, extreme anæmia. Examination of the blood remaining in those stricken showed practical elimination of the red corpuscles, and in some cases practically no arterial blood whatever. Undoubtedly, the learned doctor proceeded to explain, the remarkable statements of McGovern and others describing the feeling of a cloth being thrown over their heads and a strangling arm encircling their necks, was the result of the smothering effect of the germs entering the human system. In mild attacks—which had been extremely rare—the symptoms had all been identical in this respect. All those who had been attacked described the smothering cloth, the pressure upon the neck, the mad struggle to escape. These were precisely the mental impressions that would result so he averred—from the effects of the malady as he had described them. Pressure upon nerves and arteries, caused by the spasmodic contraction of the muscles affected by the germs, would induce pressure upon the brain and mental illusions. Hence the victims, feeling smothered, would imagine the cloth and the external pressure, and might quite reasonably be expected to imagine seeing objects that did not exist.

Hence, he argued with Teutonic logic, the fact that several persons had sworn to seeing indescribable forms rushing off when, by herculean efforts, they had recovered from the attacks, merely proved that they had been temporarily mentally deranged by the effects of the germs entering their systems. He had, he continued, made a very careful examination of all such persons, and had found them invariably excited, in a state of nervous exhaustion, and subject to violent and sudden fits of terror and to suggestion. He had endeavored to isolate the germs from samples of their blood, but so far without success, and he concluded his study almost positively that the disease was neither contagious nor transmissible; that it was in a way similar to tetanus, and that it was unquestionably the result of the alteration in climatic conditions. "In all probability," he wrote," the germs have been present but dormant in the deserts for centuries. The rainfall has invigorated and propagated them, and as they become active and dry, they are carried by the wind to find lodgement upon their living hosts. It is a notable and suggestive fact that the activity of the disease is confined to dry periods and to the hours of darkness; also that while the deaths resulting from the disease have spread southward—with the prevailing winds—they have not spread northward against the prevailing air currents, except in a few isolated cases."

As preventative measures, he recommended remaining indoors after dark—he pointed out that with one or two exceptions no one in well-closed houses had suffered—bathing in carbolic or other disinfectant solutions, and refraining from excitement, overeating, exhaustive exercises or nervousness.

Poor old Doctor Heinrich! The very morning after he had published his report—which contained nothing we did not already know—he was found dead on the steps of his own home, another victim of the "night death," as it was now called.

And as if his death had been the signal, the rains had come again, and not a death had been reported since.

"Looks to me," observed Torrens, the long, lean-jawed Texas engineer, "as if what you all need over at Negritos is a lot of firehose. The bugs don't look to bite when its wet. Just keep a lot of hose playing 'roun' the camp and the bugs'll keep away."

"I'm not at all sure that such a scheme might not work," I said, "but it would not help the rest of the world. And there's another queer feature to the whole horrible business. Not a death has been reported from any of the sections that are still dry—from this district, for example, or from Cacamaquilla or the Huaranay country."

"'Pears like to me the bugs sure like places where there's sunshine after showers," drawled Torrens. "Mebbe they'd dry up and turn into bug mummies out in the desert country—feel like I might get mummified myself if I'm here much longer. And they're night birds, too. All jokin' aside, ain't it possible they can't stand sunshine or heat and that's why they don't wander thisaway? Anyhow you look at it, it's damn bad, and I'm sure glad those bugs ain't mooning around here. Lord Amighty, it's smotherin' enough without them addin' to it."

The next news we had told a very different story. The rains had recommenced, and for ten days not a death had been reported. The doctors and specialists had reached Talara, and had been busy making an intensive investigation, but I could not see that they had reached any definite conclusions nor had they come to any agreement aside from the fact that all believed that the deaths were the result of some unknown and remarkable germ or microbe. Some held that it was a minute microscopic animal and not a true germ; others declared it the spores of some plant-like growth related to the fungi or moulds, and others were equally insistent that it was the microbe of a true disease.

Neither did they agree as to the origin, the manner of dissemination and the habits of the thing. Some claimed it was the result of the climatic changes, others that it had been introduced from some other locality, and others declared that it was a new development or form of the mysterious Chan-Chan fever.

One savant was positive that the germs were carried by night-flying insects, and in support of his theory pointed out that such insects invariably appeared in large numbers on clear nights after heavy rains. His colleagues were equally positive that the germs were blown about by the wind, and as proof called attention to the fact that the strongest winds always blew at night, that during dry weather there was always a breeze, while during the rains it was almost calm, and he further argued that wet weather would lay the germs as it did any other dust. But there could be no argument in respect to the results and the deadly character of the new malady, and all the schemes so far tested had proved ineffectual in so far as preventing attacks was concerned. No, I am mistaken in that statement; no person who had remained indoors with doors and windows closed or screened had been attacked, and as all the white residents of the district had obeyed orders and had been careful to remain indoors after nightfall, no deaths of the whites had occurred, and only Cholos and other natives, who slept in open barracks or sheds, had succumbed, aside from several members of the patrol, who had been found dead at their posts. This, declared the authorities, shed a ray of hope. If everybody kept indoors from dark until dawn, there was every reason to think that the deaths would entirely cease, and, so argued the learned doctors, if the deaths could be completely checked for a time, the germs, finding no hosts, would soon die out. And in order to prevent all possibility of the germs finding victims, all the Cholos and Indians had been rounded up and were nightly locked in barracks and no live stock of any sort was allowed at large after sundown. And as it was now established that the "Night Death" was due to microbes and to no human or outside agency, all police and patrols were abandoned, and soon after sunset the entire country was as silent and deserted as the tomb. Just how well this plan had worked out could not be determined, because, as I have said, the rains had again commenced, and no one positively could state whether the cessation of deaths was due to the weather or to the precautions taken.

These were the conditions that existed when, having completed my work at Langosta, I returned to Negritos.

As it was still rainy, and as I felt certain that there was no danger as long as it was wet weather, I decided to have a look at my long-neglected plants. There were severe penalties provided for anyone violating this rule about going abroad after dark, but I intended fully to risk it if I found my plants were about to blossom, for I was determined that I would see the strange growths while in flower. I was not greatly surprised to discover that the growths had increased amazingly. But I was surprised to find how far and how much they had spread. They were in fact everywhere, scattered through the jungles, sometimes singly, again in groups, and in some spots forming miniature forests and covering large areas of the hillsides.

I found, however, that a comparatively small portion of the plants bore buds, although those that showed no indications of approaching florescence appeared on vigorous and as fully matured as the others. This I accounted for on the theory that a certain proportion were sterile (a condition that exists commonly among many of the cacti and allied plants) and incapable of producing flowers, and my theory was more or less borne out by the fact that those that had no flower buds had developed leaves.

These leaves were remarkable growths and resembled the gray pendant lichen known as Spanish moss more than anything else. But they were quite different in structure, being composed of innumerable slightly wavy threads or filaments sprouting from a short, fleshy stem, and pale bluish-green in color. While examining these—for my interest had been transferred from the buds to the leaves—I discovered another interesting peculiarity of the remarkable plants. In every case where the growths had sprung up from the fallen decayed blossoms the stems bore the filament-like leaves and no flower buds, whereas—and this took me some time to discover—growths had sprung up from directly under the bunches of drooping, hair-like leaves. Not for some time did it dawn upon me that my strange plants had a most amazing life cycle. In other words, there was a two-phase cycle: the flowers producing non-flowering plants that in turn bore leaves (or perhaps flowers of another form) which, falling to earth, produced plants that bore only flowers. Such a mode of growth and reproduction was not, I knew, unknown among plants. Several of the parasitic tropical plants, known popularly as "air-plants," have a similar habit, the seeds producing non-flowering plants with jointed stems which break apart, each section developing a plant that bears flowers and seeds; and several ferns have a similar mode of propagating themselves; while among the marine plants the dual habit is not unusual. To me this was particularly interesting, as it tended to prove that the ancient forms of plant growth that had been brought into existence from long-dormant semi-fossil seeds by the rains had habits closely related to the marine forms of plant life. And as I had long held to a theory—and had written several monographs on the subject—that all plants originally were marine forms and that, with the receding of the waters and the increase of land, certain species and genera adapted themselves to a terrestrial existence, I was, of course, greatly pleased to find that, in my strange growths about Negritos, my theory was borne out to a certain extent. I was in fact quite convinced that many of the plants on the hillsides were very closely akin to existing marine forms and that my strange, jointed, rapid-growing, huge-flowered, night-blooming shrubs were the most closely related of all to marine growths.

Their amazingly rapid growth, their fibrous character, the semi-translucent flowers, all reminded me of bryozoans or algæ more than of true terrestrial forms of plant life.

And now this new discovery of their mode of propagation was another point in favor of my newly improvised theory.

Moreover, as I now realized for the first time, it would not be at all surprising to find the nearest air-breathing relatives of marine plants here in Peru. As I have said, all, or nearly all the plants, were extremely ancient forms that hitherto had been known only from fossils; and, in the second place, the country, as I knew from my paleontological studies, had been beneath the sea at no very remote period (geologically speaking) of the past. Hence, assuming that I was correct in my theory of the evolution of plant life, it would be natural that the earliest terrestrial forms of plant life and those most closely resembling their maritime ancestors, should be found here.

All of this of course passed through my mind far more rapidly than I have written it, and having located several plants that I judged would bloom that night—provided the rain ceased—I returned to Negritos, feeling that I had accomplished a great deal in support of my pet botanical theory. In my mind I was already composing an article on my discoveries for publication in the Journal of the International Society for Botanical Research.

It did not, however, stop raining that night nor for several nights; but at length the sun shone again, the last clouds drifted away over the Andes, and I prepared to sneak off and fulfill my long delayed desire to witness the blooming of the plants that had interested me—in fact, I might say had obsessed me for months.

There was no great difficulty in getting away from camp unseen. Everyone was within doors, there was no patrol, no police, no guards, nobody to detect me, and I chuckled to myself at the thought of how different were the present conditions to those when the first mysterious deaths had occurred and the place had been alive with armed guards searching for an imaginary murderer or maniac.

My thoughts reverted naturally to the incidents of those days, to McGovern and his terror of something that had not existed except in his overwrought and superstitious mind; to Rogers and Merivale and to the terrifying, nervous dread that had filled all of us when the nightly deaths had seemed to savor of the supernatural and uncanny. Of course I realized I was taking a risk there was a remote chance that I might be attacked by the malady that stalked its victims invisibly and unannounced on dry nights like this. But I am something of a fatalist; besides, scientific ardor is not easily dampened by thoughts of personal risks or dangers, otherwise few great scientific truths would have been discovered. But even a scientist is not always immune to vague, indefinable fears, and I felt a peculiar and far from pleasant or comfortable sensation of impending danger, as if some unseen, indescribable peril hovered near.

Once or twice as I glanced, half-nervously, at the star-bright sky, I fancied I saw dim, cloud-like, moving forms passing swiftly overhead. Little chills tingled along my spine as I recalled Rogers' horrified expression when he spoke of the "thing" he had seen vanishing from the vicinity of the dead watchman. Was it possible, I thought, that there were such things as ghosts, spirits, forces of which we knew nothing? With an effort and a forced laugh I threw off my foolish, almost superstitious feelings. Probably I had not seen anything, and if I had, what more reasonable than to suppose them drifting clouds or even large night-flying birds—herons, jabirus or wood-ibis perhaps. Still, it was dashedly lonely, eerie and mysterious out there alone, with the black loom of the Andean peaks in the distance, with the dark shadows of the hills, with the thousand and one unaccountable noises of the night on every hand, and with not a living soul, the glimmer of a light to indicate a fellow human being in the whole vast expanse. And though I had no concrete ideas nor thoughts of meeting anyone or anything, I involuntarily gripped the hilt of my machete—which I invariably carried on my trips into the jungle—and kept a keen watch on my surroundings. But nothing happened. I saw no signs of life—except an occasional night-hawk or a fluttering, burrowing owl, and presently reached the edge of the dense vegetation.

The plants that I had selected to visit were close to the edge of the jungle, and as I had already cut an open trail through the growth, I approached the spot readily, noiselessly, and came within sight of the group of tall, stout, articulated stalks. I had not come in vain; looming ghostly in the darkness I could see three of the immense white and purple flowers fully expanded and looking as large as beach umbrellas in the uncertain light of the stars. For a moment I gazed at them entranced, drinking in the wonder and beauty of this floral display; then I stepped closer to examine the details of the blooms.

Suddenly I started and stared. There was no breeze here in the shelter of the hills, not a leaf of the vegetation stirred, and yet— incredible as it seemed—the flowers were moving, vibrating, pulsing, as if alive! Could it be the effect of the light or of my eyes striving to see clearly? No, I was positive it was no optical illusion. I focused my gaze upon one blossom, watched it. It did move! The bulbous purple calyx seemed to pulse slowly, deliberately, the white membranous fringe that was now spread flat, like a gigantic plate with convoluted edges, waved and fluttered; the long, fleshy multicolored petals undulated, and the slender, attenuated stamens waved, twisted and coiled about the great, rough central pistil. To my amazed, incredulous eyes the flower actually appeared to breathe, to be endowed with sensate life, to be struggling, feeling, exploring the air about it, as if searching for something. I was fascinated and at the same time filled with a nameless fear. Still staring, I drew back, my eyes fixed as though hypnotized upon that giant flower that now, for some inexplicable reason, appeared to me a horrible, uncanny, monstrous thing. And then my hairs seemed to rise on end. I felt a gripping terror, cold chills ran over me. Before my very eyes the great palpitating flower freed itself from the stalk and softly, silently, rose in air like a white balloon, and with stamens trailing and fringe undulating, it came slowly drifting towards me. I could not take my eyes from it. My mouth seemed dry. I was incapable of movement. I could not even cry out. For an instant it hovered above me and then—God, will I ever forget it!—the monstrous thing dropped swiftly, like a descending parachute, towards me. In a flash, in the fraction of a second, I remembered McGovern's description of the smothering, clammy cloth that had dropped over his head. In a flash I realized that it had been no hallucination, that the "thing," the "ghost," which Rogers and Merivale had seen, had been no figment of their imaginations. And in the same flash of intelligence I knew that the "night death" was no malady, no microscopic germ. I knew that it was these awful, silent, monstrous, living flowers of the mysterious plants.

A trailing, slimy thread-like stamen touched my cheek, and with a hoarse, inarticulate cry I leaped back. I felt a rasping something graze my neck. The air seemed suddenly shut off from my panting lungs, and with a mad, savage yell of frenzied terror I slashed viciously upward and outward with my machete. I felt the blade bury itself in some soft, yielding body. Thick, ill-smelling, salty liquid spurted over me. A pulpy, horrible mass struck my shoulder, and clinging, twining, snaky, sticky, nightmarish fingers seemed to close upon my left arm, my throat, my body.

Screaming, struggling, slashing, almost bereft of my senses, I tore the things loose, leaped aside and freed myself of the gruesome awful thing that lay, panting, pulsating but writhing helplessly upon the ground. I felt weak, faint, almost paralysed. Then some sixth sense caused me to turn. And just in time. Two more of the terrible, silent, deadly things were drifting down upon me! Before I could run, before I could move they were dropping toward me. But my first awful, superstitious terror had left me. The things, uncanny, terrible, supernatural as they seemed, were real. They were neither ghosts, nor demons nor spirit. They could be destroyed, killed.

Alert, watchful, I waited until the trailing, writhing stamens and the great flesh-colored pistil—that even in my deadly fear and excitement I mentally likened to a great boa with weaving, ominous head—were close above me. Then with all my strength I struck and leaped aside. With a soft swish the keen steel sheared through the mass. The thing veered, canted, capsized like a rudderless airplane, and with vicious blows I slashed it; hacked it until it fell. But I almost lost my life in doing so. The third monstrous thing was upon me. I felt its hellish smothering folds about my head; the swaying, rope-like central organ rasped across my neck. Only the fact that I was stooping, bending forward, saved me. With a scream I grasped the thing, wrenched it loose and felt my hand lacerated and stung as if with a thousand red-hot needles as I did so. I thrust and lunged with a machete, and, ducking, dodged from beneath the enfolding mass.

I was sick, nauseated, weak with terror and with my efforts. Everywhere about me I knew were more of the weirdly, horrible, deadly things. At any instant a dozen, hundred might be upon me. Even the stalk from which these three had been freed bore several more ready at any moment to float free and attack me. And overcome with such fear as I never knew could exist, panting, screaming, I turned and raced towards the open country and the camp. Once or twice I glanced back, expecting to see the dim, ghostly shapes pursuing me. But I saw nothing. Perhaps there were no others, maybe only those three bloomed into life that night. But even while I ran, while I spent my breath in shrieks that could have been heard in the distant camp, the truth dawned upon me. I had escaped the "night death" by the narrowest of margins, but I had solved the mystery. I knew the truth and, bizarre, incredible, impossible as it seemed, I knew the secret of those strange plants, of the death-dealing, living blossoms. The plants were land hydroids, gigantic representatives of those puzzling marine growths that seem a connecting link between plants and animals. And, like their small marine prototypes, they bore living, carnivorous organisms—gigantic jelly-fish—that floated through the air instead of through the water.

And, like the marine jelly-fish that bud from hydroids, these gigantic man-eating things, those vampires of the desert, in their turn propagated plant-like growths that bore seeds or spores which produced hydroids with living independent organisms in place of flowers.

That I could think and could reason collectively and sanely while I raced, stumbling and fear-stricken towards the dark camp may seem strange; but there are queer kinks in the human brain, and my subconscious mind worked along scientific lines even while my conscious mental processes were devoted to striving to reach safety before some of those ghastly, vampirish, night-borne creatures overtook me. Although I was unaware of the fact, I must have yelled and screamed in my excess of terror as I ran, for presently lights glimmered in the blackness ahead, and as I reached the first buildings I saw a door open and plunged, exhausted and spent, through the portal. Even in my half-mad, half-fainting state I recognized Merivale and Johnson.

"Shut—shut the door!" I gasped. "Keep everyone inside if they value their lives! I—it—they—" I staggered forward and dropped senseless onto a couch.

I opened my eyes to find my two friends bending over me with anxious faces.

"Thank God you've come to!" cried Johnson. "What on earth has happened, Barry? Where have you been and what was that you said about 'it' and 'they'?"

With a tremendous effort I steadied my shaken nerves and, in broken, jerky sentences told than of my terrible experience, of the horrible man-eating creatures that had attacked me. The two men exchanged glances, and I could see that they thought me mad or suffering from some hallucination. My anger was aroused at their skepticism, although Heaven knows they had every reason to doubt the truth of my wild and incredible tale.

"Damn it!" I shouted, sitting up. "It's true—every word of it. Look here—" I showed them the palms of my hands, bent my head that they might examine the back of my neck. Merivale whistled. There were same red punctures that had appeared on the corpses of all those who were killed by the "Night Death."

Johnson glanced at me keenly. "By Jove, I'm beginning to believe you, Barry," he declared. "I admit the yarn sounded like the ravings of a madman at first. Gad! to think of gigantic, carnivorous jelly-fish flying through the air in the darkness—it gives me the creeps."

"And it bears out everything and solves everything!" exclaimed Merivale. "I knew that I never imagined that ghastly thing which Rogers and I saw after we found the dead watchman. And McGovern wasn't drunk or dreaming. By the Lord, Barry, you've solved the mystery. We must get Rogers and the rest and tell them."

But though Merivale and Johnson were convinced, the story was far too wild, too impossible and too fantastic for the others to swallow. Doctor Hepburn pooh-poohed it and advised Merivale to give me a sedative and put me in bed, adding that I had probably had a mild attack of the malady and had imagined the ridiculous details, but that it was my own fault for having disobeyed orders in going out after nightfall. Only Rogers, who like Merivale felt that his hitherto discredited statements were borne out by my tale, believed in my story. "Very well," I announced, "wait until daylight and I'll prove it to them. I wish to heaven some of these idiots had been with me."

And though they discredited my statements—or at least put them down to the effect of the supposed malady—a crowd assembled the next morning to listen to my story at first hand and to see me attempt to prove the truth and accuracy of my tale. But when, reaching the spot where I had fought so desperately against the awful things, I pointed to the dismembered, pulpy, discolored objects upon the ground, and they saw the swollen buds of others upon the strange plants, doubts began to give way to belief. Still stubborn, old Hepburn would not give in. He declared that in his opinion the things were flowers and nothing more, that he didn't believe they could move independently, and that having fallen a victim to the "germ" of the plague while watching the flowers expand, I had imagined all the rest when in a semi-delirious state and had blindly slashed at harmless blooms of the plants.

"Possibly," I said soothingly, "as you are supposed to be a scientist of sorts, you may know the differences between plant and animal forms of life. In that case I suggest we examine these creatures that you claim are flowers—vegetable growths."

He snorted. But he could not refuse in the presence of the others. To me it was a most repugnant undertaking, and I shuddered as we examined the mutilated things. Presently Hepburn rose and extended his hand. "I apologise, Barry," he said. "You were quite right. Gentlemen"—turning to the group about us— "Doctor Barry deserves the greatest praise and our heartfelt thanks. He has solved the mystery of the Night Death; he has laid the ghost. These—er— creatures are unquestionably invertebrate animals—much like gigantic jelly-fish in their anatomy. They are literally vampires—blood suckers and, like their marine relatives, strictly carnivorous. These slender, thread-like filaments that I mistook for stamens are tubes ending in toothed suckers and through which the blood of their prey is drawn. It was the marks of these suckers that were impressed as punctures upon the skin of those killed by the Night Death as we have called it. In all probability the creatures in life exude some powerful poisonous emanation that renders their prey almost instantly unconscious, once the things have dropped over them. Do you not agree with me, Barry?"

I nodded. "Entirely," I assured him, "or rather"—with a laugh— "you now agree with me. The things are composite, polypod jelly-fish— communities of animals similar to the Portuguese Man-of-War."

"How in thunder can they fly?" demanded one of the men. "They're heavy, they haven't any wings, and you can't tell me that petticoat arrangement can lift 'em up by waving back and forth."

"I imagine," I replied, "that the balloon-like body is filled with some sort of gas produced by the creatures themselves. As they broke off from the parent stem last night they floated upward without visible effort. I—"

"Well, what's the answer?" asked Elliott, the camp superintendent. "Now that Barry's solved the mystery of the devilish things, the question is, "How are we going to stop it?"

"Chop down and burn all the damned trees," suggested some-one.

"An excellent scheme as far as it goes," I assented. "But how are you going to destroy them all? There are thousands—perhaps tens of thousands—scattered everywhere. They grow so rapidly that by the time half are destroyed there will be as many new ones to replace them. Wherever one of these things drops to earth, a dozen shoots sprout up, and each of these produces dozens more that bear from three to ten of these vampires."

"Well, here goes to end these," cried the first speaker as, leaping forward, he commenced hacking down the thick stalks. Others joined him, and in a few moments not one of the plants was left standing in the vicinity.

"Fine!" I commented. "But by tomorrow or next day, if you return here, you'll find twice as many have grown up. And as deaths have been caused by these creatures as far away as Piura and Chancay, there is every probability that colonies of the plants have started in those distant localities."

The men gazed at one another with blank faces. "For God's sake, what are we to do?" demanded Johnson. "If those hellish things keep on increasing, the whole of South America—perhaps the entire world—will be destroyed."

"Undoubtedly—if they are not checked," I agreed. "I—we—must think of some method of exterminating them. There must be some means, if we can hit upon it. But for the present the best thing is to round up every available man and destroy every sprout, every one of the fallen creatures in the neighborhood."

It seemed a herculean task, but two thousand men can accomplish a vast amount of work, and a small army began scouring the hillsides and valleys in a desperate war upon the sources of the terrible Night Death, while full accounts of my discovery and pleas for co-operation in extirpating the things were flashed by radio to every town and settlement within a radius of more than one hundred miles.

But this hand-to-hand battle I knew would never result in the complete elimination of the things. And it could not be continued indefinitely. It was essential that some means of wiping the things from the earth should be devised, and I racked my brains and conferred for hours with the others in what appeared to be a hopeless effort to evolve or invent some such means.

Somehow I could not get the idea out of my mind that the fact that the vampires moved only at night and only in dry weather lay the key to the solution, and yet, try as I might, I could not see how we could turn these facts to our advantage. And then sudden recollection of McGovern's experience came to me. Oil! Oil had routed the thing that had attacked him. We had oil in unlimited quantities. Why not spray the entire country with oil? I dashed to my fellows and explained my scheme, and instantly all fell in with it. We had three places at Talara and a dozen more available at Lima and elsewhere. Before nightfall our planes had been equipped with spraying apparatus, and the next day they were flashing—like gigantic dragon flies—back and forth above the jungle, spraying every square foot of the country with the heavy oil.

Within a week twenty planes were at work. Soon the greenery vanished under the black coating, and far and near—to well beyond the most distant spots where the Night Death had taken its toll—the country was drenched with the shower of crude petroleum. The most careful search failed to reveal a single living plant of the terrestrial hydroids, and when no more deaths occurred, even in dry weather, and when the people, regaining confidence, remained out of doors at night, we judged that the operations had met with entire success.

Still, for weeks an airplane patrol was maintained, until Nature again took a hand and removed all danger of the recurrence of the terrible deadly plague. With the eruption of Orsini volcano in southern Chile, the ocean's bed again altered, the Humboldt Current resumed his long interrupted course and once again the west coast of South America became a rainless, barren desert. And until the climate again changes, the Night Death will be a thing of the past, the Vampires of the Desert will never reappear.

Perhaps this will never happen within the present century or again such changes may take place tomorrow or next year.

The Bees from Borneo
Will H. Gray

Silas Donaghy was by far the best beekeeper and queen breeder in the United States; not because of the amount of honey he produced but because he had bred a strain of bees that produced records. Those two hundred hives consistently averaged three hundred pounds of honey each. Naturally enough, everyone who had read about his results in the different bee journals wanted queens from his yard, and his yearly production of two thousand queens was always bought up ahead of time at two dollars each, which is just double the usual price.

Silas was a keen student of biology besides an expert beekeeper. He had tried all the usual experiments with different races of bees before falling back on Italian stock, bred for many generations in the United States for honeygathering qualities, gentleness, and color.

Although he had achieved commercial success, he still found the experimental side most fascinating, especially with regard to artificial fertilization of drone eggs—a comparatively simple matter, only requiring a little care. His greatest ambition was to crossbreed different species and even different genera. From his studies he found out that the freaks exhibited in side shows were not crosses between dog and rabbit or cat and dog, as advertised, such things being impossible, owing, it is thought, to chemical differences in the life germs.

Every beekeeper knows that the queen bee lays fertile or unfertile eggs at will. One mating is sufficient for life, and after it the queen can lay a million or more fertile eggs at the rate of as many as two thousand a day in summer. The fertile eggs become females, either workers or queens, depending on how they are fed, while the unfertile eggs hatch out into drones, which are the big, clumsy, stingless males. For the most part they are useless, for they require the labor of five workers to keep them fed, and only a very few ever perform the services for which they were created. Nature is very bounteous when it comes to reproduction, but seems to desert her children once they are safely ushered into this wicked world.

All might have gone well if someone had not sent Silas Donaghy a queen bee from the wilds of Borneo. After careful examination, he introduced it to one of his hives which he had just deprived of its own queen. In a month's time the new brood had hatched and were on the wing; pretty bees they were with a red tuft on the abdomen and long, graceful bodies with strong wings. Soon the honey began to come in and pile up on that hive, which was mounted on a weighing scale. Up and up crept the weight until Silas saw that he had something as far beyond his own strain as his own were above the ordinary black bee. In his enthusiasm for these new and beautiful creatures, he overlooked the source of their honey. Not alone did they gather from the flowers but from every plant that had sweet juice in its stems or leaves, and they did not hesitate to enter other hives and rob them of their stores. In fact, wherever there was a sign of sugar, they seemed to find it and carry it off. When that hive had piled up a thousand pounds of honey, Silas took eggs from it and put them in every hive he had. Risking everything, he bought extra hives and equipment and raised five thousand of the new queens, which he sold for five dollars each. Soon his mail was flooded with letters of two kinds: one lot praising his queens as the most wonderful honey gatherers in the world, the other abusing him for scattering a race of robbers that were ruining crops and cleaning out all other hives within a radius of five miles.

Things might have righted themselves if it had not been for a California senator who owned two thousand hives and had them completely robbed out by another beekeeper who had only five hundred, all mothered by the new Borneo strain.

By means of influence at Washington, and without consulting the Bureau of Entomology, this senator had the mails closed to Silas Donaghy's queens. It was a dreadful shock to Silas because he had already begun refunding people their money and replacing the queens free of charge. Now he could no longer make amends, but the letters of abuse continued to come in by the hundred. He said nothing, but devoted himself more and more to his experiments.

It was with an ordinary wasp or yellow jacket that he succeeded in producing a creature that soon turned the continent upside down.

Under his super-microscope he was looking at an unfertile egg of a Borneo queen. Something buzzed into the room and flew around the microscope, making a breeze that threatened to blow away the delicate egg from its glass slide. Impatiently he put out his hand and to his surprise caught something between his fingers. It was a drone wasp and he had partly crushed it. An idea suddenly struck him; he took a fine camel's-hair brush and touched it to the fluid containing the microscopic spermatazoa or life germs exuding from the dead wasp. With infinite care he applied the brush to the large end of the tiny cucumber-shaped egg on the stage of the microscope. Presently he saw several minute, eel-like creatures burrowing into the egg. One outswam the others; its long tail was replaced by protoplasmic radiations and it united with the female pronucleus. With a tense look, the experimenter sat on with his eye rigidly glued to the microscope.

Had he succeeded? Would cleavage take place? He was called to lunch, but the call went unheeded. At last the pronucleus elongated, became narrow in the middle and finally split into two.

Wonderful! Extraordinary! It would seem that he had accomplished that which no other man had ever done.

Carefully he transferred the wonderful egg to a queen cup and covered it with royal jelly, that special food that in quantity would make it a queen.

Now he must trust it to the tender mercies of the bees, for no man knows the exact constituents of the food fed to the larvae day by day. Then there is always the chance that the bees will reject the egg thus offered to them; they show their disapproval by licking up the royal jelly and devouring the delicate egg.

Silas went through agonies in those three days that it takes the egg to hatch. Everything went as it should, and in fourteen days he had a perfect queen resembling a wasp except for a few reddish hairs on the abdomen. His anxieties were not yet over, for a week after hatching the queen goes on her wedding flight. High up into the air she soars with all the drones after her in a flock. To the strong goes the victory, but his joy is short lived, for after one embrace he falls to the ground, dead, his vitals torn from him and attached to the queen. Such is the queen's first flight and after it she returns to the hive to lay countless thousands of eggs. Had he wished to, Silas could have fertilized the queen by the Sladen method, almost amounting to an operation, but he thought it wiser to let nature take her course.

On the seventh day the young queen came out of the hive, ran about the alighting board nervously for a minute, then took a short flight to get her bearings and finally shot into the air and out of sight while the drones followed in desperate haste.

Silas waited and watched, but she did not return. Days passed and his spirits fell to zero, for the chance of a lifetime had slipped from his grasp.

It was a month or so later that young Silas came running into his father's study one morning with the news:

"Oh, Father! Come quick and bring the cyanide. There's a wasp's nest bigger than a pumpkin down on a tree in the wood lot."

"Now, Silas, I've often told you not to exaggerate. You know it isn't that size."

"Well, Father, it's enormous, anyway."

When Silas, senior, went down to investigate he found his son's description not in the least exaggerated. If anything, the size was underestimated. There, to his astonishment, hung the largest wasp's nest he had ever seen or heard about. The insects going in and out seemed different from the ordinary yellow jackets. Walking over to investigate, he received a sting that temporarily knocked him out. He was well inoculated to bee stings and they hardly affected him, but this was something quite different. Some way or other he reached the house and collapsed on the doorstep.

It was three days before he was about again, feeling very shaky on his legs. He did not lack courage, for he took a butterfly net and veil and went down to see how the new insects were getting along. The nest was bigger still and the numbers of bees coming in and out had greatly increased. He managed to capture one before he was chased home, and a sting on the hand, though very painful, did not incapacitate him so badly as the first had done.

To his astonishment the captured insect had the red tip to its abdomen. Here was a great discovery. His escaped queen had settled down on her own account and started a paper-pulp nest like ordinary wasps instead of returning to her own hive. Interest in the new species overcame everything else in his mind, even the severity of the sting.

Putting the captured specimen in a queen mailing cage, he posted it to the professor of entomology at the State University, who had been friendly to him through all his late troubles. Alas for the regulations which he had quite forgotten in his excitement. The Post Office people returned his specimen with a prosecution notice. He was summoned to court and heavily fined.

While he was away from home, little Silas was stung by one of the bees and died the same evening.

Something gave way in the poor man's mind and he hated the whole world with a deadly hatred.

Making himself a perfectly bee-tight costume, he sat near the great nest for hours at a time, capturing young queens as they emerged. Next he bought a gross of little rubber balloons and some cylinders of compressed hydrogen. Making small paper cages, he attached an inflated balloon to each, put in a young queen and started them off wherever the wind would take them. When the queen got tired of her paper prison, she chewed her way out to freedom and, single-handed, started a new colony.

It was getting late in the season and the new strain of insects did not make much headway before the cold weather set in.

Early the next spring the country papers began to complain of the prevalence of deaths from bee or wasp stings. Every year some people die of stings, but now the number was greatly increased. Animals also were frequently found dead without apparent reason. Many people got stung and recovered after a week in bed.

In the cities these constant accounts from the country became a sort of joke. The words "stung," "sting," and "stings" were used on every occasion, in season and out. When a man was away from work without permission, instead of saying he was burying his grandmother he said he had been laid up with a bee sting.

At last official notice was taken of the new menace and they were recognized as being descended from the famous Borneo queens. The bees from Borneo were now discussed in every state in the Union. The cities were still joking, but the country people were getting desperate. Many had sold out for what they could get and had moved to parts not yet infested with the new pest. Those that remained wore special clothes, had all doors and windows carefully screened, and took every precaution not to let the insects into the house. It was soon discovered that even the chimneys had to be covered when fires were not burning. The new insects had to have sugar as well as insect or flesh diet, but they preferred to get their sweets in any other way rather than from the flowers. All beehives were quickly robbed and the bees killed off. Soon it was realized that there would be no fruit crop in many districts, for even if pickers could be found who would run the risk of being stung, the insects were always ahead of them devouring the fruit as soon as ripe.

The cities began to wake up when the new insects found that open fruit stalls and candy stores were theirs for the taking. They built their nests from waste paper or old wood or any fibrous material that they could find. The nests were built high up under cornices and gables where it was very difficult to find them and still more difficult to destroy them. The death toll was now greater, for the city people were not inoculated as many of the country folk were. One in every four died from the stings. The conversation became more serious, the papers had a special column for deaths from stings. A fellow worker would not turn up at the office; his friends looked at each other gravely and cast lots to see who should ring up to find out the sad news. If he did come back after being in a hospital he was hailed with enthusiasm.

All the leading scientists and doctors were working hard to devise a serum or antitoxin. Some brave men were undergoing a series of injections with formic acid to see if it would immunize them. Every newspaper had a list of so-called cures sent in by people who professed to have cured themselves or others. It was hard to judge these things, for it was impossible to know if the sting were really of a Borneo queen and not of some other hymenopterous insect. Panic alone killed many, so great was the fright of those stung by any insect. Those who recovered from a sting practically never died when stung again; this fact was of great use when recruiting began later on in the year.

A dreadful catastrophe raised the menace of the bees to an importance exceeding everything else.

A trainload of molasses was entering a suburb of a great city where the bees had obtained quite a foothold. The engineer was stung in the face and staggered back into the arms of the fireman. A lurch and both fell out on the track. On rushed the heavy train with throttle open. Soon it entered the yards at great speed, jumped the switches and collided with an outgoing passenger train. Sounds of rending steel and splintering wood filled the air. Roaring, hissing steam drowned the cries of the injured. Over track and wreckage spread a turgid amass of strong-smelling molasses.

Before the work of rescue was half completed the air was swarming with millions of buzzing insects. Doctors, nurses, railway workers, policemen and ambulance drivers were stung into insensibility and death. To complete the awful drama some well-intentioned persons bravely started smudge fires, hoping to smoke away the bees. Now fire was added and the flames licked through the seething, treacly mass, converting it into a holocaust such as had not been witnessed since the days of the Great War. Five hundred persons lost their lives through accident, fire and stings. Thirty or forty casualties, at the most, would have been the total if it had not been for the bees.

The nation was awake now. Complete destruction of this new pest was demanded in all the great newspapers. Expense could not be spared in such an emergency. There must be no half-hearted measures, for the very life of the country was being strangled by the creation of a madman.

Volunteers were organized all over the country. They were equipped with extension ladders and strong sacks, which they put over the suspended nest, drew tight the running string, and transferred the whole thing to a woven wire burner, where it was sprayed with gasoline and burnt. At first they seemed to make some headway, but a fine spell of weather and millions of emerging young queens gave the bees fresh impetus and the newly started nests could not be found so easily as the large old ones.

The national capital proved a specially happy hunting ground for the bees. The public buildings provided thousands of nooks and corners where the nests were not discovered until they were as large as barrels. Sometimes the weight would break them down. If they fell in a street, there were sure to be many deaths before traffic could be diverted, and men protected to the last degree destroyed the insects with flaming sprays and poison gas. At last things became so bad that the seat of government was moved to a town in Arizona which had not yet been invaded by bees.

Many new industries sprang into being, for anything advertised to combat the pests found a ready sale. Traps of every size, shape and description were sold; many of them more ingenious to look at than practical in use. Poison baits were sold and used by the ton, many harmless animals and not a few children fell victims to their use.

In spite of everything the pests went on increasing in numbers until the country seemed on the verge of bankruptcy. When farm mortgages, considered so safe, fell due, it was not worthwhile fore-closing them, for the land was useless. The new insects did not pollinate the fruit, but they destroyed the insects that did. Farm produce rose to unheard-of prices. Passenger traffic was reduced to a minimum, for nobody traveled who could possibly avoid it. Excursions and pleasure trips seemed to be a thing of the past. Even free insurance against stings did not stimulate travel, for no one seemed keen on being stung, however big the compensation to their heirs!

When fruit reached a certain price, large syndicates bought up fertile stretches for almost nothing and screened them in at enor-mous cost. In these enclosures the most intensive culture known was practiced with very profitable results. Not alone were there gardeners, but numerous guards patrolled the high framework with shotguns charged with salt ready to shoot any bee that should find its way in. Common bees had to be introduced from great distances for pollination purposes.

Silas Donaghy gibbered and raved in the state asylum; when he saw anyone stung he was convulsed with mirth. From morning to night he played tricks on the attendants, doctors and other pa-tients. They never could tell when he might have a bee concealed about his clothing or wrapped in his handkerchief. It was most dis-turbing to the officials to get suddenly chased by a man who held sudden death in his hand. They put him in the padded cell, but it did not disturb him in the least. When his food was brought, he imitated the buzzing of a bee so skillfully that the attendant dropped the food and ran, followed by Silas' unearthly shrieks of merriment. At times he appeared quite sane and would skillfully catch and kill every bee that accidentally got let in. When he got stung himself, which was very rarely, he would wince with the pain and fall to his knees and grope about half blinded for support while the poison coursed through his veins. Getting to his feet again, he would stagger about with the tears of agony running down his checks, the while laughing at himself and cursing his weakness. Those who saw him marveled, for most people collapsed in a writhing heap and mercifully became unconscious.

In his sane moments he begged for his beloved microscope and experimental equipment. At last, to humor him and incidentally save themselves unlimited trouble, they gave him a little hut in the grounds where he could do as he liked so long as he did not annoy anyone. The first thing he did was to tear off all the screen wire and let the bees have free access to his living and sleeping rooms. He even let them share his meals and they sat in rows on the edge of his plate. It wasn't long before there was a nest right above his bed; it remained there undisturbed, for no one went near his little abode. The official bee swatters kept clear of Silas, for they had their dignity to uphold and Silas made fun of their bee-tight costumes and elaborate equipment. He could kill more bees in a day, if he wanted to, than they could in a week.

The Government was still busy working out methods to control the plague. One that seemed to promise some success was the introduction of a large fly belonging to the hawk-like family that prey on honey bees, catching them on the wing and tearing them asunder to feed on the sweet juices within. These flies were bred in great numbers and distributed over the country. Spiders and bee-eating birds were also extensively tried out.

With the first days of autumn the nation breathed more freely, for the Borneo bees were even more sensitive to cold than the ordinary hive bees. So great was the relief that all the activities of summer began to take place in the winter. People went visiting and the railways ran excursions. Such is the spirit of the people that they quickly forget their troubles and trust that the past will bury its past. But the entomologists of the country knew and trembled at the thought of spring when the fine weather would entice from their wintering places thousands and millions of queens that would quickly construct nests and raise broods that would far exceed anything that had yet gone before. A bounty of ten cents a queen was offered and thousands of people collected the dormant insects from their hiding places. Special instructors visited all the schools, telling of the dangers that awaited them if the queens were not destroyed now.

The fine weather came and with it the queens came out of their hiding places in countless millions. Those gathered were as a drop in the bucket, compared to those left undisturbed. For a few short weeks things got steadily worse and worse. All the devices of the previous year were used and a lot of new ones. Single screen doors were no longer of any use. Double doors were better, but the most reliable system proved to be a cold passage kept at a very low temperature. In this passage the insects became chilled and could be swept up and destroyed.

Every day now seemed closer to the time when things would end. A heat wave came along and the overstrained public services collapsed. The dead lay in the streets. The frantic telephone calls went unanswered. Even the water pipes were choked with the dead insects and the water tainted with the acrid poison that also filled the air.

Those who had the means and were able fled to other parts where the breakdown had not yet occurred. The military forces of the country were fully organized for relief purposes and those who remained were rescued from the cities of the dead.

The State Lunatic Asylum collapsed with all the rest of society and patients wandered out and were soon stung to death.

Silas was undecided what to do at first. Then he thought it would be a good plan to put the screen wire back on his shack. The bees objected to the hammering, so he waited until night and did it then. He was rather disappointed at having to destroy the nest inside, but it could not be helped. Several visits to the storeroom of the asylum yielded all the food he needed. For a few days he remained in solitude, then he packed his beloved microscope, put on a light bee veil and started home over the deserted roads. He was careful not to annoy the insects in any way. He never batted at them or made quick, jerky movements and he avoided going near their nests. He took it very easy so that he would not perspire, for bees hate the smell of sweat.

Sad sights met his gaze as he trudged along. The whitened bones of cows and horses and smaller animals littered the fields, for the insects picked their victims clean, requiring as they did a partly animal diet like ordinary wasps. A disabled truck stood by the roadside and sitting in the driver's seat was a grim skeleton. Further on a cheap touring car lay on its side and four skeletons, two large and two small, told the sad tale of a family wiped out in a few minutes. These sights did not seem to affect Silas at all; he was more interested in the nests that hung from every tree and telegraph pole and from the gables and eaves of houses and barns. Once he was overtaken by an armored and screened military ambulance. He refused their aid and they hurried on, the wheels crushing a bee at every turn. A crushed bee is smelled by the other bees and they are immediately on the warpath, so Silas had to leave the road and take to the fields.

When he reached home he found his wife alone in the well-screened house. She had been ostracized by all the neighbors long before they had left, and but for Silas' letters of instruction, she could not have carried on single-handed. Somehow she had expected Silas. He entered by the cellar steps and slipped through so dexterously that only seven bees got in with him. They flew to a window, where he quickly killed them, for Mrs. Donaghy, strange to say, had never been stung. He took off his outer-clothing and found five more. Disposing of these, he went upstairs and carried his microscope to the study, where he carefully unpacked it and put a glass cover over it. He fussed about the study in an absent-minded way until Mrs. Donaghy called him to supper. Sitting down, he looked at the place where little Silas used to sit.

"Where's the boy?" he questioned. "You know I like him to be on time to his meals."

A pained look came over the poor lady's face.

"Silas, you know he's gone."

"Gone where? What do you mean?"

She looked up flushing and for the first time in her married life spoke with heat:

"Dead, you know he's dead; stung to death by one of your accursed bees."

Silas collapsed on the table. Covering his face with his hands, great sobs wracked his body. "My God, my God, what have I done?" he moaned.

Presently he was in his study again, looking at everything with a new light in his eyes. He was alert and methodical now, and there was a set appearance about his jaw that had not been there for a long, long while.

Taking the plug out of the keyhole, he waited till a bee came in and dexterously catching it by the wings, brought it to his study. His tired eyes were bright now and he appeared to be looking at something he had never seen before. Frequently he came to the living-room to ask his wife questions about what had happened in the last year or so. He seemed appalled, but a glance from any window verified all she said.

That night he visited a deep bee cellar constructed underground where he used to winter some of his colonies. He found that it had been used as an ice house while he had been away. Seeing an old hive in the corner, he went over and lifted the lid. To his utter astonishment a faint buzz greeted him that was quite different from the high note of the all-pervading pest outside. Here was the remnant of a colony of honey bees that had been forgotten. How could they have survived all this time? He didn't know, unless it was the ice making a continuous winter for two years. Shouldering the hive, he carried it out and placed it in a little screened chicken yard where Mrs. Donaghy had endeavored to raise a few vegetables. Next morning the survivors were buzzing about getting their hearings, though there wasn't much fear of their straying very far in the little enclosure.

For the next week Silas hardly slept or took time to eat. If he wasn't at the microscope he was in the small yard where the last honey bees in North America flew about and licked up the honey given them. Little they knew that the fate of a continent depended on them.

At last he produced a drone that seemed to fill the requirements. It must be able to outfly the drones of the vicious half-breeds all around. It must be able to produce grandsons, for by the laws of parthenogenesis a drone cannot have sons that would also be swift and amorous. It must produce daughters and granddaughters resembling honey bees and incapable of surviving the winter alone.

Most scientists would have waited to test out these qualities before scattering the new product broadcast. Silas, however, was always impetuous, as the sale of his first Borneo queens had shown to be. He realized now that the situation might be better but could not be worse.

Setting to work in his little enclosure, he bred drones in large numbers and liberated them. If only he had some way of distributing them quickly! Balloons and hydrogen? Alas, he had neither. He wandered about, thinking hard. There in the basement stood the little lighting plant with its neat row of batteries and a large jar of acid in the corner. Ha! There was hydrogen, either by electrolysis or more quickly still with strips of zinc or nails and the acid. Paper bags would do for the balloons.

In a day or so he was sending the drones off on the wind by the dozen together, hoping that they would seek out the young queens wherever they went and father a new race of harmless bees that would die out entirely in the winter.

In a month he noticed young queens without the familiar red tuft on their tails. Capturing a few, he put them in his enclosure and fed them carefully, even opening a precious tin of meat to help them along; but they did not respond and some died. They were incapable of living alone. However, those put into nests flourished and outdid their vicious half-sister. It was a treat to see the new drones on the wing rushing about in their wild search for virgin queens. The workers of the new breed had barbed stings and died on using them. It was not very painful either.

Every day now Silas was in his garden getting things to rights, planting and harvesting. He smiled now at the millions of bees, for they were all different from the old race that was quickly dying off.

He often wondered if there was anyone else alive. Making a trip to the deserted village, he was rummaging around looking for canned goods when he was astonished to hear a telephone ring. It was a long distance call searching for anyone alive.

"The bees have played themselves out," he was told. "The breed did not hold true. Nature righted herself automatically."

Silas went home smiling. He knew that he had started and ended the awful plague.

Coachwhip Publications

CoachwhipBooks.com

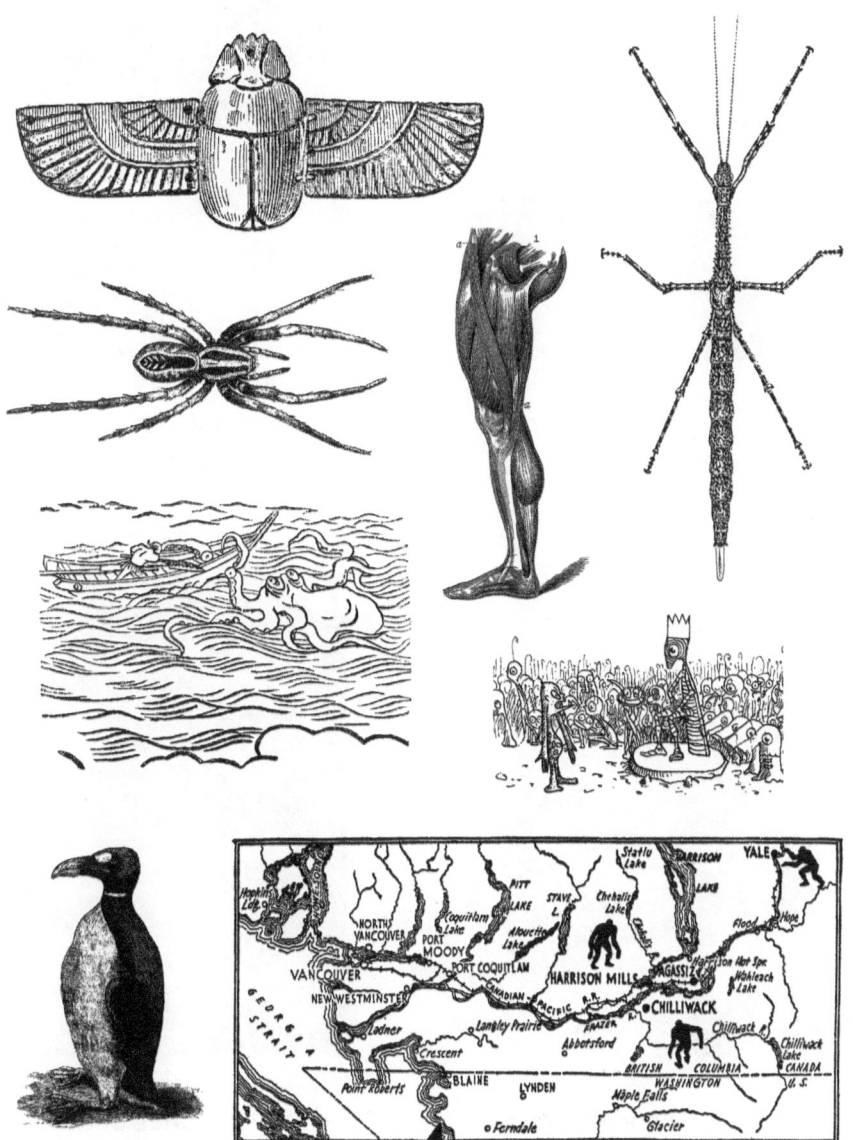

SPECULATIVE FICTION

Plants in Science Fiction
and Fantasy

Supernatural Stories in the
Christian Tradition

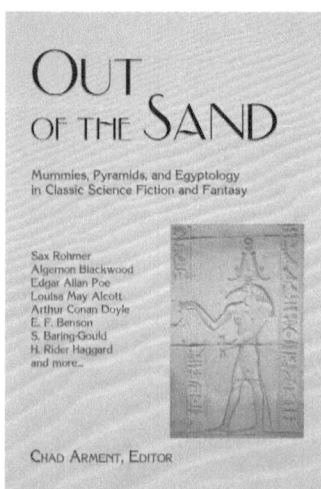

Egyptian Science Fiction
and Fantasy

Time Travel Stories in Science
Fiction and Fantasy

SHADOWS FROM A VEILED CREATION: Classic Tales of
Supernatural Fiction in the Christian Tradition
ISBN 1-930585-26-8

ABOUT TIME: The Forerunners of Time Travel and
Temporal Anomalies in Science Fiction and Fantasy
ISBN 1-930585-55-1

FLORA CURIOSA: Cryptobotany, Mysterious Fungi,
Sentient Trees, and Deadly Plants in Classic
Science Fiction and Fantasy
ISBN 1-930585-56-X

OUT OF THE SAND: Mummies, Pyramids, and Egyptology
in Classic Science Fiction and Fantasy
ISBN 1-930585-58-6

THE FANTASTIC IMAGINATION OF GEORGE MACDONALD I:
Essays, The Portent, At the Back of the North Wind,
The Flight of the Shadow
ISBN 1-930585-61-6

THE FANTASTIC IMAGINATION OF GEORGE MACDONALD II:
Phantastes, The Carasoyn, The Wise Woman, and Lilith
ISBN 1-930585-62-4

THE FANTASTIC IMAGINATION OF GEORGE MACDONALD III:
The Princess and the Goblin, The Princess and Curdie,
The Light Princess, The History of Photogen and Nycteris,
Short Stories
ISBN 1-930585-63-2

PYM: The Narrative of Arthur Gordon Pym
of Nantucket / An Antarctic Mystery
ISBN 1-930585-57-8

www.ingramcontent.com/pod-product-compliance
Lightning Source LLC
Chambersburg PA
CBHW020931020726
47495CB00002B/444